THE ACCIDENTAL PRESIDENT

THE ACCIDENTAL PRESIDENT

A Novel
By Harris I. Baseman

iUniverse, Inc.
New York Lincoln Shanghai

The Accidental President

iUniverse, Inc.

For information address:
iUniverse, Inc.
2021 Pine Lake Road, Suite 100
Lincoln, NE 68512
www.iuniverse.com

ISBN: 0-595-30688-8

Printed in the United States of America

Acknowledgement

I want to thank post Gulf War Brevet Colonel and former head of the Communications Systems Division and Vice-President of Government Systems Corporation of General Telephone Corporation, Bernard Resnick for technical advice. Whatever I got right I owe to him. Any errors are all mine.

Many thanks are also due to best selling novelist, playwright, and super writing coach, Sol Stein for his patience in trying to teach a lifetime draftsman of boring legal documents to write an entertaining story. It was a long struggle that required a lot of patience. To the extent I succeed, it's due to his perseverance. Wherever I may fail, it's because I didn't learn the lessons well enough.

CHAPTER 1

▼

When Clarence Davenport assassinated the President of the United States, he knew this day might come. Still, when he answered the phone and the caller said, "This is Agent John Wallace, United States Secret service," he was more than surprised. The voice continued, "I'd like to speak with Clarence Davenport."

Clarence didn't know what to say. He nervously glanced at his wristwatch. It was four o'clock in the afternoon.

Wallace said, "Hello, hello. Is Mr. Davenport there?"

Clarence took a deep breath to keep the anxiety he felt out of his voice. "This is Clarence Davenport. What can I do for you?"

"I'd like to meet with you tomorrow morning. Would ten o'clock at your house be convenient?"

"Will you be coming alone?"

"A White House aide, Molly Pemberton will be with me."

Wallace didn't volunteer why he wanted the meeting and Clarence decided he wouldn't ask. He took another deep breath and agreed to meet with Agent Wallace and Ms. Pemberton the next morning as requested. After he returned the phone to its cradle, Clarence walked into the living room and sat in his favorite upholstered armchair. It had been his mother's favorite. Its flowered print was faded and worn, but it had now become his favorite chair, the one where he went to sit and think.

Clarence stared into space and thought about what he had done and why. He had eagerly gone to liberate Kuwait as a young Second Lieutenant during Desert Storm and returned inexplicably ill. He could have forgiven the failure of the Army to warn him and his men that Sarin gas had been stored at the ammunition depot in Kamisiyah, Iraq when they demolished it, but he couldn't forgive General Wilson, who had ordered the mission for then covering up that mistake. He remembered how outraged he had been when the Pentagon finally admitted five years later that they had been forewarned about the presence of chemical weapons and that American soldiers, almost one hundred thousand of them, had been exposed to the release of toxic chemicals in Iraq. That was when he decided he had to avenge himself and all his men by killing General Wilson. He had thought that killing Wilson would end it, but before he could do that, he learned that the cover up of what happened at Kamisiyah went far beyond Wilson and even included President Elect Butler and Senator Jebediah Davies. That's when he decided that government corruption was so widespread that the government itself had to be destroyed. That was when he finally came up with the plan to kill President Butler and all of the legal successors to the Presidency at the Inauguration Ceremony. Planting the explosives in the TelePrompTer and speakers prior to the Inauguration Ceremony while passing himself off as a GSA electrician had worked like a charm. It would have been perfect if Education Secretary Ben Silver had only been at the ceremony like he was supposed to. The United States would have had no President. There would have been no legal successor, and there would have been the Constitutional crisis he wanted. They would have to go back to the original Constitution and correct the mistakes made by the Federal bureaucracy, the courts and the Congress during the last two hundred years. He came "Close, but no cigar", as his father used to say. He had no regrets about what he had done, but there was no sense to think about that now. He had to think about the present. He had considered this possibility and knew what he had to do.

Clarence rose from his favorite chair and looked up and down the street through the living room windows. He saw nothing unusual except for a Bell Atlantic telephone, repair truck and a workman doing something with the overhead wires, or was he? Perhaps he was already under surveillance and the lineman wasn't a lineman. He thought about calling the telephone company to see if anyone was working in the area, but decided against it. If he were under surveillance, the Feds would have advised the phone company to lie to him and say they were working in the area, and if he wasn't and there was some problem being repaired, they'd say the same thing. All he'd accomplish would be to tip them off that he was wise to them. No, he'd check again in two hours.

It was early evening when Clarence looked out of his living room window again. The telephone truck was still there and had now been joined by one from Dominion Virginia Power. He didn't waste time wondering about the presence of the utilities. Instead, he went into the basement of his house, slid the knotty pine paneling covering the rear wall aside and entered a passage way that led to a small room in the woods behind his house. Some prior owner of his house had built it as a bomb shelter during the height of the Cold War with the Soviet Union. He discovered it as a child and had used it as a secret playhouse that he shared with the Swanson children whose house backed up to his. After exiting from the bomb shelter through a tunnel that led to a small cave in the wooded area separating his house from the neighboring Swanson residence. From there he quickly made his way to the edge of the woods and then to the back door of his neighbor's raised ranch house. He looked to his right and then to his left. Nothing. He took a deep breath, then approached the house and knocked on the back door. Moments later, a gray haired woman pushed aside a lace curtain covering the glass windowpanes in the door. She peered at Clarence through her wire-rimmed eyeglasses. When she recognized him, she smiled and said, as she opened the door, "Clare, how nice to see you, but what brings you here this evening?"

"Evening, Mrs. Swanson. There's this new computer virus going around and I thought I'd install some software that prevents it from attacking your computer."

"How thoughtful of you. Come on in. I can't thank you enough for showing Mr. Swanson how to use that computer Sven and Shirley gave us. The kids were asking about you when they called on Sunday. They wanted me to be sure and thank you for fixing that computer whenever we have a problem. Mr. Swanson uses it all the time now." She smiled at him and said, "Goodness, here I am babbling away and standing in front of the door." She stepped aside.

"Glad to do it. Mr. Swanson home? I'll come back if he isn't."

"No, no. Come on in. He's in the den, and I think he's doing something on the computer right now." As she led the way towards the den, Mrs. Swanson said, "Henry, Clare's here to fix something on the computer."

"It's working just fine."

"And I want to keep it that way for you, Henry. There's a new virus making the rounds."

"Thanks Clare, that's so nice of you. Will it take long?"

"Three or four minutes to download depending on the speed of your modem. Did you order that cable connection?"

Mr. Swanson shook his head. "The telephone is quick enough for me."

Mrs. Swanson said, "I made some of that banana bread you like. You'll stay and I'll put on some coffee. We drink decaf at night. That okay for you?"

"Fine."

"I'll only be five minutes,"

Clarence turned towards Henry who was now standing beside his Dell desktop computer. "Sit yourself down, Henry. Save what you're doing, and then I'll start on the download."

While Henry sat in front of his computer and peered into the monitor with his hands resting on the keyboard, Clarence stood behind him, looking towards the doorway. Satisfied that Mrs. Swanson had left the hallway, Clarence removed a garrote from his pocket, and in one continuous movement, whipped it around Henry's neck and pulled it taught. Henry tried to rise from his seat, but Clarence pressed his elbows heavily down on Henry's shoulders as he continued pulling the ends of the cord tighter and tighter. Light reflected off Henry's balding head as he clawed at the ligature and tried to turn his head. He struggled, but was no match for the younger and stronger man. As Mr. Swanson slumped back in his chair, Clarence removed a knife from a sheath strapped to the inside of his right leg and slit Henry's throat. The blood spurted onto the computer's keyboard and monitor, ran down Henry's plaid shirt, stained his pants and pooled on the floor. Clarence wiped the blood off the blade on the back of Henry's shirt, replaced the knife and then walked into the hall towards the kitchen where he could hear the tea kettle just beginning to whistle.

As Clarence walked into the kitchen, he said, "Anything I can help you with, Mrs. Swanson?"

"Aren't you sweet. I've got everything under control, but I'll let you carry the tray into the den as soon as I finish pouring the coffee."

As Mrs. Swanson continued pouring, Clarence circled the garrote around her neck, and placed his knee against the small of her back as he pulled it tight. Mrs. Swanson dropped the kettle, reached for the cord around her neck and scratched at his hands with her fingernails. A minute later it was over. As she began to slump to the floor, Clarence held her up with his left arm, grasped his knife in his right hand and sliced across her jugular vein. Blood spurted onto the kitchen counter and the floor. Clarence smiled as he thought that if Mrs. Swanson were still alive, she'd be upset at the mess in her kitchen and would immediately start cleaning it up. He hated to cut her throat, but he could not afford to make any mistakes. He closed her dead staring eyes and then carried her body into the master bedroom and gently put her down on the bed. He straightened her dress where it had ridden up and exposed her knees and covered her body with a blanket. He then went into the den, picked up Mr. Swanson's body, wrapped it in a sheet, rolled it up in a rug and carried it into the kitchen, leaving it beside the kitchen door. Next, he went through the house closing the blinds in the living room and fixing the timer on a lamp on a living room end table to go on and off the way the Swanson's did when they went away for a vacation. Those chores finished, he fixed the telephone answering machine to answer on the second ring and prepared to leave. He glanced back into the kitchen, and noticing the pools of blood everywhere, he decided he couldn't leave Mrs. Swanson's house looking like that. Besides, someone could look in and see the mess. He returned, grabbed a roll of Bounty paper towels from the counter and wiped up the pools of blood on the counter, floor and where it spattered onto the refrigerator and the side of the electric cook top. He used up all the paper towels, threw them into the trash compactor and still wasn't satisfied. He took a pail from the utility closet near the cellar stairs, filled it with warm soapy water and washed down the kitchen counter, the floor and the appliances and then took another look back It still wasn't right. He emptied the three coffee cups, rinsed them and put them and the washed coffeepot in the dish strainer and then stepped back to survey the scene. He nodded in approval, returned the pail to the closet and then turned on the burglar alarm, picked up Mr. Swanson's body and slipped out the back door.

He timed the return from the Swanson's to his house through the woods, into the tunnel and then through the bomb shelter into his basement and up to his enclosed sun-porch. One minute and thirty-six seconds carrying the body. Tomorrow, he'd allow himself one minute and forty-five seconds. Clarence deposited Swanson's body in the bathtub and then looked out his living room window again. The telephone company and electric company trucks were still there. He regretted killing the Swanson's, but there was no time to think about that now. He had to get ready for tomorrow's meeting.

He worked at his computer, interrupting his preparations at nine P.M. and again at ten to look through the living room picture window. The telephone company and power company trucks were still there. At eleven, he made a quick trip back through the tunnel, out of the cave and woods to drop several packages in a mailbox at the end of the street and then returned home the same way. He shut down his computer and got ready for tomorrow by laying out the things he would wear and by dressing Mr. Swanson's body in nearly identical clothes.

It didn't take Secret Service Agent John Wallace and Presidential Aide Molly Pemberton long to reach Clarence Davenport's ranch house in Alexandria, Virginia. As they approached, a pleasant looking man sitting in a screened in porch on the left side of the house waved at them to come in. They entered from a side door that led out to the small side yard. The man remained seated in a flowered armchair that seemed out of place at the circular metal table. The table was painted white, and the other chairs were of white plastic that matched the table.

"I'm John Wallace, Secret Service and this is Molly Pemberton. She used to be with the FBI but she's on President Silver's staff now." They showed their I.D.'s and each tendered a business card to him.

Clarence took the cards and pointed to the chairs on both sides. He smiled. "I know who you are. Sit down."

Molly said, "Are you Mr. Clarence Davenport?"

He nodded, "Call me Clare."

"Do you know why we're here?"

"Sure, to arrest me."

"Did Mr. Hammonds say that?"

"Oh, no. He doesn't know anything about the assassination."

"Why did you mention the assassination? We didn't say anything about that."

"Grandpa Hammonds said he thinks that's what you're investigating. He's right, isn't he?"

Molly nodded. "Yes, he is."

"Why do you think we're here to arrest you?"

"Because you think I did it." Clarence poured coffee into his cup. He looked at Molly and John. "Would you like some coffee? I just made a fresh pot."

Molly shook her head. "Did you?"

"Why do you think I did?"

"We think it's possible."

"Why?"

"Because of the garrote, the bazooka, the Gulf War explosives and the Red-Eye Missiles. We know Mr. Hammonds had been a Commando in World War II and used a garrote and bazooka, that your father was in charge of a Red Eye Missile unit in Viet Nam and that you were in a demolition unit during the Gulf War."

Clarence nodded. "Do you know how I was supposed to have done it?"

Molly looked at John. He nodded at her and said, "We may as well tell him what we know."

John told him what they knew of his theft of explosives, bazookas and missile launchers from the armory, the theft of the TV van, the murders of the armory guard, the TV technician and the GSA electrician. Clarence listened without comment as John continued and recounted how they believed the explosives were in the TelePrompTer and speakers that were brought to the Capitol in a van with a GSA logo and substituted for the ones there just prior to the Inauguration Ceremony. Clarence seemed to nod in agreement while John explained that panels on the van were changed to make it look like a TV service company van and then parked near the site of Inauguration, and that the explosives were detonated from that van. Wallace continued, explaining that a Red Eye missile and a bazooka round were fired from the top of that same van.

Clarence said, "Why the missile and bazooka? And doesn't there have to be a motive? Why would I do something like that?

"Revenge," Molly said. "We know about the raid on the ammunition depot at Kamisiyah during Desert Storm and that some of your men became ill and died. We believe you killed Defense Secretary Wilson because of that. We also think that you believe there was a cover-up in the Senate arranged by President Butler when he was in the Senate and that Senator Davies continued that cover-up when he became chairman. We think that's why you killed President Butler and tried to kill Senator Davies."

Clarence smiled. "Excellent, Ms. Pemberton. That's a wonderful theory."

"Do you deny doing those things?" John said.

Clarence looked at him. "As I said, it's a wonderful theory, but do you have any evidence that ties those activities to me?"

"We haven't finished looking."

"I'm sure you haven't. Tell me, what was I trying to do. Revenge for the Desert Storm cover-up could have been achieved in a much simpler way."

"What do you mean?" Molly said.

"Defense Secretary Wilson, General Allen and my immediate superiors could have been killed in a much easier way, even President Butler. He could have been killed before he got elected, and why the bazooka and Red-Eye Missile."

"That's true," Molly said, "But you also wanted revenge for what you believe was mistreatment of your father during the Vietnam War and grandfather during World War II. That's why you used the missile launcher and bazooka."

Clarence smiled at Molly. "Why do all that at the inauguration? Do you have a theory that explains that?"

"Not yet," Molly said.

"I'm disappointed," Clare said, "but I could suggest one."

"Please do," Molly said.

"It would take far too long."

Molly smiled, "We have nothing better to do."

Clarence smiled back. "Tell you what. For the moment, I'll just hypothesize that the government that rules us all has been so corrupted by greed and special interests that it no longer operates in the best interests of the people. When that happens, the institution itself must be destroyed so that we can have a new beginning." Clarence smiled, "How's that for a two sentence explanation?"

Molly said, "It explains a lot. I think it completes the theory."

"So do I," John said.

Clarence nodded. "I'll make that unanimous."

John stood and looked down at Clarence. "I'm going to read you your rights and then ask you to accompany us. I'm placing you under arrest."

"There's no need to read me my rights. I know them as well as you do, but I'm not going anywhere."

John drew his gun. "I'm afraid I'm going to have to insist."

"Okay, but you should understand that I'm very expert in the use of explosives," Clarence smiled, "but you know that." He patted the cushion and arms of his armchair, "This chair and the house are loaded with enough explosives to blow me and both of you to kingdom come. All I have to do is press the button on this transmitter I'm holding." He turned and smiled at Molly. "Don't be alarmed, Ms Pemberton, I have no intention of harming you or Mr. Wallace unless you force me to."

"You know we can't let you go," John said.

"I have no desire to go anywhere." Clarence frowned. "That's not entirely true. There is one piece of unfinished business."

"That involve Senator Davies?" Molly said.

"Very good, Ms Pemberton. You hit the nail right on the head. I tried to kill him and missed. I don't suppose you'd give me a pass to take care of that now would you."

Molly said, "I almost wish I could, but no, we couldn't."

Clarence slid a computer disc across the table. "That contains an explanation of what was done, how I did it, why, and what I think needs to be done to change the structure of our government." It lay on the table between Clarence and Molly. "Take it." He turned towards John and slid another disc towards him. "That's a copy for you."

Molly and John took the discs.

Clarence said, "Don't worry about my trying to escape. I know you have people out there watching me." Clarence looked through the screen at the street and his small yard. "I want you to leave now and read those materials I just gave you. It's three hundred and eighty-seven pages, but I think you'll find it interesting and that it's quite well written, even if I say so myself. I had intended to e-mail copies of it to the editors of fifty newspapers across the country, but when Grandpa Hammonds called and said you were so nice, I decided I wanted to meet you. I mailed copies to CNN, Fox and the TV networks and to four news-papers. They should get it the day after tomorrow. There are parts of it that I'm going to e-mail to organizations representing Gulf War and Vietnam War veter-ans just as soon as you leave. All I got to do is click on my computer. Clarence stopped smiling. Now I want you to leave. If you don't, well, you know what will happen."

Molly stood. "One more question?"

"Sure."

"Have any help with it?"

"You mean the writing?"

"That and the whole thing?"

"Are you asking if I had an accomplice?"

Molly nodded.

"You mean like maybe President Silver?"

"Whoever."

Clarence smiled. "You'll just have to read it and see."

As Molly and John Wallace prepared to leave, Wallace warned Clarence that they would remain outside watching the house. Molly lingered a moment at the threshold, then turned and said, "Please don't do it."

Clarence smiled at her and suggested they leave while they could. They did.

Clarence peered through the bamboo blinds, watching John Wallace, and Molly Pemberton, walk back towards their black Taurus. Halfway down the walkway, Molly turned back towards the house. She could see Clarence watching them behind the blinds. She shouted, "Please don't do it, Mr. Davenport." He made no reply and closed the blinds tight."

Molly climbed into her car to call Presidential Chief of Staff Tom Andrews at the White House. While they impatiently waited to get connected, an explosion rocked the area. The porch where they had been sitting minutes before was rub-ble along with a substantial part of the ranch house. Molly and John stared at each other. Molly said, "I wish he hadn't done that."

"Think it was guilt and remorse?"

"I doubt it. I'd bet that he so strongly believes in what's on these discs that he killed himself to dramatize their importance and make sure they were listened to and taken seriously."

Before they could say more, Tom Andrews was on the line. They quickly reported what they had learned and what had happened. John said, "We asked him if he had an accomplice.

"What'd he say to that."

"He said did we mean like President Silver?"

"Did he say he was?"

"He said we'd have to read the discs to find out."

"No matter what he says on those computer discs, I won't believe the President is involved. Get the hell out of there and back here with them before some local cop detains you and grabs them. I'm going to detail some of our people to take over at the scene and then see the President. He'll want to see what's on those discs."

John said, "Do you think the President could be involved and maybe we should review them first?"

"No. We'll all do it together."

CHAPTER 2

▼

President Silver's Chief of Staff, Tom Andrews had arranged things so that as soon as Molly and John reached the White House, they were immediately ushered into the Oval office by Martha Roberts, President Silver's Administrative Assistant.

Martha took the computer disc Clarence gave Molly and started the process of making hard copies for everyone. While waiting for the copies to be brought in, Molly and John told Ben and Tom about their meeting with Clarence and his suicide.

"Both of you believe that this Clarence Davenport did it?" Ben said.

They nodded, "Yes, we do."

Molly continued, "And I'll bet those discs will confirm it and explain his reasons."

Minutes later, Martha started bringing in the still warm pages off the printers, six pages at a time in sets for Ben, Tom, Molly and John. The cover page said, *My Manifesto, by Clare Davenport.*

Everyone looked at the second page. It started off,

> *When in the course of human events, it becomes necessary for the people to rid themselves of the forces which prevent them from enjoying that which the Laws of Nature and of Nature's God entitle them, a decent respect to the opinions of mankind requires that they should declare the causes which impel them to do so.*
> *I hold these truths to be self evident, that all men are created equal, that they are endowed by their Creator with certain unalienable Rights, that among these are Life, Liberty and the pursuit of Happiness. That to*

secure these rights, Governments are instituted among Men, deriving their just powers from the consent of the governed. That whenever any Form of Government becomes destructive of these ends, it is the Right of the People to alter or to abolish it, and to institute new Government.

Molly looked up from her copy and whispered to Tom, "Excuse me, the first two paragraphs. What's that from?"

President Silver overheard her. "The Declaration of Independence, almost word for word. So are the third and fourth paragraphs."

Prudence, indeed, will dictate that Governments long established should not be changed for light and transient causes; and accordingly all experience hath shewn, that mankind are more disposed to suffer, while evils are sufferable, than to right themselves by abolishing their government. But when a long train of abuses and usurpations occur and the political leaders refuse to end them, it is the right of the people and their duty to throw off that Government, and replace it with institutions that are free of corruption. Such is now the case.

For the next four hours, President Silver's office resembled the reading room at the public library as he, Tom, Molly and John read Clarence's Manifesto. Their reading was interrupted when Martha knocked on the door and came in. She said, "Sorry to interrupt, but Mr. Evans just entered the White House. Do you want me to send him up when he gets here?"

"Yes, please do." Ben closed his copy of the Manifesto. "I don't know about the rest of you, but it saddens me to think that a basically decent person can be made into a monster. His views on campaign finance reform are remarkably similar to mine, and he's right. They were thinking about political speech when they adopted the free speech amendment. Protecting child pornography and the glorification of violence was never in the minds of the founding fathers. We'll have to think about his laundry list of grievances and his suggestions about fixing them some other time."

Tom frowned as he said, "Davenport claims that President Butler participated in a cover-up when he was a Senator and chairman of the first Senate committee that investigated the claims Davenport's men made. He also claims that Senator Davies continued the cover-up when he became chairman, and that he found evidence of the Senate cover up after he killed his commanding officer and the Senate Clerk he claims helped in the cover up. I'd love to get my hands on that."

Ben said, "Maybe you didn't get to it yet, but he has an appendix to the Manifesto that says where he stored things. The missile launcher and some of the same kind of explosives and the bazooka he used at the Inauguration are in a self-storage warehouse in Virginia. Maybe he put the evidence of the cover up in there too."

Tom flipped to the back of the Manifesto and then picked up a phone. He spoke into it a few minutes and then said, "I'll have some of our people at that warehouse in ten minutes."

Ben turned to Molly and John. "I want to thank you both. That was a magnificent job."

Before anything more could be said, there was a knock on the door and Martha entered. Secret Service Agent Rahsheed Evans and two other men followed her in. Ben greeted them and as they sat, Martha told him the Acting Attorney General Peter Lawton was on his way as requested. Moments later, Martha ushered him in. Ben said, "I asked the A.G. to be here when Mr. Evans played the tapes he took from Mr. Morton's bank vault." He turned to Martha and said, "Ask Cam to join us."

Rahsheed took a semi-translucent box out of a suitcase and placed it on the conference table. He said, as he pointed to a man standing to his left, "Mr. President, this is Mr. Brandt. He's the employee of the bank who opened Morton's vault which contained this box, and," pointing to his right, "FBI agent Perlow that found the vault key and a key that opens this box taped to the underside of a drawer in Morton's desk." Evans put his hand on the box. "This box and those keys haven't been out of our sight since we took it out of the vault."

Ben explained to the Acting Attorney General that Agent Evans had discovered the castrated body of former Assistant Defense Secretary William T. Morton and found the tapes they would now listen to in Morton's bank vault in Montgomery Alabama.

On Ben's signal, Rahsheed Evans turned the key, the lock turned and he lifted the lid. In it were two ninety-minute audiotapes and a substantial number of packages of one hundred-dollar bills. They didn't count the money, but it was obviously hundreds of thousands of dollars. Wearing gloves, Rahsheed picked up a tape marked with a "D."

Tom said, "Before we begin, I'd like the young man from the FBI who brought these tapes to make an identifying mark on each of them." He did as requested. "Now I'd like the young men from the bank and the FBI to dictate statements concerning the circumstances surrounding the finding of the box and its being brought here to the White House. After that, we'll arrange transportation for you back to Montgomery, and remember, not one word of this to any-one."

Before they could leave, Peter Lawton stood and said, "Be advised, if you do talk about this, you will be prosecuted for obstruction of justice to the full extent of the law." The bank officer stared at him a moment, nodded with his mouth hanging open and quickly left.

As they left, Spenser Cameron, Ben's press secretary walked through the open door. Ben pointed to a chair beside his desk. "Take a seat over there, Cam. You're just in time. We're going to play some tapes that Mr. Evans found in Montgomery that belonged to Bill Morton."

Rahsheed put the tape marked "D" in the player. After a few moments of silence, they heard a voice Ben recognized as Bill Morton's greeting Senator Davies. They listened to Morton refer to Ben as a "Jewish son-of-a-bitch" and then heard Davies chiding Morton for having suggested to Ben that the military leaders wouldn't follow Ben's orders as President. The Acting Attorney General, and Tom, Cam, Rahsheed and Ben remained fixed in their seats as Davies explained his scheme to discredit Ben with a planned media campaign. Their faces turned grim as they listened to Davies lay out strategies to create racial and religiously motivated violence across the country and to encourage gang wars, and to his tacit approval of Morton's intended drug importation plans. They listened with almost disbelief as Davies agreed to appoint Morton as Secretary of Defense once he was in office and agree that they might subsequently talk about splitting defense industry graft.

After a half hour, Ben said, "It sounds like they've finished the business part of the meeting. I'll arrange to have all of that tape transcribed."

Cam was the first to speak. "Mr. President, that's unbelievable. When can we release this?"

Ben shrugged. "Before we think about that, let's see what's on the other tape."

Rahsheed put the tape marked "W" in the player. The group listened to a conversation between Morton and an unidentified man. Ben interrupted the tape momentarily. "Rahsheed, do you know who that is talking with Morton?"

"Sounds like the guy that killed him, Fred Washburn. He used to be in the CIA."

Ben pushed the play button. The group listened as Morton and Washburn planned a campaign of racial violence and drug wars. As Washburn mentioned using former contacts from Columbia and Nicaragua, Evans exclaimed softly, "They must have been the guys Washburn bailed out of jail."

They listened as Washburn told Morton that he shouldn't even think about cheating the drug dealers saying, "They'll want your balls if you screw them, Bill."

Evans whispered to Tom Andrews, "Now we know what happened to Bill Morton's missing parts."

Ben smiled in spite of himself.

As the tape droned on, Ben said, "We've probably heard enough of this for now.

Cam Tom, Rahsheed, and Peter Lawton sat silently in incredulous amazement. Ben broke the silence. Sorrow and anger were etched on his face. "I'm sure you find this as incredible as I do. The assassination was bad enough, but the past three months, the lives lost, all as a result of one man's political ambitions."

Tom said, "I can't believe Davies intended what happened."

"Neither do I," Ben said. "He started something he couldn't control." Turning to Cam, Ben said, "What you don't know is I was planning to make a major announcement about the assassination this evening at 9:00 p.m. We know that a man named Clarence Davenport did it and why. The discovery of this crime may be equally as important."

Cam who hadn't yet heard about Clarence Davenport said, "Are you sure, and who the hell is Clarence Davenport?"

"We just found out about it. Davenport killed himself earlier today. The whole story is in this document." Ben handed a sheaf of papers to Cam. "Take a copy of it with you. Right now we got to think about what we do about Davies."

"Excuse me, Mr. President, but what's there to think about. Throw the bastard in jail and tell the people what he did."

Ben smiled. "I'd love to do exactly that."

Lawton said, "Sorry, sir, but that may take a while. Members of the Senate are immune from arrest."

"I know, but there's an exception for Treason, Felony and Breach of the Peace. I'm hoping an announcement will end a lot of the violence, so I don't want to delay it,"

"I'm not sure that any of those exceptions apply."

"Look into it. We need to try and stop the violence. Do the best you can as fast as you can."

"But. Mr. President..."

Ben interrupted. "No buts. Just do it. I want to make an announcement of the Davies-Morton conspiracy today."

After Peter Lawton left, Tom said, "Excuse me, Mr. President, could you delay your announcement on Davies for a day or two. The Acting A. G. grabbed me as he was leaving and said he was feeling very uncomfortable."

"I appreciate that, Tom, but you know what's going on out there. I'm hoping the announcement might stop some of the violence and save some lives. I've got to say something tonight. Tell him I'll omit naming Davies." Tom left to deliver the message.

Shortly before nine P.M., Ben Silver stood near the entrance to the media room in the West Wing of the White House. He could hear the murmur from the packed room of reporters wondering why Ben had called a press conference during the middle of TV prime time. Speculation in the District, a town built on gossip and leaks had to content itself with gossip. There were no leaks. The smart money was betting that Ben would resign the Presidency, ending his unexpected and brief tenure as the nation's chief executive. As Ben continued standing, he thought about president-elect Butler's inauguration and the explosion from the bombs that had been planted in the TelePrompTer and speakers and the missile and Bazooka shell that completed the murder of the entire cabinet and all other legal successors to the presidency, except him. His well publicized disagreement with Butler during the presidential campaign while serving as Secretary of Education under President Parsons and his unexpected absence from the inauguration ceremony resulted in his becoming the chief suspect in the FBI's investigation of the assassination of Butler and the others. Hopefully, all that will finally be ended.

At 9:00 PM, despite some grumbling by the TV networks, Ben strode on to a platform before a large bank of television cameras and an audience of puzzled journalists. Ben leaned on the podium over the seal of the United States. It was devoid of all papers. Ben could hear the whispered word "Resignation" from several members of the media. Ben remained standing while silence descended on the room. Whispers started up again as the Acting Attorney General came in followed by Ben's chief of staff, Tom Andrews and his Press Secretary, Cameron Spenser. They sat in folding wooden chairs on Ben's right. Secret Service Agents John Wallace and Rahsheed Evans and Presidential aide, Molly Pemberton followed and sat on Ben's left.

The room became tomb quiet as Ben began. "Good evening. I come before you this evening to tell you about two monstrous crimes committed against the people of the United States. One you knew about. The other, you didn't, although the results have been front-page news for many, many weeks. You see on my right Peter Lawton, the Acting Attorney General and two valued members of my administration, Tom Andrews and Cameron Spenser. They are aware of these crimes. The three on my left are respectively, John Wallace and Rahsheed Evans of the Secret Service and Molly Pemberton, formerly of the FBI and now on my staff. They are the lead investigators who brought the evidence of these crimes before us."

All eyes remained on Ben as he continued. "First, I want to talk about the murder of the President and of so many of our fellow Americans at the Inauguration. The person responsible for that was a Desert Storm veteran named Clarence Davenport."

A buzz of "Who's he?" circulated around the room.

Ben held his hands up for quiet. "He's written a three hundred and eighty-seven page explanation of what, why and how he did it which was delivered to two of the investigators sitting in front of you minutes before he killed himself." Another buzz of noise began gathering force. Ben held his hands up again. "He said he sent copies of that explanation to the TV networks and some newspapers, and that they should be getting it in the mail either tomorrow or the next day."

A hum and rustling sound permeated the room as people looked at their neighbors in the audience asking who Davenport was. Ben held his hands up for silence. "Davenport is no one that I or anyone on my staff ever heard of, and it is very likely that no one in this room ever heard of him either. Like I said, he was a veteran with Gulf War service in 1991. He became incensed at what he believed was a callous disregard and denial of responsibility for the injuries he and the men under his command suffered during that conflict. He was further alienated by what he believed was a callous disregard of his father's problems and ultimate death, which he attributed to the Vietnam conflict and neglect by the Federal government. He also was upset with the government's treatment of his grandfather, a seriously wounded World War II veteran. All of those things led him to re-examine the structure of our government and decide that it needed to be destroyed and replaced. This same person was also responsible for the murders of Defense Secretary Wilson, General Allen and Senator Davies' receptionist, Laverne Templeton, and many others. All of the investigators who worked on this matter, and especially Agent John Wallace and Ms. Molly Pemberton who are seated in back of me are owed a debt of gratitude for the excellent work they did to bring the investigation to this conclusion."

Ben stared at his stunned audience and then continued, "As unthinkable as the assassination was, there is a second crime, just as incredible that I am also going to tell you about this evening. This crime is one spawned by the political ambition of a highly respected member of the Congress and his pawn, a former Assistant Secretary of Defense, the now-deceased William T. Morton. Primarily through the perseverance and efforts of Mr. Evans over there", Ben nodded at Rahsheed Evans who acknowledged the nod with one of his own, "we have uncovered a conspiracy to foster violence, hate crimes, drug wars, anarchy and chaos. These conspirators unleashed uncontrollable forces of evil and depravity to advance their political and economic agendas. It is difficult to describe the cynical malevolence and greed that fueled this plot. The most amoral, disaffected and violent elements were sought out. One person that we know of was a discharged, ex-CIA agent. That man, recruited by William Morton purposefully encouraged the lawlessness, the violence and the hatred that spread through the land. After meeting with Mr. Morton, and at Morton's suggestion, this depraved ex-CIA agent contacted drug dealers in Colombia and Nicaragua. He fostered increased drug importation and drug wars. He encouraged crimes of violence based on racial, religious and ethnic intolerance. Those efforts by Morton and his associates threatened to destroy the creation of our founding fathers and the work of over 200 years. And how do we know that this plot took place? We know it because Mr. Evans returned here with audio tapes of the very conversations where those plans were agreed upon."

Ben paused to allow the rumble in the room to subside. "As you know, civil government has been restored in Mississippi and Alabama. There are however, in those states and in the Northwest, armed militia groups still resisting the authority of the lawful government. It is time for anarchy to end. It is time to acknowledge that the country and its people have been manipulated and victimized by evil men. I ask that all of the militiamen put down their arms and recognize that the primary purpose of the militia under Article I, Section 8 of the Constitution is to execute the Laws of the Union and suppress Insurrections, not to foment rebellion. Recognize that you have been duped into betraying the very principles that you hold most dear."

Ben took a few sheets of paper from his breast pocket and unfolded them. "I would like to read excerpts to you which were intended as advice to all of us by our first and possibly greatest president, George Washington, on his retirement from public life. He took that opportunity to warn us of some of the potential dangers we faced. Despite the changes that have taken place in the more than 200 years since, much of what he said then remains very relevant to this day We would do well to heed the advice he gave us on September 17, 1796."

Ben adjusted his glasses and then read, sections of Washington's Farewell Address urging the people, among other things, to prize their unity, avoid the divisiveness that results from the efforts of people that try to capitalize on sectional, religious or other differences, real or imagined. After Ben returned the pages to his pocket, he said, "We have all witnessed the terrible things that happen when we disregard the advice of those people who fought to provide us with the liberty and freedom we all enjoy. Living under the Constitution the founding fathers created is a blessing that made us the best and most powerful nation on the earth. It is up to you, the people of the United States, to determine just what kind of country you want to have. Is it to reflect the dreams of our founding fathers or their nightmares?"

Ben looked at his wristwatch and then said, "I see I have taken about thirty minutes. I think there is nothing more to say except that I believe that this is a time for us all to reflect. We have looked into the abyss created by a philosophy of separatism, intolerance and hatred. We have seen what can happen when those forces prevail. I think it is time for a new beginning based upon unity, understanding and tolerance of our differences. There is no other way. Thank you and good night."

As Ben started to leave, a surging wave of journalists and TV media rushed toward him, frantically shouting for attention. One reporter could be heard above the din, "Please, sir, Mr. President. Who is Morton's co-conspirator? Is it Senator Davies?"

After a look towards the Acting Attorney General and a whispered conversation with him, Ben looked at the mass of media and held his arms up requesting quiet. He waited until the voices stilled and he had their full attention. "I am now able to answer your question." He paused and again looked out over the room. "Senator Davies has been arrested and will be arraigned tomorrow."

Following his TV address, Ben enjoyed dinner in the private residence quarters of the White House with Jane Cabot. He couldn't remember any meal he had ever enjoyed more. During the meal and over Ben's favorite Key Lime Pie desert, he and Jane reviewed the events of the day. After dinner, Ben and Jane went into the bedroom where they made love for the first time in weeks, and feeling better than he had at any time since succeeding to the Presidency, Ben and Jane were ready to end the day and go to sleep. As Ben reached over to shut the table lamp next to his bed, Ben's private phone rang. Very few people had that number—Tom Andrews, Cam Spenser, Admiral Williamson, Chairman of the Joint Chiefs of Staff, Peter Clemmons, Ben's Acting Secretary of State, and Senator Robert Kendall. The call was from Kendall. After they talked for several minutes, Ben frowned and hung up the phone.

Jane took Ben's hand as she said, "What was that about?"

"Senator Kendall and I thought that tonight's announcements about Davenport and Davies would end that Impeachment proceeding they were starting in the House."

"I thought so to."

"Kendall talked with Speaker Thorsten and he's still complaining about our relationship."

"Seems to me he doesn't have much else."

"He also said he thinks the evidence against Davies must be a forgery."

Jane leaned over to rearrange Ace and Deuce, Ben's pet English bulldog and Pug. They had fallen asleep on each other and on her foot. She put her lamp on, looked at Ben and held his hand. "You know, we were talking earlier about George Washington and his Farewell Address. Let me ask you, Ben, what you want. Now that you can't be pressured to resign because of the assassination and the chaos that followed, are you ready to give your Farewell Address or do you want to stay with this job?"

"That's one hell of a question."

Jane sat up in Bed. "I'm tough enough to outlast all they can try and do to me Ben, but if you want to stay here and I'm a problem, just say the word and I'll get out of your life."

Ben shook his head. "That's definitely not what I want. I need you in my life whether I stay or go. You know I would have resigned long ago in favor of Senator Kendall if that could have been arranged, but it couldn't. Elliott Thorsten was Speaker of the House and he was next in line. That would have been too much of a disaster for me to let that happen. What's more, the gossip inside the Beltway was that Senator Davies was waiting in the wings to take over from him." Ben grimaced. "It's just that I feel so terrible about your having to put up with this crap, but if you can handle it, so can I."

"So you want to stay?"

"I was thinking that with Davenport dead and the evidence we have against Davies, as a nation, we would have a few months to lick our wounds and recuperate and an opportunity to look at our faults and correct them. I thought that maybe something positive could come out of all this."

"Do you still think so?"

"I'm not sure. I was hoping the Impeachment was dead, because I don't know if the country can take another period with the kind of chaos that Impeachment proceedings involve. Maybe Thorsten won't be able to get the Impeachment off the ground, even if he tries to move it along."

CHAPTER 3

▼

After Clarence closed the porch blinds, he stuffed the photographs of his adoptive father and mother and his computer discs in his carry-on bag and checked his pocket for his forged Irish Republic passport. He had everything he needed. He went into the bathroom, picked up Mr. Swanson's body, carried it out to the porch and quickly arranged it in his favorite armchair. He took one of John Wallace's business cards off the table, put it in his old wallet and stuffed that in Mr. Swanson's pocket. He then picked up Molly Pemberton's business card, sniffed the slight perfumed odor it had picked up in her purse and placed it inside his passport. Satisfied, he pushed the transmitter button leaving him one minute and forty-five seconds to run down to the basement and make his way through the underground tunnel and through the woods in back of his house before it would explode into a pile of ruble. He never thought he would need the fake passport when Rabbani gave it to him in London, but Rabbani had said, "just in case" he ever needed it. Seems that his uncle had been a prophet.

Clarence exited from the tunnel and made his way to the Swanson house on the other side of the woods as the explosion thundered. When he got there, he clicked the garage door opener he took from them the previous night, got into their blue Toyota Camry and drove to Ronald Reagan Washington National Airport. He parked in long-term parking, took the bus to the terminal, and from there took a free bus to a Washington hotel. It didn't matter which hotel, because he wasn't staying there. From the hotel he went to the train station and boarded the New York City express. Once in New York, he took a cab to Kennedy Airport and was on his way to Dublin, where he would arrive six and one half-hours later as Chester Dolan.

Relaxing with a Bushmill's Irish Whiskey in the Aer Lingus first class cabin, Clarence decided he'd see the country like a tourist for a few days to become comfortable with his new identity and then he'd call his uncle, Omar bin Rabbani. As he recalled the two months he spent with Rabbani, he wondered if his uncle had somehow manipulated him into doing what he had done. That possibility had crossed his mind for the first time when he pocketed the forged passport. He immediately dismissed it as a ridiculous idea, but the thought kept recurring. He'd have to think about that later, but for the next few days, as Chester Dolan, a repatriated American from New York City, he would have an expensive, good time and a cheap, bad woman.

As his flight crossed the Atlantic, Clarence tuned his armchair TV to CNN and watched President Silver's TV address naming him as the Inauguration Day assassin. His picture flashed on the tiny screen. Clarence stared at it. He had destroyed all the photographs in the house before he left except for his college graduation picture and that was the one that was on the screen. He still bore a faint resemblance to that person, but not enough to cause a problem and besides, everyone thinks Clarence Davenport is dead. Clarence smiled as he learned the details of his death, but was surprised and didn't know what to make of the disclosures about Davies. He had wanted to kill Davies because of his participation in the Kamisiyah and Gulf War Syndrome cover-up, but what Silver accused him of was even worse. Perhaps some day he might return to the United States, and if he does, he'd have to kill Davies.

He'd think about that some other time. He had to concentrate on his own situation right now. He thought about what he had just heard. Excellent, his plan had worked. Everyone thought he had died in the explosion. They'd figure it out soon enough, but so far so good. He continued listening and had to restrain himself from laughing out loud as he listened while a network pundit pronounced, in his familiar way, "Yes, Mr. And Mrs. America, today we can all breathe easier. Self-styled super-patriot Clarence Davenport took his own life, closing another bizarre chapter in the right-wing attack on our democracy. All those that thought the Inauguration Day Massacre was the product of Islamic terrorists or state-sponsored terrorism or a plot by President Ben Silver and his supporters were wrong once more. It is again, like it was in Oklahoma City, the act of a deranged, native-born, American citizen, a Gulf War Veteran, like Tim McVeigh the executed Oklahoma City bomber and like John Muhammad, the Washington D.C. sniper. Thankfully, we can now put it all to rest and get on with our lives."

After a day of playing tourist in Dublin, Clarence was already bored. He had read everything he could find about his life and presumed death in the on-line versions of the New York Times and the Washington Post and was almost eager to hear that they had discovered his escape from the ranch house. It was while having an early breakfast that the BBC's scheduled programming was interrupted by a telecast of Ben's TV press conference announcing that he had managed to deceive everyone with the explosion and escape. Clarence had expected the media to be shocked and become hostile towards Ben Silver when the truth became known and they did. None of that interested him much overly much and he continued eating his breakfast. Clarence put his tea cup down when Kim Cotton asked Ben about Clarence's last year's trip to London to see the lawyer who settled his mother's paternity case against his Saudi father. He knew that they would quickly discover that he had escaped from the house, but was surprised that they had so quickly learned of his trip to London. That means they would soon know about uncle Rabbani if they didn't already. He'd have to be careful in contacting him. It might not be safe to call Rabbani's office or his home.

Clarence opened his IBM laptop computer and looked through his address book for the home phone number of Rabbani's secretary. They had dated while he was in London and had gone to bed together a number of times. It was a relationship that could have grown, but they both knew he had to return to the United States. He dialed her number on his pre-paid disposable cell phone. When a man answered, Clarence asked for Fatima. The man told Clarence that the number he dialed was no longer Fatima's number, adding that he was damn tired of people calling his number looking for her. Clarence thought it through. He'd have to chance calling the office even if the police were watching or the phones were tapped. What the hell, they knew he was alive, and the cell phone was untraceable. He'd have to try her a little later in the morning after the office opened. Clarence left his room and purchased another pre-paid cell phone for cash, and then returned to his hotel where he got on the Internet and read the New York Times on line.

He glanced at his old Timex wristwatch and muttered, "Time to give it a go as the Brits say." He dialed the number of his uncle's office.

"Rabbani law offices, good morning."

"Is this Fatima?"

"Yes it is."

"I tried you earlier at your apartment number and some man answered and said that wasn't your number anymore."

"Ah, cousin Khalil, I should have told you I gave up the land line and just use my cell phone now. How's aunt Delia?"

Clarence frowned. He didn't have an aunt Delia. "She's fine. They're all fine."

"Mr. Rabbani doesn't like my getting personal calls in the office so give me your number and I'll call you in ten minutes."

Clarence thought quickly, was it a trap? He said, "I was just on my way somewhere. Give me your cell phone number and I'll call you in ten minutes."

"That's fine." She gave him the number.

Ten minutes later, Clarence called the number she gave him. She answered immediately.

"Thank God I answered and you said what you did. Our phones are tapped. The US FBI and Secret Service have been here and so have all the UK intelligence people including the FO."

"I thought that was why you called me Cousin Khalil. Do you know if they have the technology in the UK to listen to wireless telephone calls?"

"I don't know, but if you have it in the States, I bet they have it here, because a ton of law enforcement people from the States are here with all kinds of technical gadgets."

"Like who?"

"CIA, FBI, Secret Service at least."

"Do you know who's in charge?"

"There are three of them, a woman named Molly Pemberton, a man named John Wallace and a Negro named Rahsheed Evans. You know who they are?"

"I met the woman and Wallace. They're the ones that discovered I was the assassin, and Evans broke the case against Senator Davies." Clarence glanced at his wristwatch. "I got to terminate this call now, just in case. I'll call you later tonight."

"I'd like to see you, Clare, but it's too dangerous for you to come here. Where are you?"

"Better that I don't say."

"You can trust me, Clare."

"I'm sure I can, but someone else could be listening. Get a new untraceable cell phone. I'll call you at six thirty and get that new number from you. We'll talk then."

Clarence spent the rest of the day doing what a lot of tourists in Dublin do. He took a tour around the City of Dublin, hopping on and off the double-decker bus with the rest of the tourists to view the attractions, but seeing none of them. He had to think. He had to see if there was someplace else he should go, somewhere that he wouldn't be hunted. Maybe some Islamic country would welcome him. He'd have to think about that. When the tour ended, he hired a cab, he didn't want to be part of another tour group, and went out to Trinity College. He went into the library, took a quick look at the Exhibition of the Book of Kells, purchased a copy and then retreated to a library table with it and pretended to study it. As he flipped the pages, periodically looking at the biblical illustrations, he wondered if moving from the Bible to the Koran was a major step. When he was in London last year, he had studied the Koran with his uncle, just to learn what it was about, and thought about converting to Islam. He found it too strange to be seriously considered, but if he were to move to an Arab country he better know a lot more about it than he does now.

He glanced at his watch again. It was almost time to call Fatima. Clarence left the Trinity College Library, sat on a bench outside and dialed her number. She answered immediately, gave him the phone number of her newly purchased cell phone and pushed the end button. Clarence called that number, and again, Fatima answered immediately. "We can talk now, Clare. It's a good thing you didn't come to the office or Mr. Rabbani's house. Both places are being watched and the phones are bugged."

"I really have to figure out a way to see him or at least talk to him."

"He wants to see you too, but you'll have to be patient."

"You told him we spoke?"

"He knows I don't have a cousin Khalil. He heard me tell you that he doesn't like me getting personal calls, and he knows that's not true. He's very smart and figured it out. He told me to tell you to be careful. London is crawling with US police people and the authorities here are cooperating with them. He told me to ask you if you can get to Galway in Ireland next week?"

Clarence was immediately suspicious. Why Ireland? Do they somehow know he's in Ireland? Clarence said, "Why Galway?"

"He's playing in a golf tournament there starting a week from Friday and we don't think his minders will be going there with him."

"How come?"

"It was planned months ago, well before the police knew anything about you, and Rabbani is complaining about the surveillance ruining his business. I think they're going to have to back off a bit very soon."

"Do you know where he's staying?"

"Of course, I made the reservation."

After Fatima told him where Rabbani would be staying, Clarence said, "Tell my uncle that I'll look for him there."

"I could make a golf reservation in a foursome with Mr. Rabbani and he and you could share a golf cart." After Clarence agreed, she said, "What name."

Clarence thought quickly, he didn't want to reveal the name he was currently using. "Khalil Yomani. Ask Rabbani to bring some documents in that name that I can use."

"What country?"

"Saudi or Kuwait, whatever is easier."

"He'll have them. I could go with him, if you want?"

"Do you want to see me?"

"Yes. I could make a reservation for myself in an adjoining room and you could stay there with me."

"Do that. I want to see you, but I can't promise to stay. That might be too dangerous for you and for me."

After he ended the call, Clarence remained seated on the same bench outside the library at Trinity College. Could he trust Fatima, and what about Rabbani? He never knew Rabbani was his uncle until last year. He never knew he had been adopted and that his biological father was a Saudi prince until last year. Sure, he and Rabbani spent two months together, but did he really know him. There was an enormous reward on his head. Would Fatima or Rabbani turn him in for it? He'd have to take a chance and go to Galway, but he'd be as careful as he could. He'd have to find out if Rabbani would help him find a place to live and establish a new identity and life, or betray him to the US authorities. He had no choice. He would go to Galway, be Khalil Yomani and play golf. Wait a minute. He'd hit golf balls at a driving range years ago, but had never played on a golf course. Well, he didn't have to play like Tiger Woods. All he had to do was learn to play good enough to not draw attention to himself and learn the rules of the game. Clarence went back to his hotel and the next morning got up, and did a quick computer search for a hotel with a golf course. In short order, he booked a room at the Glenlo Abbey Hotel in Galway, a train reservation from Dublin to Galway, and then checked out of his hotel. He spent the rest of the day in a pub reading on-line newspapers. He took a cab to Heuston station in time to make the 7:05 P.M. arriving in Galway about three hours later. As he sat on the train reading a paper back book on how to play golf by Gary Player, he planned his activities for the next day. He'd buy some golf equipment, take a lesson from a professional, play eighteen holes and then check out the Waterfront Hotel where Rabbani and Fatima would be staying and the Galway Bay Golf and Country Club where he would play golf with his uncle as Khalil Yomani.

CHAPTER 4

▼

"Ladies and gentlemen, the President of the United States."

As Ben Silver strode into the media room of the West Wing of the White House, he recalled the hostility that greeted him the last time he appeared before the press corps and the triumphant feeling he had when he left. He grasped the sides of the lectern embossed with the Presidential seal and stared out at the press corps. While the room quieted, Ben wondered if he should have taken his press Secretary's advice and let him inform the media of Clarence Davenport's escape. A few of his advisors even wanted to cover-up the mistake, but no, this was his job, and the media and the public should hear the truth from their President. The last time he addressed the media, he had turned animosity into amazement and incredulity. This time he expected to leave a room full of hostility.

Before Ben could begin speaking, a few reporters stood and began rhythmically clapping their hands. The applause spread, and as Ben continued holding onto the sides of the mahogany lectern, they all stood and began applauding. Ben paused a moment, almost startled, looking at the now standing members of the media. It was the first time he had been received like that since he succeeded to the Presidency. As Ben raised his hands to still the applause, he hoped he would still enjoy their approval when he finished, but knew he wouldn't.

"Ladies and gentlemen of the press and in the radio and television audience, I appreciate the welcome. Three nights ago, in this very room, I told you that Clarence Davenport was the Inauguration Day assassin who had killed President Butler and so many other of our political leaders and that Davenport, faced with arrest, had killed himself in an explosion at his home."

Ben looked into the television cameras and took a deep breath. "It is now my painful duty to tell you that we have learned that Mr. Davenport was not in his house when he caused the explosion that destroyed it."

The crowd of reporters sprang to their feet. Ben could feel the waves of shocked disbelief as they rippled through the crowd. The roar gathered strength and assaulted Ben's ears. He held his hands up for silence. The protest got louder. The mass of media surged towards the podium, but was intercepted by a solid wall of Secret Service Agents. Ben shouted above the noise. "Please, take your seats! Please! I'll explain. I'll tell you what happened. Please! Return to your seats."

The protest continued. Ben held his hands up again. "Please! Sit down. As soon as I finish, I'll answer your questions. Now sit down and let me explain."

The media, with the assistance of the Secret Service, finally quieted down and returned to their seats. Ben said, "Thank you." He took a deep breath and continued, "When the forensics investigators went through the debris they found a mutilated body that they thought was Davenport. Subsequently, however, when Mr. Wallace and Ms. Pemberton went to Davenport's house to examine the body, they became suspicious because of what they observed. Later, they discovered the remnants of a tunnel leading from the Davenport dwelling to a nearby wooded area and a path leading to a house owned by an elderly couple, Oscar and Lucille Swanson. They discovered the body of Mrs. Swanson in the house and the body discovered in the Davenport house has now been identified through dental records as that of Oscar Swanson. We assume Davenport made his way through the tunnel and then set off the bomb electronically, destroying his house and his escape route."

Another rumble of protest began. Ben held up his hands for silence again. "We are all enormously upset and angry at his escape. The FBI, Secret Service, ATF and other law enforcement agencies have been alerted and are making every effort possible to apprehend him. I don't like it, you don't like it, nobody likes it, but that's what happened and we have to deal with that reality. Now I said I'd take some questions and I will, but please, only one question each and I'll get to as many of you as I can."

Ben pointed at one of the reporters, "Mr. Perkins."

"Mr. President, how could this happen when the house was surrounded by agents?"

"First off, the house wasn't surrounded. Secret Service Agent John Wallace and former FBI Agent Molly Pemberton received information that suggested to them that Davenport might possibly have known something about or been involved in the assassination. They tapped his phone and placed him under sur-veillance, but nothing incriminating surfaced so they called him and made an appointment with him at his house for an initial interview. During that meeting, he admitted that he was the perpetrator and they attempted to place him under arrest. He informed them that he had wired the chair he was sitting on with enough explosives to kill them all. They left while the dwelling remained under surveillance and called for instructions. While they were watching the house, Davenport apparently made his way through the tunnel, and as I said before, caused the explosion."

Ben looked to his left and said, Miss Seymour.

She rose. "Sir, don't you think the Agents should have stayed with him and if necessary been killed with him rather than allow him to escape."

"No, I don't. They made the correct decision based on what seemed to be the factual situation."

Ben pointed to a frantically waiving reporter at the back of the room. "Mr. Kelly."

"Mr. President, I saw the police report about the murder of Mrs. Swanson. It's my understanding from that report that she was killed many hours before the explosion. Why do you say that Davenport killed her and if her murder is related to Davenport's escape, maybe someone else killed her? Maybe he has accom-plices. Many of us still find it hard to believe he was acting alone just because he said so."

"I don't know that he was acting alone either, but there were clues left at the scene of the crime that persuade the investigators that Davenport killed Mr. and Mrs. Swanson. The investigators believe that Davenport planned his escape the night before and killed those people prior to the explosion, but that doesn't rule out his having accomplices." Ben nodded at a reporter sitting in the front row.

"Thank you, sir. "Do you believe Davenport assassinated President Butler and all the others for the reasons he stated in the document he sent to the media?"

"I don't know. He tells us what he did, how he did it. That checks out with what we learned during the investigation. He said he wanted to cause what he termed the Second American Revolution to force a total re-examination of the basic structure of our government and that he was acting alone. It's possible that he did everything he says, in the way and for the reasons he stated."

"Were there any clues left at the scene?"

"The authorities are keeping that confidential at the present time." Ben nod-ded at another reporter. "Next."

"Mr. President, sir, do we have any information as to where he might be."

"I wish I could say yes, but we don't. He stole the Swansons' Toyota and we found it in long-term parking at Reagan National Airport. It had been parked there two days ago so he could be almost anywhere by now. We know what time he parked there and have started the process of checking all flights leaving from there after that time. So far we haven't come up with anything helpful."

A woman reporter wearing enormous trademark glasses asked, "Mr. President, Davenport apparently left some clues when he killed his neighbors. Perhaps there are others that were similarly murdered. If we found them, that could provide a trail indicating where he went and maybe media publicity could help find him."

"That is a consideration, but it could also easily lead to misleading copy-cat killings." Ben pointed at a woman reporter in a red suit.

"Sir, he named his biological and adoptive parents in that long document you referred to. What do they know about his escape?"

"His adoptive parents are both deceased. He was their only child and we have not found any close relatives. His biological father is also deceased and we are told he never met his biological mother. We have interviewed his mother and her family and will continue investigating them, but there is no present indication of their involvement in or knowledge of any of Davenport's activities."

Ben recognized a reporter in the front row. He rose and said, "Bob Blake, CBS, Mr. President. Davenport was the illegitimate son of a Saudi prince. Do you believe the Saudis were involved in either the assassination of President Butler or Davenport's escape?"

"Nothing we presently know leads to that conclusion. We will of course continue to investigate, but the mere fact that he was the illegitimate son of a Saudi prince that he never met or even knew about until very recently does not warrant even a suspicion that the Saudis are involved."

Ben pointed at another reporter. She said, "I'd like to follow up on Bob Blake's question." Ben nodded for her to continue. "Have you investigated to see if Davenport had any contact with his Saudi relatives?"

"We have and the investigation is ongoing. Like I said, we believe he knew nothing about who his biological father was or indeed of the fact that he had been adopted until about a year ago when his adoptive mother died and left a note telling him of his adoption. We are reconstructing his activities as best we can to see who his friends and associates are." Ben turned to a frantically waving reporter on his far left, "Miss Cotton."

She momentarily fluffed her blonde hair as the cameras panned towards her. "Mr. President, Kim Cotton with the Scott Jackson News Service. "We heard that Mr. Davenport went to Europe last year and stayed in London for several months. What can you tell us about that trip and who he saw while he was there?"

Ben frowned. He knew that her asking the question would probably alert Davenport that the authorities would be looking into his activities in London. He wanted to ask her where she got that information, but instead said, "We know he visited with the lawyer who now lives in London that had represented his biological father in negotiating a settlement arrangement with his biological mother shortly after he was born. That may be all there was to that meeting, but it's something we're looking into."

Ms. Cotton remained standing, waving her arms at Ben. Ben looked away and then pointed at a reporter sitting in the second row.

"Can you tell us what leads you are currently following?"

Ben smiled. "If we had any, it would be inadvisable to discuss them."

"Why is that?" she said.

Ben looked at her over his glasses. "Wherever he is, he probably has access to television or reports of this press conference. We wouldn't want him to know what we know and what we don't know." Ben took his glasses off and pointed with them to a reporter at the back of the room and said, "My apologies. I'll try to get to know your names real soon. What's your question?"

"On a different topic. You said when you spoke to us the last time that conditions in the country were worsened by the political aspirations of Senator Davies and others. Who are the others and what's the status of the case against Davies?"

"Let's leave it with Davies for the moment. I certainly included former Assistant Secretary of Defense, Morton, but he's dead so we'll stay with Davies. As you know, Senator Davies has been released on bail. There are preliminary motions being filed in the criminal cases and I can't comment on them."

Ben pointed at a reporter in the last row. "Sir, you said that there's a tape of Senator Davies conspiring with Assistant Defense Secretary William Morton to create civil unrest throughout the country and that prosecution of Davies is being stalled by a claim of immunity because the Senate is in session. Is there a tape of that conversation and if so, when will it be released to the media?"

"The audio tapes you described are at the Department of Justice. Their release is being deferred until certain, pending court proceedings are resolved."

Before Ben could recognize anyone else, the reporter said, "There is talk about a resolution to expel Senator Davies from the Senate. Do you think he should be expelled?"

"That's for the Senate to decide." Ben glanced at his wristwatch. "That's all the time I have. Thank you all for coming and to you and the television audience for your time and attention."

Ben made his way to the exit while reporters continued shouting questions at him. As a Secret Service Agent opened the door, Ben turned and waived to the audience. Once the door closed, Ben sat heavily in a straight-backed wooden chair in front of a make-up mirror and said to Spenser Cameron, his Press Secretary, as an aide removed the thin veneer of television make-up covering his face, "That was not fun. How do you think it went?"

"As well as it could, but it was a terrible pill for the media and the public to swallow. You should have let me blame the surveillance people for his escape and break the news like I suggested. Then I'd take the heat instead of you."

"To paraphrase Truman, 'If I can't stand the heat, I ought to get out of the kitchen.' It was my job, Cam."

"Politics have changed since then, Mr. President."

"Not for me, at least in that regard."

"Yes, sir, but don't you think John Wallace and Molly Pemberton ought to have explained why they left Davenport in the house. It's hard, even for the media, to tell someone they should have stayed and been blown to bits when they're standing in front of you."

Ben nodded his head in agreement "Perhaps so, but it was more important to send them to London to see that lawyer. We'll talk more when we get to my office. Tom Andrews is waiting for me. Why don't you come too?"

Ben and Cam, accompanied, preceded and trailed by an entourage of Secret Service Agents, hurried through the corridors to the Oval Office. Once there and seated behind his desk, Ben turned towards Tom Andrews. "They finish checking the flights from Reagan to London?"

"Yes, sir. All passengers on all those flights are accounted for. We've checked everything that left Reagan for anywhere during the twelve-hour period following the explosion and so far we've come up empty. We've also started checking Dulles and Baltimore-Washington flights to London, but so far, we've come up with nothing. Some investigators think leaving the car at Reagan could be like a red herring and that he never left the country at all, so he could be almost anywhere. He could be still fixated on killing you and hiding out someplace near Washington. Some of the psychological profiles they've compiled say he could be obsessed that way."

Ben frowned. "He could be anywhere, but I still think he left the country. If he did, the only place he probably went to was London, and the person he went to see in London was most likely the lawyer who settled the paternity case for his biological father with his biological mother. That lawyer was his biological father's brother so that would make Rabbani the only relative Davenport has, except for his biological mother's family, and we know none of them has ever had anything to do with him, except for his grandfather, Walter Hammonds who we have completely exonerated."

"Do you think it's significant that the lawyer was his uncle?"

Ben frowned. "I don't know. It certainly wouldn't take two months of meetings with Rabbani to find out everything Rabbani knew about his biological father. If, as we suspect, he spent two months with Rabbani before returning to the United States and then started on his plan to assassinate President Butler and everyone at the Inauguration shortly after he returned, well yes, I think that could be significant. In any event, what else do we have?"

Ben, Tom Andrews and Spenser Cameron sat glumly silent for a moment before Spenser Cameron broke the silence. "Sorry about that Kim Cotton question, Mr. President, on the London connection. I didn't know Scott Jackson had hired her."

"That's not the issue, Cam. I want to know where she got that information about Davenport's possible London connection. We've got Agents watching his uncle's law office and home and her question had to tip him off that we know about Rabbani." Ben turned towards Tom Andrews. "Where do you think the leak came from?"

"It's got to be P.J. Winters".

"You're probably right, but why do you think so?"

"Winters is one of the very few people who knew Davenport went to London to meet with the lawyer that represented his biological father and I know that he met with Scott Jackson last night. It can't be anyone else."

"Damn it, Tom, but I've had it with that S.O.B. I should have done it already. Tomorrow morning, call Lawton and tell him to fire Winters."

"That's probably not a good idea, Mr. President. You know I think he's excrement, but as head of the FBI he has statutory protection and he's got dossiers on so many members of Congress and the bureaucracy that you won't have many allies in a fight with him."

"Tom, I can't have him compromise our efforts to find Davenport and anyone that may be working with him. Does Winters know the lawyer is Rabbani and that Rabbani is his uncle?"

"No, I told John Wallace to omit that little detail from the official report of the interview of Davenport's grandfather."

Ben frowned. "If we can't fire him, go around him. He's to know nothing about the hunt for Davenport. Restrict access to the Secret Service and the Department of Homeland Security. Nothing to the FBI, and people from those agencies working on the investigation are to be instructed that nothing goes to the FBI."

"Okay, but Winters will find out and go ballistic."

"I don't give a damn. What worries me is that keeping the FBI out of the loop will impede the investigation."

"It won't be a problem, Mr. President. There are agents in the FBI and CIA that are personal friends. They know the score and they'll report directly to me. Winters will find out about the lawyer eventually, but not until we finish looking into his background."

"That's a lousy way to have to hunt him down." Ben sighed unhappily. "Let's review what we know about him."

Tom Andrews pulled a file from his briefcase, shuffled through a few papers and said, "The name he uses now is Omar Bin Rabbani. He's a Saudi, born into the royal family, and was the brother of Davenport's biological father. He's been disinherited, by his father, and lives in London where he's been a lawyer for many years. As you know, Molly and John discovered from Davenport's grandfather, Walter Hammonds that Rabbani handled the payoff to Davenport's mother in the paternity case and that Davenport knew nothing about his being adopted until after his mother died. After Davenport discovered who his biological mother was, he called her, but she refused to see him. Davenport met her father and that's how he found out about Rabbani. We know he went to London, spent two months there and Rabbani has admitted he met with him."

Ben said, "See if you can find out what Davenport did while he was in London. We know his passport had him staying in the UK for two months. If he spent most of that time with Rabbani, then, as I said, it seems to me, that's a long time to spend with someone you never met before."

Andrews nodded in agreement. "His credit card records indicate he spent almost all of that time in London and he didn't spend much money. He moved out of his hotel after three days, and didn't check into a new one, so he had to be staying with someone and some one had to be picking up the expenses. We think it could be Rabbani."

"What else do we know about Davenport?"

"Not much."

"Review it for me."

"Okay." Andrews shuffled through the thin file folder, then looked up and said, "Before he went to London, Davenport lived very quietly in the same house in Alexandria, Virginia that he lived in with the people that adopted him when he was an infant. He was their only child. He did well in school, played high school baseball and graduated from Princeton where he majored in Government. He joined ROTC and became a demolition specialist. Service in Iraq during Desert Storm was the only time he left the United States before that trip to London." Andrews shuffled through some papers, then looked up and said, "You know the rest from his Manifesto".

Ben leaned back in his chair and shut his eyes and as he said, "Run through it anyway. Sometimes it helps to hear it again."

Tom nodded and resumed. "We know the unit Davenport commanded was the one that blew up the Iraqi munitions depot at Kamisiyah, that all of his men became ill with Gulf War Syndrome and a lot of them died. That's why he says he decided to kill Dan Wilson, but when he went to do it, he overheard Wilson talking to Davies about what he took to be a cover-up…"

Ben interrupted. "Let's not mince words, Tom. It was a cover-up. There's no question about it."

"Yes, sir. In any event, Davenport decided to see how high the cover-up went, and when he discovered it included Senator Butler who was running for President, he decided that killing Wilson would be futile. It was after that, when his mother died, that he learns he was adopted and that he found out his father was a deceased Saudi prince. Then he went to London and met with Rabbani, but we don't know what else he did during the two months he was in London. We think it was sometime after he came back that he decided to assassinate President Butler and all successors to the Presidency."

"What else do we know about Rabbani?"

"The reports we got from London don't tell us very much, only that he handles matters for Saudi and Kuwaiti businessmen in the UK and that he's not popular with the official Saudi royal family."

"Is he involved with terrorists like Al Qaeda?"

"We don't think so. The CIA thinks he's fed up with the Saudi Royals because of their corruption. They say he's a secular Muslim and opposes the Wahhabi clerics and Al Qaeda. Actually, he'd be the CIA's first choice to take over if a Saudi regime change became necessary."

"We might know more about him soon," Ben said. "I've asked Mustafa Al Sabin to find out what he can and he's coming in to the residence to see me tonight. I'd like you there, Tom, but I'll have to see him alone because he doesn't want it known that he's cooperating with us." Ben turned and said, "Cam, there can't be a word to anyone about my meeting Al Sabin, not one word. Ben looked over his glasses and smiled wryly. "What a mess. He's a Muslim and wants to help us, and I can't tell anyone because some Muslim fanatic would then decide he'd have to be killed for trying to help us. The Director of the FBI is supposed to be trying to find Davenport, but you're telling me we can't trust him and that we have to run a shadow investigation behind his back."

"Yes, I am, and there's more. I'm hearing from sources in the FBI that Winters has a meeting with Senator Davies and Scott Jackson on his calendar."

"And what do you make of that?"

"So far, nothing definite, but it confirms how Kim Cotton knew to ask the questions she did, and we think they're going to continue trying to do everything they can to bring you down."

"So, what else is new? That's been their goal from day one."

Tom shrugged. "We know from the Morton tapes that Davies started race wars and worse, so he's capable of anything. Cam and I think Davies owns Scott Jackson."

Ben nodded in agreement. "I think so too, but so what?"

Cam said, "They'll do everything they can to discredit you."

"That's what they've been doing all along."

"Yes, but now it looks like they've got Winters to give them credibility with the media and the public."

"But that's not the worst of it, Mr. President. Davies wants to see you dead and House Speaker Elliott Thurston as President.

"Perhaps you're right, Cam, but I don't think with all the security around here, he has much of a chance." Ben turned towards Tom. "What do you think? We have any security problems?"

"None that I know of, but Davenport managed to get a pass to work on the White House computers and was in the corridor with his hand on the door to your room when your dogs started barking and scared him off."

"I remembered that incident when I read about it in his Manifesto. Thank God for the dogs. Jane and I never even knew he was there."

"There's something else you ought to know. Right after you told the world that Davenport was still alive, Molly got an e-mail letter from him."

Ben sat up straight. "Interesting. Interesting. What did he want?"

"He apologized for having deceived her and said he hoped she wouldn't get in trouble because of it."

"Anything else?"

"No, sir, just that."

"I'll have to think about that. Does she have any idea why he did that?"

"She doesn't have a clue. What do you think?" Tom asked.

Ben smiled, "She is good looking and she has a nice way about her. Maybe it's that simple. Davenport doesn't have a firm grip on reality."

"I'm still worried about security at the White House. If Davenport could get as far as he did, despite all the security, so could someone recruited by Davies. If Winters is working with Davies, well he knows lots of desperate hit men and he could supply Davies with one."

Ben shook his head. "I find it hard to believe that Winters would do that."

"So do I," Tom said, "but I wouldn't rule it out, and whether Winters would or wouldn't help Davies doesn't matter very much because Davies would do it for sure and so would Davenport. Could be the people who say Davenport hasn't left are right, and whether they're right or not, if Davies were to hire someone, they could always claim Davenport did it. He'd be the perfect fall guy. They'd say he wanted to complete his original plan."

"That's nonsense. His plan was to leave the country with no legal successor to the Presidency. If he kills me now, the Speaker of the House takes over."

"I know, but remember, Davies would love to have Elliott Thurston become President."

"Okay, but would Davenport want that?"

"I don't know," Tom said as he shook his head.

Ben smiled. "Speculate all you want, but I don't think Davenport will make any new attempts to assassinate me, at least right now."

After the conclusion of the meeting in the Oval Office, Ben remained seated with his back to his desk looking out the window at the garden and seeing nothing. He had a brief telephone call from Senator Kendall, after which he returned to staring out the window. He heard the door open and looked around. It was Jane, accompanied by his English bulldog Ace and his black pug, Deuce. Ben smiled like he always did when he saw Jane.

"I brought the dogs with me. I thought you could use a few friends after the telecast."

Ben shook his head wearily "You got that right." Ben moved to the chocolate colored leather sofa and patted the adjoining cushion indicating he wanted Jane to sit next to him. The black pug took that as her invitation and jumped up onto the sofa and then onto Ben's lap. Ben smiled and scratched behind her ears. "Got at least one friend."

As Jane sat on the sofa next to Ben, the bulldog climbed up beside her. "Why is it that whenever anything goes wrong, they blame it on you?"

"As Harry Truman said, 'The buck stops here.'"

"You've been quoting him a lot these days."

"He's another one of those accidental presidents, of whom not much was expected, and he turned out to be a very good president."

"Like you?"

"I can hope." Ben smiled. "Maybe it'll rub off if I quote him. I got some of the credit when they discovered Davenport was the assassin, so I've got to get some of the blame when he manages to avoid capture."

"We talked about your resigning before we knew Davenport escaped. Does this change things?"

Ben frowned. "Not the result. Before I thought I'd stay on because I hoped I might be able to make something positive out of that mess, and now I don't see how I can quit in the middle of this mess. You know how Senator Kendall gave me the green light on my proposing him for Vice-President when we thought Davenport had killed himself, well I just spoke with him and he asked me not to."

"Don't tell me Kendall thinks you had anything to do with Davenport's escape."

"It's not that. He thinks that because of the escape, Davies and his cronies will have enough votes to prevent him from being approved. That means if I resign, House Speaker Elliott Thurston would become President, and we're pretty convinced that he's sold out to Davies."

"I don't see how you can resign now either." Jane reached for Ben's hand and held it in her lap. "I know the timing is lousy, but I'm going to have to go back to Boston."

"Do you really have to, Jane?"

"Yes, and you know I can't stay here with you while my husband is still alive."

"Jane, he's little more than a vegetable now and he won't get any better. Let's try the divorce route again."

"Fine with me, but that loathsome guardian the court appointed to represent him will only oppose it again."

"Here I am, supposedly the most powerful man in the world, and I can't persuade a scumbag lawyer in Dedham to act reasonably." Ben sighed. "I sent Tom Andrews to see him a couple of months ago and that went nowhere, maybe I could send him again, but it's most likely a fools errand."

Jane stood and took Ben's hand. "Come on. Let's forget about it all for the rest of today. Perhaps thing will look better tomorrow."

CHAPTER 5

▼

Senator Davies had by now fully recovered from his over night incarceration and the ignominy of having to post a bail bond to secure his release. A few nights in his own bed, and a day behind his desk barking instructions to his staff and cajoling, ordering, promising and doing whatever was necessary to whomever was on the other end of the telephone to get what he wanted made him feel better, but he was still in an ugly mood. His day was completed and he became ecstatic when FBI Director P.J. Winters called and leaked the news of Davenport's escape. He had to think about how he could turn that event to his best advantage, but first he'd see how Silver handles it. A few minutes later, he called Scott Jackson and told him what he wanted him to do.

After dinner that evening, Davies and his aide, Beau Lawrence, sat in front of the TV in Davies' office watching Ben's press conference. At its conclusion, Davies said, "Tell Jackson to dump that blonde reporter."

"You mean Kim Cotton?"

"Whatever."

"If he asks why?"

"She did a lousy job with that London question."

"You know it was you Davenport was trying to kill when he killed Laverne."

"Of course. What are you trying to say?"

"You want me to arrange for extra security?"

Davies adjusted his cuff links. "Yes, and I want you to move into my room. I'll take over the guest room."

"For how long?"

"Until Davenport's in jail or dead. Move my clothes and my desk." Davies stood and then walked around the room as his assistant followed him with his eyes. Davies turned and said, "You got any ideas about how I can use Davenport's escape to my advantage?"

"I'd have to give that some thought."

Davies smiled and adjusted his cuff links. "Don't strain yourself. It's obvious. Have them put the story out on the Internet that Davenport's escape from right under the noses of Silver's personally selected agents proves Silver didn't want him caught, and that Silver didn't want him caught because they were both involved in the assassination of President Butler. Have Scott say that Davenport's escape proves I was right all the time. Call him tonight."

"What exactly do you want me to tell him?"

Davies frowned. "You really are hopeless. You know I've been saying right from the beginning that either Silver was the mastermind behind the Inauguration Day assassination and that even if he wasn't, he should resign because his problems are getting in the way of the proper governance of the country. Now that we know about Davenport and that he escaped from right under the noses of the very investigators that Silver praised on TV, we can change that a little. On his next telecast, I want Scott to claim that either Silver arranged for Davenport's escape to protect his accomplice like it's rumored on the Internet, or that being unable to arrest him proves that he's incompetent and not qualified to be President. Understand?" Beau nodded that he did. Davies continued, "And make sure that no one connects me to those stories on the Internet or on Scott's program."

"Excuse me, Senator, but I wonder how you're going to beat the criminal cases against you for causing all that rioting and those race wars, and how you're going to keep from getting expelled from the Senate. Seems to me, that's more important than your continuing to take shots at Silver. Maybe you got it all figured out, but of course I don't have your giant brain."

"Don't get sarcastic with me boy. Remember what kind of trouble I can make for you."

"Sorry about that." Beau did a mental U-turn. "It's just that I'm worried about you and what might happen in court and before the Senate."

"Okay, I appreciate that cousin, Beau, but don't get uppity with me or I'll send you back home to Mississippi and let you answer to incest and murder charges for killing your sister." Davies straightened the crease in his trousers, sat back and said, "I'll try to simplify this for you. The only evidence against me for the criminal case is the tape of my conversation with Bill Morton that he recorded when we met at his house in Montgomery. Right?"

"Right, but why isn't that enough? Pardon me, but you hired him to start riots and race wars on that tape."

"Yes, but that tape was made without my consent, and under the law of Alabama, it's illegal to record a conversation without the consent of one of the participants."

"Are you saying Morton didn't consent? He taped it and the tape was found in his safe deposit box in his bank."

"No. I'll claim no such foolish thing. Morton consented to the tapes being used in proceedings he was involved in. Once he died, he couldn't be prosecuted as a co-conspirator with me and he never consented to the use of the tapes in proceedings where he wasn't involved and I didn't consent, so they can't be used against me."

"I listened very carefully to every word you said. I'm not as smart as you, but I got to say that makes no sense to me at all. You think the judges in the criminal cases will buy that argument?"

Davies smiled. "Maybe you're smarter than I thought. It is a lot of bullshit, but I got a motion to suppress that tape coming up for a hearing in Alabama next week."

"And you expect to win?"

"It's a done deal. I had to call in some markers, but it's all set."

"Okay, so you got Alabama covered. What about the other states and the federal cases? You can't possibly have all those judges everywhere in the bag."

"No need. Once Alabama is taken care of, the others got to follow."

"Why is that?"

"That's the law, my boy. The taping happened in Alabama. Once Alabama says their law makes that tape inadmissible as against me under Alabama law, every other jurisdiction has to accept that ruling."

"Why?"

"Because the Constitution of the United States says so."

"It does?"

Davies nodded. "It does. There's a provision called the 'full faith and credit clause' and that's been the law of the land forever." Davies smiled. "I love the Constitution, 'specially when it works for me. What that means is that every other jurisdiction must accept as gospel what every state says is the meaning of their own law with very few exceptions. Once Alabama says that under Alabama law the tapes can't be used against me, every other state has to go along."

"Nice going, but what about the Senate? A vote on your expulsion is scheduled there for next week. Are they bound by that full faith and credit thing?"

"You surprise me again, Beau. That's another intelligent question. Legally, maybe it doesn't apply to the Senate, but there'll be no vote in the Senate next week. They'll filibuster it if they have to, but Senator Smithers says he's lined up Daskin and that the motion to expel will not be brought up for a vote next week. I don't think it will be brought up any time soon."

"How come?"

"I just told you. Daskin is the majority leader and if he doesn't want something to come up, it doesn't come up. That's the way the Senate operates and once Alabama says the tapes are illegal, with Smithers and Senate majority leader Daskin on my side, the Senate will decide not to allow tainted evidence to be used there, especially now that Davenport is gone. I think those events will terminate the expulsion motion."

Davies adjusted his cuff links again and straightened the crease in his trouser legs.

Beau slowly nodded his head. "I think I understand. It'll have to sink in for a while, but you seem to have those things covered. What about the general public? You're not very popular at the moment."

"At the moment, that's true, but the public has a short memory. We'll discredit the tape and two months from now, it'll be old news, and six months from now, it'll be forgotten."

"Anything else you want me to do?"

"Call P. J. Winters and tell him I need a forensics expert to say that the Morton tapes aren't genuine."

"He'll do that?"

"Sure. Even if Silver had nothing to do with the assassination, we agree that Silver doesn't know how things work inside the Beltway and that he has got to go."

"Okay, anything else?"

Then call House Speaker Thurston and tell him I want him to turn the heat up on Silver's impeachment."

"Last I spoke to him, he said he wasn't sure he had a majority in the House and that Smithers said the Senate wouldn't even discuss it."

"That was before we knew Davenport escaped. And remind Thurston that we have the pictures of him murdering that boy in that San Francisco bath house."

"No need to remind him."

"Do it anyway, and tell him there's no statute of limitations for murder."

"Okay."

"One more thing, fill him in on what Jackson's doing to discredit Silver and I want him to be ready to stir up the House at the same time."

Beau frowned, "I know you think you got the expulsion and criminal cases covered, but don't you think we should have them safely behind us before we move against Silver? What's the rush?"

"You got to keep your eye on the prize."

"What prize?"

"The Presidency, of course."

"After all that's happened, you still think you can get there?"

"Absolutely. First, I got to get rid of Silver, and I don't care how." Davies paused a moment and then smiled. "Maybe with Davenport on the loose we could pin Silver's murder on him, that's a possibility and so is impeachment. With Thurston as Speaker and Daskin as Senate majority leader, I can prevent anyone from getting approved as Vice-President, so when Silver's gone, Thurston succeeds him. Once that happens we'll find evidence tying Silver to the assassination and proving I was right all along."

"What evidence?"

"Are you that stupid? With Winters on my side, I got the FBI in my pocket. What more do I need?' Davies smiled. "Then, just like I planned before, Thurston will appoint me Vice-President and resign. With what's just happened, I'll have to let Thurston stay in office a little longer to let things cool off about the tapes, but I should get it all done within a year."

"You're still serious about becoming President?"

"Dead serious."

CHAPTER 6

▼

Ben opened the door to the residential quarters in the White House and stepped aside to admit Mustafa Al-Sabin, the executive director of the Organization of Middle Eastern Oil Producers. Sabin was a heavy-set, balding man with a neat pencil line mustache and a goatee, conservatively dressed in the latest Brooks Brothers fashions. As he entered the residence, he looked around. "There's no one else here."

"No," Ben replied. "It's just you and me, as you requested."

Ben led the way through the living room to his study and to twin high-backed upholstered rocking chairs separated by a small, square, chrome and glass table in front of the fireplace. After they were comfortably seated opposite each other, Ben said, "Thank you for coming so promptly, Mr. Sabin. I'm quite anxious to learn what you know about Rabbani, but first, what's the reaction on the Arab street to Davenport's escape?"

Al-Sabin mopped his forehead nervously. "We'll have to come up with a cover story for this meeting."

"We always do.

Sabin nodded. "I hate it that I have to be so cautious."

"I know, and we will, but first, what's the talk in the Arab World?"

Sabin leaned forward. It was almost as if he were afraid someone could over-hear him. He said softly, "The fundamentalist clerics and the terrorist organizations are spreading the story that you arranged for the escape, that it's a Zionist Israeli conspiracy. There's a minority willing to believe that, but the more sophisticated Arabs, including almost all of the rulers in the region know that's not true."

"Are the leaders willing to say that publicly?"

"Sabin shook his head. "No. Most are afraid to confront the clerics."

"Does Davenport's escape cause any additional danger to US interests in the region?"

Sabin shook his head. "Not immediately. They'll try to stir up the people with talk of a Jewish conspiracy, but there is still great fear of the American armed forces. Everyone remembers the swift collapse of the Iraqi army. That defeat was a monumental blow to the Arab psyche."

"Do they take much comfort from the guerrilla warfare, suicide bombings and terrorist attacks?"

"The fanatics can praise those fools as martyrs, but sneak attacks and killing unarmed civilians is not considered very heroic by most of our people." Sabin smiled, "And of course, you make most Arab leaders very nervous."

"Because I'm Jewish?"

"In part, but more so because you've made it very plain that their continued support of terrorists could result in preemptive strikes if there's another attack on the United States. They believe you mean it. They keep hoping you'll lose the support of the military or be removed from office, but so long as you're the president and you control the military, they'll do their best to discourage terrorist activity."

"That could be the reason you came here tonight, to try and persuade me that if they fail to control the terrorists, that I should relax my position and that I should look the other way at more of their duplicitous activities."

Sabin smiled. "That is something they all want me to do. Did I succeed?"

Ben shook his head and smiled. "No. I want them to remain nervous about me. If something were to happen and I felt they had done all they could to prevent it, I might be persuaded to do nothing, but let them wonder."

"Seriously, you would listen to reason, wouldn't you?"

"Believe me, I understand that if they fail to support the radical clerics that support terrorists, they could become the object of an uprising and be deposed, but those organizations plan operations against us and our allies. I don't know how we can tolerate that appeasement program of theirs very much longer. It's an insane situation. They aid terrorists…" Sabin started to say something, but Ben interrupted. "Don't try to deny it. We know they do that and then they secretly tip us off about some planned operation against us, but they had better understand their choices. If they refuse to cooperate in our fight against radical Muslim terrorism, we might withdraw our support. I think they know that if that happens, the radical clerics will take over and that most of them would be killed.

We're coming to a point where we will make them choose to help us or try to appease the terrorists who we think will destroy them at their first opportunity. With us, they may be eventually deposed by a free society but they won't be killed."

Sabin nodded. "I agree. It's a very delicate balancing act for the rulers. They're almost ready to abandon hope that the French, Germans and Russians may be able to persuade you to modify your demands on them to take a stand, but you have got to give it a little more time. I'm reluctant to say this," Sabin paused.

"Say it," Ben said.

"Well, some think you may be forced to resign or that you may be impeached and they won't have to deal with you."

"I understand, but make sure they understand that if there's another major terrorist attack in this country from the Middle-East, I will retaliate, even if it's the last thing I do, and if they ever thought I would be distracted by the Davenport situation, they are wrong."

"The terrorists will continue trying to attack the US, but they can't do the major kind of operation like September eleven without intelligence, engineering and other kinds of assistance that only a government can provide. I think the governments in the Middle East are still too frightened of you and your military to do anything like that. They don't know your limits and think you're unpredictable."

Ben smiled. "Good. That's a fear I know you helped to spread."

Sabin shrugged. "I do what I can in my small way. You understand that the Saud Royal family and the rulers in other countries will continue to pay protection money to the terrorists to be left alone?"

"That's been going on from administration to administration." Ben frowned. "They're like the Mafia." He shook his head. "I don't know how much longer I can turn a blind eye to that kind of duplicity, but that's not a decision I'm prepared to make today." Ben sighed, and then said, "Back to Rabbani. What can you tell me about Davenport's uncle?"

"First, let's review our cover story. I'll feel much more comfortable when we dispose of that little matter."

"How's this. I requested a meeting and told you to inform all the oil producing states in the Gulf, that we consider sheltering Clarence Davenport to be a hostile act against this nation. If he shows up, they are to notify us and turn him over to us immediately. If we find any country sheltering him, there will be serious consequences unless they do, and you're pretty sure I mean it. That okay?"

Sabin nodded that it was.

"Good. You can deliver that message and you can tell them that during the meeting, you urged me to lighten up on my position that they oppose terrorists and I refused." Ben smiled. "Tell them that on this subject I'm as big a cowboy as any prior president ever was."

Sabin said, "I hate having to be so cautious."

"I understand that it's necessary that no one know of our special understanding."

"I apologize, but I live each day in fear of a small minority of my own people who wage unending *jihad* against the United States and the rest of the world. Any Muslim who doesn't accept their version of what the Koran demands is a target. They would slaughter me and my family if they knew why I was really here without a moment's hesitation."

"There are fanatics in this country that want me dead. It's just that I don't have to hide my position and that I have better protection. The worst thing about it for me isn't the fear of being killed, it's that I know what I'm doing is in the best interests of the people of this country, and if I'm stopped, there may be no one to continue what I'm trying to do."

Sabin visibly relaxed in his chair. "Forgive me. You do understand. I feel the same way about what I'm doing."

Ben continued, "Now, what did you find out about Rabbani?"

"Yes, Rabbani." Sabin frowned. "Rabbani was disinherited because of his opposition to the Royal family, but he already had a fortune."

"Our people told me that. That's like Osama Bin Laden. Did you know either or both of them?"

"I only knew Bin Laden by reputation, but I met Rabbani on several occasions when we both lived in London. I never knew him that well, and have seen him only rarely since I moved to the United States."

"Any connection between Rabbani and Osama Bin Laden?"

"They knew each other and have similar backgrounds, but they're quite different. Bin Laden is a religious fanatic. He and Al Qaeda are favored by the Wahhabi clerics who want to install a Taliban style of government throughout the Islamic world. It's my understanding that Rabbani rejected that militant, religious rhetoric and has chosen to live in the West and enjoy all that it has to offer. The only thing Osama and his followers have in common with Rabbani and his expatriate associates is hatred of the Saudi royal family. Rabbani knows I support the royal family despite their corruption because I fear that what would replace them would be Al Qaeda. Rabbani thinks the corruption is so great that he can't support them. He wants the Royal family replaced with representative government like in the UK, and believes that can be achieved with the support of the West."

"Did you know Davenport spent two months in London, we think mainly with Rabbani, shortly before he started on his plan to assassinate President Butler and the others at the Inauguration."

"No, I didn't." Sabin looked at Ben with a puzzled frown. "Did he know him before that time in London?"

"We think not."

Rabbani stared at Ben and asked incredulously, "Do you think Rabbani had anything to do with what Davenport did?'

"I don't know, but the question is what do you think?"

Sabin tugged at his goatee a moment. "That's not enough to persuade me that Rabbani had anything to do with Davenport's activities. Rabbani has a long history of friendly dealings with the West and the United States. Long before Davenport ever contacted him, Rabbani used to represent Iraqi interests in their dealings with western businesses and governments. Back when the United States supported Iraq, he dealt with many representatives of the United States and U.S. Companies. Hasn't your State Department told you of this?"

"Some, but they don't like to remember their one time advocacy of support for Iraq against Iran. Did he know Saddam Hussein?"

Sabin nodded. "It was rumored that he was close to Saddam Hussein prior to the first Gulf War, but when the war started, he terminated his representation of the government of Iraq. What I heard was that he originally started representing the Iraqi government when the United States had that hostage situation in Iran. Iraq was seen as a secular Muslim ally that could counter the spread of Islamic fundamentalism from Iran."

"Exactly what did he do for the Iraqi government?"

"I don't know exactly. All I was told was it was legal work, like contracts to build public works, power plants, roads and things like that. I know he was often in Baghdad and that he represented Iraqi interests as well as clients from Kuwait, Qatar, Oman, Bahrain and the United Arab Emirates, primarily in the UK."

Ben sat back in his Morris Chair rocker in front of the fireplace, looked at the fire for a minute and the turned to Al Sabin. He looked over the top of his glasses, frowned and said, "Did he resume his representation of the Iraqi government after the end of the War in 1991?"

"Not so far as I know, although he may have represented private individuals."

"You said Osama Bin Laden and Rabbani knew each other. Do you think Rabbani could be allied in any way with Bin Laden's Al Qaeda?"

"No. I wouldn't think so. As I said, all they share is a common hatred of the Saudi royal family. Bin Laden and the Wahhabi would combine all civil and religious rules under one authority. All law would come from the Koran as interpreted by certain of the religious leaders. So far as they're concerned, anyone who lives a personal life that doesn't comply with all the religious laws, or who believes that there should be separation between religion and the state is not a true Muslim. Rabbani is of course a Muslim, but he enjoys Western life and would like to have Arabia become a modern state with elected officials making the laws. Al Qaeda would just as soon kill him as you. This is a very old struggle in the Muslim world and unfortunately, the Bin Laden view is gaining strength. Rabbani and I have friends in common who think that Rabbani would be a wonderful pro-western replacement for the royal family."

"Is that a possibility?"

"I don't think so. The corruption in the Saudi government is staggering and there are many educated Saudis like Rabbani who would like to see them replaced with a western style democracy, but the Wahhabi clerics have too strong a hold on the people. I think it would be much more likely that Saudi Arabia would end up with religious fanatics running everything, if the royal family fell. Just look at what happened in Iran right after the Shah was deposed."

"You don't think it matters that the Iranians are Shiites and the Saudis are Sunni?"

"On that issue, they are the same. They both want Islamic fundamentalist regimes governed solely by the Koran. It's just that their respective religious leaders interpret the Koran and the succession to Mohammed differently. It's over that interpretation and that succession that they've been killing each other for over six hundred years. Saudis like Rabbani and I think that whole philosophy issue is nonsense. As I said, we differ about deposing the royal family only because I think we'll end up with something worse and he thinks that a modern democratic state would result. I wish he were right and I was wrong."

"Thanks for the explanation. From what you've just said, it seems very unlikely that Rabbani would have been in favor of what Davenport did, but yet, he was the only person Davenport knew in London and we know he spent two months there."

"That is puzzling."

"Let me ask you a few questions."

Rabbani nodded for Ben to continue.

"If the Saudi royal family fell, you think an Osama Bin Laden type of Islamic fundamentalist government unfriendly to the West would take over."

"Yes. I've explained that."

Ben smiled. "Yes. Now what do you think we should do about that? Do you think we should sit back and do nothing because it's purely internal with them? After all, who are we to tell them the kind of government they should have?"

"That's a very difficult question." Al Sabin sat back in his chair for a moment. He smoothed his mustache and then said, "I believe my people should rule themselves, but they're not ready to do so. That is the problem I've been wrestling with most of my adult life. I'm sorry to have to say that you cannot afford to do nothing. Without your support, most of the world's oil supply will fall under the control of religious fanatics who want to kill all Americans, destroy western civilization and create a world ruled by their fanaticism. With that much wealth they could buy nuclear, chemical and biological weapons, and believe me, they are willing to use them to get what they want."

"And what do you think they want?"

"I know what they want. They say they must spread Islam until everyone becomes a Muslim or agrees to be governed by an Islamic government, that the Koran and the Prophet require it. As I see it, you have no choice. Unless you prevent it, they will use the money the West pays them for oil to fund a relentless terrorist campaign against you until all Western influences in all Muslim lands are eradicated, and it will not end there. Next they will want to restore Islamic rule to all the places it had been in Europe and Asia before, and after that, to the rest of the world. As bad as that would be for you, it would be as bad for the majority of Muslims. Those fanatics would impose religious rule wherever they went. People like me and my wife, my daughters and grand-daughters, all women, everyone, we would all have to return to a world that ended more than six hundred years ago."

"I understand. Another question, do you think that withdrawing support from Israel would stop future attacks on the United States?"

Sabin looked shocked. "How could you allow that? It would be worse than allowing Hitler's Holocaust to happen again."

"That's not my question. Assume I'm not the President. Assume the United States lacks the political will to do anything to protect Israel. Does the end of Israel end the terrorism against the United States?"

Al Sabin mopped his brow with a spotless white handkerchief. "I can't be quoted, but I see it the same as the Europeans giving Czechoslovakia to Hitler. Like the Nazis, Islamic fundamentalists despise weakness. They would consider your failure to protect Israel as an admission of weakness and a signal to increase the attack, just as Hitler did."

Ben looked over his glasses at al Sabin. "So, bottom line, you think we should invade Arabia if the fundamentalists take over?"

Mustafa al-Sabin sat quietly nodding his head and staring into the fireplace. He finally faced Ben and said, "Yes. You would have to seize the Saudi oil fields to prevent a worldwide depression and total chaos and to keep them out of the hands of Al Qaeda. You would of course be despised in much of the Islamic world, but you are now."

"And what do we do about the royal family?"

"You'd have to restore them to power."

"Even if they were deposed by a popular internal revolution and most of them were killed?"

"You would still have to take control of the oil fields. You can not risk that resource being controlled by the Wahhabi clerics. So, under those circumstances I guess you would have to replace them."

"Replace them with?"

Sabin paused, "Perhaps I begin to see where you're going. Rabbani would certainly be a possible choice to become the new President of a democratic Arabia. He would have support from some remaining members of the royal family, being one of them, and that would give him some legitimacy with segments of the general population. The Wahhabi would be a problem, but they always are."

"You know Rabbani. Is he smart enough to have figured that out?"

Al Sabin pulled at his goatee and stared into the fireplace. "I don't know. He's very clever. I hear he's a world-class chess player, but I don't know. It's possible, I suppose."

"Everyone knows that American foreign policy has been dedicated to keeping the royal family in power and excusing their corruption and even their aid to terrorist organizations because we're afraid that if we don't, we end up with something worse."

"As have I."

Ben continued, "That's been going on for a long time. Maybe Rabbani is becoming impatient."

"Okay."

"Assume he wants to force a change. He knows that all that prevents Al Qaeda and the radical clerics from taking over is fear that the royal family backed up by the United States would prevail. But, if Al Qaeda were persuaded that the US would do nothing, then Al Qaeda could engineer a popular uprising against the royal family and an Al Qaeda take over." Sabin nodded in agreement as Ben continued, "Maybe Rabbani thinks that an Al Qaeda take over in Arabia would eventually force the United States to remove Al Qaeda and then put him and his group in power. What do you think?"

Al Sabin frowned. "I admit all that's possible, not probable, but possible. The Al Qaeda and the terrorists won't try to depose the royal family so long as they have your support."

"Now think about Clarence Davenport."

"Okay, but I don't see the connection."

"We agreed that what keeps Al Qaeda from seizing power in Saudi Arabia is fear of the United States. But what if the United States was in such turmoil that they couldn't immediately do anything? Then an internal uprising sponsored by the clerics and Al Qaeda might succeed."

"I agree. That would present a set of circumstances that would be very tempting to Al Qaeda."

"Isn't that precisely what Davenport would have accomplished if he had fully succeeded with his plan to leave this country without a legal President by killing all Presidential successors at the Inauguration? Davenport said it was to force a re-examination of our Constitution and a return to what he says are the real purposes of the founding fathers. Accept that as Davenport's motive. But wouldn't it also set the stage for Al Qaeda's take over of Saudi Arabia."

Al-Sabin sat back in his chair smoothing his mustache, then turned towards Ben, shaking his head. "I confess I never thought about it that way. I see the possibilities. I've heard that some Al Qaeda say that they will first get rid of the far enemy, meaning the West and then they will destroy the near enemy, meaning all secular Muslim states like Egypt and Turkey and even Shiite fundamentalist states like Iran."

"I think that might well be the Al Qaeda plan. They somehow immobilize the United States, seize control of the oil wealth of Arabia and the rest of the Middle East. With that, they can buy all the nuclear bombs and military equipment they would ever need from France, Germany and Russia who may be stupid enough to believe it wouldn't be used against them. That would position them to move against the rest of the world."

Al-Sabin shook his head, "I just can't imagine Rabbani being a part of that, but I suppose it's possible. Now that we're talking about that, there's something else you should know that may influence your thinking. There's a belief that many of the man-in-the-street fundamentalists have that all that's needed to get the Islamic take-over of the world started is one cataclysmic defeat of the West. That would be a sign from God to start a spontaneous Muslim uprising that God will then reward with total victory. They could think that leaving the United

States without a President could be that kind of cataclysmic event. So even if the more sophisticated in Al Qaeda expect that the United States would eventually move militarily, they wouldn't care because that could easily be the event that unites Muslims everywhere in a battle to the death with the West, and that is what I think they want. They believe the West has no stomach for a prolonged bloody war. If they can keep the United States immobilized long enough to acquire nuclear weapons, they think they will succeed in their goal and reestablish the Caliphate that collapsed after World War One. Many Muslims believe that without the United States, NATO and the rest of Europe is a paper tiger. It's only the United States and Great Britain that keep the fanatics from taking control. If the terrorists take over in the Middle East, the world wide death toll will be in the many millions even though it's only a small minority of Muslims who support that kind of genocide."

"I agree that most Muslims oppose terrorist activities, but even if that minority is only 10%, that's still over ten million people in the Middle East that are willing to support terrorism and attack U.S. citizens and institutions. We saw what a small number of those fanatics can do on September 11. Many people in the CIA and State Department concluded that there was no connection between Saddam Hussein and Osama Bin Laden because Iraq was a secular regime and Al Qaeda are religious fanatics."

"You think otherwise."

"I do. Nobody thought Hitler and Stalin would ever co-operate with each other, but they did and they then divided up Poland. Later, of course, Germany invaded the Soviet Union."

Sabin nodded. "That's history."

"I think Hussein and Bin Laden dealt with each other despite their religious differences because they were united by their hatred of the United States, Israel and the Saudi royal family. They could make temporary alliances while each pursued their separate goals of becoming the predominant power in the region. After that, they each may have had plans to destroy the other."

Sabin nodded in agreement. "My enemy's enemy is my friend,—at least until our common enemy is destroyed."

"Exactly, and then I'll betray my former ally. Similarly why couldn't Rabbani and Al Qaeda form a temporary alliance despite their differences?"

Ben and Al-Sabin sat quietly, each absorbed in his own thoughts, Ben rocking slowly in his rocking chair and Al-Sabin smoothing his mustache and pulling at his goatee while staring at the blaze in the fireplace. Al-Sabin broke the silence. "I can't find a hole in the scenario you laid out. I searched my memory for everything I could remember about Rabbani. Perhaps he's capable of dreaming up that kind of a plan, and I suppose if he spent two months with Davenport, well it's possible he somehow recruited him to do it. Do you have any proof that he did?"

"Not a shred."

"Let me say that personally, I find it hard to believe that Rabbani could have been involved that way with Davenport. There were too many years when they didn't know each other."

"You're probably right, and you're not alone in that. Practically everyone in the Department of Justice, the CIA and the FBI decided that Davenport did it and that he was acting alone," Ben smiled, "except for a loud minority that claim that he was part of a conspiracy that I headed up."

Al-Sabin shook his head. "I know. That story is also spread throughout the Arab world."

Ben shook his head, "Ever since I learned about Davenport and his connection to Rabbani, I've been trying to make some sense out of it. Everybody on the Middle-East desk in the State Department and in the CIA thinks that for the last twenty-five years, Rabbani has been as good a friend to the United States as it could have and that his relationship with Davenport that began just last year is irrelevant."

"In the absence of any proof of anything else, I suppose you have to give him the benefit of the doubt."

"I don't know. We are so used to evaluating any claim of wrongdoing in the context of the criminal justice system, that our whole culture looks at things from that perspective. I've always done that myself. But ever since terrorism attacks started in this country, I've forced myself to look at things a little differently. Just think about the investigation that led to our finding out about Davenport. Because of the way Davenport carried out his plan, the investigators thought that the assassin could be someone who had some kind of connection to Gulf War explosives, British commando training, the use of an American World War II bazooka, and Vietnam War rocket launchers. All they knew when they went to see Davenport's maternal grandfather was that the grandfather had been a commando with the Brits early in the war, and that he switched to the US Army as a bazooka operator when we got into it. The first time the grandfather met with the investigators, they were convinced that he knew nothing about the Inauguration Day massacre and they looked into his family. Davenport's name never surfaced."

"Oh, how come?"

"The grandfather didn't really think of him as a grandchild because Davenport was illegitimate, had been put up for adoption and then never heard from for many years. It was pure luck that they finally learned about him from the old man. When they did they thought there was a possibility that he could be involved as the grandfather's knowing or unknowing surrogate because of the use of the garrote and the bazooka. Then they found out that Davenport was in the Gulf War as a demolition officer and that his adoptive father had been in Vietnam with a rocket launcher group. With what they had, in an ordinary case, they wouldn't even have gotten permission for a wiretap, but they did here because it was such an important case, and then, the wiretap provided nothing. So they really had very little when they went to see Davenport. All they had was that he fit the profile of a person they were looking for. If he didn't supply us with that long document telling us everything he did and where to find the evidence, we probably couldn't have convicted him in a criminal court. When you realize that, it makes you look at these terrorism cases differently. When you're dealing with terrorists, the focus has got to be on preventing terrorist acts rather than catching, trying and convicting someone for a criminal act. That requires a change in the basic culture of the FBI and the Justice Department, which they haven't done yet. I don't know, but Davenport's visiting with Rabbani and Rabbani's possible connection to Iraq could be coincidental, but perhaps it isn't. It's something worth considering and I'd appreciate a renewed effort on your part to find out everything you can about Rabbani."

"Okay, but I still doubt Rabbani had anything to do with what Davenport did."

"Good. As much as I'd like to get Davenport and see that he's punished for what he did, I'm much more interested in finding out if he was involved with Rabbani so that we could stop any further terrorist attacks that Rabbani may be planning. Frankly, I hope it turns out that Rabbani had nothing to do with what Davenport did because from what I'm told by people in the State Department, he would be our first choice to take over in Arabia if the royal family were deposed."

CHAPTER 7

▼

Clarence Davenport had been a decent high school athlete, not good enough to play varsity sports at Princeton, but better than the average guy. He had now taken three lessons from a fine Irish golf pro, hit a million golf balls and purchased the latest Taylor Made woods and Callaway irons. The golf course was still winning and Clarence was not used to losing. This was the last hole for today. He'd relax and try to enjoy it. After a decent drive, and a five iron to the fringe in front of the green, Clarence chipped in close and then tapped in to save par. He trudged off the course and added up his score, 104. He shrugged and thought maybe tomorrow would be a better day. He didn't know it at the time, but it was a break through for him. By Wednesday, he was breaking one hundred and pronounced respectable by his golf pro, Bill Begley, a smiling Irishman who loved to laugh and managed to make Clarence relax and enjoy the game. On Thursday morning he drove over to the Waterfront Hotel where Rabbani and Fatima would be staying. He checked out the entrances and exits and then played the Galway Bay Golf and Country Club where they would play golf. Begley had told him that familiarity with the course would help. He had let his beard grow, darkened his brown hair and the sun had tanned his normal fair complexion to a point where he could be taken for someone with some Middle-Eastern antecedents. Today was the day, he would have to chance everything and meet with Uncle Rabbani.

Clarence arrived at the Waterfront Hotel early on Friday and checked the grounds and the lobby for anything suspicious. Satisfied, he registered as Khalil Yomani and entered the room he had reserved across from Rabbani and Fatima's suite. He left the door open a crack and kept one eye on the Rabbani suite while he had lunch in his room and then while he sat in front of his laptop computer, checking one news source after another. He read stories reporting that the authorities in the UK were looking for him, but nothing to indicate that anyone suspected he could be in Ireland.

It was four thirty when he heard Rabbani's familiar voice. "Here's our suite, Fatima. Did you see the look the clerk gave me when we checked in? I'm flattered that he thinks we may be doing naughty things up here."

"Well, we could be, Uncle?" Clarence heard Fatima laugh as she said, "I'm a pretty sexy looking package. Don't you agree?"

As Rabbani, fumbled with the key to the suite, Clarence left his room across the hall. They both looked up at him, nodded and then looked away. They didn't recognize him. Clarence continued down the hall, then to the lobby where he checked to see if he could discern anything suspicious and next, a quick tour of the grounds. Nothing to be concerned with. He had a view of most of the parking area from his room, but it wouldn't hurt to check the small area he couldn't see. That was okay too. Ten minutes after he left his room, he was back standing in front of the Rabbani suite. He took a deep breath and then knocked gently on the door. Rabbani said, "Yes. Who is it?"

Clarence said, with a slight Irish brogue, "From the golf course, sir. The starter on the tee times."

"I'm all set, thanks."

"Things have gotten in a bit of a muddle. I can come back if it's inconvenient."

"Right there," Rabbani said through the door as he unlocked it. He stepped aside to let Clarence enter and then stared at him. "You're the man across the hall." He stared at him harder. "My God, you're Cl…"

Before he could finish the word, Clarence clapped his hand over Rabbani's mouth. "Shh. Quiet uncle, I wanted to surprise you. We can talk in my room without disturbing Fatima."

The two men went across the hall to Clarence's room. Rabbani said, "It's good to see you, but I wouldn't have recognized you if we passed in the street."

"That's what I was hoping for."

"Why all the cloak and dagger?"

"How can you ask me that?"

"I'm sorry, you're absolutely right to be cautious and suspicious of everyone."

"Even you, my uncle?"

"Yes. Even me, until you have reason to believe otherwise. Fatima told you your Secret Service and even a female representative from your President Silver have visited with me."

"John Wallace and Molly Pemberton?"

"Yes. They know I am your uncle. They were accompanied by representatives from the PM's office. I was told they expect me to cooperate fully with the U.S. authorities. You know your press reports that you did what you did all by yourself."

"Well, that's what I told them."

"I know, I read the document you sent to the media."

"What did you think of it?"

"The government reforms were the things we discussed when you were in London, so nothing surprised me except some of the details about how you did it, very ingenious."

"Did you think I would do what I did?"

Rabbani shrugged. "When you left London, I thought you would do something and that it would be at the Inauguration ceremony. I thought it might be a shoulder-held missile of some sort. I must congratulate you. I hadn't thought of planting explosives in the TelePrompTer and in the speakers. That was very creative."

"Thank you, uncle. You know I got the idea of doing it at the Inauguration from you." Clarence smiled. "Do you want some of the credit for what I did? Should I tell the world we were in this together? All it takes is a few minutes on my computer."

Rabbani's face turned red.

Before Rabbani could say anything, Clarence said, "Don't get upset, uncle. I was only joking."

"I know that, but there's no humor in it. Someone could take you seriously. Really, Clarence do you think there's any truth to that idea at all."

"Of course not. When we met, I was very angry at what had been done to me and my men at Kamisiyah, and at the government for covering it up. All you did was commiserate with me and tell me that you were upset with your government because of their support of the very corrupt Saudi royal family and that you thought it would be pointless for me to kill my commanding officer while leaving the government responsible intact. I could have decided to forget the whole thing."

"True."

"Did you think I would?"

"Perhaps."

"It was your suggestion that I look at the line of succession to the Presidency if I wanted to strike an effective blow against the government. That showed me the way. I recall you approached it like a theoretical problem to be intellectually solved."

"Was that not good advice? If Silver had gone to the Inauguration like he was supposed to, you would have succeeded in striking the blow you wanted."

"Yes."

"Are you having regrets?"

"No, only that I didn't succeed."

"Good, but I've got to ask you. Did you ever tell anyone that we spoke of these things?"

"You needn't worry, uncle. I've mentioned your name to no one, but I'd be surprised if you didn't. Wouldn't it make you very popular in much of the Muslim world?"

Rabbani shrugged. "To certain factions, but not to the ones I'm interested in. You're quite sure you've not spoken of this to anyone?"

"No one. Who would I tell? Who would believe me and what good would it do me? Maybe someday you will tell the world you gave me the idea."

"No. I need to maintain good relations with the West, especially the United States."

"Why?"

"Some day I may be in a position to rule Arabia, and for that, I would need their support."

"Their oil revenues are very attractive."

"That and the power it commands. That's what's important."

Clarence smiled. "Killing me and turning my dead body over to the United States should go a long way to establishing you as a United States favorite. Is that something you plan, uncle?"

"Frankly, Clarence, if it would make me the ruler of Arabia, I wouldn't hesitate a moment, but it wouldn't, and actually I'm glad of it."

"Glad to know where I stand with you."

"Don't be childish." Rabbani smiled "I've become fond of you Clarence, but for that much power I'd kill my mother, and what's more, I think you can be very useful."

"How?"

"You have the potential to contribute greatly to my ultimate success and perhaps some day, even be my successor."

"Are you serious?"

"Yes. You know I have no children. I have many nieces and nephews, but most are worthless, except for you, Fatima and Neil. Time alone can bring the answers, but yes, I would like us to work together."

Clarence shrugged. "I don't know what to say."

"Say nothing. Let it develop." Rabbani glanced at his wristwatch. "Fatima will wonder where I am, but we have time." He looked at Clarence. "You know of course that your United States government wants to believe that you did this alone, without any foreign involvement. There are many in your government who would suppress all suggestions that I or any other member of the expatriate group I represent had anything to do with the Inauguration Day assassination even if they were certain of it."

"And why is that?"

"Not knowing what might happen following the assassination, we solidified our relationships with many United States officials at all levels."

"How did you do that?"

"There's no one way. Whatever it takes. For some it's money, for some women, boys or young girls, but for most, it's power. Some simply concluded that it was in the best interest of the United States that we become the successor to the House of Saud and they wouldn't care what we had done. Everybody wants to believe you did it by yourself and that no one else was involved. It was just our bad luck that Silver was Secretary of Education and that he decided to skip the Inauguration."

"You're probably right. After the assassination, some of the U.S. media wondered whether Al Qaeda or some other foreign group or state was involved, and almost immediately, the FBI and the other law enforcement agencies said they believed it was homegrown. The only foreign involvement theory that kept circulating was the possibility that the Israelis were involved in some plot to put Silver into the Presidency."

"Yes, and as soon as you were discovered and they read your document, all of them, media and law enforcement, they immediately breathed a sigh of relief and congratulated themselves for stating right at the beginning that no foreign terrorist, or state sponsored terrorism was involved. It was the case of another angry Gulf War veteran acting alone, just like Tim McVeigh in Oklahoma City and John Muhammad, the Washington D.C. area sniper." Rabbani shrugged as he continued. "Why did they come to that conclusion so quickly? Just because you said so? It's ludicrous. You kill thousands of people, but you wouldn't tell a lie. They do it all the time. I think it's because it makes them feel better to be able to say that the crisis is over, resume your normal activities, go to the mall, by a new TV, go have a drink." Rabbani smiled, "So if you changed your mind and some day wanted to say that I and my exiled group of Arab friends were involved with you, tell me, Clarence, who would believe you? Who would admit they were wrong? No one in the U.S. Government ever admits they were wrong about anything."

Clarence shook his head. "You've got nothing to worry about. I'll never change my story. It would make me a traitor and a fool, and I am neither. It's true that when I arrived in London and met you, I was angry. I may have been drifting towards a decision to do nothing, but that was because I couldn't think of anything that would have been effective. When you suggested I look at the law of Presidential succession, and I thought about it in the context of the Inauguration Day Ceremony, I realized it presented me with an opportunity to kill President Butler and all his successors. That would have created the kind of constitutional crisis that required them to re-examine the structure of the federal government. For me to say it was part of some Islamic plot destroys my message, but I admit that there are times I wonder if I would have thought of it without your tip."

"I think you would have, but perhaps it's something we can never know for certain."

"When I found out they always keep one person in the line of succession from attending and that Defense Secretary Wilson wasn't going to be there, I almost canceled the plan. Did you know they never allow all the successors to be at the same place at the same time?"

Rabbani smiled. "Actually I did."

"You should have told me."

"I didn't know what you would do, and besides, if you wanted to do something, I knew you'd figure it out without me. I suggest you forget that I perhaps played some minor role in what you did. The truth of it is that you did it all alone." Rabbani poured himself a glass of water. "This Jewish president of yours interests me. I never thought I'd have to deal with a Jew in the White House. I hear that the Jew didn't want to become President and that that early on he wanted to resign. I also understand that there are many of your politicians who want him to resign. Do you know that when they thought you were dead, his popularity rose, but now that they know you escaped, he is once again a pariah to the public and the media, and that some of them are saying he must have helped you escape?"

Clarence nodded and pointed to the laptop computer on the small desk in front of the window. "I've kept up with the news from the United States."

"What can you tell me about him?"

"Sorry, but I can't help you there. All I know is what appears in the news."

"You learned nothing more when you had your White House pass and serviced the computers?

Clarence shrugged, "Nothing important."

"I'm disappointed. I never thought I'd have to deal with such an unknown. Based on what his envoy, this Molly Pemberton had to say, it's possible that this accidental President of yours may think I may be more involved with you than the people in your State Department and CIA." Clarence shrugged, indicating he had nothing useful to add. Rabbani continued, "What do you know of this envoy?"

"Not much, except that she's very smart and very good-looking."

Rabbani smiled, "Don't say that in front of Fatima. She'll want to scratch her eyes out. But what is her position in the Silver administration? Is she someone of real importance?"

"All I know is she used to be with the FBI and was very instrumental in discovering who I was. My grandfather liked her and so did I." Clarence patted his back pocket. "She gave me her card with her e-mail address on it. I kept it here in my wallet."

"Why did you do that?"

"I sent her a message right after they announced my escape."

Rabbani looked shocked. "Are you mad? They may have ways of tracing you."

"Don't worry, not the way I do it."

"But why take a chance?"

"Just a whim. I liked her. I just wanted to say I hope my deceiving her didn't get her in too much trouble with the President."

"Apparently it didn't. She's still working for him, but you have got to be more careful."

"Agreed."

"This Molly Pemberton told me Silver thinks you will contact me. After they left, a representative of the Crown threatened to expel me from the country if I don't cooperate."

"Is that why you don't want anyone to know about the role you played."?

"In part, but the real reason is more complicated."

"Would you tell me?"

Rabbani glanced at his wristwatch. "Why not. Let me start at the beginning, before the first Gulf War in 1991. You know that many expatriate Saudis are opposed to the Royal family in Saudi Arabia because of their corruption. Let us assume that those expatriates wanted the Royal family to be replaced, but that they feared that if the Royal family fell, it would be replaced by a religious regime headed by Osama Bin Laden with the approval of the Wahhabi clerics like that of the Taliban in Afghanistan. That would be a disaster for secular Muslims and the whole, civilized world." Rabbani took a sip of water and then continued. "We had a plan that we were just about to implement. First we would stage an uprising in Saudi Arabia that would depose the Royal family and put Osama Bin Laden and Al Qaeda in charge. To do that, some members of our expatriate community would cooperate with Osama Bin Laden and Al Qaeda. They encourage him to start an uprising against the Royal family. He knows that many of us have influence with the Saudi military leaders so we agree to persuade them to stand aside while the clerics whip the people into a frenzy. So, Al Qaeda takes over in Arabia and establishes an Islamic government like the Taliban. Next, the world is horrified at what's occurring in Arabia and with the tacit approval of everyone, Saddam Hussein was to move his army into Arabia, to destroy Al Qaeda and then we, the expatriates would assume power. All that was needed was for Al Qaeda to make the first move. All that held them back was fear that the United States or Iraq might intervene. Al Qaeda had negotiated an arrangement with Iraq and planned to use our organization as a front to keep the U.S. from intervening. We knew that Saddam Hussein would double-cross Al Qaeda because we brokered an arrangement where, Iraq goes into Arabia, deposes Al Qaeda, and we take over from them. Under those circumstances, the United States agrees to do nothing."

Clarence could see Rabbani becoming more excited as he continued. "While many in the United States wouldn't like Osama Bin Laden seizing control of Arabia, with our assurances that Iraq would move in and then turn over the government to our group, we were certain the U.S, would welcome Iraq doing the job for them. It was perfect

"Do you really think Iraq would have moved out. I mean what's in it for them?"

"We suggested that the Iraqis get Kuwait. That's what Saddam Hussein always wanted. We expected the U.S. would have been so happy to have been spared the job of invading Arabia, they wouldn't have responded to Iraq's take-over of Kuwait."

"I don't know, Uncle. Iraq might have still decided to stay in Arabia. You know you can't trust Saddam Hussein."

Rabbani smiled. "I know him very well, and I agree. He's not known as Saddam the generous. He's a snake. He probably would refuse to get out, but it wouldn't take long before the Wahhabi clerics and the people of Arabia would want him gone. As a secular Muslim and a foreigner, he's hated as much as the Americans. After a taste of his cruelty and sadism, it'll probably be more. They know the Americans are only interested in the oil and don't really want to rule Arabia. With Saddam Hussein it's different. If he refused to leave it would be because Saddam wants an empire. In any event, we were certain that if Saddam double crossed us and refused to leave, before long, the Arabians would have been begging the Americans to come and throw him out, and we would then have taken over from the Americans. It was a win-win strategy for us."

"So what happened?"

Rabbani smiled. "Let me use your bathroom for a minute. This damn prostate of mine has a mind of its own these days, and why don't you send for some fruit juice, cranberry juice if they have it, it's supposed to be good for this problem."

When Rabbani returned, he resumed his seat on the sofa. "You know what happened. Saddam got tired of waiting for Bin Laden to make his move. He misread the entire situation. He thought the West and the UN were nothing to worry about and invaded Kuwait."

Moments later, they were interrupted by a knock on the door as a waiter arrived with the cranberry juice Clarence ordered. Once the waiter left, Rabbani sipped his juice and said, "So you understand the history?"

"I didn't know the intrigue in the background, but it makes sense to me."

"Good," Rabbani said. "Faced with what Saddam did in Kuwait and his expulsion from there, we had a new reality to deal with. The United States made it clear that it would not allow Saddam to control Kuwait and that of course included Saudi Arabia, and the U.S. solidified its support of the Royal family during the Gulf War. It became clear that if we were to rid ourselves of the Royal family, we would have to come up with a new plan."

"And you participated in that new plan?"

Rabbani smiled. "Am I not a leading member of the expatriate community?" Rabbani leaned back in his chair a moment, then turned and looked at Clarence, "To succeed, we would have to persuade Al Qaeda that they could depose the Saud Royal Family and they wouldn't do that so long as the family had U. S. support. We knew that given time, the Royal family's cowardice and corruption would weaken that U.S. commitment to them." Rabbani smiled, "And sure enough, they did. Members of the Royal family financed terrorist organizations, they gave money to suicide bombers, fifteen of the nineteen September 11th hijackers were Saudis. Bin Laden and his supporters miscalculated. They thought the terrorist attacks in the United States and its embassies and on the Cole would persuade the Americans to withdraw from the Middle East. Instead, the September 11 attack resulted in Americans becoming fed up with international terrorism. In another setback, the U.S. invaded Bin Laden's home base in Afghanistan and then got rid of Saddam Hussein with no help from the Saudis and against the wishes of the UN and many of its powerful members like France, Russia and Germany. Despite those setbacks, Al Qaeda kept going, but they were looking for a time where they could safely make their move and depose the Saud Family without US interference. After seeing how easily the U.S. got rid of Saddam Hussein in 2003, Al Qaeda wouldn't consider moving into Saudi Arabia unless they believed the United States was too preoccupied with its own problems to intervene. That's where you came in. If you had succeeded in destroying the U. S. Presidency the way you intended, that would have been taken as a sign to proceed by Osama Bin Laden's followers. That's what you almost accomplished for us. If Silver had only gone to the Inauguration like he was supposed to, the United States would not have had a President. Al Qaeda was convinced that if you succeeded there would have been chaos in the United States for years, more than enough time to rid the country of the Royal Family. He said he would install us in power to keep the rest of the world from objecting like they would to a foreign invasion"

Clarence shook his head. "You'd just be a puppet. You don't really believe that Al Qaeda would turn the country over to you and your friends do you?"

"Of course not." Rabbani sipped his juice and leaned back. "After a few weeks, we would break with Al Qaeda and advise the world of Al Qaeda's plan to impose their kind of religious fanaticism on the rest of the world. Soon the rest of the Middle East, Europe, Asia, the United Nations, the whole world would be begging the United States to invade Arabia and destroy Al Qaeda. What Al Qaeda fails to understand is that the United States is very resilient. No matter what kind of trouble was going on in the United States, it would respond to that kind of plea and move into Arabia. It would be no contest, and we would take over with the blessing of most of the Arab world and most of the world's Muslims. We would have the protection of the United States, and, consider this, the United States would be owed a debt of gratitude by everyone." Rabbani smiled, "Don't you think that would be the best of all possible solutions?"

Clarence nodded. "Pretty neat, but maybe the U.S. would just restore the Royal family."

"I don't think so. First, I expect that Al Qaeda would have all of them they could find slaughtered. Second, as I said before, support for the Royal family in your country since the 2003 Iraq War has pretty much disappeared."

"So, do you have a current plan?"

Rabbani glanced at his wristwatch. "We can talk about that later. For the moment, we have more pressing decisions to make about your future."

"Just what do you have in mind?"

"Like where are you to go? Where can you live when so many police forces are looking for you? What are you going to do with the rest of your life?"

Clarence smiled. "Those questions are of course of great interest to me also."

"Do you have anything in mind?"

"I thought I might move to a Moslem country, maybe in the Middle East. I thought maybe I'd be considered some kind of hero by those people."

"Forget it. They'd kill you and sell your head to the Americans. You know that many in the Middle East believe you acted in consort with President Silver and those that don't, hold you responsible for saddling them with a Jewish President committed to supporting Israel. Some of the members of the expatriate family here in the UK who know better, think the safest thing to do is to kill you."

"And what do you think, my uncle."

"I told you. I think someone with your talent can be very useful to us in achieving our goals and in ruling Arabia afterwards. We'll have to do some plastic surgery to change your appearance even more, and we'll have to think of a way for me to convince my associates that you are a valuable asset. In the meantime, we'll have to decide where you should stay."

Do you have any suggestions?"

"I have some thoughts, but let's not rush into anything. For the moment, I don't see any problem with this weekend. I have some identity papers and passports for you from Saudi Arabia, Iraq, Syria, Jordan and Iran. I didn't have much time and they were easy for me. The problem is that you only speak English." Rabbani stared at Clarence. "I used your old picture on them. Now that I see how well you changed your appearance, I think I may have to destroy them and do new ones. I was also working on papers from former British colonies like Jamaica, Trinidad, and South Africa. They should be easier for you. When they're ready, I'll see to it that you get them. But for this golf outing and until things quiet down a little, why don't you stay here as Khalil Yomani. I have a complete set of Saudi papers in his name for you in my room."

"Good, I'll use that for now and take the others when they're ready."

"I'll need some new pictures of you before I can finish them. Fatima brought a digital camera. Now let me tell you about the other men in our foursome. They will know you as Khalil Yomani and think you are the son of a friend, that you were brought up in the UK and that you spent the last ten years living in the United States. I told them I wasn't sure exactly where you lived and what you did in the U.S., that I met you in Washington quite by accident, found out you were going to be in Ireland this week and invited you to play in this tournament."

Clarence nodded. "Good. That should be easy."

"In a couple of hours, we'll go down to dinner, just you, me and Fatima. She's quite anxious to see you again and has been primping all day." Rabbani smiled. "At dinner, I'll ask you what you've been doing. You think about it for now, and whatever story you tell us will be who you are and Fatima and I will know nothing else."

After Rabbani left, Clarence removed the knife he had strapped to his calf. He didn't think about constructing a cover story as he had been told. He didn't need Rabbani to tell him that, he'd already taken care of it, but he remained seated in the upholstered armchair reviewing what he had learned. He didn't know where he fit in to his uncle's plans. If he didn't have a major role to play, he better expect Rabbani to try and have him killed because it would be too dangerous to ever let him talk to the U.S. authorities. He'd go along with things for the moment and see what develops.

CHAPTER 8

▼

Clarence was relieved when the golf weekend ended. He had been needlessly nervous about his golf game and being accepted as Khalil Yomani. He had not played good enough or bad enough to be noticed, and his story about living in the United States for most of the past ten years was accepted without question. Most of the other golfers had now gone and nothing suspicious had occurred.

Clarence and Rabbani were seated in Clarence's room. It had been difficult for Clarence to get through the last two days with all the questions he had. He spent the day on the golf course, his evenings socializing with Rabbani and the other golfers and his nights with Fatima. It felt good being with a woman again and perhaps they could have a life together someplace, but he needed to ask his questions. What did Rabbani want him to do and would it be something he would want to do?

Rabbani poured himself a glass of cranberry juice, took a sip and then said, "So my young nephew, now we can talk. For what you accomplished, considering the odds against it, you should be praised. Unfortunately, you left one man standing and as I said, it is your bad luck that he's a Jew and even worse that he's a smart one."

"You surprise me, uncle. I thought about our two months together in London and can't recall one time when you said anything that was even remotely anti Semitic. What's more, I distinctly remember your saying that the Arab world should make peace with the Israelis. Frankly, I thought you paid about as much attention to being a Muslim as I did to being a Christian. Was that an act for my benefit?"

"No, not at all. I have no personal problem with Jews. For me, religion is only a useful tool in uniting an unruly populace. Most Muslims are not the religious fanatics you see throwing stones or blowing themselves up as suicide bombers. It's primarily the poor and uneducated among them with no hope that you read about, and for them and their families, the suicide death of one of them produces a better life for the other family members that survive. Who are we to tell them that it's wrong to do that?"

"But they kill innocent people, Uncle."

"And you didn't."

"My cause was just."

"And in their minds, their cause is equally as just."

Clarence rocked back and forth in his chair a moment. "I guess it's the same thing."

"Yes, it is."

"I'm curious. What do you have in mind for me."

"For the next few days, you will stay in Ireland while I prepare some new passports for you. Then we have to change your appearance even more. You will go to Switzerland for some plastic surgery. That all right with you?"

Clarence nodded in agreement. "You're sure I can trust those people?"

"With the Swiss, for money, everything is possible, and they know we have tons of it. They would never betray us."

"I don't know, there's a big price on my head, and the United States has more money than you and your Saudi friends."

"True, but they can't quietly spend their money the way we can, and what's more, they won't know who you are."

"Very good, and what after that?"

"I have plans, big plans for you, but you will have to do something to help me persuade my associates to accept you as one of our little inner circle."

"And what would that be?"

"You have unfinished business with President Silver."

"If you mean you want me to kill him, I don't know. That's very hard to do, maybe a suicide bomber could do it, but I'm not a suicide bomber."

"I understand."

"And what would it accomplish? There are successors to the Presidency now. The first one would be the Speaker of the House, Elliott Thurston."

"We would rather see him in the Oval Office than Silver. Silver is not manageable. Thurston is, but you're missing the point. Your figuring out a way to get rid of Silver will establish your credibility. We have plenty of potential martyrs to carry out the actual killing. You are too valuable to waste that way. Perhaps a suicide bomber with foreign press credentials. We shall see. You think about how we can get rid of him. After we change your appearance, and while you are recuperating from that, we'll create a whole new person for you. I think you will be a citizen of what used to be Rhodesia, or perhaps British Honduras. That will make the language easier and we'll give you a whole background that'll allow you to go everywhere we want without difficulty." Rabbani looked at him appraisingly for a moment. "Yes, I think it will be Rhodesia. Most of the old British records were destroyed after it became Zimbabwe in nineteen-eighty. You'll be the sole survivor of some Arab family that was killed in a black uprising, but for now, you'll be Khalil Yomani."

"And where will I go and what will I do as this person you invent?"

"For starters, I'll have to second you to Al Qaeda training for a while. That will help establish you with them and with our group because you will let us know what's they're up to. While you're recuperating in Switzerland for a few weeks, you will have two jobs. One will be to come up with a plan to kill President Silver and the other to learn enough about Islam to pass as a Muslim."

"And just where do I go when I'm 'seconded' to Al Qaeda and what am I supposed to do for them?"

"As someone who has lived in the United States for over ten years, you will help train Al Qaeda operatives who are to be sent there with what life is like so they won't stick out like a sore thumb. With our backing, they will accept you, especially if you can come up with a good plan to kill President Silver."

"Where am I supposed to do this training?"

"There's a training base for terrorists at a place called New Salman Pak."

"And what kind of assignments will they have?"

"Does it matter?"

"It could. There are regional differences and getting around in a city would be very different from moving around in rural areas."

"I see your point, but frankly, I don't know what Al Qaeda has in mind. They talked about sending a force of one hundred snipers out to terrorize the people in all your major cities. They also talked about infecting one hundred martyrs with smallpox and having them wander around in you big cities, to attend sporting events, concerts and classes in your universities." Rabbani shrugged. "I don't know exactly what they have in mind and I doubt it would be either of those two actions. They like something more dramatic. Once they get to know you and learn that you have lived in the U.S. for many years, they may ask you to suggest some targets. Think about it. It would help you and me if you came up with something really good. So, what do you think? You will join us?"

"Well of course, but my goal was to restore the United States to its original principles under the Constitution, not to destroy it with terrorism".

"I understand, but that mission has failed, at least for now, so you must fight our battle with us. To do that, it is as I told you. Al Qaeda must be convinced that the U.S. military will not interfere with their take over of Arabia. Once that happens and Al Qaeda is ruling in Arabia and spreading terrorism everywhere, the entire world will beg the United States to rid us all of Al Qaeda and then we will rule Arabia."

"Joining you is fine with me, uncle, but cooperating with Al Qaeda. Is that really necessary?"

"Unfortunately yes, but it's only temporary. We all make alliances and use all the tools we can, including terrorism to achieve our goals. For Al Qaeda, it's to destroy the West and create a worldwide radical Islamic order ruled by them. For the Saud Royal Family, it's to be allowed to continue their rule and they support terrorism as the price for being left alone. For the Iraqis, it was to gain political control of the entire Middle East and use the oil power of the region to economically enslave the west. For my fellow expatriates, and me it's much, more simple. All we want is to rule Arabia and make proper use of its wealth. We must prepare for the eventuality that some day, the oil will be gone, and to do that, we need the help of the West. Unfortunately, terrible things must happen before the world will demand that the United States and the West move in and assist us in establishing a new group of democratic rulers for the region."

"So in the meantime, we cooperate with the lunatics in Al Qaeda."

"As I said, it's only a temporary alliance. We'll help the United States get rid of them when we have secured power."

"That's a dangerous game you're playing, uncle. The moneyed interests in Germany thought they could manipulate Hitler and the Nazis, and it turned out the other way around."

"I don't need you to tell me that. I know they consider me a heretic and they'd just as soon kill me as an Israeli or an American, but for now they need us for money and support from certain elements within the kingdom. We can be as ruthless as they can, so when the time comes, we'll be rid of those fanatics. For now, we must use them, but if it became known that we were cooperating with them, I'd lose all Western support."

"I don't like it that much, but I'm sure you're right that it's a necessary temporary expedient. I'll be a spy for you and help them out all I can for as long as it's necessary. When that is no longer necessary, your role will be unknown to the West, but what about me?"

"Al Qaeda will value you as the person we create for that purpose. Once that assignment is finished, Khalil Yomani will die a martyr's death and you will reappear as a former Rhodesian, and as that person, you will play an important role with our new governing group. Trust me on that. I will make it happen."

Clarence nodded in agreement. "I hope it won't take too long. What else do I do while I'm with those people?"

"As I said, it's very important that Al Qaeda succeed with whatever it is they decide to do. It may not seem like much to you, but the big problem in all the activities of their foot soldiers, whether they be snipers, the suicide bombers or walking germ factories or whatever their plan may be is a lack of familiarity with life in the United States. They will stick out like a boil on the end of your nose. You will tell them enough so once they are in the United States, they will be able to go to Las Vegas, to New York, Chicago and Los Angeles, wherever they are sent. Perhaps you will teach them enough so they can enter a Cathedral or a Synagogue and do all the things Al Qaeda wants them to do. Once the plan is adopted and those foot soldiers of the *jihad* are sent to the United States, you will come back to London, tell us where they are going and what they are planning and then you can prepare to rule Arabia and the region with me. I read the Manifesto you sent to the media with great interest, especially the parts that dealt with the changes you want in your Constitution and the way it has been interpreted. I will want to establish a Constitutional republic in Arabia. It seems to me that there's no one better than you in knowing what's necessary and what's to be avoided. You interested?"

Clarence nodded. "You know I am."

"Good, and you can have Fatima for one of your wives if she pleases you." Rabbani took a sip of cranberry juice. "We can make use of some of the ancient *sharia* laws when it suits us and that will assuage the general population."

"Is the United States the only country being targeted?"

"At the moment, the United States and the UK are Al Qaeda's principal targets. Some of the operatives may do something in Europe in a smaller scale. But, if the Russians, or the French, or the Germans try to impede the United States from acting to replace Al Qaeda, we will give them a taste of Al Qaeda style Islamic terrorism to bring them around. For now, the plan is to restrict major activities to the United States, the UK and Israel, but those fools in Al Qaeda are not manageable. There are so many terrorist organizations, and we are only loosely allied with some of them. They select targets of opportunity from time to time." Rabbani glanced at his wristwatch again. "That pretty much tells the story. So what do you say? Are you ready to get started?"

"Of course."

"Good. Tomorrow we must make this Chester Dolan that you were when you left the United States and arrived here disappear and be presumed dead. They will discover who that was eventually."

"And how do you intend to do that?"

"I think we've worked it all out. Do you know how to operate a small power boat or perhaps a small sailboat?"

"Both."

"Excellent. Then it's all set. Tomorrow, as that person, you will rent a small boat. You will go to one of the Aran Islands, Fatima will show you exactly where. You will capsize the boat in a cove we picked out. There are only a few hundred people that live on the whole island. A body will be recovered with your wallet and identified as the person who rented the boat, and the body will be cremated."

"Whose body?"

"What do you care? It'll be some drunk. God knows there are enough of them in this country. When the United States authorities discover the name you used to escape and trace him to Ireland and to the rental of that boat, that person will already be officially dead and cremated."

"You really think they'll buy that identification?"

"Oh yes. The United States authorities will be quick to accept the idea that you're dead and claim credit for solving the case of your disappearance, and the American public will accept it so they can feel better and get on with their lives. They always do. They did it with the 1993 attack on the World Trade Center, the Oklahoma City bombing and the nine eleven attacks on the World Trade Center and the Pentagon. And remember, in each case, the U.S. authorities refused to consider that other governments might have been involved in those attacks. For example, they were very quick to say that the anthrax scare and the Washington sniper had nothing to do with foreign or state sponsored terrorism."

"Are you saying that Al Qaeda or Iraq was involved in those matters?"

"No. I don't know, but I ask you, how could the authorities have known that so fast?"

"I wondered about that myself. While we were talking, I had an idea about how we could kill Silver."

"I'm listening."

"It's quite simple. I'm almost mad at myself for not thinking of it before."

"Could it still be done?"

"Yes, I think so, and very easily." I can't go back to Washington to do it, but I can tell you how. All you got to do is provide a small amount of explosives, a miniature TV camera and TV receiver, and a GPS system."

"What's a GPS system?"

"Global Positioning System. They install them in lots of automobiles. You may even have it in your Mercedes."

"I do have it. You're saying that's all I need to supply to kill Silver?"

"That, and maybe some good luck."

"I'm more than interested. What do we do with those things?"

"We install them in a model airplane."

"A child's toy?"

"Sort of, but there are adults who build and fly them as a hobby and some are quite sophisticated and large. Someone can fly a plane equipped that way to the White House and when he sees President Silver in the Rose Garden, he brings it in and detonates it."

"Don't those little model planes make a lot of noise?"

"Not if they're battery powered."

"You think you can put enough explosives in one of those small planes?"

"I'm pretty sure we could. Give me a few hours with some Army manuals and I could figure out exactly what's required. I can explain exactly how it should be done to an engineer or technician in ten minutes. You supply the materials I indicate and everything else he needs he can get very easily and without raising any suspicions in the United States. Damn, I wish I had thought of it. I could have killed him so easily when there still wasn't anyone to succeed to the Presidency, and my whole plan would have worked."

"I will check this out with my associates. We have people who will know if it could work. If we approve, you will explain this plan to engineers when you get to the training camp. They will also evaluate it. I hope you're right. The plan sounds simple and feasible to me, but I'm not an expert in those matters." Rabbani nodded and then smiled. "Yes, I'll tell my associates. If it works like you say, they will be very impressed." Rabbani rose and walked towards the door. With one hand on the doorknob, he looked back and said as he prepared to leave, "Your plan, I like it. It's very creative. You know, Clarence, that I've truly come to like you and appreciate your unique talents, and now when I tell my associates of your suggestion, they'll be enormously impressed, and that means they'll stop telling me that I have to kill you." Rabbani smiled and shut the door to Clarence's room behind him.

Clarence remained seated for a few minutes as the door closed and patted the knife in the sheath strapped to his calf. He muttered, under his breath, to the now empty room, "I'm glad to hear that uncle, because you would have found that easier said than done, and I've become fond of you too."

CHAPTER 9

▼

It didn't take long for FBI Director P.J. Winters to discover that he wasn't getting any information about the Davenport investigation. No amount of blustering at the Secret Service Agents involved or at the head of Homeland Security worked. By the time Senator Davies' assistant, Beau Lawrence returned Winters' call to Davies, Winters' foul mood had turned ugly and he was near apoplectic when informed that Davies was unavailable until Beau told him that Davies was at his weekend retreat. At Winter's insistence, Beau agreed to call Davies and tell him Winters had to speak with him immediately. Davies called Winters and the two agreed to meet at Davies' palatial estate on Chesapeake Bay that evening. What they had to discuss could not be talked about on the phone and meeting at Davies' country home suited him just fine.

When Winters arrived, Davies was seated on the veranda sipping mineral water and listening to a Wagnerian opera. An elderly woman was sitting next to him. As he motioned for Winters to join him, he said, "Say hello to my mother. She came up from Mississippi for a little visit."

Winters removed his hat and nodded at the woman. "Pleased to meet you, Mrs. Davies. I'm P.J. Winters."

Davies' mother smiled. "I know that and I'm mighty pleased to meet you too." Mrs. Davies rose from he seat next to her son. "I'll leave you two to talk business."

As Mrs. Davies left, Winters said, "Your mother is a fine looking woman, Senator."

"Mother had a little stroke last year and I had her come up to be checked out at Walter Reed. Medicine in Mississippi isn't the finest. You still drinking Chivas on the rocks?"

"That'll be fine." Winters took the seat opposite Davies. Impatient to talk about what brought him there, he said, "Why'd that idiot in your office take so damn long to call me back?"

"Beau doesn't know anything about what we're planning and I don't think you'd want me to tell him." Davies smiled, "Or perhaps you don't care."

"Don't be ridiculous. You know that the bastard in the White House has managed to cut me out of all information on the Davenport investigation?"

"No, but I'm not surprised. He knows you've been sniping away at him since he took office. Say what you will about him, but you got to admit he's pretty damn smart."

"I'll grant you that, but I have to know what's going on. I want you to get an investigation going in the Senate and for the Congress to insist that the FBI know everything they're doing about finding out what's going on in the Davenport investigation in Europe."

"You know I would if I could, but there's a lot of Senators and Representatives that think the CIA can't operate inside the country and that the FBI has no business acting outside the country."

"Don't give me that. You guys can do whatever you want."

"Sure, but you know damn well I got my own problems right now. I'd do it if I could, but I'll have to rely on Smithers in the Senate and Thurston in the House, and right now, I don't have the control over them that I used to."

"I know. Silver is just pissing me off. I was just hoping you could do something. What's the status of the cases against you?"

"I think I have it under control, but it'll take a little while. Thanks for that information on those judges."

"Glad to help. You've been saying all along that Silver was the brains behind Davenport. Even though I know you didn't believe it, but with him cutting me out of the investigation, I'm beginning to wonder if it could be true."

Davies shrugged as he adjusted his cuff links. "Don't be ridiculous, P.J. It doesn't become you. We both know that he can't do the job properly and we that we have to get rid of him, and what difference does it make anyway?"

Winters smiled, "I know it's bullshit, but more and more of my people are willing to believe it."

"I've been telling you for a long time, that for the good of the country, we got to get rid of Silver."

"So long as we're all telling the truth, I think you're beginning to believe your own bullshit, Senator. What you mean is for the good of Senator Davies we should get rid of Silver."

"Fair enough, and for the good of FBI Director Winters."

"Agreed, we both want to see it happen." Winters pulled a pair of Cuban cigars out of his pocket and offered one to Davies. Davies put his hands up, palms out, refusing the offer. "You mind if I smoke?"

"I'd prefer that you didn't."

Winters returned the cigars to his pocket. "Fine, but you are a fussy little prig."

Davies smiled. "It's never been necessary that we be friends. I use you. You use me. When we have common interests we work together, and when we don't we go our separate ways."

"That suits me just fine."

Davies ignored Winters' reply. "Do you have anyone in mind for the little jobs we discussed?"

"Which job?"

"Both."

"We understand that no mention is ever made as to where the names came from?"

"Look, P.J., if I ever admit you provided the people we used to kill Silver or his girl friend's husband, I cut my own throat and if you admit I supplied you with the money for them, you cut your throat. We're each too big a fish for anyone to give us immunity for ratting out the other, and besides, it'd finish us politically."

"You got it all figured out."

"You see any problems?"

"No."

"Good, so what do you have?"

"Getting Silver is tough. There are guys that would do it, but the chances for success are slim with all the protection the Secret Service is now providing. There's a TV cameraman with White House accreditation. He's a Palestinian and says he could wear a bomb and put enough explosives in his equipment to kill himself and Silver when Silver walks by during a press conference."

"Why would he do it?"

"He's dying from an inoperable brain tumor and he hates Jews."

"That all he wants?"

"No. He wants ten million in a Swiss bank account for his family before he does it."

"No Problem, but what if he doesn't do it or he fails?"

P.J. laughed. "What do you want, a warranty deed? You going to sue him for non-performance?"

"What are his chances for success?"

"You heard the plan. He could be stopped by the Secret Service before he even gets into the room. Scott Jackson tells me the Secret Service have some dogs with them right outside the pressroom in the West Wing and he thinks they are bomb sniffers."

"So I risk ten million and maybe get nothing. I'll have to think it over. What about the other one?"

"Whacking the broad's husband is easy. He's in a nursing home and doesn't know which end is up anyway. You can get him done for ten large."

"Are you aware that you're talking like some hoodlum in a 'B' movie?"

"And what do you think you're doing, planning a tea party? If it offends you I'll talk like a Harvard professor."

"Okay, forget it. What about the rest of it?"

"One of my people will do it, and we've figured out how we can get a guy to confess and implicate Silver."

"How the hell do you do that?"

"It'll be managed. Trust me on this. Better you don't know."

"I want to know how you're going to get that done."

P.J. stared at his manicured fingernails a moment. Then looked up and stared at Davies. "I'm telling you I'll take care of it, and that's all I'm telling you. If you don't trust me to do this, get someone else."

"Cool it, I just like to know how things are done."

"I've said all I intend to."

"And this guy that's going to confess, he can't connect anything back to you or me?"

"What do you think I am, stupid? He won't be able to because he won't know anything."

"How do you arrange that?"

"I'll arrange it. Don't worry about it. You said yourself, we're in this together."

"Who's going to do it?"

"One of my men."

"Who?"

"If you have to know, Walter Wagner."

"You trust him that much?"

"He's done jobs like this for me before." P.J. grinned. "He's convinced that getting rid of Silver is good for the country."

"He's not to know about me, agreed?"

"Agreed. He may suspect something at some point, but he'll never know anything for sure." Winters poured himself another two fingers of Chivas.

"Does he know what's on the tape of me and Morton?"

P. J. nodded. "We've heard rumors. I told him that if it's true that you agreed to look the other way about some drug dealing, that we've all made deals with criminals to further some investigation or prosecution. I told him that if you did what it says in the tape, you did it in the best interests of the country." P.J. grinned. "He hopes the scuttlebutt he's heard about you starting Klan riots against the blacks is true and, as far as he's concerned, that makes you his choice for President. You still think you can get there."

"Don't see why not. Like I said, I've got all the cases covered, and six months from now, it'll all be ancient history. Once my position in the Senate is confirmed, I'll be able to take care of you like I said. You got my word on that."

"That's fine with me, Senator. I know with Silver gone, Thurston is his successor and becomes President and that you're going to be the Vice-President, but I don't know why Thurston resigns and you become President, but you're telling me that happens."

"Right."

"You want to tell me why that happens?"

"No."

"Okay, but just so we're clear on this. You serve your time as President and then you back me for the job. If it doesn't happen for you, you back me anyway."

"That's the deal."

"Agreed."

Davies adjusted his cuff links. "I got a question for you. When Silver said they knew Davenport killed the Swansons because of evidence at the crime scene, do you know what he was talking about?"

"Sure. Davenport kills people by garroting them and then slicing their throats with a serrated blade."

"Very interesting."

"Why is that interesting?"

"Suppose the guy that kills the Silver's girl friend's husband does it like that, so it looks like Davenport did it. That would reinforce the case that Davenport did it and that he did it for Silver and form a strong case for impeachment."

P.J shook his head. "Stick to what you know, Senator. It'd be easy to do it that way, but it's too risky. We may not be able to place Davenport in the country when it's done. Nobody knows where the hell he is. No, I don't think it's a good idea."

"Okay, it was just an idea."

"Now you're sure you want to do this?"

"For sure with the girl friend's husband, but I'll let you know when."

"Why the delay?"

"I want to be sure the cases against me get handled the right way."

"And what about killing Silver?"

"I don't know about risking the ten million. What do you think?"

"I wouldn't risk my ten million on that guy, but I don't have your kind of money."

"Keep that on the back burner. We may do it if the other thing fizzles."

CHAPTER 10

▼

Ben looked up from the reports he was reading from the Intelligence Services on the search for Clarence Davenport as Tom Andrews and Spenser Cameron approached. He waived them towards the sofa to the right of his desk. As they sat, Ben rose from behind his desk, picked up the armchair in front of his desk, and moved it opposite the sofa. He sat in it and said over the pile of files spread out on the coffee table, "I assume you have read the reports from the Intelligence people?"

Tom and Cam nodded that they had.

"We don't know any more about where Davenport is now than we did five minutes after the house blew up." Ben pointed to a separate smaller and slimmer pile of files. "According to the information in these files from Counter Terrorism, Al Qaeda and various Muslim extremist groups may be planning something major. Instead of concentrating on that, practically every investigative resource we have is employed in finding Clarence Davenport."

"We can't very well order them to reduce the hunt for Davenport. There's already talk trying to connect you to him saying that you arranged his escape to keep him from implicating you." Tom Andrews turned to Spenser Cameron. "You agree with that Cam?"

"No question. An increasing number of Internet web sites are raising that issue and it's spreading to the more responsible media outlets." Cam turned towards Ben, "If you reduce the force involved in the search for Davenport, you'll create a greater media storm and that'll play right into the hands of the Impeachment crowd. They're already saying that you're not really trying to find him."

Ben shook his head. "You know I don't want to leave any stone unturned in finding Davenport, but it's more important that we investigate these warnings about planned terrorist attacks. It's my job to stop these future disasters."

"I agree," Tom said, "but maybe we can divert some of those resources without the media knowing about it."

"Impossible," Cam said.

Ben held his hands up for silence. "Look, I can't kowtow to possible or even likely media fallout and impeachment concerns. The media will do what they're going to do no matter what I do and those members of Congress that want me impeached will continue pushing that no matter what I do. The only thing that'll stop them is getting Davenport, but," Ben waived at the piles of files and folders, "what they're doing is a complete waste of time. Investigators are falling over each other and the information in these files is laughable. I can't let this continue and possibly risk thousands of innocent lives." Pointing at the slimmer pile of files on the coffee table, Ben said, "We need to give this information the attention it deserves."

Ben rose from his chair and looked out the window at the rose garden. He sighed and returned to his chair behind his desk. "Whoever sits behind the desk in the Oval Office is faced with difficult decisions. We can only do what we think best and must accept that we can make colossal mistakes. A prior occupant of this office wanted to bring peace to the Middle East, resolve the Palestinian-Israeli conflict and make that his legacy. I think because of that he disregarded evidence of an Iraqi connection to the 1993 World Trade Center bombing and to the bombing of the Murrah building in Oklahoma City in 1995. After all, you don't bring peace to a region by going to war." Ben shook his head. "I may be wrong, but I think the investigative people in the FBI and CIA accommodated that decision when they all said the 1993 World Trade Center attack was the work of a few nutty Islamic extremists and that there was no state sponsorship. They did it again when they convicted McVeigh and Nicholls of the Oklahoma City bombing, and again said they were not involved with anyone else. In both cases there was a lot of evidence indicating that Iraq may have played a significant role in both attacks. The judge in the McVeigh case said he hoped the conviction wouldn't end the investigation of what really happened in Oklahoma City, but it did." Ben took off his glasses and squeezed between his eyes before continuing. "Then, when the September 11 attack on the World Trade Center and the Pentagon happened, all the bureaucrats were still committed to denying that any state sponsorship was involved. It was Al Qaeda, but there was no state sponsorship. God forbid anyone ever admits they made a mistake. At that point, no one wanted the finger pointed at them, but maybe if they acted differently, we could have prevented nine eleven, probably not, but that's something we'll never know. I'm not going to make that mistake and disregard these warnings."

Spenser Cameron looked at Ben with a puzzled look on his face.

Ben said, "What's troubling you, Cam?"

"This may not be the time to talk about it, but I thought the 1993 World Trade Center attack was the work of a few unconnected fanatic Muslims. And didn't McVeigh and Nicholls carry out the Oklahoma City bombing because of the Federal Government actions at Waco or Ruby Ridge. I always thought that had nothing to do with anything else."

"There's a ton of evidence that says otherwise. When some of the respected media like the Wall Street Journal, and members of Congress, like Senator Specter and Representative Burton, began to take notice and called for explanations from the FBI and others, the bureaucratic reaction was to cover your rear by denial and cover-up rather than admitting to a mistake. But this isn't the time to get into all that."

Cam said, "No disrespect intended, sir. All that happened in the nineties. You can't use that to try to explain your pulling away from the Davenport investigation. It's too complicated, controversial and the public has a short memory."

"I give the people more credit than that." Ben looked at Tom and then Cam. "There's a lesson to be learned. Cover-ups don't work. They backfire, often with totally unexpected results. It's like the situation with Davenport. You see the similarity between all those cover-ups, don't you?"

Tom frowned. "Actually, sir, I don't."

"Okay, when the Federal government bought into the ideas that it was only the religious fanatic they had arrested and his followers that were involved in the 1993 World Trade center, they didn't follow up on other leads they had. They did the same thing with McVeigh and Nicholls in the Oklahoma City bombing case. In that case, those convictions ended the investigation even though the judge said he hoped it wouldn't. Their failure to follow up and investigate the likely Al Qaeda and Iraqi involvement has to be justified by the entrenched bureaucracy that failed to do what they're supposed to do. The similarity to the Davenport situation is in the treatment of unwanted information by the Federal bureaucracy. In Davenport's case, no one in the Army or the Pentagon was willing to admit to responsibility for sending our troops to demolish the Kamisiyah munitions depot when they knew or should have known that Sarin gas and other chemical weapons were kept there. As a result of that error, many of our troops were exposed to those chemicals and, as bad as that was, the cover-up made it even worse. You remember that the Army and the Pentagon denied that and claimed they lost the military logs for that period. It took over five years for them to admit about 100,000 of our people had been exposed to chemical contaminants." Ben shook his head. "I believe we acted shamefully in refusing to pay proper attention to the Gulf War Syndrome claims of many of our troops, but it's the reaction of the bureaucracy that I'm focused on and the unintended result. It's because of that cover-up that Davenport says he carried out the Inauguration Day assassination. I will not be a party to any cover-up of..."

Ben was interrupted by a knock on the door. His assistant, Martha Roberts entered. "Sorry, Mr. President, but I thought you would want to know. FBI director Winters is going to address the nation on TV right now. He told the networks it was a matter of extreme importance."

"Thank you, Martha."

Cam said, "I wonder what that's all about."

"We'll soon see." Ben clicked on the TV set in his office. P.J. Winters was standing outside in front of the Hoover Building, surrounded by a horde of media. He held his hand up for silence. "Thank you all for coming. I want to announce that the FBI has determined that Clarence Davenport left the United States with a forged passport using the name of Chester Dolan from New York's Kennedy airport, arriving in Dublin Ireland. From there he went to Galway and a few days later rented a boat and made for the Aran Islands. He ran into some bad weather, his boat capsized and he drowned..." A rumble started in the crowd of media. P.J. held his hands up for silence. "His body was recovered and identified as that of Chester Dolan. Thanks to the excellent work of the FBI, we can bring to a close, the hunt for Clarence Davenport."

"As Winters began to leave, a reporter shouted, "Where's his body?"

Winters stooped and turned back to the microphone. "There is no body. He was cremated."

"How come so fast?"

"Those were his instructions." P. J. held his hands up for silence again as a rumble of protest began to form. "It was pretty straight forward. Davenport, as this Chester Dolan, was going to start a business in Galway as a computer consultant. You all remember how he infiltrated the Butler election campaign in that capacity. He called on a lawyer in Galway to draw up corporate papers, and while he was there, the lawyer asked him if he needed a will. They talked about it and the lawyer drew up a will expressing the desire that he be cremated if anything happened to him. Davenport signed it just before he left for the Aran Islands."

"How do you know it was him?"

"Handwriting experts and fingerprints on the will say it was him."

"Who were the beneficiaries?"

"Good question, but it doesn't lead anywhere. The beneficiaries were charities suggested by the lawyer. He had about twenty-seven thousand dollars in his account when he died and that's who'll be getting the money."

"You're certain it was him?"

"As certain as you can be about anything."

"Who was the lawyer?"

"The lawyer never saw him before. Davenport walked in off the street, said his name was Dolan and that's all he knows. We checked everything before we concluded it was genuine."

At the conclusion of the telecast, Ben said, "What do you make of that?"

"Fortuitous," Tom said, "very fortuitous. Now we can concentrate on the intelligence materials."

Cam nodded in agreement. "Saves you from a big problem. What do you think, Mr. President?"

"The Aran Islands are off the coast of Galway."

"That's right," Tom said. "My grand-father was from Galway. Does that mean anything?"

"Perhaps not. I don't know. It's almost too fortuitous for me, and I don't like the cremation story. I hope it's true, but I think we shouldn't accept that story too quickly." Ben turned towards Tom. "See if you can find out how they got onto that Chester Dolan identity, how they traced him to Ireland and found him in Galway and in the Aran Islands. Ben looked at his watch, that'll have to be it for today, gentlemen. I've got a meeting with Senator Kendall in about five minutes."

Later that evening, Tom Called Ben and informed him that an anonymous phone call from London to the FBI led them to the Galway lawyer and the Aran Islands. Ben was not surprised that the call came from London.

CHAPTER 11

▼

It had been a week since Clarence had rented a small skiff from the marina in Galway recommended by his lawyer and set out for the Aran Islands. The Connacht Tribune had carried the story of the boat sinking and the unfortunate death of poor Mr. Dolan. With no mourners to consider, the funeral and cremation arrangements had been quickly scheduled and completed. Clarence had been tempted to go to the funeral, but instead left for Switzerland where plastic surgery had been scheduled to change his appearance and he was now recuperating in the brisk air of the Swiss Alps. Fatima phoned him each day to see how he was and assure him that everyone believed he was dead.

Doing nothing never suited Clarence and he asked her each time she phoned about the status of his plan to kill President Silver with the model plane, and each time she had to tell him that she didn't know and that he should be patient. Finally, She told him someone would see him later that day to talk about his plan and start him on his journey to the New Salman Pak training center.

A quiet knock on his hospital room door interrupted his browsing the news on his computer.

"Come in. It's open."

A man in his middle twenties, impeccably dressed straight out of the latest issue of GQ entered and shut the door carefully behind him. He had the dark, good looks of an Italian film star. He said as he approached, "You must be Khalil Yomani, or would you prefer that I call you Clarence?"

Before another word could be said, Clarence leaped from his chair. As he did, he pulled a knife from a sheath strapped to his right leg and spun the young man around, pushing his face against the wall. With the blade of the knife pressed against the man's throat, Clarence hissed. "Keep it quiet, very quiet or the next sound you make will be your last. Who are you?"

The young man whispered, "Easy. I'm a nephew of your uncle Rabbani and your half brother."

Clarence eased the pressure on the knife blade. "I want to see some I.D."

"My passport is in my jacket pocket."

As he started to reach into his pocket, Clarence pushed the young man's face harder against the wall and reached around to feel the pocket. Satisfied that it didn't contain a weapon, he released the pressure on the young man. "Get it and hand it to me."

Clarence looked at the passport and read the name. Neil Rabbani. Clarence stepped back. "Uncle mentioned your name to me. He must have sent you."

"Yes, he did." Clarence backed off a few steps. The young man rubbed his cheek that had been pressed against the wall. He said, "Sorry I spooked you. Jesus, but your face is still a mess. Rabbani says that when you finish healing we're going to look like we could be brothers." Clarence holstered his knife.

The young man breathed a sigh. "Uncle sent me to tell you that the engineers went over your plan to kill Silver with the model plane. They think it could work. An amusing title for a murder mystery, don't you think, ***Death by Model Airplane.***"

Clarence was not amused. "How long have you been living in England?"

"Every chance I get. Can't stand it in Riyahd or anyplace else in Saudi Arabia for that matter. No pubs, no dancing, nothing. Frightfully boring."

"Who are the engineers who reviewed my plan?"

"The main one is an Iraqi chap who used to work in Saddam Hussein's weapons program. He's with Al Qaeda now."

"What's your real name?"

"Nadil, but here, in the UK and in the rest of the Continent, I'm known as Neil Rabbani, which I must say I prefer."

"Uncle trusts you enough to tell you who I am?"

The young man's face changed dramatically. He loosened his silk tie and removed his jacket. "Got you, didn't I? The effete person you just saw is the role I play in England and the Continent. I don't have your track record, but believe me, I can take care of myself. I also have a part to play in Uncle's over all plan."

"What's that?"

"For now, helping you. I'm to go to New Salman Pak with you and vouch for you."

"What is New Salman Pak?"

"It's a training base named after the one that used to be in Iraq."

"Where is it?"

"It's mobile now, but is currently located in a no man's land in northern Iran."

"Who runs it?"

"Al Qaeda and a group of former Iraqi officials, but there are volunteers there from all over the Muslim world. You okay with working with Al Qaeda for a bit?"

"Yes. Uncle told me I would."

Neil smiled. "I know." His face became serious as he continued. "Now listen to me. This is important. Uncle created this cover story for you with them. Your name is Khalil Yomani. You have lived in the United States for many years. You were injured while testing some explosives for the model airplane assassination of President Silver. You were doing this on your own and were not affiliated with any other group. You are recuperating from restorative facial surgery done in Switzerland and are going to New Salman Pak so they can carry out your plan. You will help Al Qaeda in any way you can while you're there. They will check everything you tell them because they're not sure they can trust either of us. The story is that Rabbani recruited you while you were together in Galway. You will also be vouched for by one of the men you played golf with. Understood?"

Clarence nodded in agreement.

"Good. You will wear bandages and keep your face covered at all times while you are there. Once this assignment ends, we will see to it that Khalil Yomani dies a martyr's death. After that, the bandages come off and you become a new person and return to London with me."

After Neil left, Clarence remained seated in his hospital room armchair reviewing the conversation with Neil. He decided that what he was told sounded reasonable, but that if after he accomplished what they wanted, it could be Neil's job to see to it that he really died. Could he really trust Rabbani and Neil? Well, he'd be careful, and it would take a better man than Neil to do that job.

Two days later, as Khalil Yomani, Clarence and Neil Rabbani arrived at New Salman Pak via Rome, then to Istanbul and Ankara, with the last leg by automobile and finally helicopter into the camp. Word that Khalil had a plan to kill the hated, American Jewish President had preceded their arrival. They were greeted by the Al Qaeda and Iraqi leaders of the camp. The Iraqi was clean-shaven, except for a large black mustache. He wore an Army uniform with the shirtsleeves rolled up, exposing a tattoo Neil later identified as signifying membership in the elite Republican Guards unit of the former Iraqi Army. The Al Qaeda leader had a long graying beard and wore traditional robes and headdress. The two leaders conducted Neil and Khalil to a tent that they entered and then sat down cross-legged on a beautifully made Persian rug that was spread over the dirt floor. As they entered, the Al Qaeda leader explained that the tent they entered would be for them for as long as they were in the camp.

Once they were seated, Neil explained in halting Arabic that his associate with the bandaged face, like him, had spent so much of his life living in the United States that he no longer comfortably spoke Arabic. He added that Rabbani thought that would be no problem since all the people that Khalil would work with would be sent to the U.S on various missions and will have to be somewhat fluent in English. After the two camp leaders conferred a moment in Arabic, the Iraqi said that was fine and they were aware of that problem. The Iraqi then asked how Khalil planned to kill the American President.

Neil said, "You don't know the plan?"

The Iraqi answered, "No, you are to tell us. We know some engineers think it could be a good plan, but we need to see it demonstrated to prove that it works."

Neil told them Clarence's plan in bad Arabic and with swooping, airplane-like gestures of Clarence's plan to do it with a model airplane filled with explosives. When he finished his explanation, a puzzled frown spread across the faces of the Iraqi and Al Qaeda leaders. After a hasty conference between them, the Iraqi said, in broken English, "We don't understand what you are trying to tell us. Are you telling us that he intends to kill the U.S. President with a toy airplane?"

Neil nodded affirmatively.

After another brief conference with his associate, the Iraqi continued, "We don't know how this is possible. You will explain to our engineer who in the Camp and is supposed to help test the device and then carry out the plan if it works. He will tell us what you plan." After the Iraqi finished his statement, he and the Al Qaeda leader both stood and immediately left the tent.

Minutes later, a man with swarthy skin, black, curly hair and a brush mustache opened the flap of the tent. He was dressed in a clean, but threadbare Iraqi army uniform. He hesitantly entered and said something in Arabic. The only thing Clarence understood was the name, Khalil Yomani. Neil said, pointing towards Clarence, "He is Khalil Yomani. I am Nadil, but I prefer Neil, Neil Rabbani. If you are going to the United States to carry out this plan, then starting right now, the only language you will speak is English."

The man said in Arabic that he spoke a little English.

"Good. It is part of your training so you can get around successfully in the United States when you are sent."

The man smiled. "In Gaza, I studied the accursed language. I can speak it."

Clarence said, "You will not say accursed. That immediately makes you suspicious to the authorities."

"Very good. I shall remember."

Neil said, "You don't need me for any more of this. I'll scout around and see some of my old friends and vouch for you with them."

Clarence turned to his visitor and invited him to sit and he immediately squatted down on the rug. Once he did, Clarence offered him some water or fruit juice, but the offer was declined. Clarence said, do you speak Spanish?"

"No Spanish. Only a little English."

"Then we can't pass you off as a Spaniard or a Latino. You'll have to trim back that mustache and get a hair cut."

"Allah be praised. Whatever you say."

"I say you never mention Allah again until you've completed your mission and you're back in whatever country you came from."

"As you say."

"What's your name?"

"Akmed."

"Okay, Akmed, what were you told about this assignment?"

"Only that I am to be told of your plan to kill the Jewish dog of a President and to then explain it to our leaders. If, as an engineer I and other engineers from Iraq and Al Qaeda see it demonstrated and it works like you say, you will tell me exactly how to do it. Then, I'm to go to the United States to carry it out when the leaders think the time is right. Once you have told me what I am to do, I am never to mention it again and then, only to the specified person I will be working with."

"Did they tell you anything about who I am?"

"Just that you are either crazy or a genius."

Clarence looked puzzled, "Why crazy?"

"They say you want to kill the American President with a toy. They don't see how."

Khalil nodded. "What kind of engineer are you?"

"Electrical."

"Good. You know how to work with explosives?"

"Yes."

"Do you know about detonating explosives with radio waves?"

"Yes."

"You are familiar with miniaturized TV equipment?"

"Yes."

"Do you know anything about flying model airplanes?"

"No."

"Do you know what they are?"

"Yes. I know rich, crazy English play with them. It is a hobby."

"Did you know that some are powered by a combustion motor and some by battery powered electric motors?"

"No I did not."

Clarence rummaged through his luggage and removed a thin sheaf of papers. "These are technical specifications of various battery powered model airplanes. You will study them. We will build several models, we will install in them explosives, a miniature TV camera and a GPS. We will determine their load factor, range and flight time and once we're satisfied, we will demonstrate our ability to destroy our target."

"Excuse me, but what is GPS?"

"A Global Positioning System."

"Ah, yes, yes. Now I see. You guide it to the target location with the GPS and see the actual target through the TV camera. You detonate electronically. Yes, that would work. Yes, yes, it's a wonderful plan. Not crazy, a genius. I will check with associates more knowledgeable than I about explosives, but I can see how that could work. Where would this glorious event take place?"

"Once everyone is convinced and they think the time is right and they're ready to send you to the United States, I'll tell them to send you to Baltimore, Maryland. I know a rental development there where you can stay without drawing too much attention to yourself. There, you can be supplied with equipment and a model airplane. You will use the same kind of battery-powered model airplane we test here." Clarence stood, stretched and walked around the tent a minute. He turned back to Akmed. "I think that watching the screen and flying the plane is a two-man job. Tell that to my hosts."

Several hours later, Akmed returned. He was smiling from ear to ear. "They have agreed that you are a genius. All of the engineers say the plan should work depending on distance from the launch site, the amount of the charge and proximity to the target. They want to participate in the testing so they can determine the amount of explosives to be installed and how close to the target it must fly. They have selected, subject to your approval, the person who will accompany me to the United States and that will actually fly the plane after I assemble it. You are to meet with him and satisfy yourself that he is the right person for that job."

After Akmed finished his report, the now happy terrorist backed his way out of the tent, saluting Clarence repeatedly as he did so."

Minutes later, a voice from outside of Khalil's tent said, "May I come in?"

A man with a light mocha complexion entered following Clarence's "Come in."

He was much better dressed than the prior visitor in sports clothes that looked like they could have come from the Gap or some other store in the United States. "Good evening, you must be Khalil Yomani." He put his hand out to shake Clarence's hand. "My name is Yusif Ahmed, but everyone here and at school in the United States calls me Joseph. I was told to see you and find out what I'm supposed to do when I go back to school."

"What school is that?"

"American University."

"Where are you from?"

"Does it matter?"

"I suppose not."

"Good. At the moment I'm using a Lebanese passport. What am I supposed to do?"

"You don't know?"

"No. I was told that you'd tell me if you thought I was right for the assignment."

"Okay. I want this to succeed, so I want to know if you are prepared to do something dangerous and to kill someone? Frankly, you don't look like the type."

"I'm more than ready. Don't be fooled by my manner of dress or anything else. All I've been told is that capture is not an option on this assignment. If I'm about to be captured, I'm to kill my associate if he's with me and in any event, bite down on a cyanide pill."

"You are prepared to do that?"

"Of course, but how can you ask me that?"

"My state of mind is not the issue. It's you and what you're willing to do that is my concern. You say you are prepared to kill innocent people and even take your life if necessary. Why?"

"If they are American lives, Jewish lives, any unbeliever, I would kill them without hesitation. What does my death matter if it's in the service of Allah. I will go straight to Paradise."

"Why do you hate Americans so much?"

"I have lived in the United States for three years now. I have seen their movies, their television, listened to their music and lived that life like an American student and seen how it corrupts everyone and everything. It even corrupted me for a time. Pornography is everywhere, the women are all whores and everyone is obsessed with sex. They live only for their pleasure. Even in the Christian religion, how can they deny that New York and London are the modern times Sodom and Gomorrah? Because of the power of the West, that culture spreads through the world like a plague. It threatens our Muslim values. It must be stopped and it is the duty of every true believer to stop it. Do you not agree?"

"As I said before, what I think is not the issue."

"What if there are Muslims at the target site when you are to act. Will you be able to do so?"

"Of course. If they are with the enemy, they are probably traitors to Islam, and if they are true believers, they will be pleased to die as martyrs and go to Paradise. This we were taught."

"Where?"

"In Pakistan."

"Very good."

"Well then, do I pass the test?"

"Almost. Do you know what a radio-controlled model plane is?"

Yusif nodded. "Yes."

"Have you ever flown one?"

"No."

Clarence told Yusif his plan of equipping a plane with explosives, a GPS system and a miniature TV camera so they could follow the flight on a television screen. Clarence asked, "Think you could become proficient in flying that plane to a target."

"Sounds a little like playing a video game."

"There are some similarities. Are you good at them?"

"Expert."

"Then, I think you should be good at this."

Yusif nodded. "What's this all about?"

Clarence smiled. "You are going to become a historic figure, and if you do it right, a big hero. Once it has been demonstrated that the plane will do what I say it will do, you will practice with it until you are expert in flying it. Then you will go to Baltimore Maryland with an engineer who will construct a duplicate of that radio-controlled model airplane which will be similarly equipped with a miniaturized TV camera, GPS equipment and explosives. At some point, you will fly that model airplane where you are told and you and that model airplane will change the course of history. With it, you will kill the President of the United States."

Yusif sat in his chair for a moment looking stunned. Then he rose from his chair, approached Clarence, and then knelt and kissed the cuff of Clarence's trousers. "I must do this. All my life I knew I had a purpose. That event will show the whole Muslim world that we can defeat the great Satan. It will give them the courage everywhere to do battle with the Crusaders who have robbed us of our just power for hundreds of years. It is the will of Allah that I do this and spread the true word of Allah as revealed to his prophet throughout the world."

Clarence looked down at Yusif. "Get up. You are the one, but I have to tell you about the White House and the lay out of the grounds. I think this may be done in the Rose Garden. President Silver likes to spend time out there. The Secret Service provides personal security, but if we use the electric powered model, they'll be unable to hear it and it's probably too small for them to spot it, especially if it comes out of the sun."

Clarence and Yusif went over plans of the White House and grounds and of Camp David where Silver occasionally went on weekends. Everything was in his computer and he printed copies for Yusif. As Yusif prepared to leave, he again knelt in front of Clarence. He took Clarence's hand and kissed it. "I thank you for this opportunity. I will do it, and you will be proud. The names of Khalil Yomani and Yusif Ahmed will be revered throughout the Muslim world. Mothers everywhere will name their children after us. You will see. The sword of Islam will triumph everywhere. The world will belong to Islam and you will be its greatest hero."

After Yusif left, Clarence leaned back on a pile of cushions. It wasn't comfortable like that old flowered armchair he used to sit on, but it would have to do. He had to think about Yusif. He didn't share Yusif's hatred for Western Culture, but agreed that freedom had gone too far and turned to licentiousness. He wanted to return freedom and democracy to what the founders and the Constitution proclaimed, not destroy it and replace it with the values of an Islamic state. Perhaps it's like Rabbani said, temporary alliances must be made with enemies to vanquish a common foe. No matter what he did, there was no danger of the United States becoming an Islamic state, but perhaps it would sober them up so they looked at where they had gone astray and return to where they had been. He needed to think about this some more and this was a good time to do it. Damn, but he couldn't think straight lying on these cushions. Maybe he could tell them that his tent should be furnished like a western style living room so he could instruct his students properly about life in the United States. Perhaps they'd get him one like the one he had at home.

CHAPTER 12

▼

Davies didn't like it when Judge Badderly telephoned from Alabama and said he needed to talk to Davies about the proposed rulings in the criminal case against Davies pending before him. Stripped of the legal verbiage, it was simply that, under the laws of the state of Alabama, the consent implied by law, of a person surreptitiously recording a conversation to its subsequent use is terminated on that person's death. Badderley had agreed to rule as follows:

1. *Under Alabama law, the consent of at least one party must be given to the taping of a conversation;*

2. *Senator Davies had not consented to the taping or the use of the audio-tape made in these proceedings;*

3. *the consent of William Morton to the original taping and the use of such tapes in proceedings against the said William Morton may be implied as he made the audio tape in question;*

4. *no implication of consent exists as to the use of the tapes in any proceeding against any other party;*

5. *with the death of William Morton, that implied consent to the original taping expired;*

6. *that the implied consent by the now deceased William Morton to the use of the taped materials original taping was not consent to the use of the audio tape of the alleged conversation he had with Senator Davies in any proceeding to which he was not a party; and*

7. ***Now Therefore, it is the judgment of the court that the audiotape of the alleged conversation between Senator Davies and William Morton is inadmissible in all judicial proceedings.***

Those rulings by Badderly were to form the basis for arguments that would prevent their use under the Full Faith and Credit clause of the United States Constitution in any other court in the United States. Davies knew that was exactly what Badderly was supposed to rule, because he had prepared the rulings.

"Don't say anything more, judge. I don't discuss sensitive things on the phone and you shouldn't either. I can go down to visit my mother in Jackson tomorrow. Why don't I meet you tomorrow evening? Beau will call you at home this evening and tell you where and when."

After completing his call, Davies rang his intercom buzzer summoning his assistant, Beau. "That scumbag Badderly called. I don't know whether he's getting cold feet or not, but were going down to Mississippi. He's at a judicial conference in Vicksburg, so we'll make a little side trip and straighten him out. Tell the press I'm going home for a visit with my mother, and I'll be right back. Tell them it's got nothing to do with the charges pending against me. My mother's been having some medical problems, so that ought to go down okay. Oh, and I want to take that file on the Alabama judges that Winters put together for me."

The next afternoon, Davies and his assistant, Beau drove in their rented Lincoln Town Car from the airport west towards Vicksburg, stopping at the Holiday Inn to meet Badderly as agreed. Beau met him in the parking lot, ran an electronic wand over him, explaining that he was checking for recording devices, and then opened the back door of the Lincoln. Davies was seated in the back. Beau shut the door and went and sat in the judges Chrysler.

Davies said, "What's so urgent? We had a deal and I don't like hold ups."

"It's not that. I thought the only thing involved was the case before me in Alabama. Now I understand that the ruling I make is going to be precedent all over the country. There's this rule that says," Badderly pulled a scrap of paper from his pocket and read, "Full faith and credit shall be given in each state to the public acts, records, and judicial proceedings of every other state."

"I know all about it."

"Well, if I ever knew it, I forgot it and so did the other appeals court judges."

"How could you not know, you're lawyers, aren't you?"

"We're just country lawyers down here. Lots of us forgot it or never knew. Don't matter, but me and the judges that are up for re-election are very nervous because what we do will get a lot of national media attention, and we think it probably won't be favorable. I don't want to be reversed on appeal and they're afraid to take the risk."

"How much will it take to get rid of that fear."

"Costs a lot of money these days to get elected a judge in Alabama. The one hundred thousand you're paying won't be enough for me and the other judges if there's all that bad publicity about this case."

"I said how much?"

"Now don't shoot the messenger."

"For Christ sakes, how much?"

"They want a million each."

"Get out of the car."

Badderley moved forward in his seat, and with one hand on the door handle said, "Okay, but you'll regret it, Senator."

"You think so, what about you and the rest of those bums? What'll you regret when I leak the contents of these files to the media?" Davies handed a half inch thick folder of files with the name of each of the judges on one of them to Badderly. "You all better start looking for a job."

Badderly opened the file with his name on it. He gasped as he looked at the first color photograph. He was with his Secretary at a Holiday Inn. They'd been meeting there twice a week for the past two years, but he thought he'd been careful. Next was a synopsis of a real estate deal he went into. He made fifty thousand in two weeks on it. He knew it was a disguised pay-off and so would everyone else if it went public. He turned the page. Damn, they traced the history of the deal and came to the same conclusion. He opened another file. It had the name of one of the appeals court judges on it. He looked inside. "Jesus" he said aloud. "He's porking judge Paulson's wife." Badderly opened another and looked at the picture of another of the judges. "Always thought he was a bit fruity, but with a black guy, Jesus H. Christ." He looked through the remaining files. Each contained damaging personal information about the judge whose name was on the folder.

Badderly wrung his hands as he turned to Davies. "What can we do, Jeb. We're really worried about getting re-elected. I'm sure you can understand that. When they see what you got, they'll have to go along, but can you do anything to help us out?"

"When you put it that way, you can tell them I'll keep the original deal, and I'll run a fund raiser for each of them. If anybody loses their seat on the bench, I'll get them something else. It's the best I can do. I'll be at my mother's house tonight. Call me and let me know if there are any problems."

"Okay, but what happens with those files? Where that stuff come from?"

"Don't worry about it. I'll have it. You fellows do the right thing, and you can continue on just the way it's always been with no one the wiser. I'm going back to Washington tomorrow. Don't call me unless you have a problem, and if you have to call, use a pay phone. Remember, no cell phones, ever. One more thing. Never try and hold me up again. You and the rest of the good old boys down here are out of your weight class. Try it and I'll bury you."

After his meeting with Badderly, Davies continued on to his mother's house outside of Jackson. "Momma, I've been telling you. You really ought to move on out of here. We had a nice little visit up at my country place last month. Come and stay there. You'll be closer to good medical care. And besides, this neighborhood has changed. If you don't want to be out in the country, I'll get you a nice place right outside of Washington. Then I'll be able to see you more often and take care of you better."

"Thank you Jeb, darling, but I imagine you got enough on your mind with all the troubles you got right now, and besides, all my friends are here, your daddy's grave is only a quarter mile down the road, and I'm happy right here where I've always been."

"Whatever you say, Momma, but don't worry about all the talk you been hearing about me being in trouble. Don't tell anyone, but day after tomorrow, there'll be a hearing in court in Alabama and that ought to end all my troubles."

"I hope so, but it said in the paper that Judge Badderly got the case and I hear tell that he isn't any friend of yours."

"Have I ever lied to you, Momma?"

"No. You've been a good boy Jeb."

"I promise you, there's nothing to worry about. You just take care of your health and don't even think about that case before Badderly. You'll see, a couple of days and I'll be sitting on top of the world again."

The next afternoon, Davies and Beau were on their way back to Washington. The day after that, Davies watched with satisfaction as an excited reporter announced to his TV audience the unexpected result of the hearing before Judge Badderly on the motion to suppress the audiotape of his conversation with Bill Morton. He had a single solitary glass of Champagne to celebrate and then called P.J. Winters on a secure line.

"You see the TV?"

"The decision by Badderly?"

"Yes. Thanks for your help with the judges. That information you gave me was very persuasive."

"Glad to help. Anything else on your mind."

"Yes. We can go ahead with the plan to kill Jane Cabot's husband. The Badderly decision was what I was waiting for."

"You're sure you want this done."

"Absolutely."

"You can consider the broad's husband is a dead man."

"When?"

"I don't know exactly. There's a few things I have to set up first."

"Can you say what?"

P.J. was silent for a moment. When your sources tell you that Tom Andrews is going to Massachusetts, you'll know that it's going down. Once that happens, there's no changing your mind."

"What's Andrews got to do with anything and when and why is he going to Massachusetts?"

"That's all I'm going to tell you."

"Can you tell me about when, like in a few days, a week, a month?"

"Don't press me, but I think it'll be less than a month."

CHAPTER 13

▼

The man steadied his arm on his parked car as he looked through the sniper scope on his rifle and said, "Which one is he?"

His companion, FBI Agent and P.J. Winters confidant, Walter Wagner, looked through binoculars. "See the guy bouncing the tennis ball off the wall and trying to catch it?"

"Yeah. What's the matter with him? He misses more than he catches."

"Brain damage. He got shot in the head during a convenience store hold up."

"He a cop?"

"No."

"He do it?"

"No, just in the wrong place at the wrong time."

"You sure this is good for the country?"

"I told you. We got to get rid of Silver. I know you can't be happy with a Jew running the country."

"No, just wondering if it's necessary to hit that guy. He looks like he's in his fifties, but he acts like he was five."

"Four actually, but stop wondering." Wagner adjusted the focus of his binoculars. "He'll be alone in a few minutes, except for the other loonies. The nurse always goes off for a smoke about now and is gone for five or ten minutes. We'll be long gone before anybody knows he's been hit." Wagner drew a cellophane envelope out of his pocket, put on white, plastic surgeons gloves and removed a book of matches from the envelope. He placed the matchbook carefully on the ground next to where the shooter's knee made a slight impression in the soft soil.

Next he took a cartridge casing of the same caliber as the one in the rifle out of the envelope and held it in his gloved hand.

His companion with the rifle said, "Whose stuff is that?"

"Don't worry about it. He's a real bad guy that should have been put away a long time ago. This will make it happen." Wagner looked through his binoculars again and said, "Looks good. Whenever your ready."

"I'm ready."

"Do it."

The silencered rifle went phhtt and three hundred and fifty yards away, Lindsay Cabot fell to the ground. The shooter said, "Done. Head shot. The poor bastard never knew he got hit. Well, at least he didn't suffer."

The man in the gloves watched as the shell casing was ejected. He picked it up and dropped the one he had previously removed from the cellophane envelope. "Let's get the hell out of here."

Once they were in the car, Wagner dialed a number on his cell phone. "It's Walter, P.J. Done. Ezra and I are on our way to Providence. We'll be there when the news breaks."

Winters called and repeated the message he received from Walter Wagner to Senator Davies. Davies wanted to call someone and tell them, but there was no one he could tell, not even Beau. He'd have to wait until the news went public."

He put the TV on and impatiently waited for confirmation. Finally, a half-hour later, an excited reporter broke into the scheduled programming on CNN. "Breaking news from Quincy, Massachusetts. Lindsay Cabot, the estranged husband of presidential girl friend, Jane Cabot, was murdered this morning at a Quincy Nursing Home. Sources in the Quincy Police Department have informed CNN that death was instantaneous as a result of a gun shot wound to the head."

At the end of the announcement, Davies called House Speaker Elliott Thurston. "Jeb, here Elliott. You hear the news. No, well Jane Cabot's husband was murdered. Do I think President Silver could have had anything to do with it? How the hell should I know, but I do think the FBI ought to move in on it. You know the way those local police forces can screw things up. Great idea, why don't you call Winters and suggest it. You can tell Winters we talked if you want, but so far as I'm concerned, it was your idea and Winters can announce that the request came from you. Given my situation, it's probably better that the request not come from me anyway."

Davies remained seated in front of the TV and was rewarded one hour and forty-five minutes later when scheduled broadcasting was again interrupted, this time by a remote unit. A young woman reporter identified herself and then said, "We're coming to you from the Hoover Building where we've been told Director P.J. Winters will be appearing momentarily with an announcement concerning the murder this morning of Lindsay Cabot in Quincy, Massachusetts. Mr. Cabot was the husband of Jane Cabot who is known to be, romantically involved with President Silver."

Moments later, the camera panned to the front of the room where P. J. Winters was now standing in front of a bank of microphones. "Thank you all for coming but this is all a little premature. All I can tell you is that I got the news the way all of you did of the Lindsay Cabot murder. Right after that, House Speaker Thurston called and suggested that the FBI cooperate with the Quincy, Massachusetts Police Department in the investigation, in view of the possible interest of the President and Mrs. Cabot in the matter. I agreed. I called the Quincy Chief of Police and we will work the case jointly. Fortunately, Deputy Director Walter Wagner was in Providence, Rhode Island at the time. He has been instructed to go to Quincy and assist local law enforcement in the investigation of the crime. All I can tell you now is that the police have found a shell casing and a matchbook at the scene. They are being checked for fingerprints. If there are any and we can identify them, we'll let you all know. That's all I have to say for now." With that, Winters nodded grimly in the direction of the media and started to leave. A shouted question brought him back to the microphones. "I was just asked if President Silver or Mrs. Jane Cabot is a suspect in the murder. We all know about the relationship between the President and Mrs. Cabot, but there is nothing at this time, to indicate any involvement by either of them in this murder. However, you can rest assured that if that evidence were to develop, high office is no protection to anyone so far as either the FBI or the Quincy Police department are concerned."

As Winters returned to his office, his Secretary said, "Senator Davies is on hold on the first line and he sounds upset."

"Okay, I'll take it. Tell him I'm on my way in and that I'll speak with him in a minute." Winters went into his office, shut the door and sat behind his massive mahogany desk, plunked his feet on top of his desk, and then picked up his phone.

Davies said, "What the hell is going on? You held a press conference and you didn't say anything, and how does that connect back to Silver?"

Winters examined his manicured and polished fingernails a moment before responding. "Stop acting like a hound in heat. It'll all be done in an orderly way. I told you to leave it all to me. I'm going to have another press conference and announce that we identified the prints and have the perp under arrest. It'll be done in time for the eleven o'clock news tonight."

P.J. was good at his word. At ten o'clock his office issued a press release. It said,

> *"The FBI and Quincy, Massachusetts Police Department announce the arrest of Charles 'Red' Kelly in connection with the murder of Lindsay Cabot. Kelly was apprehended in Worcester, Massachusetts at the home of a female friend. Due to the sensitive nature of this particular homicide and with the agreement of local law enforcement, the FBI has retained custody of the prisoner. The FBI will continue to interrogate Mr. Kelly further tomorrow morning."*

After hearing the news of the press release, Davies called P.J. at his home The phone rang five times and then was answered by a machine. Davies slammed the phone down and then called the number again, with the same result. He repeated the call four more times before P.J. finally picked it up and said, "What the hell you calling me for? It's after eleven, for Christ sake."

"When we talked, you said you'd identify the prints and announce you made the arrest. You didn't say anything about the fingerprints in the press release, and who the hell is Kelly?"

"Oh for Christ sake. I decided not to say what we had yet and identify Kelly as the actual shooter. Did you expect me to say Silver somehow managed to avoid everybody and traveled to Massachusetts, shot Cabot and then reappeared in Washington without being missed?"

"No, but I want to know what's going on."

"Go screw yourself. I don't work for you. We got a deal and I said I'd handle this. Now bug off."

"But I got to know…"

"We been through this. I said I'd handle it. Now forget it and go to sleep. I mean it."

"God damn it, P.J. I trust you to handle things, but I just don't see how this is going to implicate Silver. You're telling me it will and it all went as planned?"

"Yes."

"Good. I'm sorry for calling so late."

"That's okay. It's just that you caught me in the act with Celeste. Forget about it. I'll call you tomorrow after we finish the interrogation."

The next morning, Deputy Director Walter Wagner continued the interrogation of Charles "Red" Kelly in the Federal courthouse in Boston. Kelly was manacled to the leg of a steel table screwed into the floor and Wagner was seated opposite him. Kelly said, "I don't know what you're trying to pull here, but I was in Worcester when that Cabot guy got iced. My sister was talking to me on the phone and she called the house so I had to be there to get the call. Ask her. She'll tell you. Check the phone records. No way I could get from Worcester to Quincy in time to do that job."

"Look, Red, don't get your sister in trouble. She's never had any before. We found a matchbook and a cartridge case with your fingerprints at the scene. How do you explain that?"

"It's not mine. Someone planted it."

"Sure, and how do you explain this pen we found where you've been staying with your girl friend?"

"What pen?"

"This pen with the Presidential seal on it."

"How the hell do I know? Must have been the last time I got invited to the White House."

"Don't get sarcastic with me. I'm going to show you a little video on the TV we brought in, just for you. Not your usual porn, but watch it closely, because you're the star." Wagner clicked the TV on and then clicked the VCR. It was a grainy surveillance tape from a liquor store. "Recognize the store, Red? It's the one you held up last January. And there's you coming in the door. And there's you looking around and waiting for the other customer to leave. And there's you, Red, holding up the clerk and putting the money in your pocket. And there's you, Red, shooting the clerk in the head. Camera work is a little shabby but good enough to put you away forever. What do you say now, Red." Wagner smiled and then snapped his fingers. "I know what happened, you were on the phone with your sister when someone with your face shot and killed the clerk, just like someone with your fingerprints killed Cabot. What's the matter, Red? Cat got your tongue?"

"I want a lawyer."

"Anything you say, Red, you got your rights, but you decide that after you hear what I've got to say."

"Okay."

"We like you for killing Lindsay Cabot. We found the shell casing and we got the matchbook. They put you at the scene. We found the pen with the Presidential seal on it at your girlfriend's. We found a fifty thousand-dollar cash deposit in your name at Citizen's Bank." Kelly started to say something, but before he could say one word, Wagner interrupted him. "Shut up, Red. Just listen. We figure it this way. Someone, we think it was Tom Andrews that works for President Silver, hired you to hit Cabot. Andrews is a pretty smart guy and you may not be able to identify him, but we think it was him. We think it was him because he used to live in Worcester, was once with the Worcester police and he knew you from back then. We know that he called on Lindsay's lawyer and tried to persuade him to let Mrs. Cabot divorce her husband and got turned down. We know he went there again this week to see that lawyer and got turned down again. After that he went to Worcester and visited his parents. We think that while he was there, you met somewhere. He's smart so he probably chose someplace dark for the meet, so you couldn't identify him. He hired you to murder Mr. Cabot. He probably gave you a picture of him and he wrote down the man's name and address for you. He must have used a pen with the Presidential seal on it, forgot, and you must have picked it up and put it in your pocket. You may not even remember it, but we think that's how it went down."

"Bullshit," Red scowled and started to say something.

But before he could, Walter interrupted again. "We don't care that much about the liquor store killing. What we want is a quick solution to the Cabot case. The country needs it and that makes this your lucky day. You cop to the Cabot murder and give us Andrews and we'll deal on both cases, but we got to do it now."

"What's the deal?"

"Ten years on each."

"Consecutive or concurrent?"

"We'll go concurrently."

"You recommend parole after five?"

"We won't oppose it and we can forget about knowing about where the fifty is if you give us what we want. Maybe you owed it to someone and paid them before we arrested you, but you got to decide right now."

"Where do I do the time?"

"You got preferences?"

"Yes."

"Okay, the country club lock up of your choice."

"What do I have to say.

"Did it happen like I said?"

"Is that what you want me to say?"

"It's not what I want. Is that what happened?"

"Yeah, just like you had been watching."

Wagner pulled a yellow legal pad and a ballpoint pen with an FBI logo on it out of his briefcase. He slid them across the table to Kelly. "Write it all down, we'll go over it and then get it typed so you can sign it. Once you do that, I'll contact Director Winters. He'll want to make an announcement to the media and we don't want anyone talking to you until you're arraigned tomorrow and you plead guilty. After you do that, we'll go back to Washington so the Director can talk with you."

An hour and a half later at two P.M., Walter Wagner faxed a copy of Kelly's statement to P.J and called him on his private line. "Kelly's statement is on its way to your fax machine. It's just like what we said and by tonight, Kelly will believe it happened just like it says in his signed statement. He'll plead guilty tomorrow morning. We let him call his sister and he told her to keep her mouth shut about talking to him when Cabot was taken out."

"Good job, Walter. You nervous about Kelly changing his mind?" Walter said he was not and P.J. continued. If you get nervous about him, see to it Kelly gets killed while trying to escape when we bring him to Washington."

After ending the call with Wagner, P.J. pushed the button on his phone for Senator Davies' private line. Davies had been pacing back and forth in his office all morning waiting for the call. Not being in charge and pulling all the strings was difficult for him to manage. He started to call P.J. a dozen times, but managed to restrain himself. The minute the phone rang, he steeled himself to let it ring twice more before he picked it up, and then said as casually as he could. "Hello. Oh, P.J. I was expecting another call. What's happening?"

"We got a confession from Kelly. Don't ask me why. No sense to talk about how we got it. All you or anybody else has to know is in the document. He'll plead guilty tomorrow morning, and after that, I'll release copies of the confession to the media. I'll fax a copy to you tomorrow right after he pleads. No. Not now, tomorrow. We can't have any leaks until after he pleads, but I can tell you this, there's enough of a suggestion of White House involvement to warrant a House inquiry. Whether the inquiry is in an Impeachment hearing or not is up to you and Thurston to manage."

For the second time in less than a month, Senator Davies drank a solitary single glass of champagne. He enjoyed it and was tempted to have a second, but didn't.

CHAPTER 14

▼

Ben was in the bathroom getting ready for bed. He looked into the mirror while brushing his teeth and was surprised at how tired and haggard he looked. He was thinking that perhaps a good night's sleep would fix that when the phone beside his bed rang. Ben glanced at his wristwatch. It was almost eleven. Ben wondered what new disaster had occurred.

It was Tom Andrews. "Sorry to bother you, Mr. President, but Molly just showed me something that I think you ought to see. It could wait until morning but if you're still up, we can be there in ten minutes."

"See you in ten in the residence."

Ben was tempted to meet them wearing his robe and slippers, but decided that wasn't very presidential and got dressed again.

Ben greeted them in his living room. His bulldog, Ace, greeted Molly, bringing her a stuffed animal, while the black pug waited impatiently for Ben to sit down so she could reclaim his lap. "Don't pay any attention to Ace, Molly. He brought you a toy just in case you might want to play with him. Sit down over here and tell me what this is all about."

Molly sat in the designated chair. As she pulled a folded piece of paper out of her purse, she said, "I received this e-mail from Clarence Davenport."

"When did he send it?" Ben said.

"Before he went to the Aran Islands."

"Why the delay in telling me?"

"It was miss-filed."

"You'll have to tell me how that happened, but let me see what he says."

As Molly handed the paper to Ben, Tom said, "We checked and it's a Yahoo account he set up that day, and no other messages were sent or received by that account."

Ben took the folded paper, and read it.

Dear Molly,

I hope you don't mind my calling you, Molly but I know you've been chasing me a long time and I've gotten to admire the way you finally managed to find me. Grandpa Hammonds told me all about you.

I want to apologize for deceiving you about my intentions when you came to arrest me. I heard you when you told me not to kill myself. Thank you for caring. I hope I didn't cause too much embarrassment and trouble for you, but I saw no other alternative.

For some reason, it's important to me that you understand that it wasn't hatred for my country that required me to do what I did. It was the opposite. It was love of my country that required that I destroy the structure that had become rotted with corruption so it could be restored to what it was created to be.

Perhaps under different circumstances, we may have met and become friends, maybe more than friends. I would like to think so.
Clare

After Ben finished reading the letter, he refolded it and put it on the glass and chrome end table beside his chair. He shook his head, saying nothing. Tom Andrews broke the silence, "What do you make of it, Mr. President?"

"It'd take a convention of psychiatrists to figure that one out."

"Why the delay in telling me about this, Molly?"

"It came in while I was in London meeting with Mr. Rabbani and the British intelligence and law enforcement people. When I'm away, my assistant reads and assembles my regular mail and calls me about it, She forwards my e-mail and then prints it out and files it."

"Can't you access your e-mail when you're away?"

"Not that e-mail address. It's security protected and they change the password every day." Ben motioned for Molly to continue. Molly said, "She was out that day and the intern filling in for her called me about the mail, but forgot to forward the e-mail and misplaced the entire day's mail including the copies of the e-mail. This afternoon I tried to find one of the letters she called about and couldn't find it, and then I finally realized I couldn't find any mail for that day. I went back to the office tonight to look some more and when I found it I saw the e-mail from Clarence Davenport. Sorry about the foul up."

"Forget it. Do you think she read the Davenport message?"

"I doubt it, and if she did she wouldn't have understood what it said. She's a particularly brainless intern."

"Good. I hope she didn't read it. I don't want a word of this to be mentioned to anyone right now. We have to concentrate on trying to prevent a major terrorist attack and I don't want this distraction. You ever hear from him before?"

"No, sir."

"How did he happen to have your e-mail address?"

"When we went to his house to interview him, John Wallace and I gave him our cards at the beginning of the interview. Mine has my e-mail address on it. He must have kept it."

"Have you responded to this letter?"

"No, sir."

Ben looked over his glasses at Molly. "You think he's really dead now?"

"I don't know. He deceived me once about being dead."

"Deceived us all," Ben said. "I don't like the fact that the body was cremated the way it was. That whole story never rang true with me."

"Me neither," Molly said. "We went to Galway and I talked with the boat rental people. It was Davenport that rented the boat. That, I'm sure of. I showed them his picture. He was using a different name, but it was he. I also interviewed the attorney that did that will. He was cooperative and turned over the wallet and personal effects they found on the body. One of Wallace's cards was in the wallet."

"John's, not yours." Ben took his glasses off and looked at the ceiling a moment. "That's interesting."

"What's interesting about that?" Tom asked.

"Perhaps he just couldn't part with Molly's card. I don't know." Ben turned to Molly. "You think he could have staged this death all by himself."

"It would have been very difficult. We know he rented the boat. He'd have no trouble murdering someone, stowing the body on the boat, and sailing off to the Aran Islands and sinking the boat, but what then? Assume he has a rubber boat and rows ashore. From where they found the boat off of Inis Oirr, he could have easily made it onto the Island, but what then? The island has a population of about 300, and I doubt a stranger could show up and not be noticed. If he made for Inis Meain, it has an even smaller population and the third island, Inis Mor, only has a population of around 900. There's no indication he was ever on any of those islands. The closest mainland points are in Counties Clare and Connemara and they're about seven miles away. Maybe he could make it in a rubber boat, but the seas were pretty rough when he started out, and even if he gets there, what then? He's in the middle of nowhere. He'd have to find a way to get back to at least Galway City and I don't know how he does that without someone seeing him."

"So you think if he staged his death again, this time he had to have an accomplice."

Molly frowned. "I don't see how he could have done it alone, so either that's him that got cremated or he had some help, and if I had to guess, I'd say that's not him that was pulled out of the ocean."

"Thanks, Molly, I'm glad you called and came over. I'm betting that Davenport is still alive and that since he needed help, it was Rabbani that helped him arrange this second death. I recall that one of the reports I read indicated that Rabbani was in Galway the weekend before this supposed boating accident. I'll be that's no coincidence."

"I don't know, sir," Molly said. "He went there for a golf tournament that he plays in every year that had been scheduled more than a year ago."

Ben turned to Tom, "I don't know if this is possible, but could we test the ashes for DNA and see if it matches Davenport's?"

"Forget it," Molly said. "The lawyer dutifully followed the instructions in Davenport's will and scattered the ashes into the Irish Sea."

"How convenient. Tom how did the FBI find out about Davenport's body being found?"

"They received an anonymous tip that someone resembling Davenport was seen renting a sailboat in Galway. By the time they got the message, processed it and got someone to Galway to investigate, Davenport was dead, cremated and his ashes scattered in the ocean. I can't really blame them for that delay because the FBI and the Secret Service have received thousands of anonymous tips about Davenport from all over the world."

Ben nodded. "And how did they find out about that lawyer in Galway?"

"The boat rental people had the lawyer as a contact so they got to him and found out about the will and all that quite easily"

Ben leaned forwards towards Molly and Tom, "Thank you for coming over. I'll have to think about it, but for what it's worth, I was never satisfied that Davenport was killed in that boating accident. It and that fast cremation are just too convenient and Rabbani being in the area, it's all too much, but I want to put these suspicions on the back burner for now. We are getting intelligence reports about increasing Al Qaeda activity and meetings between Al Qaeda operatives and former Iraqi agents. Something seems to be going on, and as much as I'd like to get Davenport, our resources must be dedicated to trying to stop whatever the new attack is that seems to be in the works. Does anyone other than the two of you know about this e-mail?"

"We came straight here," Molly said.

Ben looked into Molly's eyes. "I want you and John Wallace and Rahsheed Evans working on finding Davenport. I think he's still alive and out there somewhere. You and John found him before with some help from Rahsheed, so if anyone can find him it'll be the three of you. Tom, I want you and Molly to bring Wallace and Evans up to speed on this, and remember, not a word to anyone else."

"Anything else before Tom and I leave, Mr. President?"

"One more thing, Molly. I think you should maybe answer that e-mail/"

"What would you want me to say?"

"If he's still alive like I think, he may check that e-mail address he used. He probably won't respond now, but there may come a time when he wants to say something more to you. He obviously likes you and thinks there's some kind of relationship there. What if you wrote him that you believe he's still alive and that you're glad that he managed to deceive the world again and that his secret is safe with you?"

"I think it's a good idea, but I don't think he'd buy that part about his secret being safe with me. He's too smart to fall for that."

Ben nodded, "You're probably right. Okay, give it some thought and put something together and let's get together tomorrow and review it. Call Martha tomorrow morning and have her put it on my calendar. Tell her to set the meeting in the Rose Garden."

The next afternoon, Ben met with Molly and Tom in the Rose Garden. Molly handed Ben the draft e-mail letter to Clarence she had prepared. It read,

Clare,

I read the reports of your death. I was wrong about that the last time and found that I was not unhappy when I learned that you were still alive. For some strange reason, while I can't condone what you did, I hope these reports of your death are also wrong. If you ever wish to return to this country to accept your punishment, contact me and I will arrange it, provided I can guarantee your personal safety.
Molly Pemberton

Ben nodded as he read the letter. When he finished reading it he handed it back to Molly and told her to send it. Molly opened her laptop computer, tapped a few keys and then clicked the send icon. Ben said, "Good, and let's plan on sending Davenport a little note, say once a week."

"What would we say?"

"Nothing very special. Just a few words to let him know you think about him every now and then, no regular pattern. Maybe we can provoke a mistake."

Ben turned towards Tom. "You know Jane's husband, Lindsay was shot and killed and they arrested some guy for it?" Tom nodded that he did. "What do you make of it?"

"I don't know, sir. We're getting no information from the FBI or local law enforcement so we don't know anything, but it's damned strange. One of my friends in the bureau said that when P.J heard about it, he remarked that it was very convenient for you. I got a bad feeling about it. How's Jane taking it?"

"She feels terrible. It's easy to say that he's been dead for all practical purposes since he got shot four years ago, but she feels terrible. She was still married to him so she's making the funeral arrangements. I told her I'd try and get up to Boston for the funeral?"

"You think that's wise, sir?"

"Probably not, and she told me not to, but my kids and her son will go and I'm not sure she means it."

"I could call her and really find out," Molly said.

"No, I'll ask her again when it has become a little more real. She doesn't play games."

Tom said, "There's something I want to mention before we go." Ben nodded for Tom to continue. "The man they arrested for Lindsay's murder is a guy named, "Red" Kelly. He was arrested in Worcester. You know I was with the Worcester police before I joined the FBI?" Ben nodded that he did. "There was a kid there I arrested a few times named "Red" Kelly. I always figured he was a hoodlum in training, but, we lived in the same parish and I knew his parents so I gave him some breaks and tried to straighten him out. When I heard about the murder, I wondered if it was the same guy. I tried to find out from someone in the FBI, but ever since we shut them out on the Davenport investigation, they've shut us out on everything, and the guys I know in the Bureau are not as willing as they used to be to share information. We ought to find out more tomorrow when they go to court."

"Why would he have done it? Lindsay was totally harmless. Could this Kelly have known Lindsay from before? Lindsay was originally from Framingham, and that's not so far from Worcester?"

"It's possible, but I doubt it. We ought to know more tomorrow. They're due in court at nine and P.J. is expected to hold a press conference around ten."

Later that evening, Molly contacted and advised him that her e-mail letter to Clarence Davenport had not been returned as undeliverable and that Davenport's e-mail service provider had indicated that the account had been periodically accessed by someone after the date of Davenport's supposed death. Ben knew that the message didn't necessarily mean that Davenport was alive and had received her message, but someone who knew of the account and the password for it was using the account.

As Ben got ready for bed, he wondered where Davenport could be and what P.J. Winters was going to say in his press conference. Both thoughts gave him a bad feeling.

CHAPTER 15

▼

At ten A.M. FBI Director Winters stood on the steps of the J. Edgar Hoover Building in front of a battery of microphones. On signal from the director he said, "I'm pleased to tell you all that Charles "Red" Kelly has confessed to the murder of Lindsay Cabot. Excellent police work by the FBI and the Quincy, Massachusetts police force resulted in our solving this terrible crime this quickly. Kelly confessed because the Quincy police found a cartridge casing and a matchbook cover at the scene with fingerprints that we identified as those of Mr. Kelly. His confession, however, only solves a part of the crime. This was a murder for hire." A reporter started to ask a question. Winters shot him a withering stare that would have stopped a Sherman tank. Winters looked away and then continued. "Agents examined the apartment in Worcester, Massachusetts where Kelly had been living. They found in that apartment a pen with the Presidential seal on it. In his statement under oath, Kelly stated that he met with a man who disguised his voice and obscured his features, and that the man he met paid him fifty thousand dollars to kill Lindsay Cabot. The meeting took place in a public park in Worcester, Massachusetts six days ago. That man wrote the address where Kelly could find Cabot on a scrap of paper and showed him a picture of Cabot. Kelly wasn't sufficiently sure of it to swear to it, but he believes the man used the pen to write the address, that he accidentally left the pen on the park bench where they met and that Kelly inadvertently picked up the pen and put it in his pocket. We wish Kelly could be certain of that and that he could identify the person that contacted him, but he can't. I said I'd take some questions." P.J. pointed at a reporter from CBS, "Mr. Simmons?"

"Are you suggesting that the President or the White House is involved in the Lindsay murder."

"You're making that connection, not me, Mr. Simmons. I deal in facts and evidence." Winters pointed at another reporter.

"Andy Roper, ABC, Director Winters. "I have one of those White House ball-points. Is there any evidence in addition to the pen you mentioned that indicates a White House connection?"

"There's circumstantial evidence that suggests a certain person in the White House may have been the contact, but it's probably insufficient to get a conviction." P.J looked past Roper and said, "You over there from NBC. Sorry I don't know your name."

"It's Carter, sir, Jeff Carter. I'm new at the Washington office. Can you tell us what that circumstantial evidence may be?"

"Sorry, but I don't think that's advisable. I'll take one more question. Over there, Scott, Scott Jackson."

"Mr. Director, I happen to know that six days ago when that meeting took place in a park in Worcester, Massachusetts, the President's chief of staff, Tom Andrews was in Worcester. Don't you think that it's very possible and maybe likely that Andrews met with Kelly and arranged for the murder of Lindsay Cabot? That certainly would be convenient for the President and Mrs. Cabot, and might impede the movement to impeach the President. Does the FBI know if that meeting between Kelly and Andrews took place?"

Winters scowled at Scott Jackson. "I don't know how you know what you know, but yes, the FBI does know the facts you recited. We have no proof that the meeting you referred to took place. We know Kelly met with someone in Worcester, Massachusetts that hired him to kill Cabot on that day and that Tom Andrews was in Worcester that day, but that is only circumstantial evidence and would probably not be sufficient to convict in a criminal trial."

"Mr. Director," Jackson continued, "We know Andrews was on the Worcester Police Force early in his career and that Kelly has a police record in Worcester going back to that period. Do you know if Andrews knew Kelly back then?"

"We have reason to believe they were acquainted, and we're checking that out right now.

An unidentified reporter in the back of the room shouted, "Why the hell aren't he and his boss in the White House and the President's girl friend being interrogated?"

Another reporter shouted. "Right. They got to be in it together."

Winters held his hand up for silence. "I've been through all this with lawyers from the Department of Justice. There's circumstantial evidence that Mr. Andrews may be involved in this. If he is, well you all know who he works for, but that's only circumstantial evidence that the President and or Mrs. Cabot may be involved, and as I said, the attorneys at the D.O.J. tell me it is not sufficient to convict any of them in the criminal courts. Maybe somebody who knew of the President's relationship with Mrs. Cabot wanted to do him a favor. Maybe someone thought the way they were carrying on in the White House was wrong and thought it would be better if Mrs. Cabot's husband were no longer alive. Could be lots of things, and any defense lawyer worth his salt would be able to come up with a theory of how someone else could have done it."

"What about Tom Andrews?" Jackson said.

"What about Tom Andrews?"

The camera panned over to Scott Jackson. "You told us that Andrews was in Worcester a few days before Cabot was murdered and that it was on the same day that Kelly says he met the man that paid him to kill Lindsay Cabot. If you think that's a coincidence then you must also believe in the tooth fairy."

Winters smiled. "What I believe personally and what I can act on as the head of the FBI are two different things. I'm sure you can appreciate the difference, Scott. That will have to be all for today."

A half-hour later, Winters was back at FBI headquarters. As he walked towards his office, he got approving nods from the staff. Walter Wagner greeted him. "Nice performance. Davies called and asked if you'd call him when you came in."

"How'd he sound?"

"Hard to tell, but he was pretty calm."

Okay, I'll call him."

"Jeb, P.J. I understand you called. I assume the press conference answered all your questions."

"I called to congratulate you. It was a great job. The performances by you and Scott deserve Oscars. At first I was disappointed. I thought he should have named Andrews as the bagman and that he should have claimed Andrews said he was doing it for the President. Then I thought it through, and I realized that Andrews couldn't be that stupid."

"That's why we arranged it like we did. It's got to ring true or it won't fly. Wrap it up and tie it with a ribbon and nobody would believe it. Life is messy."

"I won't question how you do things again. I'm used to dealing with idiots like Senator Smithers, Representative Thurston and my assistant, Beau. I got to micro-manage those guys."

"You know what Mark Twain said about guys like them?"

"What?"

"He's supposed to have said, 'Suppose you were an idiot, and suppose you were a member of Congress, but I repeat myself." P.J. laughed.

Davies joined in and laughed with him. "There's more to you than I thought, and I have to say it's been a real pleasure working with a first class professional villain like you."

"You're a damn good villain yourself, Jeb. Let's remember where we're heading. You're goal is the White House. If you get there, I'm your Vice-President and once you're done, you support me for the Presidency. If you don't get there, you support me to the party for the Presidency and fund raise and campaign for me."

"That's the deal."

CHAPTER 16

▼

Clarence watched his Uncle Rabbani, followed by the Swiss surgeon who had operated on his face, disembark from their helicopter on the short tarmac at New Salman Pak. He was anxious to see them, especially the surgeon, because that meant the bandages covering his face would be removed and he'd get to see what he would look like for the rest of his life.

Minutes later, Rabbani and the surgeon were in the tent Clarence shared with his half-brother. Clarence sat quietly while the surgeon snipped away at the bandages covering his face. As the surgeon removed the bandage wrappings, he told Clarence that his face should be sufficiently healed so that they'd be able to see what he was going to look like, but here would still be some bruising and raw looking areas that would quickly heal, and that he should stay out of the sun. As the last piece of gauze was snipped off, Clarence opened his eyes and stared at the face looking back at him in the mirror. He didn't recognize himself. He studied the mirror some more. His receding hairline had been pushed forward with hair taken from the back of his head. His formerly blue eyes were more prominent and blacker with the permanent implants than they were with the lenses he had been using. His weak chin had been strengthened, but his most prominent feature was a new nose. It was larger and slightly hooked. Somehow, it seemed to suit him better. His face still looked like he had been in a losing prizefight, but he decided he was pleased with what he saw. He turned towards his uncle Rabbani and his half-brother Neil who were both still studying his face. "What do you think, Uncle, and you, Neil?"

Rabbani said, "I think you look more like an Arab than I do. You know that I gave them pictures of my brother, your father, and asked them to create a family resemblance? Clarence nodded that he did. "They succeeded admirably. You look like you could be my son or Neil's older brother." Rabbani turned Clarence's chair and looked directly at his face. "Yes, it'll do. I'll have a variety of passports with your new face ready when you're ready to leave here. Heal up some more and then e-mail me some photos. For now, you will remain as Khalil Yomani and continue to wear the bandages. The doctors want you to stay out of the sun and I think it would be good if no one here saw your new face. Continue to keep your face covered when you deal with any one here."

Clarence nodded. "Fine, it's a little warm under the wrappings but I've gotten used to it. What brings you here, uncle? I'm sure it wasn't to preview my new face."

"No, it wasn't. I understand you are ready to demonstrate that your plan for killing President Silver will work. I understand all the preliminary testing has been successfully completed and the Iraqi and Al Qaeda engineers all think it will work, but they are doing field tests to be certain that it will succeed. We've all had experience with engineers making claims and then finding in the real world that they were wrong. Do you know how they plan to test it?"

Clarence nodded that he did. "They have ten fully equipped model planes carrying varying amounts of explosives. They will explode them at different distances from the target and see what the results are."

"And how will they know what amount is required to kill a human?

Clarence frowned. "They captured a group of about thirty Kurds in a border skirmish. They'll chain them to a stake, three at a time and explode one of the model planes. If any survive, they'll know they have to increase the amount of the charge and or bring the model plane in closer to the target. The engineers have computed what will give them the maximum airtime and range with the optimum amount of explosives and distance from the target. They'll start with that and do variations up and down from there. It's not very scientific, but that's the way the camp leaders want it to be tested."

"You're not happy with testing it like that?" Rabbani said.

"We know what's required without that. I figured it out and know how much explosives we have to use and how close we have to get to be certain we make the kill. Killing those people is not necessary."

"Those people were dead the minute they were captured. Don't waste any sympathy on them."

"I won't."

"You know there are still some of the camp leaders who think the test will fail."

"Then they're very stupid."

"They're not stupid, just unsophisticated. When do they do the test?

Clarence looked at his wristwatch. "About an hour."

"Excellent. That gives me enough time."

"Time for what, uncle?"

"Time to tell you a little story and then to talk with Almihidi. Listen to this story very carefully. There was a Saudi woman. Say she was the daughter of my half sister"

Clarence nodded. "Your cousin."

"Yes, exactly. Her family arranged a marriage for her that she didn't want. Under Islamic custom, her refusal to follow their wishes would dishonor the family. Her mother who had that kind of arranged marriage was sympathetic, and on a family trip to London, she helped her daughter run away. She gave her valuable jewels and secretly sent her to me in London, and I sent her to another relative in the United States. There, she enrolled in a college under a fictitious name and began to become westernized. Her father and her brothers looked for her, but she couldn't be found. While there, she attended a party, someone put drugs in her drink, she was raped and had a child. She loved her child and it became the focus of her life. Then she made a mistake. She wanted her mother to know of her happiness and sent her a message. The message was intercepted by her brother who informed her father of what had occurred. Her mother found out and warned her. She left the baby with a friend and went to the police. She told them who she was, that her family was coming to kidnap her and asked them for protection. She was a minor and the police called the State Department. The State Department called the Saudi Ambassador. In accordance with instructions from the State Department, the police turned her over to the Saudis and she was taken against her will, put on a private jet and taken back to Saudi Arabia. Once there, she was promptly stoned to death in accordance with Islamic *sharia* laws by her father and other family members. It was considered an honor killing and was excused by the Saudi authorities." Rabbani leaned back and smiled at Clarence. "You will remember that story?"

"Yes, but why?"

"Almihidi no longer believes the story we told him about who you are. He is much smarter than most of those Al Qaeda and Iraqis. I am going to tell him that you are the child of the woman in the story, that you hate the U.S. government for betraying your mother's trust and you hate the Saudi government for shipping her back to her death." Finished with the telling of that story, Rabbani rose and left Clarence's tent.

Shortly before one P.M., Clarence, with his face once more wrapped in bandages, led his uncle to the temporary viewing stand built for the occasion. As they walked towards their seats, several Iraqi engineers greeted Clarence, saying in broken English, "Good luck with the test, Khalil." Clarence, Uncle Rabbani and Neil finally sat down in the seats set aside for them in the viewing stands among all the important camp leaders. Everyone had their binoculars trained on a trio of Kurds chained to an iron stake seven hundred meters from the viewing area. Five minutes later, one of the Iraqi lieutenants shouted, there's the plane. Seconds later and twenty meters from the chained Kurds, the plane exploded. After the dust settled, the camp doctor approached the iron stake. The legs of the Kurds were still attached to the stake but the rest of their torsos were scattered over an area of twenty meters. Every fifteen minutes for the next two hours and fifteen minutes, three Kurds were chained to the iron stake and the assembly of Al Qaeda and Iraqi leaders watched as model plane after model plane carrying varied loads of explosives was exploded at varying distances from the stake. Of the thirty Kurds, only five who were the furthest from the point of explosion survived the blast. Their wounds were so bad it was an act of mercy when an Iraqi soldier shot each of them through the head.

At the end of the demonstration, the Iraqi and Al Qaeda camp leaders walked over to where Clarence was sitting. The Iraqi said, 'Khalil, you are to be congratulated. The test has removed all doubt that anyone had. It was a brilliant idea and you have trained Akmed and Yusif how to build those toy planes and fly them. We think you have also prepared them to be sent to the United States to carry out their assignment. Do you agree?"

"They're ready. I assume they have a contact in the area and a place to stay."

"Yes, we have that worked out and they will stay in Baltimore as you suggested." The Iraqi turned to Rabbani. Gesturing to include his Al Qaeda counterpart, he said, "We thank you for sending this young man to us and we hope that the doctor you brought has done a fine job on repairing his face." Turning to Clarence he said, "If you are not satisfied, Khalil, tell us and we will kill him."

"No, he did a very good job."

"Good." Turning back to Rabbani, the Iraqi leader said, "We understand that Khalil is your man and that he is with us on loan, but we would like to discuss some of our other plans to attack the West with him, if that meets with your approval." Rabbani said nothing and the Iraqi looked at him quizzically. "Is it required that you know what these matters are before you allow this?"

"Certainly not," Rabbani said. "It's just that I'm a little surprised after what I told you about him today. You know how important he is to me and I had been planning on his leaving with me today."

"Perhaps you can spare him for a little while? I also have some important things to discuss with him."

"There are other things that we must prepare for after we succeed in driving all the westerners from Arabia, and I want Khalil to help me with those matters, but your work is more pressing and there are others that I can work with. He can stay until he finishes with you."

"Thank you, Rabbani. We have come to agree with you that this nephew of yours has some extraordinary talents."

"I have many talented nephews."

After they had finished talking with the camp commanders, Clarence, Neil and Rabbani returned to Clarence's tent. Reclining on the cushions scattered on the Persian rugs, Clarence said, "I'm impressed. You knew before we came here that they'd ask me to review their attack plans."

"I like to think ahead and plan for all possibilities. This one was easy."

Neil said, "Don't play chess with uncle. He's unbeatable."

Rabbani motioned for Neil to play some music on the battery powered CD system and then lowered his voice and whispered, "You will know what these fanatics are planning and perhaps when, and other details. It may be in our interest to forewarn the Americans of some of them to prove our friendship and we don't want them to be so hurt that they will be unable to respond for many years. They think Silver would respond too quickly and they may be right, so it may be important that your plan to kill him succeeds. If you have to stay here longer than I want you to, you will tell Neil their plans. I can always insist that I need him for something. Have you been able to learn anything more about what they plan from training their people?"

"Not much. It's been pretty general. What they do in an airport when they want to fly somewhere. What to order in a restaurant. How to rent an apartment and establish a bank account. How to use an ATM, a urinal, a television remote. How much to tip a waiter. What you do when you enter a church. Nothing that would tell me what the planned targets might be, it's just things they should know in order to travel and live in the United States."

"That it?"

"No. I've been teaching them how to get and receive instructions by e-mail. How to get and use disposable cellular phones."

"That it?"

"So far."

"You know New York well?"

Clarence shrugged. "I've been to New York many times. You know I went to Princeton and that's not too far away from New York, so I used to go into the city quite often."

"Good. This is mainly an Al Qaeda operation, but we've pledged our cooperation. I know from the way they think that New York will be a major target. I'll tell them you know the city well, and then they'll probably let you know what they plan. We have friends and family there. If I know what they plan and approximately when, I can act accordingly."

"You mean inform the Americans?"

"Not necessarily. Assume they plan to contaminate Madison Square Garden with anthrax, or VF or Sarin, that alone could kill more than the World Trade Center. That's the kind of thing that would interest Al Qaeda. We would just stay away. I heard that they intend to send hundreds of suicide bombers, snipers and people infected with small pox to the United States to cause chaos there. They were amused at how two deranged snipers immobilized the D.C. area for weeks, so they could do something like that, but personally, I doubt that could be the main part of their plan. It's not dramatic enough to truly interest Al Qaeda. The leaders of Al Qaeda want a cataclysmic event in the West that would be seen by the rank and file as a God given sign. TV footage of someone shot by a sniper or sick and dying in a hospital doesn't excite people very much. Explosions, buildings, toppling, fires, those would be the kinds of omens that they believe would give Muslims all over the world the courage to rise up against the West. They dream of the creation of a new Muslim Caliphate to rule the world under Muslim law as interpreted by the Wahhabi and Al Qaeda."

Clarence nodded. "I heard something like that from Yusif, the young man that will be flying the model plane. Most of the people here are devoted to that cause. Could it happen?"

"You know better than that. It may give them the courage, but they can not succeed." Rabbani looked at him with a half-amused expression on his face. "I knew you would think it might succeed. You thought, through some kind of magic, that killing the President of the United States and all legal successors to him would destroy the legal government of the United States and result in the creation of your new Second Republic. You believed that if you succeeded, that would cure all the defects in the present U.S. system."

"You never thought my plan could succeed?"

"Sorry, nephew. I thought you might accomplish your goal of killing all successors to the presidency and cause a constitutional crisis, but changing the fundamental structure of the United States government. No, I didn't believe that would happen. But don't feel bad. Many fanatic Muslims believe in that same kind of magic. They believe that a crushing defeat of the West will bring their dreams for the restoration of a world wide Caliphate to fruition." Rabbani laughed. "Both dreams are impossible. The divisions among secular Muslims, the religious fanatics, the Sunni and the Shiites are too deep to disappear for long. As soon as the victory is won, the truce between the religious Islamic forces and the secular Islamic governments will unravel and Sunni and Shiites will resume killing each other. While the West begins to recover, Muslims will be killing Muslims and there will be total chaos throughout the Muslim world. When that happens, Muslims everywhere will look to us to bring order to chaos. After a taste of the brutality practiced by a religious or secular Muslim dictatorship, Muslims, Christians, Jews, Buddhists, Hindus, they all will beg us to rule the Middle East."

"I thought you were only interested in Arabia?"

"It is my main interest, but we will have to help other Muslims in the region to retain our power. We will have to be careful because we can't burden ourselves with their poverty and their problems, but you needn't be concerned. We have it worked out. There is one other thing I wish to discuss with you. You were trained in demolition by the United States Army, were you not?"

"You know I was."

"Yes, yes that's right. You destroyed the Iraqi munitions depot at Kamisiyah. I would like to tell the camp leaders that you are expert in demolition. Perhaps that will open another door for you to learn what they plan. You are willing that I tell them that?"

"Yes."

"They may want to check their computations with you. There is some distrust of the technical competence of the Iraqi engineers by some of the Salman Pak camp leaders. They were correct on their second effort at the New York World Trade Center on September 11,2001, but many Al Qaeda believe the Iraqis miscalculated on the failed first try in 1993. Now that you have been accepted as a 'brilliant technical leader' they may consult with you about any plans like that, and you will of course let me know. It's important that we know as much as possible about what Al Qaeda and the Iraqis are planning so we can use it to our advantage. I'm sure you understand. They must succeed in hitting the United States hard, but not so hard that either the U.S. is unable to respond or that it responds with nuclear strikes." Clarence sat staring at Rabbani saying nothing. Rabbani said, "What's the matter? Are you upset at something?"

"No" It just that I never fully appreciated how complicated, but yet how perfect your plan is. There is much I can learn from you," Clarence smiled, "but I'll take Neil's warning and never play chess with you."

"I'll take that as a compliment."

"You should, Uncle. Do you think the United States would act alone without the rest of the West if the Europeans object?"

"Of course they would. It depends on who's the President. Silver would respond very quickly and let the U.S. Military do the job. Others might delay, but the American people demonstrated they would want to retaliate. There can be no mistake about that. They demonstrated that with the massive support they gave to the Afghanistan and Iraq campaigns. Sooner or later, no matter who the President may be, the U.S. will move against the terrorists. But we have covered that before. Let me know if they are planning anything for Europe. We can't have the French, Germans and Russians talking appeasement again when the time comes to act. Even if they aren't there are other affiliated terror groups that want to attack in those countries, and we can encourage them if the Europeans prove troublesome. The Arc de Triomphe or the Eiffel Tower in Paris would be perfect targets, but I hope that's not necessary. I like those old landmarks and there are other symbolic targets possible elsewhere. They think the French and Germans will be no problem but they may do it anyway." Rabbani shook his head. Al Qaeda can't control all of the Muslim extremist organizations. Some of them are anxious to do something and they have suggested sending groups of martyrs to European cities that have large Muslim populations and infect them with smallpox and other communicable diseases to keep the Europeans from supporting any action against them. They like the idea of sending a small army of small pox infected idiots wandering around in the subways and bistros infecting everyone until they drop dead. They think that would discourage those Europeans from supporting the Americans and get rid of a large number of rabid and uneducated fanatics that they've had to support."

"They would kill their own people that way."

"Of course, they would die as martyrs. For them, nothing could be better."

"You seem to have everything covered, uncle."

"I believe I do. There may be symbolic attacks like those in France planned for other cities in the U.S., but I assume the major planned attack will be on New York City. Any other attacks would not be as complicated as the New York City one. There are rumors that they are considering the Alamo in Texas, the Sears

Tower in Chicago, the Golden Gate and Oakland bridges and the Hollywood sign in California, and churches and synagogues throughout the United States. I would like to know where."

"It could have the opposite result and persuade the Germans and French to support the Americans and British."

Rabbani shrugged. "That's a risk, but there's nothing I can do to stop them. There are all kinds of radical groups that want to participate in the attack and all kinds of animosities against their host countries by many immigrant Muslims. Does that bother you more than the other activities?"

"I suppose not. Every war has civilian casualties. When this is all over, what do you see me doing?"

"As I said before. You will be very important and will help shape the government we construct in the mold of the Second American Republic you wrote about. I expect you to become my second in command, or if you want, you could even return to the United States as our ambassador. Whatever you want, but first, I must leave here tomorrow and you must finish your job here."

CHAPTER 17

▼

Rabbani had been correct. The New Salman Pak leadership, Al Qaeda and Iraqi, treated Clarence with new respect and deference as he continued training Al Qaeda terrorists on what they had to know to live unobtrusively among their victims. They instructed his students that his every word was to be treated as if it were ordered by the Koran. They didn't like him any better, but he had their attention. Two nights later, he and Neil Rabbani were summoned to a meeting with Fawzi Almihdi, the Al Qaeda supreme camp leader. Neil and Clarence exchanged worried glances and then Clarence rose uncomfortably from where he had been reclining on a grouping of cushions spread on his Persian rug, slipped into his Khalil personality and accompanied the messenger to Al Qaeda headquarters hut. As he entered the hut, he saw Almihdi in the middle of a group of his lieutenants. They were all wearing traditional robes and headdresses. They were all Saudis and Wahhabi Muslims, none of whom had ever previously spoken directly to him without an interpreter. Clarence looked around, but didn't see the interpreter in the small group. Clarence looked towards Almihdi and it seemed to him that his usual fierce, black eyes appeared somehow more friendly. Almihdi motioned for Clarence to sit down opposite him on a pile of cushions. Clarence did as ordered and squatted across from the bearded Al Qaeda leaders. He listened with amazement as Almihdi informed him in perfect English that his calculation of the amount of explosive required at different distances from the target was more accurate than the computations made by the Iraqi engineers and demolition experts. Almihdi smiled at him and Clarence then thanked him for his kind words as the rest of the Saudis nodded with approval. Almihdi then asked if he would be willing to expand his role beyond the plan to kill Ben Silver and the training of terrorist foot soldiers by reviewing their plans to attack the United States and perhaps suggest other things they might do. Clarence had been among them long enough and knew what he had to say. Clarence said in halting Arabic, "It is the will of Allah that I assist you in *jihad* against the United States. I will do whatever task you ask of me."

Almihdi and the other Saudis beamed their approval. Satisfied with Clarence's answer, Fawzi told him of their plan to send the people he trained to the United States. "One group is to be infected with small pox after they arrive and is then to attend sports competitions, church and synagogue services, concerts, movies and other events in cities across the country, spreading the disease until they dropped dead from it themselves. Another group of one hundred will be sent to the United States, split into fifty two-man, sniper squads and simultaneously attack random targets in each of the fifty states. You have trained those people. But I want to ask you, what do you think of those plans?"

"They are good plans and they will create chaos across the United States until the small pox carriers die and the general public is vaccinated and until the snipers are caught or killed. Is that the result you want?"

After a brief conversation in Arabic among the Saudis, Almihdi said, "I think you understand my problem. What we wish to accomplish is the removal of all western influences from the Middle East so we can establish our new Islamic state. From the Middle East, it will spread from Siberia to Spain, into Africa, Europe, Asia, Indonesia, Malaysia and the Philippines. Everywhere that Muslims live will be part of our state, and we will rid it of all Jews, Christians, Hindus, Buddhists and other non-believers and restore the laws of *sharia*. That is Allah's will." Clarence remained silent. He knew he was expected to say something, but was unsure about what kind of response they wanted. Almihdi said to his lieutenants, "Khalil seems reluctant to say anything. Leave us for a few minutes."

When they were alone, Almihdi said, "Excuse me my young friend. It was insensitive of me. Rabbani informed me of the so-called honor slaying of your mother, so I understand that there are aspects of the *sharia* laws that offend you, but you must understand that their adoption is central to our cause. Can you forget about it to work with us?"

Clarence nodded that he could.

"Good. I will call the others back. They do not know of your true background. I will tell them that you were reluctant to be critical of the plans made by the Iraqi-Saudi joint planning group."

When the other Al Qaeda leaders returned, Almihdi said, "I have advised Khalil that he is to be open and candid with us, even if he's not impressed with our plans." Turning back to Clarence, Almihidi said. "So, do you agree that our plan will force the Americans to leave the region as we hope? Once we are rid of them, the European cowards will be no problem. We have so many of our people living in those countries now, they quake with fear at the threat we pose and have no courage to resist us. Little by little they will surrender to us. Britain alone can do nothing and the few who resist will be overwhelmed without American assistance. It is only the accursed United States that stands in our way." Almihidi hastily conferred with his lieutenants and then turned back to Clarence. "We know you are reluctant to say anything negative, but we want your honest opinion."

Clarence nodded. "It is a good plan, but it would not accomplish what you want. The small pox phase would soon be controlled and while thousands might become infected, they would be treated. We saw what one pair of snipers did and multiplied by fifty, it would create a huge problem, but the cost in lives and dollars is relatively small. Those events would not dissuade the United States government from doing something it wanted to do and in my opinion, it would increase their resolve to act against you. To accomplish what you want it has to be much more dramatic and costly."

After the Al Qaeda leaders conferred for at least five minutes while Clarence sat there not understanding very much of what was said despite his diligent study of United States State Department Arabic tapes, Almihidi dismissed his lieutenants and told Clarence to remain. When they had all filed out, Almihidi said, "I believe as you do that the plan wouldn't accomplish what needs to be done, but we must do something to satisfy our supporters that we are waging *jihad* against the Americans. The destruction of the Saddam Hussein regime did much to upset our organization and we are still rebuilding. This new Jewish President works with the Israelis and disrupts us as well. If we do nothing, the Saudis and others will stop fearing us, and the donations that we need to support our movement will slow down. Rabbani tells me you have the sophistication to understand these things." He paused a moment and then said, "What do you think would work? What can we do that would stop the United States from interfering with us that is within our reduced capabilities? It should be something dramatic, something costly in lives and money, something more than nine eleven. We wanted to combine the killing of Silver with the simultaneous destruction of the Congress and the Supreme Court, but we have finally admitted to ourselves that doings so is beyond our present abilities. What do you think would enable us to force the Americans to withdraw?"

Clarence nodded in agreement. "Destroying the three branches of the United States government would create the kind of chaos you want. Short of that, I'm not sure."

"We have a list of more easily manageable targets." Almihidi drew a folio of thin files from a box of files behind him and handed it to Clarence. "Take these Khalil. They have been translated into English. They are all targets in the United states that we have the ability to act against. Do you think destroying other targets could accomplish our purpose?"

"If they are the right targets. There are many in the United States who think they shouldn't be the world's police force and that they should just look after themselves. That sets up the kind of debate that would immobilize them, at least for some time, perhaps long enough for you to achieve what you want."

"Many of us think the same way, but we've been unable to come up with a suitable plan. You know the United States better than we do. You think about it. I want to know what you think of the targets we selected and, I also want you to feel free to add to it. We will talk more in one week." As Almihidi started to rise he said. "I know you were anxious to leave and I appreciate your willingness to remain here, so is there something we could do to make your time here more comfortable?"

"Well, perhaps there is. I have been so long in the west that I can't get comfortable squatting or reclining on cushions anymore, and I've always done my best thinking sitting in an armchair."

Almihidi called to one of his lieutenants who had been waiting outside the hut and said a few words in Arabic to his associate. Rising, he turned back to Clarence and said, "After I leave, describe what you want to my assistant and we'll fly it in from Istanbul tomorrow. When we meet again in one week, I'm confident that you'll have a good plan for us."

During the week, Clarence spent many hours sitting in his new flowered armchair in front of his tent in deep thought. He set up a table and his computer and worked at the idea that he had. At the end of the week, Clarence and Neil were summoned to return to the Al Qaeda hut. After exchanging greetings, Clarence said, "I have thought over what you told me and you can continue with what you have planned, but I think I've thought of something that has a much better chance of immobilizing them long enough so you can achieve your goals."

Almihidi impatiently waived for him to continue.

Clarence nodded and said, "First you would immobilize Manhattan from the rest of the country. It's an island, connected to the mainland by bridges and tunnels. There are eleven across the East River, twelve across the Harlem River, nine across the Hudson River, eight to Long Island and the South Shore and seven others to Staten Island and New Jersey. That's a total of forty-seven. I haven't finished the calculation to determine how many tons of explosives are needed for each of them and it may be more than you could assemble, but I don't think you would need to do all of them. If you blew up the Brooklyn, the Queensboro, the Throg's Neck, the Triborough, the Henry Hudson, the George Washington, the Tappan Zee and the Verrazano bridges and the Queens-Midtown, the Holland and the Lincoln tunnels, that should be enough to effectively shut down the city for a long time and cost many billions of dollars to replace. Anything more would be a bonus. That could be done using truck bombs, and if you do it during the evening rush hour, it ought to kill many thousands more than in nine eleven. That would be an enormous blow. But if you expand that and explode a nuclear bomb over Manhattan, even a small dirty bomb when no one can leave, that would go a long way towards knocking the United States out of world affairs for a very long time, maybe forever."

"Sadly, we do not have a nuclear capability as yet. Do we then fail?"

"Not necessarily. There's something else you might consider. Destroying the bridges and tunnels alone could be enough, but if you sprayed the city with anthrax, Sarin or VF gas, that could be almost as effective as exploding a nuclear bomb."

"And how would we do that. We have no ability to spray that island with those toxins."

"But I think you may."

"How?"

"In a way that is similar to the plan to kill the president with the model airplane. Your Iraqi friends developed several different kinds of drone aircraft. They disappeared and were never accounted for to the weapons inspectors. The Iraqis here may know where they are and be able to get them for you."

The Al Qaeda leader looked at him with an uncomprehending stare. "What is a drone aircraft?"

"Unmanned planes. Iraq has developed a large one with that ability. It has a twenty-five foot wingspan and a five hundred-mile range. You could launch it from a freighter in international waters hundreds of miles from New York City. It's slow and is large enough to be picked up on radar, but with all the chaos I would expect after the bridges and tunnels are blown, if it flies low, it might not get picked up and it might get through. Even if it doesn't, they also have small aircraft planes outfitted for biological and chemical warfare that are practically invisible with a range of about three hundred miles. Coordinate that with the launch of a few hundred, model airplanes from within the city and most of the drones should get through. I would also suggest you consider launching a few drones to let the rest of the country know that they can be targets, and that's important. Some Americans think that bad things that happen to New York don't effect them. You can launch some drones from ships against San Diego, Los Angeles, San Francisco, Seattle, New Orleans, Houston, Miami, and from Canada against Detroit and from Mexico against San Antonio. It seems to me that you might be able to do that if the Iraqis cooperate. What do you think?"

Almihidi smiled. "Yes, it sounds easier than nine—eleven. Come back at eight o'clock tonight. I will speak with the Iraqis and tell you what they say."

"Before I go, there's one more thing I'm still working on which I also think is well within your capabilities. It would be to destroy selected electrical generating plants. With no electricity on the island of Manhattan, the chaos would multiply and it would make it all the more difficult to intercept the drone aircraft."

Almihidi nodded at Clarence. "There can be no question about it. Allah has brought you to us at this time for this purpose. Go now in peace and return at eight."

When Clarence returned he saw that the Al Qaeda leadership had been joined by the Iraqi camp leaders. Almihidi smiled as Clarence was ushered in. After he sat where directed, Almihidi told him that they would proceed with his plan to blow up New York's tunnels and bridges, all of them and the power plants. When he finished, the Iraqi camp leader spoke in halting English and confirmed that they managed to remove one large drone aircraft with a five hundred-mile range and five dozen of the smaller ones with a three hundred-mile range before Baghdad fell to the Americans. They would be provided in furtherance of Clarence's plan. Near the end of the meeting, the Al Qaeda leader nodded and said, "We like your approach to things, Khalil. Our technical people find that everything you say is true. We also have decided to attack some European targets so they will understand that by siding with the Americans they will bring similar destruction on themselves. Iraqi intelligence has selected the Arc De Triomphe in Paris and targets in Germany and Russia to deliver the message. Look at this list and tell me whether you agree with them?"

Clarence glanced at the list, then shrugged and said as he handed the list back to Almhidi, "I don't know enough as yet to agree or disagree."

Almihidi smiled and nodded. "It pleases me that you do not pretend to have expertise that you don't have. Keep the list. When you have time, would you be willing to check the calculations of the Iraqi engineers of what's necessary to destroy the selected targets."

Clarence nodded. "If you want, I'll be pleased to do that."

"Very good." The Al Qaeda leader rose to leave the meeting. He paused and turned towards Clarence. "You will have whatever assistance you need in completing your calculations. The Iraqi engineers in camp are available to you. I also want you to know that the men you trained to kill the Jew president have arrived in Baltimore. They were met by our contacts there and will acquire the necessary equipment and begin testing the planes they construct to be sure they work like the ones we built here. They will then fly it over to the White House a few times to see if it's intercepted before we load on the explosives. When they fly it over the White House, it will record what the camera sees and the film will be returned to us here. We will want you to review the film to make sure that everything is working correctly and that the calculations of distances and the amounts of explosives we will use are sufficient. That is all right with you?"

"Glad to help out."

CHAPTER 18

▼

Akmed had taken three days to purchase the correct battery powered model airplanes, GPS systems, miniaturized TV cameras and other electronic equipment. Actually, it was his job to read the specifications and decide what equipment to buy and Yusif's job to find the store and purchase it. Not all of the equipment they had used at the Camp could be readily found in the United States, but they were prepared for that problem. Clarence had trained them well. After Yusif bought the plane and all the equipment, it then became Akmed's job to fit the GPS, the TV camera and the package of explosives into each model plane, just as he had at New Salman Pak. Then it was his and Yusif's job to test the completed devices by flying them to make sure that they all would work. They had a half dozen different models they had tested and decided upon the one that they'd use to kill Ben Silver. It was a model of a P-51. Akmed had wanted to use a MIG fighter and paint an old Iraqi flag or a scimitar on the wings, but was overruled.

They had flown the selected plane a number of times, and now had even flown it over the White House and Rose Garden and filmed everything. They were ready and so was the plane. They had gingerly installed the package of explosives in the fuselage and carefully drove to Washington with the plane resting on Akmed's lap.

They set up near the Railroad Bridge between the Washington Channel and the Tidal Basin around nine-thirty A. M. From there, it was pretty much a straight shot past the Washington Monument and the Ellipse, around the Executive Office Building and on to the White House. They followed the flight on TV and recorded every minute. Akmed and Yusif agreed that it would be glorious when they played the tape on Al Jazeera. Crowds would cheer, maybe even more than when the twin towers of the World trade Center crumbled. They peered at the TV screen. There, they could see the Rose Garden. It was just like Khalil Yomani said. Truly, he seemed to know where every bush and shrub would be. Akmed said, "There's the Jewish Satan himself."

Akmed was right. Ben Silver was sitting in the Rose Garden between Tom Andrews and Molly Pemberton. Akmed continued, "He's with a man and a woman. They're sitting at a small table talking looking at something and drinking and eating."

Yusif said that if they installed a microphone, they might have been able to hear what was being said. Akmed, missing a sense of humor, protested that a microphone would have made the plane too heavy. Yusif told him to forget it.

Akmed said, "Allah be willing, we could do it right now. Fly the plane two hundred meters closer and we push the button and all three are dead."

"Allah got nothing to do with this, and didn't Khalil tell you to forget about Allah until the assignment was over and you were back in Baghdad?"

"You are right."

"I'll fly it in a couple of hundred meters, but don't you push that button. Is the camera recording everything?"

"Yes, even the woman's revealed face and body. She is quite beautiful, but she dresses like a whore. You can see the outline of her breasts and the space between them."

"Okay, I'm going to bring the plane back in. You grab it when it gets here. I don't want it to crash and get damaged or maybe even blow up. With what we got on that baby, we'd be history."

"No matter. We would die as martyrs and go straight to Paradise."

"I got some things I want to do first."

"Like what?"

"Like live. I'm only twenty-two."

After they brought the plane in safely and they were on their way back to Baltimore, Akmed said, "I know you told me that we would not do it today, but why? That you did not tell me."

"This was a dress rehearsal. I have to send all the tapes with all the weights and specifications of the plane fully loaded, and the exact weight of the explosives in grams to New Salman Pak for the experts to evaluate. They want to be certain that the explosion will be strong enough to kill Silver. Some of the Iraqi engineers and clerics don't trust Khalil Yomani."

"Why not?"

"The engineers are jealous and he is too western and not religious enough for the Wahhabi clerics."

Akmed grunted. "He is not pious, but this will kill the American president. This will show the world and all our people what we are capable of. Those Iraqis are fools. It is perfect, just as Yomani said."

"You say so but they think they know best. It doesn't pay to disagree with them."

"The Iraqis are not true believers. I know. I lived among them in Baghdad before the Americans came and they are still a secular government under what the Americans established. They remain the near enemy and we will destroy them and all the other non-believers when we establish the new Caliphate. But first, we must destroy the far enemy that stands in our way." Akmed smiled one of his rare smiles. "Who could believe that we could so easily arrive here in the land of the great Satan, the biggest of the far enemy and wander around so easily? No one notices us. No one cares that we are here."

"You are Palestinian?"

"Yes and you are what?"

"Saudi."

"When we defeat the United States, it will be time to establish a true Islamic state in Iraq. As a Wahhabi, you must agree."

"Of course."

"These experts who criticize Yomani at New Salman Pak, are they the same ones who failed in the first attempt to destroy the World Trade Center in 1993?"

"Not their mistake, according to them. They say the effort would have been a joke without them, and that the people who did it were very stupid and wouldn't wait until they could do it the right way. And if they are, remember, they are the people who figured out that the planes loaded with the fuel they had hitting the World Trade Center Towers where they did would bring those buildings down, and they were right. Stop just ahead in that Burger King parking lot."

Ten minutes after they stopped. A stretch limousine with diplomatic license plates pulled along side of them. The driver rolled down the smoked glass window and a swarthy man wearing a black and white checked Arab headdress looked at them. Yusif got out of his Toyota, walked over to the limousine and delivered a package to the man sitting in the front passenger seat. The smoked glass window went back up and the limousine accelerated out of the Burger King lot." Nobody had said a word.

"Who was that?" Akmed said.

"No idea, probably a Saudi. He'll see to it that the video tape and the measurements are at New Salman Pak no later than the day after tomorrow."

"Then what?"

"Then they'll tell us to do it, unless they think you calculated wrong on the amount of explosives that are required or they see something in the pictures they don't like, or they change their mind."

"Change their mind. No, that can not be. If they change their mind, I say we do it anyway."

"No need to talk about that possibility. Do you think they could find any mistakes in your computations?"

"No. I made no mistake. The distances from the target are calibrated correctly. They'll see that, then we'll do it and we'll be able to leave this land of fornicators and whores."

"What do you say, so long as we're here, why don't we go in and have a Whopper with some fries and a coke." Yusif smiled. "We won't hear anything for a few days, so maybe tomorrow night we ought to go out and do some whoreing and fornicating. That's something these American women are very good at. We won't get too many chances to do that once we have to leave."

Akmed frowned. "I don't know. I welcome leaving, but perhaps I should see what it's like so I can tell everyone at the Mosque about the kind of life they lead here."

"Definitely. You owe it to yourself as a scientist to investigate this lifestyle so you can hate it more accurately."

Akmed nodded his head. "You're right Yusif. It's the scientific thing to do. We should do it."

Yusif blew his nose and turned away so Akmed couldn't see him laughing. When he recovered his composure, Yusif said with as straight a face as he could manage, "What kind of women do you like?"

"I do not know. I have only been with one woman, my wife."

"And she has only been with one man, you."

"Of course."

"In your dreams, what kind of woman would you like to have?"

"What do you mean?"

"Tall, short, white, yellow, black, brunette, blonde hair, red-head, what? Big teats, small ones, big ass? You like it oral, anal, missionary style? What's your fantasy?"

"I have no such fantasies."

"If you have to, what would you choose?"

Akmed furrowed his brow and thought about the question. After a few minutes he said, "In the interest of scientific inquiry."

"Of course, what else could it be?"

"Then, perhaps a slim woman with blonde hair and breasts like melons. I should like to test that combination."

"I'll see what I can do, and what way would you like this female to do it?

Akmed again gave serious thought to the question before he answered, "Each of the ways you mentioned, and if there are more, those ways also. Is that possible?"

"I've been a student here for almost four years. I may be able to introduce you to someone like that, and if she likes you, everything is possible. I'll introduce you as a second cousin from Kurdistan."

"You would do this for me?"

"In the interests of science."

Yusif made some phone calls, and then excused himself for the rest of the afternoon. He returned three and a half-hours later after making arrangements with a George Washington University coed that satisfied the physical requirements and for a thousand dollars promised Yusif that she'd fulfill all of Akmed's sexual fantasies and throw in a freebie for Yusif before he left her apartment. The deal was made and Yusif returned to the Baltimore apartment trying to decide if he would disclose to his Al Qaeda banker how he had spent a thousand dollars of their money.

After their night out, Akmed was so tired that he slept until two o'clock in the afternoon. When he woke, and finally wandered out into the apartment he was sharing with Yusif holding his head, Yusif said, "Amy called so I know you had a good time, but I can see you must have been drinking too."

"Yes, Amy suggested that I try alcoholic beverages, and I wanted to please her, and in the interests of scientific inquiry, I tried them, but I think I will not try them again. When we conquer these snakes and dogs I just might take this Amy for a concubine for a time."

"Maybe so, but for now, you've got to clear your head. I heard from New Salman Pak and we'll have to re-configure things. The Iraqi engineers think the load of explosives is too small and that it requires that the model plane gets closer to Silver than we thought."

"I made no mistake. Does Khalil Yomani agree with them?"

"No. He thinks what you have is enough, but the Al Qaeda leader decided to be cautious and agreed that we should do as the Iraqis want, and Khalil didn't think bringing it in five meters more with a slightly greater load would hurt our chances for success."

They're giving us up to two weeks to buy a new model plane, equip it properly and test it. We're going to have to delay killing Silver for a little while. Sorry, I know you're anxious to get home to your wife, but this has to be done their way."

Yusif thought Akmed would be upset and was surprised when Akmed said, "I agree. It must be done properly. Did they tell you the weight of the package of explosives we are to use?"

"Yes, we are to increase it by one hundred grams and decrease the distance from the target by five meters."

"That will require a larger plane and a larger motor. I will tell you exactly what we will need, and then I'll get right to work on it. If we have some free time at night, would it be possible for me to continue my experiments with the sexual abilities of these Western women. There may be something we could learn from them and teach our wives"

"Good idea, would you want to continue with Amy or would you like to try another type, like a black woman or an Asian?"

"That is truly a difficult question. I could know more by an intense study of this Amy, but in the interests of science, perhaps a different type altogether would reveal more. What do you think?

"I vote for the survey course. Try something different. I know this Vietnamese girl. She's very small and I think you could learn a lot from her, but first we've got to build the new model, equip it and test it."

"I will do that most diligently. It will be done well before schedule and it will have enough explosives in it to assure everyone that it will destroy that Jewish president."

CHAPTER 19

▼

Ben and his chief of staff, Tom Andrews, were seated in comfortable maroon leather armchairs in the Oval Office. They had just completed a meeting with the National Security Advisor. It had been a frustrating meeting. He reported increased terrorist activity and chatter, but no specific information upon which any action could be taken.

Ben said, "The only good thing I can say about that is that at least we're not diverting a lot of our resources looking for Davenport. I hope we can avoid a disaster, but there's nothing more that I can think of that we ought to be doing. How about you?"

Tom Andrews shook his head and pushed back the big shock of his white hair, "I was up half the night trying to see if there were anything more we could be doing."

"No sense to torture ourselves." After Tom nodded in agreement, Ben continued, "Let's discuss the Lindsay Cabot murder for a few minutes. A few days ago, you told me you knew someone named Red Kelly back when you were with the Worcester Police, but didn't know if he was the Red Kelly that killed Jane's husband, and now we know it is." Tom again nodded in agreement. "Tell me, Tom, how did you happen to be in Worcester on the day that Kelly says he met with someone who hired him to kill Jane's husband?"

"You remember we talked about the possibility of my going to Massachusetts to discuss with Mr. Cabot's court appointed attorney the possibility of his letting her divorce go through?"

Ben nodded, "Of course."

"That was the day I met with him, and after that I went to Worcester to visit my folks."

"I didn't know you went to see him."

"I didn't tell you because I knew you thought talking with Mr. Cabot's court appointed attorney was a waste of time, so when he called me and suggested we might be able to solve that problem, I decided to look into it. I should have mentioned it to you, but I didn't want to get your hopes up."

"What did he want?"

"Instead of an appointment to the Federal District Court, he said you could arrange an appointment to the Massachusetts Superior Court and he'd resign as Mr. Cabot's attorney. He said he thought some other court appointed attorney might see things your way."

"You never told me about it."

"I knew you wouldn't listen."

"You're right, I wouldn't. You know, I find it a very strange coincidence that he'd call you and set up an appointment in Boston for the same day Kelly says he met with someone in Worcester who hired him to kill Cabot."

"Maybe so, but it's creating trouble for you that you don't need, and that's why I think I ought to resign."

"Forget it. Who knew you were going to be in Worcester?"

"Anyone that knew I was going to Boston, and that was no secret. Most of official Washington and the media know that whenever I go to Massachusetts I manage to sneak in a visit to my parents."

"Interesting." At that moment, Ben's phone buzzed. Ben answered it, listened a moment and said, bring him in." He turned to Tom. "We'll have to continue this later. Senator Kendall will be arriving any minute now. Stay for the meeting."

Moments later, Martha ushered Senator Kendall into the Oval Office. Wasting no time, Kendall sat tall, perched on the edge of his seat like he was riding a horse on his New Mexico ranch and updated Ben on the effect of the Cabot murder and the Badderley decision on the Congress, becoming more upset by the minute. "Once that decision came down in Alabama, that S.O.B. Thurston sold out to Davies completely. He's using his position as House Speaker to get the House to start an investigation into the Cabot murder, but his real purpose is to harass you and make it impossible for you to function as President. He'll get you and Tom and Mrs. Cabot up to testify and they'll keep squeezing, hoping they can force you to resign."

"Let's think about that for a minute, Senator. I've got to think about what's best for the country. If it gets so bad that I can't do the job then I got to consider it. If they want me gone that much would they make a deal? Say, I nominate you as my Vice President, they approve and then I resign."

Kendall sat back in his chair shaking his head. "No way. First of all, I'm not interested in becoming President in that manner. Secondly, now that Davies won that case suppressing the tape of him planning the terrible things Morton did, he thinks he has regained enough clout to prevent me or anyone else from being approved. I think Davies still believes he can become President. We don't know what it is, but he seems to have some kind of a hold over Elliott Thurston"

"That makes it easy for me. I sure as hell don't want to see Thurston in the White House."

"I agree. He's a Davies lapdog. What you got to do is issue a statement that you know nothing about the murder of Lindsay Cabot, that you don't believe Tom Andrews had anything to do with, and if it turns he did, Tom was perhaps acting out of misguided loyalty to you." Kendall turned towards Andrews, "Sorry about this, Tom, but for now, maybe you ought to resign."

"Nothing doing," Ben said. "That's like saying I think he did it. I refuse."

Tom said, "Senator Kendall is right. The smart thing politically is for you to do that and for me to resign."

"It's not open for discussion. I'm the President, and I make the decisions around here. Tom will not be the sacrificial lamb, and not one more word about that from either of you."

Kendall smiled, "It may be politically dumb, excuse me for saying that, but I applaud the decision. The media want the headline, but frankly, I don't think it would change anything with the Congress, one way or the other."

Ben nodded. "Okay, Tom and I will endure the harassment. I'll talk to Jane, but I'll be surprised if she wants me to back down. The big question is, do they have the votes in the House to impeach?"

"Not this minute. There's a group in the House who hopes that you resign as a result of the harassment. They plan to send an emissary, to tell you they'll issue a statement clearing you and Jane of any involvement in the murder and that you're resigning for the good of the country because of the wholly unwarranted cloud of suspicion about the murder. They will, if you press them, include Tom in the deal. If you still refuse and the media pressure builds, it looks like they'll flip and that Thurston will have the majority he needs to go ahead with the impeachment."

"What happens when it gets to the Senate?"

"That's a tough one. Before the Alabama decision and before that circumstantial evidence tying Tom to the murder came out, they didn't even have a majority, never mind two thirds, but now, it's close. I'm not asking you to do it, but that's why I said it was politically smart to distance yourself from Tom."

"I understood it the first time."

"Sir, you can't prevent me from resigning."

"Yes I can. If you resign, then maybe I will and we all end up with Thurston in the White House."

"You wouldn't do that," Tom said.

"Don't force my hand, Tom. I may not be bluffing."

"After Senator Kendall left, Ben said, "I appreciate your willingness to try and protect me, Tom, and I agree that Thurston is not an acceptable alternative. So, between us, for the good of the country, I might even let you do that if I thought it would stop the effort to force me to resign or be impeached, but it won't. They'll continue trying until they get what they want and that's me out and Thurston sitting in this office, and I don't believe that's their final objective."

"What is?"

"I don't know, but it involves Davies, I don't know what he's up to, but I just know he's pulling all the strings. The only way to put a stop to all this is by discrediting Davies once and for all. I thought we had done that, but that decision in Alabama undoes that. Well, let's think about it. Maybe we'll be able to come up with something."

Later that evening, Ben called Jane. "Sorry I couldn't make it to Lindsay's funeral. It must have been a tough day for you."

"It would only have been a worse media circus if you came. Most of Lindsay's family tried to be helpful, but there's always one person who, for God knows what reason, has to make trouble. Lindsay's younger sister has always been a little peculiar. The media found her and she loves the attention."

"I know. Cam told me."

"I don't think you heard this one. She told a Herald reporter that the convenience store hold-up where Lindsay was shot was another time when we tried to have him killed."

"That's totally crazy. We didn't even know each other when that happened."

"That's why you haven't seen it in print yet. The Herald reporter knew that, but you can bet that she'll tell that story to some tabloid and they'll print it."

"Sorry about all the trouble this is causing. How did the funeral itself go?"

"I'm still the wife and next of kin, so I had to make all of the burial arrangements. The undertaker is convinced that I arranged poor Lindsay's murder. It was surreal. I wanted to scream at the unctuous bastard, but with reporters lurking right outside his office, I couldn't even do that. At the service, I said a few words and so did his mother. She, at least was wonderful. She knows I had nothing to do with the murder."

"Sounds like you've had a terrible day."

"There have been worse, but it easily makes the top ten."

"I keep feeling like I have to apologize. I'm sure it's all got something to do with my being President"

"It probably does, but that doesn't make it your fault."

"I suppose not. You need any help with the funeral bills?"

"Thanks, Ben, but no. I had forgotten, but Lindsay had a prepaid life insurance policy from his old job and I'm the beneficiary. It's a big policy, two million dollars. The press will love that when they hear about it. The agent called right before the funeral to say there would be a delay in payment because of the allegations Kelly made, but I can take care of the bills without it. After the funeral I spent three hours with the Quincy police. They wanted to know, among other things if I could persuade you to come in for questioning."

"What did you tell them?"

"I remembered what you always did when you were pissed. I stayed under control and was very nice. I told them I didn't have the ability to influence you one way or the other."

"Are you in trouble with them?"

"I don't know? You think I need a lawyer?"

"It's probably a good idea."

"Should I call Gary Rosenthal from your old office?"

"No. You need a trial lawyer. You know Peter McGlynn, don't you?"

"Not really. I met him and his wife at one of that charity fundraiser Gary Finegold sponsors every year."

"He's the right lawyer for this. I'll call Peter tomorrow morning and then you call him tomorrow afternoon."

"Okay. What a mess." Jane laughed, "And how was your day, the lady said ever so sweetly?"

"Not good, but not as bad as yours. I had a meeting here this evening with Tom and Bob Kendall. One of the things we discussed was the possibility of my resigning the Presidency. I'd love to do just that, but I told them I didn't much like the idea. You know how I feel about turning the country over to Thurston and his crowd." Ben paused and sighed. "I don't know Jane, after talking to you, I'm thinking that maybe I should say the hell with it and just quit. It kills me to think about the trouble I'm causing you, and Kendall tells me its going to get worse, because the House is going to start investigating your husband's murder to force me to resign and if I don't, they'll probably start impeachment proceedings. They'll be harassing you, Tom and me. Say the word and I'm history. I never wanted this damn job anyway."

"Ben, we've been through this. I'm not that fragile. I appreciate your concern, but screw them. Let them do their worst. I'll take it in stride."

"How about our getting married now and your moving in?"

"That's sweet, even if it's not quite the romantic proposal I've always dreamed of, but you know as well as I do that our getting married right now would only make things look worse."

"I know I can't do it, but I'd love to quit this whole mess and become anonymous again. I loved the life we had planned before this all happened. Work a little bit from wherever I am, mainly on my computer and by fax and phone, most of the winter in St. Croix, summer on the Cape and the rest of the time in Brookline."

"Sounds good to me too, Ben, but it's not to be now and it never can be. Whenever you leave office and no matter the circumstances, you can never again be just a private citizen, so let's make the best of it."

"You are the realist."

"So tell me. What else is going on? I don't understand how Davies got that tape of him and Morton thrown out. I bet that judge in Alabama was paid off, and why does that mean it can't be used in other courts."

Ben explained that the law of Alabama, as interpreted by the judge, required that at least one party to tape-recorded conversation consent to its use before it could be used in court, and that since Morton was dead he couldn't consent, and Davies didn't. Therefore, since no one consented, it was inadmissible.

"That doesn't make sense to me, but so much of the law doesn't. I'll let you go in a minute, but first I have to ask you about where this nonsense about Tom hiring Red Kelly comes from?"

"You heard what Winters said. Kelly's from Worcester. Tom was with the Worcester police while he was going to law school, and he was in Boston meeting with Lindsay's lawyer and then went to Worcester to visit his parents the same day Kelly claims he met with someone that hired him to kill Lindsay. I feel even worse about it because Tom went to Boston to see that lawyer who was appointed Lindsay's guardian."

"I didn't know he went to see that scumbag."

"Neither did I. Tom didn't tell me before he went and didn't say anything when he came back because it went nowhere."

"Odd that he went there. How come he did?"

The lawyer called him and suggested the meeting."

"That whole thing stinks."

"I agree, but those are the facts and we can't seem to make any sense out of it. I also learned that they found one of those pens from my office in Kelly's apartment? They're using those circumstances to build a case against Tom, but the objective is to start Impeachment proceedings in the House to force me to resign."

"Could the FBI have manufactured the whole case? That P.J. Winters hates your guts."

"I suppose it's possible, but that would mean that he arranged Lindsay's murder. That's going pretty far. I don't believe even Winters would do that."

"Come on Ben. You've seen what the FBI did in the Whitey Bulger case right here in Boston, and there have been plenty of other scandals that are just as bad."

"I don't know. Winters is no good. I suppose you could be right. I may discuss that with Tom. He knows him very well."

CHAPTER 20

▼

"The plane is ready," Akmed announced. "We have tested it and it now has more than enough explosives to kill the infidel President five times. I thank Allah that at last we have permission to do it. I will miss finishing my research with the American whores, but it is time to go home and be heroes."

Yusif shook his head. "Let's hope he's in the Rose Garden. We were lucky on our last dress rehearsal to find him there."

"If he's not, we'll have to keep trying until we succeed, but with the help of Allah, we will complete our mission today."

"Fine with me."

Akmed carried the plane down from their Baltimore apartment to their rented Ford Expedition and gingerly loaded it into the back of their SUV with the rest of the electronics required for their mission. As Yusif carefully drove the Ford Expedition out of the apartment development parking lot, Akmed said, "They have been driving me crazy changing the amount of explosives they want us to use. Let's get it done before they change it again. I still think the smaller plane with the smaller package of explosives would have been enough to kill the Jew and then we wouldn't need this beast of a car. You could put ten Renaults like the one I use in Baghdad in here and still have plenty of room."

"I like this better than the shit-box we had before. Don't take it personally. They agreed that the other plane and charge would have been enough and that they were wrong, but then they decided on the bigger payload so we won't have to fly the plane so close."

Akmed agreed that was an advantage. He had the package of explosives in his lap and would install it in the model P-51 and connect the detonator wires just before take-off. As they drove towards Washington, Akmed said, "This Khalil Yomani, he is truly inspired by Allah, but do you know his background?"

"No. I don't know anything more than you do, but I don't think he's who he said he was. He didn't act or talk like an Arab or a Muslim."

"And what of the man who brought us to him? Do you know who he is?"

"Neil Rabbani?"

"Yes."

"Yes. I've seen pictures of him with some Arab big shots in London. He was an assistant for someone. I think it was that visitor who watched the tests at New Salman Pak, but I can't be sure of that. He knew several of the Saudis at the Camp so I think he's who he said he was. Perhaps when we get back I'll be able to figure it out, but if not, I won't worry about it. Why are you so interested?"

"No special reason."

"Did they give you a cyanide pill and tell you to take it if you get caught?" Akmed nodded that they did. Yusif continued, "And would you do it?"

Without hesitating a moment, Akmed said "Of course. I would then go straight to Paradise." Akmed said almost incredulously, "And you would not?"

Yusif thought that probably means they told you to kill me if you think I wouldn't, just like they told me to kill you. He said, "Oh sure I would. I wouldn't like to, but of course I would do it. Let's not think of these unpleasant things. We will do the job, and then we will leave and be heroes wherever we go in the Muslim world."

An hour and a half later, Akmed and Yusif were at their selected place near the railroad bridge. Yusif said as he squatted on the ground next to Akmed, "We could have done this from the roof top of a hotel near here and been comfortable while we did this."

"Khalil Yomani himself picked this location. A little discomfort for our cause will make our victory even better."

"Is that in the Koran?"

"I don't know, but whenever times are difficult, so are we told by our clerics."

At ten A.M. they flew the plane over to the White House. The cameras sent a view of the Rose Garden back to the watching assassins. They saw no one. After the plane returned, they installed fresh batteries, checked all the connections and then flew the plane back to the White House again at noon without luck. They repeated the procedure again at two and again at four o'clock with similar results. As the model approached the White House, shortly after six P.M., Yusif said, "This will have to be the final flight for today. We will recharge all the batteries and try again tomorrow."

"Quiet! Quiet," Akmed said. "I see something. Allah be praised. It is the infidel President. He is with that same woman and three men. She is shameless, see how she is dressed. One of the men is a Negro."

Yusif stared at the screen. "You're right. That's Silver. He's with that Molly Pemberton again. I wonder if there's anything going on between them. The men are Tom Andrews, John Wallace and the nigger is Rahsheed Evans."

"That Rahsheed, is he a Muslim?"

"I believe he is. You have a problem killing him?"

"No, if he's a true believer he will go straight to Paradise and if not, he deserves to die. Fly it in closer. Hurry, everything is perfect. You're almost there. Don't turn that way. Turn left, left."

"Easy. Take it easy. We have our instructions to bring it in out of the sun. You know that."

"Hurry! Look, they're standing up. Quickly! Do it! Now."

"Damn it," Yusif said. "They're still out of range."

"No, I think they're close enough." Quick! They're moving into the building."

"Damn, they've moved inside."

"You should have done it."

"No. Our instructions required us to be ten meters closer."

"We had enough explosives to do it. You should have done it. We would have killed them all."

"And what if you're wrong and Silver escaped. Some would say it's a sign that Allah was not with us. And what would be our fate. We would have disobeyed our orders. We would have failed. We would have exposed our plan so that we could never try it again. And when we return, we wouldn't be treated as heroes. We'd be laughed at or maybe even killed, and all because we didn't follow the plan. There would be no trip to Paradise for you, my friend."

"A thousand pardons, Yusif. You are right. We have to succeed. We will continue until we do."

When Yusif and Akmed returned to Baltimore, he prepared a report of the day's attempt to kill President Silver, explaining why they had to defer the assassination. As he had done after every flight, he then delivered his report and the film of that day's flight to the man in the stretch limousine, meeting him this time in a KFC parking lot. For the next two days, they returned to their spot near the Railroad Bridge and flew the 747 model to the White House, but Ben failed to appear in the Rose Garden during any of their fly-overs. Disappointed, they welcomed a two-day interruption necessitated by rainy weather that would have prevented anyone from sitting outside.

CHAPTER 21

▼

Clarence had sat out in front of his tent in his new armchair covered in a flowery damask silk flown in from Istanbul every day for over a week. In the morning his chair would be placed in the shade of the west side of his tent and in the afternoon on the east side. Sitting in the shade, in front of a table on which he had his laptop and a printer, he pored over information about Manhattan's bridges and tunnels and the U.S. electric power grid. He computed the amount of the explosive charge required to destroy each target and where they should be placed. He had all the help he could want from a squad of five Iraqi engineers who were assigned to help him. The Al Qaeda and Iraqi leadership were pleased with his plan. It was low tech and could be easily accomplished using truck bombs. Last night they had discussed whether the attacks should be carried out during rush hour to maximize the number killed during the attack or during the middle of the day to maximize the number of people who would be trapped on Manhattan Island. He was going to recommend that the attack take place during the evening rush hour to maximize the expected chaos from the loss of electric power and hide the incoming Iraqi drone airplanes carrying Sarin gas, VF and other toxic chemicals. Some commuters leaving early would escape, but proceeding at that time would maximize the chances for the overall success of the plan.

Clarence stretched and looked at the pile of tapes of the fly-overs of the White House Rose Garden that Yusif and Akmed had made. The tapes had been digitized, transferred onto DVD and finally given to him to review. He'd take a break and do that now. Moments later he had them on his screen. Ben Silver was in eleven of the fly-overs and Molly Pemberton was sitting beside him in ten of them. He had thought about Molly on many occasions, but now, busy with the tasks assigned to him, he had managed to banish all thoughts of her from his mind. Seeing her grainy image on the videotapes brought it back and he wasn't sure exactly how he felt about her. He took her business card out of his wallet and thought about the last time he saw her in the driveway of his house in Alexandria. He smiled as he remembered the way she had turned towards where they had met and the earnest plea in her voice as she asked him not to kill himself. He stared at her business card and then sniffed it and wished it had retained the scent of her perfume.

If Yusif and Akmed killed Silver, they'd most likely kill Molly too. How would he feel about being responsible for her death? He'd killed hundreds, but no one he really cared about. Did he care about her? Somehow the idea of his killing her didn't feel right. As he thought about it, he frowned and remembered that yesterday he had worked with Iraqi intelligence officers and engineers and reviewed their calculations of the amounts of explosives required to destroy selected targets in France, Germany and Russia. That was no problem. Killing the people who had the misfortune to be at those landmarks was also no problem. Killing his own countrymen in the tunnels and on the bridges of New York was no problem. Killing even more with toxic chemicals didn't present a problem either. Why did he feel bad about Molly Pemberton? Why did thinking about killing her make him feel ill? He decided he would have to think about that later as he saw Fawzi Almihidi, the Al Qaeda camp leader approaching. He welcomed the interruption. Almihidi asked, "You have completed the computations for the destruction of the New York and the European targets?"

"Yes, except for the George Washington Bridge in New York and I still have to check the computations made by the Iraqis for the Piet Hein Tunnel in Holland and the Cross Harbour Tunnel in Hong Kong. All I need is another hour or so."

"The explosives designated for the other Hong Kong harbor tunnels are sufficient?"

"Yes. They can probably isolate the sections destroyed and repair them in a few weeks, but it will demonstrate how vulnerable they are."

"Excellent. Exactly what we intend. I have told your uncle how pleased we are with you. We are indebted to him because of what you have done." Almihidi smiled. "Is there something else I can do to make your stay more pleasant? I see that you make use of the armchair we brought in for you. The fabric covering it pleases you?"

"Perfect. I once had one very much like this one when I lived in the United States. I find I work more efficiently this way."

"I have ordered one for myself and I agree that it is very comfortable. Is there anything else I can do for you to make your stay among us more pleasant? Perhaps a young woman, or a child, or if you prefer, a young man. Whatever you might want, we will happily supply it."

"Perhaps a young woman." Clarence's glance fell on Molly Pemberton's business card resting on the table beside his chair, "but not right now."

"As you wish. There may be one more thing. Some of the Al Qaeda leadership would like to coordinate the killing of President Silver with the attack on New York. Do you think that could be done."

Clarence didn't think it was possible and hesitated a moment, not sure how he wanted to respond. He then said, "Perhaps if we do the bridges and tunnels at a different time when Silver would be in bed. I read that the redecorating of the residence in the White House has been completed so I believe I know where he'll be sleeping, but it is unlikely that it could be done with a single model airplane like the one we selected for the Rose Garden attack. That one is designed to work when he's someplace where the model plane can get close enough to him to kill him with the moderate explosive charge the plane carries. With walls or windows between him and the explosion, a greater amount of explosives would have to be used."

"Can you think of another way? You think it could be done with a shoulder fired rocket?"

"I thought about that before. It's a gamble. But perhaps one of the small, Iraqi drone planes could get through without being noticed. Let me think it over and do some calculations."

"Come take a walk with me, my young friend. There are those in this camp who consider you to be nothing more than another infidel. I want them to see that you have my protection, and I want to ask you something."

Clarence and Almihidi began a slow walk through the training base. Everyone stopped what they were doing and stared as he and Almihidi approached, arm in arm. Clarence could hear a conversational buzz as they passed. Almihidi barely acknowledged the greetings of other camp participants as they walked and chatted about life in the United States. After a time, Almihidi stopped and pulled a small portable radio, about the size of two cellular telephones from beneath his robes. He handed it to Clarence. "Do you know what this is"

Clarence examined the radio. He pushed the on switch and heard some Arabic music. Puzzled, Clarence said, "It looks like a portable radio."

"It is, but it is something else as well."

"What?"

"It is a device that jams radio frequencies. It was developed by our Iraqi friends when they controlled their government. They want us to hijack several planes like we did on September 11 and crash them into the White House at the same time that we blow the bridges and tunnels in Manhattan. They want use to use their achievement in electronics once more, and that plan for killing the President appeals to many of my associates, but I would be interested in your opinion."

"I understand that the radio frequencies used by the airlines en route are still published and that they can easily be jammed, but now there are electronic transmitters and receivers that cannot be jammed. I don't know whether they have installed them, probably not because they're really expensive, but that's not really the problem I see."

"Then tell me what you do see. I want you to be brutally frank with me."

Clarence nodded. "It would certainly kill him if you succeeded in crashing the plane into the White House, but I don't think that plan will succeed. Before September 11, the airlines instructed their crews to not threaten the safety of the passengers and the plane by resisting a hijacking. They thought the plane would be landed safely and that all the hijackers wanted was to get somewhere, or to achieve the release of political prisoners or be paid a lot of money. That's all changed now. They have armed air marshals on some flights, and with flights originating or terminating in the D.C. area or passing nearby, there's a good chance one will be on any flight you attempt to hijack."

"We have an inexhaustible supply of willing martyrs. Assume we have enough of our people on board to overcome the crew and any air marshal and that we have trained someone to fly the plane."

"The military will shoot the plane down."

"If they know and they can get there in time. We believe we can jam their radios successfully. Any other problems?"

"Even if you jam the radios, many passengers will have cellular phones. That's how we learned what we did about the hijacking on September 11."

Almihidi frowned. "You say 'we' not they?"

Clarence's face turned red under his bandages. He had made a mistake. "I was in the United States, living there on September 11, 2002. That's how I and everyone else living in the United States learned of our glorious victory on that date."

"Are you aware of any additional difficulties with the hijacking plan?"

"You still want me to be frank?"

"Of course."

"Assuming you can breach the now reinforced locked cockpit doors and take control of the plane and avoid being shot down by the military, the biggest problem still exists. The other passengers will react as they did on the flight that crashed in Pennsylvania. They will not sit by and let our people crash the plane into the White House without a struggle, but perhaps they have considered that problem." Clarence congratulated himself for saying, "our people".

Almihidi smiled. "They have considered it but not solved it to my satisfaction. They consider all Americans to be fat and lazy cowards. I know better. I don't think the Iraqi plan can work. That's the trouble with them. They always underestimated the Americans and fought them with the prior war's strategy. It lost them their country."

Clarence and Almihidi continued walking in silence. As they approached Clarence's tent, Almihidi said. "Let's go in. We'll have a drink and there's something else I want to ask you." They went inside, opened a couple of cans of Coke from Clarence's refrigerator and squatted on the Persian rug covering the dirt floor. "There's something I don't understand. The *jihad* against the U.S. began well before Sept 11. Iraq attempted to assassinate the senior Bush in Kuwait, trained the terrorists in charge of the 1993 bombing of the World Trade Center and the bombing of the Oklahoma City federal building and there were other attacks against the Cole and American embassies. Why did they do almost nothing until the September 11 hijacking of the airliners?"

"There is no generally accepted answer to that question."

"Is there an answer that you accept?"

"There's an explanation that I find reasonable."

"Tell me and I'll tell you if I find it reasonable."

"There was credible evidence that the 1993 attack on the World Trade Center and the 1995 attack in Oklahoma City were combined operations by Al Qaeda and Iraq. The official explanation from the CIA and FBI was that 1993 attack was the work of an extreme Islamic fundamentalist group based in the United states and that Oklahoma City was done by a right wing Gulf War vet named Tim McVeigh and a service buddy, Terry Nicholls, and that they were acting alone. They said there was no state sponsorship of those attacks or any of the others."

"Why did the CIA and FBI say that. How could they know there was no state sponsorship? How do they think these things happen? No, I'm sure they knew that it was at least possible that some foreign governments played a role if they didn't know it to a certainty. Did you believe that," Almihidi searched for the correct word, then said, "fairy story? I can't believe you did Khalil."

Clarence smiled. "At first I did, but then I came to believe those who thought otherwise."

"I understand that most Americans still don't believe foreign states were involved in those attacks or the one on September 11 and that most officials still maintain that there was no foreign state involvement. How can they do that? I don't understand."

"Bill Clinton was the President at the time those events occurred."

"Are you saying that his involvement with that young woman prevented him from responding?"

Clarence shook his head. "It may have played a role, but I doubt it."

"What then? They say he was a very intelligent. If so, he had to know better."

"I share your opinion of him. I think he did know better, but he had a goal. It was to bring peace to the Middle East. He had a large ego and thought he would succeed where everyone else failed. He couldn't bring peace to the region and go to war against Iraq. That's why I think he told the CIA and the FBI that he didn't want to hear about foreign government involvement and those agencies obliged. It suited them to say they caught the persons responsible for the attacks against the United States and that the threat was over. Clinton almost succeeded at Oslo. In any event, the people in those agencies were forever after bound to the statements they made and unwilling to say they had been wrong. That's the way those bureaucracies operate."

Almihidi shook his head. "I suppose it's better to claim you should be praised for removing the threat and people want to believe that and resume their normal activities."

Clarence agreed. "Americans want to be able to resume their soft, easy way of life and feel free to go the mall and buy things they don't need."

Almihidi smiled. "You understand them well. Perhaps Clinton isn't as smart as I thought he was. He had no chance of success at Oslo." With that statement, Almihidi rose, thanked Clarence for the explanation, gave him a western style handshake and prepared to leave Clarence's tent. At the entrance flap, he paused, turned and said, "You think about using multiple model airplanes or the Iraqi drone plane for killing President Silver, maybe there's some other way that you will think of. We will talk again."

After Almihidi left, Clarence went outside and sat in his armchair. He felt relieved. Was it because he could stop thinking about Molly? No, he was still thinking about her. Was it because he could stop thinking about how he would feel if he were responsible for killing her. Yes, that must be it. Knowing they wouldn't make the attempt to kill Silver until he reported back to them and thinking about killing Silver in some way that wouldn't put Molly at risk seemed to make him feel better.

He quickly finished the remaining computations for the bridges and tunnels and then turned back to his laptop and began working on the problem Almihidi gave him. Could they use an Iraqi drone aircraft and crash it through Ben Silver's bedroom window in the wee hours. He knew the dimensions of every room in the White House. He knew the capacity of the drone and the demolition power of the explosives, but he didn't know what the window was made of. It was probably bulletproof. What was the position of the bed in the bedroom? What are the chances that a plane that large could approach the White House undetected?

Clarence knew before he started that the kind of coordination Al Qaeda wanted was not possible and if they blew the tunnels and bridges at two in the morning, the people trapped on Manhattan would primarily be the people who lived there. That would minimize the number killed in the attack and thereafter. He'd have to tell Almihidi the truth, but Almihdi would be away for a few days, and perhaps he wouldn't have to tell him immediately, and maybe they'd decide to try and kill Silver in the bedroom instead of the Rose Garden, even if it weren't a sure thing. He still felt relieved, but not as much as before.

While Clarence sat in his flowered armchair in front of his tent at New Salman Pak thinking about the coming Al Qaeda attacks, Akmed woke to bright skies in his Maryland apartment. He decided that this would be the day to kill Ben Silver. After days of rainy weather, Silver would probably be anxious to get some fresh air in the Rose Garden. As he prepared the plane and all the equipment for today's trial, Yusif sat at his Dell laptop computer checking his e-mail for any new instructions. Yusif frowned as he opened a coded message from New Salman Pak. He printed it, took out his codebook and deciphered the message. He called Akmed. "Akmed hold it. We have new instructions."

"What is it?"

"Come here and I'll tell you. Sit down."

Akmed sat on a barstool at a small table opposite from Yusif. "What do they want?"

"I don't know what to make of it. They are preparing a massive attack against the U. S. on the anniversary of the September 11 attack. They may cancel this operation. They want to know if we think we can kill Silver on that date."

"Are they mad? That's almost two months from now, and how can we be sure that Silver will be outside on that date?"

"They suggest that we fly the plane to the White House at two o'clock in the morning on that date and explode it outside the window of his bedroom. They are re-computing the amount of explosives and the size of the model plane required to cause a big enough explosion to kill him while he sleeps."

"I can tell you right now, there's no model plane large enough to carry a sufficient charge to assure us of success."

"Interesting. Khalil Yomani has said the same thing. They ask if you think it could be done if we used more than one plane. What do you think would be the result if we each flew a plane like the one we have? We're capable of doing that."

"I would have to figure it out, but I don't think two planes will be enough. Maybe four planes would do it. I could figure it out. We'd need more equipment and a truck to carry everything. There are many problems."

"Let it be their job at New Salman Pak to figure it out. Let's not get discouraged by this delay. At the end of the message, they say if they find the new plan doesn't work, they will tell us so we can return to the original plan. In the meantime we can enjoy what this country has to offer."

Akmed nodded in agreement. "We will wait. We must all suffer for Islam." Akmed sat quietly a moment. "I know why they choose that September 11 date, but what else do they plan to do?"

"I don't know."

"It must be something glorious."

CHAPTER 22

▼

House Speaker Elliott Thurston checked the time on his wristwatch, and then rose from his seat, adjusted his microphone, tapped his gavel on his desk, and said, "This House will be in order. These proceedings are being televised and will demonstrate our democracy in action to the people of this country and throughout the world. For their benefit, I'll briefly explain the nature of the process in which we are now engaged." Thurston shuffled the papers on his Speaker's platform a moment and then continued, "We are here to determine whether Benjamin Silver, President of the United States, should be impeached. Under the Constitution of this great republic, the President of the United States is to be removed from office on conviction of 'treason, bribery, or other high crimes and misdemeanors.' Today's proceeding is not to determine whether the President should be removed from office. That function is, by our Constitution, vested in the United States Senate which 'has the sole power to try all impeachments'. We have 'the sole power of impeachment' which means that it is our responsibility to determine if the President should be charged with treason, bribery, or other high crimes and misdemeanors, and if so to present those charges to the United States Senate for trial. Copies of the Rules applicable to these proceedings as adopted by the Rules Committee have been provided to the members of the House and will be provided to the members of the media. Prior to the presentation of evidence, I'd like to describe and synopsize some of those rules for the benefit of the television media and the audience here and at home."

Thurston turned towards his aide to receive the slim file that was being offered to him, and then put on the horn rimmed reading glasses that had been resting on the table. He peered through them and began reading:

"One. The rules of evidence generally applicable to criminal trials shall not apply in these proceedings;

Two. No objections as to relevancy or materiality shall be made to questions propounded by the members of the House;

Three. To sustain a charge made in these proceedings and send this cause to the Senate for disposition, it shall only be necessary that it appear more likely than not that the President is guilty of the offense charged by the House; and

Four. Any information, claims, evidence or argument relating to the alleged misconduct of any member of the Congress is irrelevant, immaterial and inadmissible in these proceedings unless directly related to the charges filed against the President."

After Thurston finished reading the applicable rules, the clerk read the charges and the evidentiary phase of the proceedings began. The presentation began with the charge of malfeasance in office as a result of Ben's inability to nominate a vice-president, fill Cabinet appointments and appoint judges to fill vacancies in the courts. Even Ben's severest critics knew that it was the Senate that was holding up all nominations, but they knew that Senator Smithers insisted on those charge being made as there was at least one Senator who would vote to remove Ben from office on that charge and not the others. What the media and the public were waiting for, however, was the presentation of charges and evidence relating to Ben's relationship with Jane Cabot and the Lindsay Cabot murder. The official complaint was that Ben was a co-conspirator with Jane Cabot and Tom Andrews or other unnamed persons in the murder of Lindsay Cabot.

Speaker Thurston managed the proceedings skillfully. Walter Wagner presented the matchbook and shell casing he had planted and removed from the crime scene. A forensics expert identified the fingerprints on the matchbook and shell casing as Red Kelly's.

Kelly was then produced He told his story of the murder and of his being hired to commit it. After Ben's counsel tried to discredit Kelly's testimony by pointing out that Kelly had received a very light sentence, Speaker Thurston allowed Winters to explain that the light sentence was warranted in the public interest so as to quickly get at the truth behind the Cabot murder. Instant on-line polling indicated that the public agreed that the public interest in knowing the facts concerning the Cabot murder warranted the FBI making the arrangements it did with Kelly.

At long last, Ben was called to testify. On his direct testimony, Ben stated he knew nothing about the murder of Lindsay Cabot and that he would not testify about his relationship with Jane Cabot, except to say that they had an adult relationship that included all of the activities in which adults in love normally engage.

Counsel for the House wasted no time. She started her interrogation of Ben by asking him to describe the sexual activities he engaged in with Jane in the White House. When Ben refused to do so, House Counsel said, "Our interest in your sexual relationship is very germane to these proceedings. We are interested in knowing whether you have engaged in oral or anal sex since those activities violate the criminal law and are felonies. Indeed sir, your entire relationship with that married woman may have violated laws against fornication."

Ben said, "I'm well aware of what your motives are. It's to harass and embarrass me. I will not be harassed. I will not be embarrassed. I will not answer those questions."

"Are you exercising your right against self incrimination?"

"No, I'm exercising my right as a human to not play your game."

After a brief, whispered and heated conference among committee members and their counsel, the senior attorney in charge of interrogating Ben said, "You are excused for now, but we may return to this issue at a later time. You may leave."

As Ben started to leave, the House clerk said, "We call Mrs. Jane Cabot."

As Ben and Jane approached each other in the corridor, Ben said, "I'm so sorry I got you into this mess."

Jane took his hand, "It's not your doing, and don't worry about it."

Like Ben, Jane testified that she had an adult relationship with Ben. When asked to describe the kinds of sexual relations in which they had engaged and if they took place in the White House, Jane said, "He's a healthy man. I'm a healthy woman, and we'll privately have any kind of sexual relations we are both willing to have whenever and wherever we want. As to exactly where, when and what, it's none of your business, and that's all I'm going to say about that."

The attorney interrogating her said, "You know we can hold you in contempt and put you in jail until you answer my questions."

Jane said, "Do what you want. I shall not answer those questions."

Attorney McGlynn sitting beside Jane said, "Mr. Speaker, those questions are irrelevant. They have nothing to do with treason, bribery or high crimes and misdemeanors for impeachment of the President of the United States."

"You heard the rules governing these proceedings," Thurston said. "Relevancy is not grounds for an objection and besides, those are felonious acts we believe she committed with the President. Answer the question."

The interrogating attorney said to Jane, "The witness is directed to answer."

McGlynn stood and said, "Mr. Speaker and madam prosecutor, have you no shame? Are there no limits to which you will descend?"

The prosecutor replied, "Another word from you, Mr. McGlynn and I'll have you removed from this chamber. Those are proper questions and the witness is required to answer them."

"I shall not answer them." Jane then rose from her seat and began to walk out of the House chamber.

As Jane proceeded down the corridor, the attorney shouted after her, "Come back here. I've not finished with you."

Jane paused, turned and said, "Well I've finished with you," and continued up the aisle to the exit.

"We'll see about that. Stop her. Sergeant of arms! Stop her. You just wait there Mrs. Cabot while I ask the House to hold you in contempt."

As the doorkeeper started to attempt to restrain her, Jane was joined by Ben and his entourage of Secret Service Agents. They didn't stop and the doorkeeper stepped aside as House Counsel shouted after them and to the small army of news photographers snapping away, "You better bring your toothbrush with you when we drag you back in here to answer these questions."

It was eleven-thirty when Jane walked out of the House chamber with counsel for the committee shouting after her. After a lengthy conference among attorneys and House members, it was decided to adjourn until three o'clock.

Speaker Thurston, finally arrived in the House at three forty-five PM. He called the House to order and then said, "I want to apologize to the media and to the membership for the delay. We've decided that we would not question Mrs. Cabot any further with respect to her relationship with the President. We all know what it means when they say they have an adult relationship and it is therefore unnecessary to question Mrs. Cabot or the President any further with respect to that issue. We had originally intended to call Lindsay Cabot's mother and sister at this point in the proceedings and finish up with Presidential Chief of Staff Tom Andrews tomorrow. Counsel for Lindsay Cabot's mother has informed us that she does not wish to testify and out of respect to her at the loss of her son we have decided not to require that she appear. Her testimony was intended to show that since her son's injury, there has not been a loving relationship between her son and his wife, Mrs. Cabot. We have decided to forego that testimony as again, we all know by Mrs. Cabot's own statements that she has not honored her marriage vows. The other witness scheduled for this afternoon, Lindsay Cabot's sister, has apparently had some medical difficulty and is under the care of a physician. That left us with only Mr. Andrews, and we had some preparatory work to do before questioning him. Congressman Alden Broadhurst and I and our staffs worked together during the extended recess so we could move the proceedings along and hopefully end the evidentiary phase today. I apologize again and thank you for your understanding. Now, let me turn the proceedings over to Congressman Broadhurst."

What Thurston didn't tell anyone was that during the recess, the telephone lines, e-mail and fax machines of most of the House members had lit up with messages from irate constituents complaining about the interrogation of the President and Jane Cabot by House counsel. The callers were mainly women, but it was clear from the mail and from Internet polling that the American public decided that the interrogation by House Counsel had stepped over the line.

Broadhurst strode briskly to the microphones, nodded grimly to the media and whispered to his aide, "I've been waiting a long time to get even with that Jew bastard, Silver, and his arrogant Mick sidekick." The Clerk called for Tom Andrews and as Andrews approached the witness chair, Broadhurst finished straightening out his notes. Broadhurst quickly elicited from Andrews that he had at one time met with Lindsay Cabot's lawyer in Boston at the request of President Silver. Tom stated that at that meeting, he had inquired as to the possibility of Mrs. Cabot obtaining a divorce and that the meeting had not produced the result desired by the President. Tom then testified that there was a second meeting with Cabot's lawyers at the lawyer's request, and that it too did not produce the result desired by the President. Tom next confirmed that after the second meeting with the lawyer in Boston he did in fact travel to Worcester, but denied that he met with Kelly on the afternoon that Kelly claimed someone hired him to murder Lindsay Cabot. At that point, Broadhurst rose from his chair, looking shocked. Holding his wireless microphone, he walked over to where Tom was sitting and said, "You admit you were in Worcester on the day Kelly claims he was hired by someone acting in behalf of the President to kill Mr. Cabot."

"Right."

"Are you in Worcester frequently?"

"No."

"When was the last time you were in Worcester before the day on which Kelly says he met with someone who hired him to murder Mr. Cabot?"

"I don't know exactly."

"Would you say less than six months?"

"No, probably a little more."

"So you hadn't been to Worcester for more than six months, and you want us to believe that you just happened to be in Worcester on the date that someone hired Kelly to accomplish what the President wanted to accomplish by killing Lindsay Cabot?"

"That's the way it is."

"Now do I understand that you want us to believe that the person he met with on that very day when you were both in Worcester wasn't you? Would you have us believe that he met with some other person representing the President?"

"If I heard Mr. Kelly's testimony correctly, he never claimed that the person who hired him said he was acting in behalf of the President."

"You're quite right Mr. Andrews, he never did. I apologize. I forgot exactly what Kelly said, but I guess you didn't. I'd guess you'd never forget what Kelly said, would you, because you're the man that heard it." Broadhurst didn't wait for Tom to respond. He continued. "So, Mr. Andrews, you're saying that when you, excuse me, someone hired Kelly to kill Mr. Cabot, you, excuse me, that person that hired Kelly may not have been acting for President Silver or his mistress, Mrs. Cabot. You'd have us believe if you or whoever it was that hired Kelly was just acting as a Good Samaritan, doing a favor for the lovers so they could be together. Was that it?"

"No I'm not saying that. I'm saying I never spoke with Kelly and I know nothing about anyone hiring him to kill Mr. Cabot."

"Then tell me, sir. How did your pen happen to be found in Kelly's apartment in Worcester?"

"That's not my pen. We buy those pens in the thousands at the White House and they are often taken by people as souvenirs."

"Guests take them as souvenirs, you say. Interesting. So far as we know, Kelly has never been on any guest list at the White House. Are you saying the President invited Kelly to the White House without informing the Secret Service?"

"So far as I know, the President doesn't know Kelly and has never invited him to the White House."

"Perhaps the President doesn't know Kelly, but you're an old friend of his aren't you, Mr. Andrews?"

"No."

Broadhurst shouted, "You haven't known Mr. Kelly for many years?"

"I knew him many years ago."

"I apologize Mr. Andrews. Perhaps I selected the wrong tense. I'll rephrase my question. It seems to me if you were a friend of someone many years ago, that makes you an old friend, but I won't quibble. You once were a friend of Mr. Kelly? Is that better, Mr. Andrews?"

"No, I was never his friend."

"Fine. When you knew Mr. Kelly you were a police officer with the Worcester, Massachusetts police force, were you not?"

"Yes."

"And you arrested Kelly for breaking into the home of an elderly Worcester couple and assaulting them."

"Yes."

"During the course of that assault the husband suffered a broken rib and his wife a broken arm, and after assaulting them, Kelly robbed them of one hundred and eighty-seven dollars in cash, two watches, three rings and a television set." Tom nodded affirmatively. Broadhurst continued, "According to the record, you recommended two years probation, and Kelly never served a day in jail for that crime." Tom nodded in agreement. Broadhurst stepped back a pace. "Seems to me that's pretty friendly treatment, but as I said before, I don't want to quibble with you, so I'll ask you, isn't that a pretty lenient sentence for such a violent crime, Mr. Andrews, especially when it's a second offense?"

"Yes, but he was only nineteen at the time, and I don't think I knew it was a second offense."

"Now you said you weren't a friend of Kelly, right?"

"Yes."

"Yet, isn't true you spent a lot of time with Kelly after the crime? Isn't it true that you and he had coffee together once a week for about two months? Isn't that true, Mr. Andrews?"

"Yes, that is true."

"You must have been good friends, at least at that time?"

"No, it wasn't like that. We lived in the same parish and his parents and the parish priest asked me to spend a little time with him, hoping I could straighten him out. That's why I had met with him."

Broadhurst smiled at Tom. "You certainly seem to enjoy going around and being a Good Samaritan. You should be better rewarded for your good works. Well, Mr. Andrews, I have some good news and some bad news for you. The good news is that this proceeding is not concerned with deciding your guilt or innocence in the Lindsay Cabot murder. We are sitting here to examine the conduct of the President of the United States to determine whether these proceedings should be taken to the Senate of the United States for them to determine whether the President of the United States should be removed from office. The bad new is that when you leave here, you will be arrested for the murder of Lindsay Cabot and proceedings for extradition to Massachusetts will be immediately commenced, unless you want to waive that technicality." Broadhurst turned his back on Tom and then turned back and said. "You are dismissed."

Following the proceedings in the House, Tom Andrews made arrangements to appear in the Norfolk County Superior Court in Dedham, Massachusetts the next morning at nine A.M. He appeared as scheduled, was arraigned, released on bail and was back in Washington in time for an eight PM meeting in the Oval Office with Ben, Senator Bob Kendall, Molly Pemberton, Rahsheed Evans and John Wallace.

As Tom entered the anteroom to the Oval Office, Molly saw him, and ran over and kissed him. "Not here," Tom said pointing to Ben's administrative assistant.

"Martha knows we're living together, and so does everyone else."

Martha smiled, "Don't stop on my account."

Tom turned crimson to the roots of his white hair. "Still, they'll all be coming in any minute."

"Okay, but I'm so worried, Tom. I wasn't sure they'd let you come back. An attorney in the D.O. J. told me that they usually don't allow people to be released on bail in murder cases."

"Peter McGlynn represented me and managed to get it done."

"Did you see your folks at the court house?"

"No. I had my brother-in law pick me up outside. We drove out to Worcester for a short visit and then he drove me back to Logan."

"I thought your parents were going to meet you at the court house. Are they okay?"

"Fine, but, even though McGlynn told me not to worry about it, I didn't want them there, just in case the judge decided that I wasn't going to be released on bail. I didn't want them to see me being led away in handcuffs."

Molly nodded. "This is so crazy. I was afraid they'd keep you in jail and at the same time I was hoping the judge would dismiss it. The case against you is absurd. The judge should dismiss it."

Tom shook his head, "That's not the way the system works. Suspicion is enough at this stage and you have a politically ambitious District Attorney who can make some headlines by proceeding. There's no way they can ever get a conviction. All the time I was in Worcester on the day I was supposed to have met with Kelly, I was with someone. My brother-in-law picked me up at the airport, drove me to the meeting with Cabot's lawyer, waited for me and then drove me out to Worcester. We visited with the folks and then we all went to my sister's house where we had dinner. Then my folks drove me back to Logan where I caught the last shuttle to Washington. There's no way I could have met with Kelly. Who are people going to believe, me with my record and my family with theirs or Kelly, a convict with a criminal record as long as your arm? Broadhurst and Thurston know it. I'm not sure the Norfolk County District Attorney does, or if he does that he cares. It's not really about me, Molly. All Thurston wants is to get the President, and we can't let him do that."

Moments later, Rahsheed Evans and John Wallace entered the anteroom in front of the Oval Office, and a minute later Ben came in with Senator Kendall. After handshakes all around they entered Ben's office.

Ben started the meeting saying, "Sorry about the mess you're in Tom."

"I'm not really worried about it, Mr. President. We all understand what's behind it, and thanks for getting Peter McGlynn to represent me. It went just like he said it would."

"Peter is a good lawyer. He knows all the judges and they all know him and trust him. I felt sure you'd be released, but it must be tough on your folks. The press has you convicted and in jail."

"It's difficult for them because they know I couldn't have done what the media are saying I did, but let's not waste any time on that right now. After this, if it's okay with you Mr. President, I'll get together with Cam and we'll issue a statement to the press."

"Do that." Ben turned towards Senator Kendall. "What do you think the Senate's going to do if it gets the Impeachment from the House."

Kendall said, "Sorry, but that's when, not if. They got a majority in the House to vote to impeach when it comes up. The politicking and arm-twisting is all going on in the Senate right now."

Ben frowned. "What's the score?"

"Too close to call. With the case against Davies falling apart, he's a tough force to deal with. That son of a bitch in the FBI, Winters, is feeding him information about some of the Senators and if it's not them, maybe it's a son or daughter or some other relative. Winters has files on a lot of them and their families and Davies knows how to use it. Damn, but I wish there was some way to knock Davies out of the box again."

"So, the way it is now, if they remove me, it's going to be Thurston."

"That's the way it looks, and Davies is a lock for Vice President if that happens."

"We can't let that happen. We've talked about this before, but is there any chance that if I save them the trouble and agree to resign that we could get you or someone else that's acceptable instead of those two?"

"There's no change in that. Davies, Smithers and the rest won't let it happen. They want to see Thurston become President and I believe that after Davies becomes vice president, Thurston will resign."

"Why?" Ben said, "as bad as Thurston is, Davies is worse."

"I don't know, and it may not happen, but a source I respect thinks that's what Davies is planning."

Ben shook his head. "I don't know how fast things may happen in the Senate, Bob. Do you think I should acquaint Thurston and Davies with some critical information about the escalation in terrorist activity? The intelligence services have been reporting a dramatic increase in traffic over the last few weeks, and it's important that we be prepared for what could happen."

"What specifics do we have?"

"Not much. Only that various radical Islamic groups that have previously engaged in terrorist activities are talking to each other much more than usual."

"Is that S.O.B. Winters holding back information?"

"We can't be certain with him, but the people we trust in the FBI don't think so. The CIA thinks they're planning something and that what's going to happen is slated to take place mainly in the United States. The anniversary of September 11 is coming up so it could be planned for around then. I asked Secret Service Agent Rahsheed Evans to this meeting because he also thinks they're planning something terrible and I have a lot of respect for his hunches." Ben turned to Rahsheed, "Tell everyone what you believe may be going on and why."

"I think you all know I was brought up in the Muslim religion and that most members of my family and many of my friends are Muslims. All of us, with maybe one or two exceptions, are appalled at the terrible things being done in the name of Islam by small groups of fundamentalist Muslim fanatics. I don't have anything definite, but I've heard a few things that are disturbing. I believe a series of major events is being planned for probably the anniversary of the September eleven attack. My source doesn't know what's planned, but believes it will be centered in New York again, but not restricted to New York, and that it may be a variety of different kinds of things."

"How are you getting this information?" Ben asked.

"Very confidentially, my cousin is married to a man who used to be like the rest of us. We follow our faith, but we separate the religion from the rest of our life. After my cousin's husband returned from a pilgrimage to Mecca, he changed. He started to pray five times a day and insist that my cousin wear a headscarf whenever she goes out. He's convinced that the answer to all problems is to be found in strict adherence to the Koran as interpreted by certain Wahhabi clerics that I know believe in the Al Qaeda philosophy. He's been telling their children outrageous things, and my cousin is ready to divorce him, but I asked her to stick it out a little longer, and she agreed. He and his friends talk when they think she's asleep. One of them is a little hard of hearing and sometimes they talk loud enough that she can overhear them."

"You think we ought to bring them in and sweat them?" John Wallace asked.

"I thought about that, John. I think we're better off leaving them in place. My cousin is in no danger. She'll pretend to go along with them for a while and she'll be able to do better with them than we can. If I thought it could help us prevent whatever is being planned I'd say bring them in, but they probably don't have that knowledge right now. Frankly, maybe they never will. They're very small fish in that pond. What we need is our people on the inside with some of these fundamentalist clerics and inside the Al Qaeda organization. I'd do it if I thought I could pull it off, but they know where I stand on those issues. They hate me as much as they hate the Jews and the Crusaders." Rahsheed gestured at Senator Kendall, Tom Andrews and John Wallace. "That's what they call Christians, 'Crusaders'."

Ben shook his head, "Thanks Rahsheed. Continue with that for as long as you and your cousin feel comfortable with it. I've met with the CIA Director, the Secretary of Homeland Security and a Deputy in the FBI that we trust, and we hear similar things from all of them. They're supposed to have people on the inside and they don't know anything more than what your cousin told you."

"Give me five per cent of their budget and I'll turn some of those bearded fanatics in the mosques into capitalists and consumerists in love with all this country has to offer."

Ben smiled. "I believe you could." Ben turned to Senator Davies. "What do you think, Senator, should I brief Thurston and Davies on what we're hearing?"

"No. It'll tell the people fighting to keep you in office that you've quit on them and frankly, with the access they have to Winters and other people in the bureaucracy, anything you're hearing from the CIA, Homeland Security or the FBI, they can get if they want it. I would suggest, however, that you have a meeting with a bipartisan leadership group from the Senate and let them know what's going on. They ought to know and it'll help politically."

"Good, let Martha know who I should invite."

"Will do."

"Okay, it's not much but we have to try and do whatever we can to prevent what looks like multiple disasters looming on the horizon, and on that cheery note, I guess we'll have to end this meeting." As everyone started to leave, Ben said, "John, Molly, Rahsheed, I'd like to talk to the three of you about an idea I just got and might want to send one of you to Montgomery. There's a few calls I've got to make right now, so could you come back in about a half hour?"

"Of course, Mr. President."

CHAPTER 23

▼————————

When Martha ushered Molly, John and Rahsheed back into the Oval Office, Ben motioned them into the armchairs in front of the sofa as he concluded his telephone conversation with the British Prime Minister. Moments later, Martha returned and placed a pot of coffee and cups and saucers on the coffee table between the armchairs and the sofa as Ben ended his phone call. Ben sat staring at the phone for a minute, then sighed, walked over, sat on the sofa and said, "As you know, when the Impeachment case gets to the Senate it's going to be very close. Davies' vote alone could be crucial and Senator Kendall is convinced that he's the one putting the pressure on the other Senators. If we can immobilize him, we can improve our chances. I had an idea about how we may be able to do that and I want to go over it with the three of you."

Ben poured himself a cup of coffee while telling Molly, John and Rahsheed to help themselves. "It's decaf, I can't drink regular after five o'clock if I want to get any sleep." Ben continued, "What brought Davies back from the brink was that decision in Alabama by Judge Badderley."

"I'm not sure I understand how that works," Molly said.

Badderley decided that the consent implied from Morton's making of the tapes of his conversations with Davies and Washburn didn't apply to their use in proceedings that he's not involved in, and that being dead, he can no longer consent. There's a bit of a stink surrounding that decision, but it's still the law of the land and has to be followed in all other jurisdictions under the Full Faith and Credit Clause of the United States Constitution until it gets reversed on appeal, and the appeals court judges in Alabama don't seem to be in any rush to reverse it."

"Even when the decision is so stupid?" Molly said.

"There's no exception for stupid decisions, but there may be a way around it. I want to find out who the executor or administrator of Bill Morton's estate is. If that person, acting as Morton's representative consents and we get the case before the right judge, we can get a decision that the consent by the estate is consent to the use of the tapes in all proceedings, including the case against Davies."

"Great idea," John said. "Do you think that would let us use the tape of Morton's conversation with Washburn where they talked about causing civil unrest and importing drugs?"

"They said the rules of evidence wouldn't apply so maybe we can. Do we know who's the executor or administrator of Morton's Estate?"

Rahsheed said, "Mrs. Morton was appointed administratrix of the Estate. He died intestate and his divorce wasn't final so his wife got herself appointed. I heard that there's a lot of litigation down there with local people making claims against the Estate."

"Did you have the same idea I had?" Ben asked.

"No sir. I have family down there and a nephew of mine is one of the claimants. The Morton murder and gossip about the money Morton had accumulated is still the big news down there."

"That's interesting," Ben said. "Find out what's going on in Montgomery, all the gossip, and then let's discuss it again at nine o'clock tomorrow morning. It's supposed to be a nice day so let's all meet in the Rose Garden."

The next morning, Molly, John and Rahsheed were seated under the umbrella table in the Rose Garden when Ben joined them shortly after nine AM. Rahsheed said, "Mrs. Morton's none too popular in Montgomery. The Morton family was once quite prominent in the community and those people always considered Mrs. Morton and her people 'white trash'. She had an affair with a black man and that's just not done down there. Some of the white folks down there blame her affair for causing Bill Morton to do all the terrible things he did. The black community doesn't like her either because of all the trouble she caused. Because of that, there's a lot of local talk about finding a way to prevent her from receiving his government pension benefits that she says she's entitled to as his surviving spouse and the money that he accumulated for dealing drugs. I hear she's plenty worried about it. There's also a lot of talk around the community that Judge Badderley is dirty and had a private meeting somewhere with Senator Davies before deciding that case the way he did."

"There's not enough time to do anything about Badderley right now." Ben frowned and turned to Molly. "Molly, call Mrs. Morton. Tell her what we want and that we'll help her get that government pension and the cash in the bank if she cooperates with us. Do that this morning and call me after you speak to her."

Molly called Ben's office at two o'clock. When she called, Ben was meeting with his National Security advisor and the heads of the Intelligence Services. Martha told Molly that Ben wanted to meet her at three o'clock in the Rose Garden. Ben was a half-hour late for the meeting and looked even more worried than usual when he arrived. He apologized to Molly for being late and asked her what Mrs. Morton had said. Molly said, "It went the way we expected. She's worried that the local's will find a way to take the cash in the bank, the pension benefits and the house and leave her with nothing. She'll consent in behalf of Morton's Estate so we can use the tapes against Davies."

"That's good news." Ben picked up the phone and said to Martha, "Get Lydia Green for me." Moments later Ben said, "Lyd, Molly Pemberton will be down to see you in a few minutes and tell you what we need. Draw the necessary documents as quickly as you can. I'd like Molly to talk with Mrs. Morton tonight and maybe meet with her tomorrow to get it signed. Great and thanks." Ben turned back to Molly. "You know Chief White House Counsel Lydia Green, don't you?"

"We've been introduced."

"Good. She's terrific and will get it done. Tell her the whole story and tell her to call me if she has any questions you can't answer." Ben sat back and smiled for the first time that day. "This could turn out to be very important, Molly so let me know immediately if you have any problems."

At seven o'clock that evening, Molly called Ben and advised him that she had gone over the agreement with Mrs. Morton and that she was making arrangements to fly down to Montgomery the next morning to meet with Mrs. Morton and get it signed. Ben thanked Molly, called Lydia and thanked her for getting the agreement done expeditiously, and then called Jane to give her the good news. Ben was sipping a lonely after dinner glass of shiraz wine in the Residence dining room to celebrate what he hoped would change the bleak looking future that many expected when Molly called for the second time that evening.

"I'm so sorry, Mr. President," she said. "I called Mrs. Morton to confirm our meeting for tomorrow. She told me we'd have to up the payment to her if we want to get that consent."

"To what?"

"Ten million."

"What happened?"

"She called Senator Davies and told him about our deal. He told her all the judges were friends of his and he could fix things with them so all those claims and law suits would be dismissed."

"Damn," Ben said.

"Got any idea about what we can do now?"

"Not at the moment."

Ben poured his wine down the drain and then sat in the living room and called Jane. "Sorry to call so late." Ben told Jane what Davies had done. "Damn it, Jane. I thought we finally managed to put a muzzle on that bastard, but Davies always seems to find a way to avoid trouble. He's like a cat with nine lives. No matter what I do, he continues destroying me. Times like this I begin to wonder if it's really worth it.

"I don't like hearing you talk that way, Ben. You've never been a quitter, so don't start now."

"You're right, Jane. I just hope I haven't run out of miracles. I can't think of anything worse for all of us than putting the country in the hands of Elliott Thurston and Jeb Davies. I had a meeting with the heads of the Intelligence Services today and one of the things I learned is that Davies and Thurston are talking about adopting a new appeasement philosophy in dealing with terrorist states. They'll sell out the Brits, the Spaniards the people we support in Afghanistan and Iraq and the Israelis."

"They can't be serious."

"But they are. Short term, oil will be dirt cheap and cheap energy will bring a degree of increased prosperity. While the Islamic fundamentalists reestablish their rule in Afghanistan, make Iraq into another Islamic state like Afghanistan and then do the same with Saudi Arabia, the world will settle down. But it'll be like the calm before the storm. After that, the religious fanatics will destroy the secular governments in Egypt and Turkey and look to expand into other regions while increasing terrorism attacks on the West. Their goal is to establish a fundamentalist Islamic dictatorship throughout the Middle East, Europe, Asia, Africa and wherever there are any Muslims. Davies and Thurston are playing a very dangerous game. The French, and the Russians and Germans have been playing that same game. They're scared to death of the sizable Muslim communities in their countries and are taking economic advantage out of playing along with the terrorist organizations. They can play the appeasement card because they know the United States will do what must be done, but if we're going to sit on the sidelines, there's no one to stop those fanatics. The Brits can't do it alone."

After a moment of silence, Jane said, "I don't know what to say, Ben. I just hope and pray you'll find a way to stop them."

"Me too. Some of the military people want me to pick a region and nuke it."

"They can't be serious."

"But they are. They point out that it worked to end World War II and say it will end this one."

"You wouldn't do that, would you?"

"Another major attack on the us and it may be what a majority will want."

"But you wouldn't do it?"

"I hope I never have to seriously consider it, but it's the job of the President to protect the people of the United States." Ben sighed. "This is a lousy job. I wish you could be here with me. It's pretty lonely rattling around here by myself."

"You know that's inadvisable while the impeachment is pending."

"I know, but I don't like it much."

"Me neither. Good night, Ben, perhaps things will look brighter tomorrow."

"Hope so. We'll talk tomorrow. Good night."

CHAPTER 24

▼

As soon as the small door in the confessional slid open, the white haired woman said, "Forgive me, Father, for I have sinned. It's been four days since my last confession and I need…I need…I. need…Oh God, I don't know what I need. You must help me, Father."

Father Jim looked through the mesh curtain separating him from the penitent on the other side of the confessional. "What is it you need, Mrs. Kelly? What brings you here so troubled and so soon after your last confession?"

"I am sorely troubled, Father. I don't know what to do. I lied to that nice Mrs. Andrews."

"Lying is a sin, Mrs. Kelly, but perhaps it's not so terrible a sin as you think. Why don't you tell me about it?"

"It's what I lied about, Father. You remember that Mrs. Andrews? She's the mother of that nice boy, Thomas who used to be on the Worcester police force. He's the one we asked to help Red that time."

"Tom Andrews, yes. I remember."

"He's all grown up now and works for the President of the United States."

"I know."

"Three days ago Red said he had been hired to kill that poor Mr. Cabot that's married to the President's girl friend and that he met with someone who hired him to do the killing in Worcester on the day that Mr. Andrews was in Worcester. Everyone says the man that hired Red was Mr. Andrews."

"Yes, I'm aware of that."

"Mrs. Andrews was waiting outside my house to talk with me this morning. She phoned me last night but I wouldn't talk to her. She stopped me and said her

Tommy couldn't have met with Red that day because Tommy was in Worcester visiting with her and her husband when he was supposed to be meeting with Red. She asked me if I knew anything that could help her son."

"Yes. Please continue."

Mrs. Kelly sobbed. "I lied to her. I told her I couldn't help her. Her Tommy is the President's chief helper now. Being so powerful like he is, nothing bad could happen to him, could it, Father?"

"Powerful or not, Red's testimony could get him convicted of murder and the President impeached. Margaret, if you know something that would help Mr. Andrews, you should tell the authorities. Do you want to tell me about it?"

"Yes, Father, but it can go no further."

"You know that I can't reveal anything you tell me in the confessional."

"Yes, I know that."

"Go on."

"Red had ended a two week bender just before the day Mr. Andrews came to Worcester. He was asleep at my house the entire day he was supposed to have met with someone and been hired to kill that Mr. Cabot."

"Are you saying he didn't kill Mr. Cabot?"

"He had no reason to."

"But Red confessed that he did."

"I know, but he didn't."

"Okay, so whether Red did or didn't kill Mr. Cabot, if Mr. Andrews didn't meet with Red, go to the authorities and tell them." Father Jim shook his head. "Sorry, Margaret, but I don't understand. Why did you think you had to lie to Mrs. Andrews."

"You don't understand, Father. I spoke to Red. He didn't do it, but the FBI said he did."

"Then why did he confess."

"Red said the FBI offered him too good a deal to turn down, and that's why he confessed."

"I still don't understand. Why don't you go to the authorities and clear Tom Andrews?"

"Red said that if I did, the deal he made with the FBI would be cancelled and he'd be in worse trouble than he is now."

"The trouble he has is of his own making, Margaret. He should take responsibility for his own actions, but if he refuses, you have to do the right thing. You cannot allow Tom Andrews to be tried for murder and the President to be impeached when you know something that might prevent those terrible things from happening."

I'm sorry, Father. Red told me that if his arrangement with the FBI falls through, he could get a life sentence or even worse."

"That's too bad, Margaret, but you have to go to the authorities."

"I can't do that, Father. He's my son. He may be no good, but he is my son." Mrs. Kelly wept softly behind the screen. "What am I to do?"

"You know what you should do."

"I can't do that. Will you grant me absolution, Father?"

"For lying to Mrs. Andrews, yes. For possibly causing the imprisonment of Tom Andrews and the impeachment of the President, I don't know. I will pray that some way is found to clear Mr. Andrews and prevent the impeachment of the President that doesn't require that you reveal what you know to the authorities."

Mrs. Kelly said, "Thank you, Father." She rose from the kneeler and left the confessional.

Father Jim remained seated behind the screen feeling immobilized by the weight of the secret she had told him. He took off his wire-rimmed glasses and pinched the area between his eyes. Mrs. Kelly didn't know it, but Father Jim had met the President when Ben had taught at the Boston College Law School. Father Jim was the parish priest at St. Ignatius and he had audited Ben's courses on Constitutional Law and Legal Ethics. They had become friends and often dined and played golf together. He remembered grieving with Ben when Ben's first wife died and being happy with him when Ben told him about Jane coming into his life. He had dinner with Ben and Jane a month before Ben became President. At that moment, Father Jim hated the rules of the Catholic Church, but they were his life and he had to follow them. Finally, Father Jim left the Confessional. He prayed long and hard for guidance. None was immediately forthcoming.

CHAPTER 25

▼

Weeks had passed since Clarence last saw Rabbani. He had quickly finished the computations required to determine the amount of explosives required and their positioning for all the Al Qaeda selected targets and then spent endless hours training cadres of fanatics to make their way around in the United States. Dealing with the foot soldiers of the terrorist force was very different than discussing philosophy and geo-politics with the upper echelon camp leaders. At times Clarence wondered whether he was doing the right thing, but the time for wondering had long since passed. For better or for worse, when he caused the explosion at the inauguration that killed President Butler and all legal successors to the presidency except Ben Silver, he had taken an irreversible step. Damn Ben Silver. His plan to force a re-examination of the founding principles of American government would have worked, despite what Rabbani says, if Silver had gone to the inauguration like he was supposed to have done. That was a cause worth dying for. This one wasn't, but his only choice now was to see this through.

Reports had come through that some operatives he trained had already arrived in the United States, been welcomed by members of existing Al Qaeda cells and helped to rent apartments in Brooklyn, Chicago, Oklahoma City, Phoenix, Las Vegas, Los Angeles and San Francisco. They in turn were meeting additional trained operatives who had graduated from the New Salman Pak training school as they arrived. They were all being readied to play their part in the planned attacks on the United States.

Some of the chemists and biologists Clarence trained were busy compounding poisons and toxic chemicals like ricin, VF and Sarin while others brewed quantities of smallpox virus and busied themselves in their bomb factories. Technicians rented trucks and automobiles and modified them into rolling bombs, carefully installing the bombs made by their associates in the rented vehicles. Other technical experts were studying photographs and all the construction documents they could find to determine the best places on the targeted tunnels, bridges and electric power grid facilities for the explosions that would maximize the deaths and destruction. Clarence's routine was occasionally interrupted with questions about the proposed demolition of the selected targets as he was recognized as the most knowledgeable demolition expert in the entire camp. No one suspected that his expertise was obtained through U.S. Army training during the 1991 Gulf War. Despite being so busy, he was becoming bored. While Clarence had always been a loner, he couldn't help but be impressed by the comradeship he found among his students. For the moment, at least, Sunni, Shiite, Wahhabi, all shades of Islamic fanaticism seemed to come together for the purpose of attacking the United States. All his students had willingly dedicated their lives to that single cause and he was impressed. He tried befriending some of his students, but found that their views of the United States, and of life in general were so warped by their education in the religious schools they had all attended, that it was impossible to establish any kind of relationship with them. Clarence spent his nights in solitary isolation. He also found that some of the Iraqis were becoming jealous of the respect his expertise had gained for him at their expense and that some of the Saudis were jealous of his growing relationship with Almihidi. Clarence's tent was sumptuous compared to most of the other tents in the training center, but despite the expensive and colorful Persian rugs, it was a dusty place to live, periodically invaded by all kinds of flying and crawling insects. He often thought he'd pay a thousand dollars for a can of Raid.

Clarence had never minded being alone when he was growing up. When he had been a young Second Lieutenant during the Gulf War, he had stayed somewhat apart from the men under his command and that felt right. They had respected him and included him in their conversations by asking him questions or asking him to settle an argument. That also felt right. This was different. These men respected him for what he could teach them, but they were not interested in talking to him about anything other than their hatred for the United States and how he could help them succeed in their assignment of bringing death and destruction to its citizens.

The group he was training now was the lowest level of suicide personnel. Some were destined to be injected with small pox and become walking germ factories until they were no longer able to move around from one crowded venue to another. Others would open canisters of nerve gas and other toxic substances in subways, trains, churches, and at sporting events, anyplace that was a tightly closed facility. That they too would be killed or made ill was of no significance, even to them. He had to include rudimentary elements of personal hygiene in many of his classes and introduce tooth brushing and the use of under arm deodorants to most of them so they could pass unnoticed. This particular group was particularly odoriferous, and Clarence arranged to teach his class standing upwind of them

The camp was wearing thin on Clarence and he was impatiently awaiting Rabbani's next visit, scheduled for this evening. Clarence was finding it difficult to wait, but at last he saw his uncle's familiar face. Clarence said, "It's good to see you, uncle. It's been a long time."

"I know, but I had to have a little surgery and went to the United States for it."

"I didn't know. Was it something serious?"

"It could have been, but, fortunately, it wasn't. You know I'd been having prostate trouble. I thought it might have been cancerous, but it wasn't, just enlarged. It's been taken care of and I feel wonderful again."

"I'm glad to hear it."

"Thank you. I understand you've been doing a terrific job here. I've seen reports from some of the people you trained. They all say you prepared them well for what they encountered when they arrived at their destination."

"Good, but when can I end this phase. Life here is primitive."

"Another week, two at most and then you can come back to London. I would send Fatima to keep you company at night, but I need her in London right now." Rabbani smiled. "I could send someone else if you need a bed companion."

"Thanks, but I'm just anxious to get out of here and back to civilization."

Rabbani smiled. "I understand. This life is not to my taste either. It'll be London for you. The Americans think you're dead, so no ones looking for you anymore."

For a moment, Clarence thought about telling Rabbani about the e-mail letters he was receiving from Molly Pemberton. She, at least, wasn't so sure he was dead, but he decided not to mention it. Instead, he said, "With the way I look now, they wouldn't recognize me if they were looking for me and I was standing in front of them."

"That was the idea, but don't press it too much. There's something else I'd like your expert opinion on. Some of the Al Qaeda and Iraqis put your plan to kill Silver in the Rose Garden on hold because they would like the killing of the President to coincide with the plan to destroy the tunnels and bridges to Manhattan and the electric power grid. They've been considering other alternatives but need to be satisfied that they will assure Silver's death if they postpone the model airplane attack until then. They promised to make a decision today."

Clarence scratched his head a moment. "These sand fleas are driving me nuts." He frowned. "Frankly, I don't see how that's possible. There's no set time that Silver is in the Rose Garden."

"Perhaps not, but what of the plans do kill him in some other place. They mentioned a bomb right outside his bedroom or perhaps the Oval Office. He's in that office every day. Couldn't the model plane just as easily fly there."

Clarence leaned back in his armchair. "I've considered all those possibilities." Clarence picked up a file on his worktable. "The computations are in here. It doesn't work. The amount of explosives required would have to be substantially increased." He shook his head. "The model plane would have to be so large that I'm sure it would be noticed and destroyed before it could do the job, and multiple planes present the same and additional problems."

Rabbani started pulling papers and documents out of his briefcase. "I'm going to give you a file of the computations of some engineering groups. You're probably right, but double-check them. After you do that, look at these copies of the surveillance tapes from Akmed and Yusif. We had them fly other models at a higher altitude and further away, but with better resolution and close enough to see the Rose Garden every day. Al Qaeda was hoping they'd find some daily pattern to Silver's appearances in the Rose Garden. They didn't find any, but they want you to take a look." Rabbani looked at his wristwatch, "I've got to meet with the camp leaders now. We'll talk later."

Clarence sat down and studied the engineering and demolition information. The math was right. It was possible to build five model planes large enough to carry the large amount of explosives indicated, but the White House was not built like a normal "sticks and bricks" residence. The demolition engineer who thought that the five planes simultaneously exploded would be sufficient was probably wrong and the one that said it would probably fail was, in Clarence's opinion, probably right. Besides, they had to change to gasoline powered motors to carry the required amount of explosives. And how do you simultaneously maneuver five planes to the correct position outside the bedroom window without their colliding? And what about the noise from five planes? That might draw too much attention. The Rose Garden with one battery powered model plane flying in close from out of the sun was the only way to go. Clarence started to review the surveillance tapes Akmed and Yusif provided. Rabbani was right. There was no pattern to Ben Silver's use of the Rose Garden. The only pattern

Clarence could see was that on almost every occasion that Ben was in the Rose Garden, Molly Pemberton sat next to him. Clarence stopped the tape and studied Molly's picture. He looked at more of the tapes. There she was again, showing a little leg in that shot, and then tugging her skirt down. He lingered over the portions she was in and decided he'd make copies of some of the better pictures that she was in before returning the tapes to Rabbani. He especially liked the picture where she was standing besides the President and leaning forward, pointing to some document on the table. It must have been warm and he could see the slight rise of her breasts through the gauzy v-neck blouse she was wearing. He stared at the picture and then decided to copy that picture and edit the President out of it.

That evening, Rabbani called on Clarence. He said, "They have tentatively modified your plan and want to kill him in his bedroom using five planes. What do you think? Is attacking Silver's bedroom a good way to kill him?"

Clarence thought about lying but couldn't. "I disagree. The White House structure is too strong, and I think there would be so much noise from the motors that it's likely that some of the five planes would be intercepted. I doubt that all five exploded together would have enough fire power to accomplish the result and if any one of them didn't make it, then for sure it wouldn't work. No one mentioned it, but to concentrate the attack the way they indicate would require flying all five planes in close formation. One little miscalculation by one of the people flying anyone of them could cause a collision where one crashes into another and that would destroy the whole plan. I don't know that much about flying those model planes, but I doubt they can be operated precisely enough to cover that risk."

"One more thing. One of the Iraqi engineers took your computation of the amount of explosives required to be put in the model plane. He says you miscalculated the distance using your own formula and that this is the right distance. That's why they postponed the attack the first time." Rabbani pulled a sheet of paper full of mathematical computations from his pocket and handed it to Clarence. "He says it's not a big mistake, but he says you're not so smart as they think you are and he has Almihidi's ear right now. Look it over and let me know."

Clarence handed the paper back to Rabbani. "I already did."

"Did you make a mistake?"

"No. My computation was in feet. He used meters. Convert them properly and they are the same."

Rabbani rose from the rug he had been sitting on. "I'll make sure Almihidi knows. It would be nice to have the dramatic effect and the additional chaos from those attacks happening at the same time, but we'll see. I'll be back."

When Rabbani returned, he was all smiles. "They agree you're right. They didn't consider the difficulty of flying the models the way they would have to. When they did, they decided the risk of failure was too great. But, I have some good news. Al Qaeda leadership have decided that since they don't trust the computation that says they can change your plan, they have reinstated your original plan." Rabbani stared at Clarence. "What's the matter? I thought you'd be pleased."

"I am. I'm very pleased. You know how much I want to get Silver. It's just that I'm surprised. I had reconciled myself to the thought that the model airplane idea wasn't going to happen and I'm curious. Was the Iraqi who criticized my computations there?"

"Yes."

"What did he say when his error was pointed out to him?"

"We'll never know. Almihidi cut his throat."

Clarence shrugged. "I'll have to remember not to make any mistakes."

"For picking up that flaw in the plan, your stature in our group has again sky-rocketed. You will play an important role when we take over, but now, I must be off so I'll say goodbye. See you in a week, maybe two, in London."

When Rabbani left, Clarence felt like he should be pleased, but he wasn't. Why should he care if Molly were killed by a bomb in the Rose Garden? He had killed plenty of other people. Of course he didn't really know any of the people he killed, except for the Swansons. Killing them bothered him too, but he had to do it, and they were old and he got over it. Molly was young and pretty, and then, she was glad that he hadn't killed himself. Damn, why is this still bothering me. Clarence decided that he would have to get over feeling responsible for Molly's death when that happened, but he wasn't feeling good about it. He decided that in the morning, he'd look at those pictures of her again. Perhaps he'd see something about her he didn't like. If he did, then killing her wouldn't bother him. He sneaked another look at a still of one of the pictures he had copied. But what if it still bothered him. Could he live with that? He'd have to decide, maybe tomorrow.

The next morning, Clarence looked at the photographs of Molly again. He edited Ben out of more of the ones he liked, printed his favorite on photographic paper and put it in his wallet. He then opened the file with the e-mail letters she sent him. He hadn't answered any of them, but looked forward to receiving them. It had been a week since the last one so the next one should be arriving in two or three days. He read the letters again, added the photographs to the file and saved them on a disc he could take with him when the time came to leave the camp. Damn. He decided that it would be very difficult if not impossible to be responsible for Molly's death, but there was nothing he could do about it, or was there?

CHAPTER 26

▼

"I will now sum up the case for the Impeachment of President Benjamin Silver. The first Article states that President Benjamin Silver is an accessory to the murder of Lindsay Cabot, the then husband of the President's mistress. You may decide, as I have, that the first charge is proved beyond a reasonable doubt although there is no need that we do so. In considering murder cases in our criminal courts, the factors generally considered are means, motive and opportunity. We have suggested that the actual perpetrator of this crime is President Silver's chief of staff, Tom Andrews. He has been indicted for that crime so there is obviously probable cause to believe that he did in fact shoot Lindsay Cabot in the head thereby causing his death. Let us independently consider with relation to Mr. Andrews, means, motive and opportunity. The weapon used to murder Mr. Cabot has not been recovered, but as a former Secret Service Agent, Mr. Andrews had access to weapons of all kinds. We have placed before you his service record indicating his proficiency and accuracy with all types of firearms, including the very type used in the commission of this murder. There can be no doubt that Tom Andrews had access to a murder weapon of the type used and therefore had the means to commit this murder. As Tom Andrews had the means to commit the murder, so did the President, because Andrews was President Silver's means to accomplish the result he wanted. Accordingly, we have demonstrated that Tom Andrews and President Silver had the means to commit this murder."

Thurston took a sip from a glass on his desk before continuing. "Let us now consider motive. Tom Andrews didn't know Lindsay Cabot. He had nothing against him personally. Why should he kill Cabot? Before Benjamin Silver became President of the United States, Tom Andrews was the Secret Service

Agent in charge of protecting President Butler from assassination. We all know how badly he failed in that assignment. He should have been fired and removed from the Federal payroll. Instead, President Silver rewarded that failure by making Andrews his Chief of Staff. It should be expected that Andrews would feel a debt of gratitude to the person who removed him from the trash heap of Federal service to which he should have been relegated and instead rewarded him with a far more powerful role. From bodyguard to chief presidential advisor, a strong motive to do a favor for the man who did so much for him."

Thurston took another sip from his cup. "We all know of the President's relationship with Mrs. Cabot. They wanted to be together. She wanted to divorce her husband of twenty-seven years and marry President Silver. We know that because President Silver has said so and so has she. You have seen the evidence we put before you showing that President Silver asked his good friend and confidant to arrange a divorce for Mrs. Cabot from her husband and that he visited with Mr. Cabot's lawyer and was turned down. We know he went there a second time for the same purpose, and was again turned down. Do you think he wanted to return to Washington and admit failure to the man who saved his political life? I think not. Since he couldn't arrange the divorce, the only alternative he had was to arrange for the murder of the man that stood in the way and was preventing President Silver from being with the woman he wanted. This sordid motive is among the most common motives for murder that there is. I conclude that Tom Andrews and, more importantly, President Silver had a strong motive for the murder of Lindsay Cabot. We do not believe that Mr. Andrews would have arranged this murder without the President's approval, and if you believe that like I do, you must vote to Impeach the President."

Thurston glanced at his watch again. "Sorry to be taking so long, but this responsibility is among the most awesome that there can be and I, like you feel the responsibility that goes with it. The final piece we must consider is opportunity. Beyond any doubt, Tom Andrews knew the confessed shooter that killed Lindsay Cabot for many years. Beyond doubt, Andrews was in Worcester when the confessed killer said he met with someone meeting Andrews' description and was hired to do the murder, and we all know about the pen with the presidential seal on it that the killer had. You can believe in coincidence if you like. I do not. I conclude that Andrews had the opportunity to hire the killer and that he did so. You can believe that Tom Andrews hired Mr. Cabot's assassin without the knowledge of the President, and that when he came back to Washington to report that he had failed to arrange for Mrs. Cabot's divorce, he said nothing to President Silver about solving the problem by arranging for Mr. Cabot's murder.

I do not. I believe the President engaged in a criminal conspiracy with Tom Andrews and through him with Red Kelly. That conspiracy resulted in the commission of the high crime of murder and the President is an accessory to that murder." I will now yield to Congressman Broadhurst who will present Article Two.

Broadhurst a heavyset, baldheaded man with a perpetually flushed face, heaved himself to his feet. "Thank you, Mr. Speaker. It's no secret that I don't like Ben Silver very much, but it was never personal. It was that he didn't understand the way this government works. Some of you may not like the way it works, but if you want to get anything accomplished, you better know how to go about it. I believe Speaker Thurston has made out all the case that's necessary to move this case to the Senate. However, there may be some members of that august body who feel that the high crimes and misdemeanors necessary for removal from office should pertain to the official functions of the President and that his involvement in the murder was personal and not governmental. As you may recall, that argument was made during the impeachment of William Jefferson Clinton. In the event some of you or some members of the Senate feel that way, it is my intention to put before you additional facts concerning his official activities. I regard the failure to comply with the clear mandates of the Constitution and the duly passed laws of these United States to be an impeachable offense. We are supposed to have a vice-president and a cabinet, we have neither. We have vacancies on the Supreme Court and in many other Federal Courts. This President has been unable to fill them. It's as I said, he can't get anything done because he doesn't know how. Some of you may think that's not an impeachable offense. Bear in mind, he was never elected and we have no other way to rid ourselves of this accidental president. If you don't like that, I implore you to look at Article Three. Beyond doubt, Benjamin Silver was having illicit sexual relations with a married woman in the White House. Where I come from that's a serious crime and I bet it is where you come from too. If any of us did that and flaunted our actions in the face of the American people like he does, you know damn well the voters would remove us from office at their earliest opportunity. That's what they want us and the Senate to do. If we don't, then maybe we deserve to be removed from office ourselves. Thank you for your time and attention." Broadhurst lowered himself into his seat, mopped the sweat from his head and said to Congressman Lionel Dover, forgetting his microphone was still on, "I told you someday I'd get even with that bastard for turning me down on those fundraising appearances."

Thurston hurriedly reclaimed the microphone lead. "Thank you Congress-man Broadhurst. I recognize that emotions run high in these proceedings, so I'm sure you didn't mean that last remark, and I'll see that it's stricken from the record of these proceedings."

"Thank you Mr. Speaker. You are of course quite right." Broadhurst nodded and smiled at the TV camera that had panned back towards him.

Addressing the television cameras, Thurston said, "We will end the presenta-tion of charges and the television coverage of these proceedings at this time. I see by my watch that we are approaching the noon hour and accordingly, we will recess at this point. When we resume this afternoon, the House members who want to be heard in opposition to this Impeachment will have an opportunity to express their views. Once that is finished, we will recess to deliberate the charges." Thurston didn't say it, but the main purpose of the recess would be to try and force Ben to resign.

Like almost everyone in the country, Ben had watched almost every minute of the televised Impeachment proceedings. It was potentially history in the making. The press was predicting while he would not be the first President to be impeached in the House, it was likely that Ben Silver would be the first President to be removed from office by the Senate unless he resigned first the way Richard Nixon did. Ben interrupted his TV watching only to accept phone calls from the Israeli Prime Minister and the Prime Minister of the UK. Both called to wish him good luck. Watching with him was Senator Bob Kendall who sat quietly shaking his head. At the conclusion of the televised portion of the hearing, Ben said, "They know they have the votes in the House without the nonsense that Broad-hurst brought up. Why are they pushing that crap?"

"There are a few odd ball Rep's that may be opposed to the main Article on Cabot that will buy into the other. They have the required majority without it, but they want to deliver a message to the Senate by getting more than two thirds of the House."

"What do you think the House vote will be?"

"They'll either have the two thirds by two or three votes or be short by about that number. It may matter to the press, but it won't matter in the Senate."

"What's you latest count there?"

"The same as it was, too close to call."

Ben grimaced and shook his head. "Sometimes I think I should just resign. There are so many important things we have to do that we can't do while we're distracted by this circus. You know the CIA and our other sources have been reporting increasing activity from suspected terrorist organizations they've been tracking and I'm becoming nervous that Al Qaeda and its allies will see this as an opportunity to try something colossal. The FBI is at best a very poor source of information on domestic activities and with what's going on now, if Winters could prevent it, they wouldn't tell me even if they had important information."

"Let's not worry about things we can't do anything about. What we got to do is find a way to derail Senator Davies. How did you make out with Mrs. Morton? She okay your using the tapes?"

Ben shook his head. "She agreed when Molly called, but after that she called Davies and reneged."

"Damn. That could cook your goose. Just before coming over here I heard that Davies was now saying that the reason the judge found the Morton tape inadmissible was because it wasn't genuine and the judge knew it even though some forensics people said it was." Kendall frowned. "That's too bad. I was counting on neutralizing Davies. The SOB still has the ability to twist a few arms so he could give them the two or three votes they need to get to the two thirds." Kendall shrugged, "Anyway about that judge's decision? I really don't understand it. Make any sense to you?"

"Not really. It seems to most lawyers that since Morton made the tape, he had to have consented to it, and that's usually enough. They expect the decision to be reversed on appeal, but the Alabama courts have refused to expedite the appeal process, and until it's reversed, the decision stands as the law of the land and we're stymied."

"In the meantime, the impeachment proceeds at its own pace."

Ben nodded his head affirmatively. "Right."

"And you're telling me that all other judges have to pay attention to that lousy decision."

"Well, they're supposed to."

"No matter what else is going on?"

"Yes, unless some factual change occurs."

"Like what?"

"With Morton dead and his wife bought by Davies, it's hard to see what factual change could occur."

Kendall nodded. "I see what you mean. I guess there's no way around it. We're about through for now anyway, so I'll get out of your way. I hope something happens to derail that bastard and soon." Senator Kendall rose from his seat, and started to walk towards the door, he paused and said, "Let's pray for a miracle and it better be a quick one. I'll try to stall things and they'll try to persuade you to resign, but there's only so much I can do."

"How long before the appeal gets heard?"

Ben shook his head. "I don't know exactly, but it could take months."

"I can't stall things that long." Kendall stood in the doorway a moment. Let's hope something good happens."

"Let me know if you get any brilliant ideas," Ben said.

CHAPTER 27

▼

It was another warm summer day in Washington. Ben had been sitting outside in the Rose Garden for about five minutes reviewing a series of satellite photographs while waiting for Molly Pemberton.

Molly walked towards Ben. She was out of breath. "Sorry to be late, Mr. President."

"Nonsense. You couldn't have got here any faster if you had wheels." Ben pointed at the pile of photographs he had been studying. "I didn't want the intelligence people I met with to know that I wanted you to look at some of these so I had to wait until they left to call you."

"What are they?"

"They're satellite surveillance photographs of what some of us think could be a terrorist training camp. We named it New Salman Pak after the one that used to be in Iraq." Ben handed Molly a photograph. "Look at the man with the bandaged face sitting outside in an armchair."

Molly looked at it. She gasped and then stared at the photograph. "Good lord. That chair looks like the chair Davenport was sitting in when we went to his house and tried to arrest him." She looked at it again and nodded. "Yes it looks a lot like it."

Ben handed her another photograph. "This is one of the chair that's been enhanced. Take a look."

Molly examined the picture. "A flowered fabric, very similar to the fabric on Davenport's chair." She looked up at Ben. "I bet that's him. Maybe he had plastic surgery on his face. What do the intelligence people say?"

"They say Davenport died near the Aran Islands and was cremated. They're not going to admit they were wrong. And a majority of the intelligence group thinks this is some kind of religious retreat. They don't want to believe there could be a terrorist training facility in that location. I believe the minority and I had them stay a little longer after the main group left."

"What are you going to do?"

"For the moment, nothing. The military agree with the minority and some of them want me to order the launch of a bunch of missiles to destroy the camp and kill everyone in it, men women and children."

"There are women and children in the camp?"

"Yes."

"That makes it tougher, but maybe you have to do it anyway." Molly took off the sweater she had been wearing revealing a tight, sleeveless blouse, open at the throat. "It's so cool in the air-conditioned offices and so nice and warm out here."

"Make no mistake, Molly. I would hate to see innocent women and children killed, but it's my job to protect the innocent men, women and children of this country. I'd give that order this minute if I didn't think it was more important that we find out what's going on at that base. The intelligence analysts have concluded that they don't know the identity of the man with the bandaged face, but they have identified some of the other people at that camp. There are Iraqi fugitives from Saddam's regime, high-ranking Al Qaeda planners and top terrorists from many other organizations. Something big is being planned there and we're trying to find out what so we can maybe prevent it."

"Can we put someone in there?"

"They've tried to infiltrate one or two spies, but security has been too tight."

"Is a raid by a small force possible?"

"That's being considered, but planning that operation will take time. Right now they're enhancing the photographs they have and increasing the number of satellite sweeps of the area. On one of the enhanced photographs I saw something that looked like a picture of the Sagamore Bridge. That's one of the two bridges that connect Cape Cod to the rest of Massachusetts. I know that area well because I used to cross that bridge almost every weekend during the summer for about twenty years."

"Could that be what they're planning?"

Ben shrugged. "Could be one of the things they're planning, but I doubt that it's the main event. Destroying that bridge, even if they destroy the other one at the same time would be an enormous inconvenience, but they could be quickly rebuilt and it wouldn't have the dramatic effect that Al Qaeda likes to get from their major operations. The intelligence analysts saw some kind of a vehicle on another shot that they say is probably a mobile chemical weapons lab, and they identified some of the people in the picture as scientists that worked with biological weapons in Iraq. Our top intelligence analysts think a major chemical and biological attack is being planned, but at this point, we don't know what's planned, when it's supposed to happen or where, although they expect New York and Washington would be two of the major targets, as usual. We'll have to continue surveillance as best we can. That's our best chance of finding out what they're planning. Catching Davenport, if that's him, will have to wait. If that's not possible, or it takes too long, we may have to attack the base with some missiles and hope we can disrupt whatever they're planning. Speaking of Davenport, have you prepared a new letter to him? Isn't it about time for one?"

Molly pulled a sheet of paper out of her bag. "I wrote this before I knew about those pictures. Do you think that changes anything?

Ben read the letter.

Clare,

I remain certain that you are still alive. I've heard nothing of you and I think that's good news. I hope it means that you have abandoned your efforts to destroy the United States and that you are at peace with yourself. My offer still stands to negotiate your surrender, but as always, only if I can guarantee your personal safety.
Molly

Ben nodded and then looked at his wristwatch. "That's fine. Send it. You'll have to excuse me for a minute, but don't go. I've got to make one phone call and then there's something else I want to talk to you about."

Ben picked up the phone. "Martha would you please get Senator Kendall for me." Moments later the phone rang. Ben picked it up. "Bob, I had an idea about Davies. I'll fill you in later. What's the score in the Senate? No change. That's good news and thanks for that. I'm not sure it'll work, but let's stall for a while. I agree. It's not a good idea to tell them I'm thinking about resigning. I'm sure you'll think of some stall. Let me know what it was at some point."

As Ben ended the call, Molly said, "Perhaps it's none of my business, and I'm reluctant to ask, but you were talking about the Impeachment."

"Yes. The situation is the same. A delegation from Congress, supposedly bipartisan, has formed to try and persuade me to resign. According to Senator Kendall, if they are difficult about putting off the meeting, it means they think they have the two thirds of the Senate they need. He thinks no one is sure of the vote yet. Some of the people who I thought would vote against me are holding out and looking to get some advantage for casting their vote against me."

"Can you sweeten the pot for the holdouts so they don't get the votes they need?"

"I'm reluctant to do that, but I promised Kendall that I'd keep my mouth shut and let him handle the stall tactics."

Ben leaned back in his chair. Let's talk about Mrs. Morton."

Molly's eyes blazed. "I hate that lying bitch."

Ben smiled. "I'm not fond of her either, but I have an idea. I'll explain it to you. I'm going to have the United States sue Morton's estate to recover the money we found in his safe deposit box that he made dealing drugs and put liens on his house and all his other assets because of what Morton did. Then we can put the Estate in Bankruptcy and get a Federal Bankruptcy judge to remove her and appoint a new Administrator who can give us the consent we need."

Molly sat quietly absorbing what Ben had just said. "I'm not a lawyer, but if you do that, is there anything that Davies can do to mess it up?"

"Not if we do it right. I'll send Rahsheed and John Wallace down to Montgomery and get some lawyer from the DOJ we can trust to go down there with them. They'll line things up with the local bar and the Federal Bankruptcy judge so that we can be sure we can get what we want. I'll have Rahsheed buy up the local claims so we have enough numbers to control the bankruptcy case and that will keep all those state court judges that Davies knows totally out of the picture."

"It sounds good to me, but what do you want me to do? Sounds like you don't need me for anything."

"Lining that up can be fast, but the filing in the bankruptcy court and getting decrees can take a while, maybe more time than I have."

"Do you want me to go to Montgomery and threaten her before you send the others down there?"

"No. I'll have Rahsheed and the others fly down tomorrow. Unless something unusual comes up, they ought to be able to get what I want done in a day or two. Then you come down and talk with Mrs. Morton. When Mrs. Morton and her attorney understand that we can put the Estate into bankruptcy and she can lose everything, I think she'll sign that consent."

"You don't want me threaten her with that right now? I can't wait to let her have it, and it may save a few days."

"No. As Yogi Berra said, 'It ain't over 'till it's over.' I want to make sure it's all set up and her lawyer knows it when you talk with her."

After Molly left, Ben went into the Oval Office, got Rahsheed and John Wallace on a conference call and explained to them what he wanted done. He told them to select a lawyer from the Department of Justice and get down to Montgomery as early as possible tomorrow. They didn't want to call attention to their mission and took the first available flight to Montgomery via Atlanta.

While John and Rahsheed were flying to Montgomery, Senator Kendall was concluding a meeting with a group of his Senate colleagues. It was not collegial. At the end of the meeting, Kendall called Ben. "Sorry to tell you this, Mr. President, but they got the two thirds they need."

"Do they still want to see me or are they going to bring it before the Senate right away?"

"They'll want to see you first, but they insist on it being right away."

"I've got the group going down to Montgomery right now. They'll need about three days. Can we stall that long?"

"No. They want to meet today. I'll tell them I'm having trouble reaching you, but it will have to be tomorrow."

"That's not enough time. Tell them you told me what they want and you think that maybe I want an extra day or two to think about whether it's best for the country that I resign and what I might want. You think I may want a deal to get a pardon for Tom Andrews if he's convicted of killing Lindsay Cabot."

Kendall laughed through the phone. "That's the kind of thing they'd understand, but it would have to be something for yourself, like a judgeship, or maybe a Cabinet post to heal the country. Let me think about how I present something. I'll do my best to get you another few days."

"So you think if they get the consent so we can discredit Davies by using his conversation with Morton that we can beat back the Impeachment?"

"I didn't say that, but it may change a few votes I'll do the best I can."

After ending the call with Kendall, Ben called Molly and told her to take the next flight down to Montgomery and then he called Rahsheed on his cell phone. He told him that Molly was on her way to Montgomery and asked him to speed up his Montgomery assignment as much as possible. Rahsheed was telling John about his conversation with the President as they heard the steward announce, "Fasten your seat belts for our approach to Montgomery's Dannelly Field." A smiling flight attendant walked through the cabin as Rahsheed automatically fastened his seat belt and thought about his last visit to Montgomery, Alabama. That time he had found former Assistant Defense Secretary William T. Morton brutally murdered in his den and discovered the audio tapes of Morton's conversations with Senator Davies and Fred Washburn. They had their assignments.

John Wallace was to talk with the Federal District Court Judge, the Bankruptcy Court Judges and the white supremacist lawyer for one of the claimants and they'd start today instead of tomorrow. The attorney from the Justice Department in Washington was to call on his counterparts in the local office and make sure they were on board. It was Rahsheed's job to buy up the local claims. Once the bankruptcy case and liens were pending, Rahsheed was to talk with the local probate judge and acquaint him with what was going on.

A day later, they had accomplished what they had been sent down to Montgomery to do. Rahsheed had his talk with the local probate court judge who immediately understood that there was no way out for Mrs. Morton and no way for Davies to do anything about it. Rahsheed, John and Molly then called Ben to fill him in. When Rahsheed finished his report, Ben asked to speak with Molly. Ben said, "Everything set?"

Molly replied, "The DOJ attorney has an appointment with Mrs. Morton's lawyer for the same time I'm meeting with her. Rahsheed and John will be standing by to expedite things in the bankruptcy court if that's necessary. The bankruptcy judge was very cooperative. He's willing to approve the appointment of a lawyer friend of Rahsheed's as a temporary receiver of Morton's estate if it would help."

"Thank him for me. Make sure they all know that. Tell everyone they did a great job, and, Molly, make sure Mrs. Morton understands that unless she signs immediately, she'll never see a dime from the estate. I don't want her calling Davies and him having the chance to buy her off again."

Two hours later, Molly called Ben to report that she met with Mrs. Morton, and that after meetings with her attorney, the probate judge and the bankruptcy court judge, the document consenting to the use of the tapes was signed.

"Have any problems, Molly?"

"Not really. She wanted to call Davies before signing it, but I threatened to leave and terminate the deal unless she signed it immediately and everyone else did what they were supposed to do to help out. She complained to her lawyer that we were being unfair, but he told her to shut up and sign it. Rahsheed is faxing a copy to you."

"Glad her lawyer was cooperative."

"He knew he wouldn't be paid if the estate went into bankruptcy."

"Excellent. See you when you get back."

As soon as Ben ended the call, he called Senator Kendall. "Bob, it's signed. I just heard and received a fax copy. I'll get one over to you. See what the reaction is in the Senate and let me know. Okay, I'll keep my fingers crossed."

CHAPTER 28

▼

"Senator Kendall wants to see you as soon as possible, Mr. President. He says it's important."

"Tell him to come right over, Martha."

Forty-five minutes later, Ben, Senator Bob Kendall and Tom Andrews were seated around the coffee table in the Oval Office. Kendall said, "The impeachment freight train is stalled, at least for the moment. Yesterday it looked like they had sixty-eight votes and that you were gone and Thurston was in the White House. They lost three when Morton's wife consented to the release of the tape."

"That's good news," Tom said.

Kendall looked at Ben. "I hope you'll back me up on this. I had to promise them that they would get to hear what Davies said to Morton on that tape."

"I wish you hadn't," Ben said. "The A.G. doesn't want it released."

"I know, but it's only to a small group of Senators who can go either way. They'll promise to keep it confidential, and we got to keep Davies from recovering two of those votes or that impeachment train starts up again. They want to hear what Davies said to Morton. They find it hard to believe that he okayed drug dealing and that campaign of racial violence."

"Tom, what's the rationale for the position of the Acting A.G. on that?"

"He's delighted you got Mrs. Morton's consent and they're proceeding with the criminal case against Davies again, but he doesn't want the tape to be released. He thinks it might hurt the prosecution of the case."

"How?" Ben said.

"They're confident that the exclusionary ruling by Judge Badderley will eventually be reversed on appeal. If the contents of the tapes are released now before he's reversed, they think it may be so prejudicial that it might end up being excluded from evidence."

Ben sat back in his chair. "I suppose it might, but the operative word is might. Much as I don't want to take any chances with the prosecution of the case against Davies, it would be worse to end up with me impeached and Thurston in the Oval Office. From what I'm hearing, if that happens, the case against Davies would be killed or he'd get a full pardon from Thurston if he ever got convicted."

"You're absolutely right," Kendall said. "When they hear the tape, they'll have to consider that it could be disastrous to ally themselves with Davies if the public gets to hear it at some point."

Ben said. "Tom, do you remember whether Badderley issued a "gag order" in his opinion about the tapes?"

Tom shook his head. "No."

Ben sent for a copy of the order, and minutes later, Martha handed Ben a copy of Badderley's decision. Ben quickly scanned it. "Good, he didn't." He turned to Tom. "I want a copy of the Morton tapes released to Senator Kendall immediately. You let the Attorney General know we've done so." Ben looked towards Kendall. "Bob, Martha made copies of the tape. You'll have one when you leave and I suggest you play it for your Senate colleagues first thing tomorrow, before Davies can do anything about it. Get their agreement that they keep it to themselves."

"Hell, I'll do it tonight. I know just who I got to call, but understand, this could be temporary. Davies quit pressuring and blackmailing members of the Senate when he had the votes he needed. He probably could have got more, but he didn't need them and probably saw no need to spend that political capital."

"What's it take to permanently stop the impeachment?"

"Not sure, Mr. President. It might take Tom being acquitted on the Lindsay murder case, and that might not be enough. What's that look like?"

Tom said, "It's my word and that of my mother, father, sister and brother-in law against the word of a career criminal and circumstantial evidence of doubtful value."

"What evidence?" Kendall asked.

"The evidence that ties Kelly to the murder scene and that stupid pen that the police found in Kelly's apartment."

Kendall said, "That's not much to find a man guilty beyond a reasonable doubt. Could you get the case tried quickly? A not guilty verdict would be a big help."

"Tom's attorney doesn't think it should be rushed. The Worcester police are looking into Kelly's activities during the day he says he met with Tom, and looking to see if there are any non-family members who remember seeing Tom on that day. They hope they can come up with something like that to back-up Tom's family or somebody placing Kelly somewhere to prove that Tom and Kelly couldn't have met where and when Kelly says the meeting took place. Tom was well liked from his days on the Worcester police force and so are his parents, but it's pretty unusual for the police to try and prove someone's innocence. We also have a P.I. looking into where Kelly was before and after Kelly was supposed to have killed Mr. Cabot. Nobody seems to know where he was, or what he was doing."

"If Senator Kendall thinks an acquittal will help you, I think I ought to demand an early trial."

"I don't think that's a good idea, Tom."

"It's my decision, Mr. President."

"Yes, but I know your attorney very well. If he thinks it's not a good idea, you ought to listen to him."

"I'll discuss it with him, but it's ultimately for me to decide."

Ben had to agree.

Later that night, Senator Kendall met with a half dozen of his colleagues in the Senate. He played the tape of Bill Morton's conversation with Senator Davies. When the tape ended, Kendall said, "No need to say much to you gentlemen. You all been around the block a few times and know that no matter what Davies promised you or has on you, he'll be in no position to do much once this tape becomes a public document. If he doesn't go to jail, and lose his seat in the Senate, he'll at least lose his power base. I can't promise you anything because you know President Silver doesn't operate that way, but if any of you get hurt by Davies, I'll do what I can and talk with the President on your behalf. You're all experienced members of the Senate, and I'm sure something appropriate can be found for you in government if that's what you want."

As the group began to leave, Senator Salvatore Grilli delayed. He said, "Can I talk with you privately for a few minutes?"

Kendall agreed and after the others left, Grilli was standing waiting for Senator Kendall to return to his den. Grilli said, "Can this be just between us?"

"Of course. What's on your mind?"

"You got to believe me, Bob. I swear on my mother's head, I knew nothing about this until the impeachment thing started and Davies told me about it."

Kendall said, "Sit down, Sal. Relax, I'll get you a drink and then you can tell me about it. You still drink that Skye vodka and tonic?"

"Don't trouble yourself, Bob. I just want to get this over with."

"No trouble. I got it all right here. Go on."

Grilli sat down. He sighed and waited until Kendall handed him his drink. "Thanks, Bob." He took a deep drink and then squared his shoulders. "I guess I needed that." He took another deep breath and then said, "A couple of years ago, my son was a young associate with a New York law firm that represented a corporation listed on the New York Stock Exchange. He got some inside information about the company and he told his girl friend, her brother, my daughter and her husband and my ex wife, and they all made some money because of it, but so did a lot of other people. There was an investigation by the FBI and the SEC brought some civil cases against a few of the corporations officers, but that was as far as it went. Nothing was filed against any of the people my son talked with." Grilli took another sip of his drink and then continued, "When Davies told me about it, at first I didn't believe it. But then I checked with my son and my daughter and her husband and they admitted it. Davies says he can keep it buried, but if I don't vote against President Silver, my son and daughter will end up in jail."

Kendall shook his head. "I wondered why you voted the way you did, Sal."

"What could I do, Bob? I can't send my son and daughter to jail."

"I doubt anyone would go to jail for a first offense if they come forward and pay the profit into court as a penalty."

Grilli looked down at his hands and studied the vodka and tonic he was holding as if it held the answers to his question. He looked up at Kendall. "It wasn't the first time or the last time. My son admitted that he set up a Cayman Islands account in a fictitious name and that he's made over two million dollars like that."

Kendall remained still, looking at Grilli. He finally said, "I'm so sorry, Sal. Probably doesn't matter, but I knew your son when he was at Georgetown. I'm just astounded that he'd do that. What happened?"

Grilli shook his head. "Maybe it was my fault for not paying enough attention to him. I don't know. You know what happens during an election campaign. I was distracted and trying to keep my marriage from falling apart before the election. Both stupid decisions."

"Don't blame yourself. You didn't make him do it. Must have been something going on in his life. What's the story?"

"The usual. He started making some money and began running with a fast crowd that introduced him to drugs. I never saw it. The habit got more and more expensive, and as he got away with it, his respect for right and wrong went to hell. God, I just don't know what I can do. He swears to me that if I let it slide, he'll never do any drugs or do anything wrong again. Even if I decide that my son has to accept the consequences of what he did, what do I do about my daughter and her husband. They were twenty-two at the time and didn't even know what they were doing was wrong."

Kendall poured himself a drink and freshened Grilli's. "I don't know what to say, Sal. I wouldn't want to have been in your shoes. It's easy to say that your son ought to take his punishment for what he did and that you do your best to settle your daughters problems as best you can, but I don't know what I'd do if it were my son and daughter. I hope to God I never have to find out. I could ask Silver if he'd be willing to grant pardons to your family if you want."

"Think he would?"

"Probably would for your daughter, but I doubt it for your son."

"He's the one that has the big problem."

"Sorry, but just let me know where you stand when I have to count noses to advise the President."

"I will. When you get to me, let me know what the count is. If I'm lucky, maybe the President won't need my vote and I can avoid having the problem with Davies."

"I'll do that."

Grilli smiled grimly. "Thanks, but I was wondering. What's the story with that murder? Was Silver involved in it with Tom Andrews? Maybe Davies is right and he should be impeached."

"Sorry, Sal. I'd give you a pass on this if I could, but I've gotten to know President Silver pretty well since he became President. I'm telling you there's absolutely no way he could have been involved in the Lindsay Cabot murder, and I doubt that Tom Andrews had anything to do with it either."

Grilli nodded. "I didn't really think the President had anything to do with it either, but Senator Smithers was saying that whether he did or not, we should remove him from office on whatever basis we can live with because Silver doesn't understand the system and can't do the job. Some of the Senators went along with that approach on the last caucus when we went over sixty-six votes before you set up this meeting."

"Smithers is wrong on both counts. And what kind of precedent does that set? Whenever two thirds of the Senate doesn't like a President we kick him out. And if we don't like the Vice President that succeeds him we kick him out and we keep going down the line of succession until we come to a puppet President we can control. That's not the Constitution we swore to uphold and you know it."

"You're right, Bob. Forget it. I want to thank you for listening. I hope this can be the end of Davies pushing the impeachment." Grilli rose from his seat beside the sofa and walked towards the door. Kendall trailed behind. When they got to the exit door, Grilli turned and said, "I wish I could promise you that if this surfaces again that I wouldn't vote against President Silver, but I just can't. I'm hoping I won't have to make that decision."

"Me too." Kendall said as they shook hands at the door, "That's a decision I'd sure as hell never want to make for myself."

Early the next afternoon, Kendall was back in Ben's office. Ben postponed a lunch meeting with Molly in the Rose Garden to find out how the Senate was standing on the impeachment question. Kendall said with a smile, "Don't break out the champagne yet because it's still pretty close. There are now thirty Senators who are opposed to Davies and they can't be moved, but still, if the Senate were to vote today, Davies would have sixty-four votes, so he only needs to pick up three of the remaining six votes to have you removed. Davies knows the count as well as I do and he is fuming. He's spread the word that this isn't over yet. I don't know what he has in mind but he has access to a lot of personal information on members of the Senate and their families. One of the Senators who voted against you told me that Davies has blackmailed him with damaging information involving his children that could only have come from P.J Winters. I'd love to tell you about it, but I promised I'd keep it confidential."

"You have any idea about what Davies intends to do?"

"No, and I'd bet he doesn't know himself, but there's not much comfort in that because he's a resourceful bastard."

"Agreed," Ben said.

CHAPTER 29

▼

Clarence didn't know how much more time he could spend at New Salman Pak without losing his sanity or his life. He always had a way with languages, and his study of State Department Arabic tapes coupled with his day by day association with his Arabic speaking students had taught him enough to begin to surreptitiously follow their conversations. He was not totally surprised to learn that a minority of the camp leaders still didn't trust him. They could accept his inability to speak Arabic, but his absenting himself from the camp's daily prayer rituals was not acceptable. They all agreed it was blasphemous. Even those who were not suspicious of his background had to agree that his conduct was no better than that of an infidel, and that if he wasn't a true believer, when his usefulness was over, there was no reason why they should let him live any longer. The more secular Iraqis also had become increasingly hostile after the summary execution of one of their group by Almihidi. They didn't understand what happened and spread the story that Khalil had lied to Almihidi about him, causing his death. There hadn't been any decision made as yet, but Clarence wasn't sure that the camp leaders that supported him could control the religious fanatics if they decided to kill him. Clarence wondered if he could trust Neil Rabbani, but decided he'd have to talk with him. There was no one else.

When Neil came back to the tent that evening, Clarence said, "Tell me, Neil, I've been wondering if I ought to trust these people to live up to their word, and I'm a little nervous about my personal safety? You think I'm nuts to be concerned?"

Neil looked at Clarence and frowned. "For the moment we're both okay, but no, I don't trust them completely either. Neither of us are acceptable to the fanatics."

"But you're really a Muslim and you participate in the prayers some of the time."

Neil smiled. "I'm not nearly religious enough for them. So far as the fanatics are concerned, I'm not a true believer and that means I'm no better than a Jew or a Crusader. I have some friends here. I think they'll tip me off if anything is being planned, provided they know about it."

"You expected this before we came here, didn't you?"

"Yes."

"Did uncle?"

"Of course. He knew it was a risk, but a risk that had to be taken. Uncle's goal is to run Arabia and after that all of the Middle East. It's a high stakes game and we have to take a lot of major risks, but it's worth it."

"Worth it to who?"

"To uncle, to me, to you and to the people of the region."

"We know what uncle Rabbani wants. What's in it for you?"

"I'll rule some place like Iraq or Syria, maybe Jordan, and I'm next in line after you to take over when Rabbani retires from office."

"Why didn't he tell me about it?"

"He thought it would be better not to worry you about it. I was to tell you when the time was right."

"And when was that supposed to be?"

"Either when the mission was over or the natives got too restless."

"What's our escape plan."

"You've seen me riding around at night on that Honda bike. We take a ride on the bike. Then a short helicopter ride. Then a Lear and we'll be back in London."

"That's we, not just you? Why should I trust you? If they kill me, you move up a notch."

"Uncle would have my head if I left without you. Honest."

"Tell you what, Neil. I believe you, but from now on, when you go for your nightly ride, I'll go with you, and I'll keep the keys to the Honda."

"Fine with me." Neil threw the keys to Clarence."

"Both sets." Neil threw him the second set of keys. "I'll take both sets of keys to the helicopter also." Neil handed them over. "I'll keep these some place where I'll be the only one that can find them."

"You don't trust me yet, do you. We can take a ride tonight to the helicopter pad, and if you know how to fly one, then you could leave here without me."

"I don't know how, and I don't know where we're supposed to meet the Lear, so there's no danger of that."

Neil smiled. "I know. Seriously, if you think something bad is about to happen or you become uncomfortable, give me the word and we're out of here."

With that assurance and the keys to the motorbike and the helicopter in his possession, Clarence felt less anxious.

Later that night, Neil and Clarence rode out of the training base due east for about thirty minutes. Neil led the way through a wooded area to a clearing and pulled camouflage netting off of a green and brown painted helicopter. It was a small two-seater. Clarence had to admit that it was well hidden. He had almost bumped into the helicopter before he saw it. Neil started the engine and Clarence noted that it ran more quietly than he had expected.

On the way back to the base, Clarence felt a little more at ease, as he felt the weight of the keys in his pocket. Yes, he'd keep all the keys. After they returned, Neil left the tent to spend the night with his current bed companion and Clarence sat at his computer looking at pictures of Molly and reading the notes she had sent him. He got the weather forecast for Washington, D.C. They were in for a stretch of good weather. That means Molly might be sitting outside in the Rose Garden with the President, and that means maybe she would be killed by Akmed and Yusif. He didn't want that. She was the only person who really cared whether he lived or died. He took her picture and her business card out of his wallet, stared at them a moment and impulsively typed out her e-mail address. He typed a message.

> *If you know what's good for you, you'll stay out of the Rose Garden when the President goes out there. A Friend.*

He sat staring at the message, ready to send. Should he send it? It could be dangerous. He had an escape route and if he insisted, he and Neil could leave. Before he could think about it any more, he clicked, "send". He didn't have to wait long. As soon as he sent it, he felt a wave if relief. It was the right thing to do.

It was early afternoon in Washington, D.C. when the computer on Molly's desk notified her of incoming mail. At first she didn't know what it was since that computer had never received any mail before. It was set up when Molly first received the one communication she had received shortly before P.J. Winters had announced Clarence Davenport's death by drowning in the Aran Islands. Molly had changed her e-mail address and nothing had been received at that old address for months.

Molly read the message. She was stunned for a moment, then hit the print icon and picked up the phone. She called Ben's administrative aide. "Martha, where's the President?"

"He's tied up right now Molly. Unless it's an emergency, he doesn't want to be disturbed. Jane came in and they want to have a little time together. Lord knows…"

Molly interrupted. "Just tell me where he is. It's urgent."

"They're in the Rose Garden."

"Get them out of there."

"I'll do no such thing."

"Just do it." Molly hung up the phone, ripped the message out of the printer and raced through the corridors from the West Wing to the White House. She passed startled clerks and bureaucrats and finally burst out of the French doors leading to the Rose Garden. Ben looked up and saw Molly. He waved to her, "Come join us. Jane just arrived and we're having a very civilized English tea."

Jane said, "Come do. It's almost like being in the English countryside. We must even have some youngster or eccentric old timer flying a model airplane off at the other end of the garden. Didn't you notice it, Ben?"

"No one's flying any model planes around here that I know of."

"Well there it is," Jane said. "It's coming right toward us."

Molly said, "Excuse me sir. We've got to leave here immediately."

"Why?"

"I've heard from Clarence."

"Really," Ben said.

"Please sir. Do as I ask. Leave here immediately. Please sir. Now."

Ben could here the panic in Molly's voice.

Through the lens of the miniature TV camera Akmed and Yusif watched as Molly had sprinted towards the President and Jane.

Yusif said, "Can't that thing fly any faster. I want to finish this job today."

"It goes as fast as it goes. Another thirty seconds and we'll be in range."

Ben and Jane rose from the table. As they joined Molly and slowly walked towards the French doors, Molly said, "Hurry please."

"What's the rush, Molly," Ben said.

"I don't know, but what I do know is I've got to get you out of the Rose Garden."

As they watched Ben shut the Rose Garden door behind him, Akmed said to Yusif, "Another ten seconds and it would have been over. What do you think happened that made them leave? They didn't even get to drink their tea or eat any of those little sandwiches. The woman that came in was holding a piece of paper. She must have received an important message."

"Allah decided they can have another day to walk this earth.

Inside the Oval Office, Molly said, "Read this sir. I'm sure it's from Clarence Davenport."

Ben read the message. "He wants you to stay out of the Rose Garden. I wonder why." Ben shook his head. "There must be some danger there. Maybe someone is planning some attack through the Rose Garden, a missile, maybe a suicide bomber. Who knows? I suppose we ought to take the warning. Let's see what Tom has to say."

Moments later, Tom Andrews had joined Ben, Jane and Molly and read the message. After Molly explained how she received the message, Ben said, "What do you make of it?"

Andrews said. "I agree that it's probably from Davenport and that we have to take it seriously. Do you still think that Davenport is the guy with the bandaged face sitting in the armchair at that camp we have under surveillance."

"I think so," Ben said.

"Why don't we just take it out. A couple of missiles and they're history."

Ben shook his head. "No can do. Some analysts agree that the camp is a terrorist training base, but there's another group that think it's just a place where they're having a religious retreat. More importantly, if this warning came from Davenport and that is a terrorist training camp, we don't want to kill him or destroy it yet. Maybe he'll give us some more information and maybe through surveillance we can figure out what they're planning."

"I don't know, sir. That message doesn't tell us very much. We don't know what he's warning us against or when whatever it is he's warning us against is supposed to happen. I bet if you talk to Military Intelligence they'll tell you to do something."

"I know they will. We've been trying to put together a possible small raid on that camp for over a week now without success. We went over it with State and they're opposed to our doing anything without UN approval and Senator Kendall says that under the present circumstances it would guarantee that the Senate would vote to Impeach if I authorized an attack. Admiral Williamson offered to do it on his own without authorization and take the heat, but I can't let him do that. If I thought it would really be a major victory against terrorism or perhaps prevent an attack on this country, I'd authorize it anyway, but I don't think that's the way to go right now."

"You think we should reply to the message?" Molly said.

Ben nodded. "Yes, I do."

"What should we say?"

"Think about it over night and draft a reply. We'll meet tomorrow morning and finalize something together. When you're working on it, remember that we don't want to say anything to indicate that we have any idea about where he might be, and remember, you too, Tom, not a word about this to anyone."

The next morning, Ben and Molly huddled at Ben's desk. The brief e-mail warning from Clarence and Molly's draft response was in front of them. Ben put them aside and said with a smile, "We don't know what's going on in his mind, but it seems that Mr. Davenport has a serious case of the 'hots' for you."

Molly's face turned crimson. "I assure you I don't know why, but I guess I have to agree."

Ben continued, "Aside from the fact that you're a good looking woman, think. Did you say anything to him of a personal nature when you first met him at his house?"

Molly furrowed her forehead. "Not really. When John and I left, we thought he was going to commit suicide. As we were walking down to the car, I looked back and saw him watching us and I yelled back to him and said he shouldn't kill himself."

"Interesting. Let's remember that." Ben leaned back in his chair. "Somehow, Davenport knows of some plan to kill me and that it's to take place in the Rose Garden. He's telling you because he's concerned about you. He's certainly not interested in warning me, but I'd love to know what that plan is."

"Yes, sir, but he's not about to tell us."

"Maybe he will if he thinks you'll be killed. We already agreed that's got to be the reason he sent that e-mail. He must know, probably from the media, that you spend a lot of time with me and often in the Rose Garden. That's what we have to keep in mind when you reply."

Ben and Molly returned to Molly's draft response and spent the next forty-five minutes discussing and redrafting. They were both almost finally satisfied. Ben read the suggested response:

Dear Friend,

Thanks for the warning. I told President Silver I received a warning note about the Rose Garden from a friend and that I just know you are that friend. Like everyone, he says you're dead, but I know you're not.

The President told me not to mention to anyone my thinking the warning came from you. He said that the press and the FBI would make my life miserable if I repeated what I believed, so you're still officially dead. Perhaps it's better that way.

It must be very dangerous for you to write to me. Thank you.

I wish I could follow your advice. I tried to persuade the President to stay out of the Rose Garden, but he says that even if the warning is serious, he will not give in to terrorist tactics and change his life. I thought of refusing to go out into the Rose Garden, but if that's what the President wants that's what I have to do. I used to be an FBI agent but was fired after my fight with FBI Director Winters. Winters wanted to put me in jail, but President Silver interceded and hired me as his assistant. I was fortunate to get this job and I love it. I'll have to take my chances. I hope nothing bad happens to me or the President. He's read and re-read your manifesto. Many of the reforms you wanted are the reforms he'd like to see happen. Too bad things worked out the way they did. You and he think alike about so many things.

Thanks again for your concern about me. I appreciate it.

Your friend,
Molly Pemberton.

Ben looked up and sat back in his chair. "I think it's good. Send it. If he's infatuated with you like I think he is, maybe he'll give something more away. You'll let me know immediately if you hear anything."

Molly nodded that she would and rose to leave. Ben said, "Before you go, take a look at these latest satellite photos of that camp. The man sitting outside in the upholstered armchair isn't wearing any bandages." Molly peered over Ben's shoulder and then leaned over closer to the picture. "Look through the magnifying glass."

Molly took the picture and the glass, sat back down in her chair and stared at the photograph. "That's not Clarence Davenport. No amount of plastic surgery could turn him into that gorilla."

"I agree, and if he had facial surgery, he could never have grown that beard in the time that passed."

Molly stared at the picture some more. "Do you have the other picture we looked at the other day?" Ben rummaged in his desk a moment, and then slid another photograph to Molly. Molly stared at one, then the other through the glass. "That's not the same chair and that's not the same tent."

After Molly slid the photographs back across the desk, Ben stared at them. "You're right. I told the Intel people I was especially interested in blowups of the man in the armchair and that's what they brought in. I was beginning to think that the man in the armchair wasn't Clarence, but you're right, that's not the same chair or the same tent." Ben pointed at the old picture. "So it's still possible that it's Clarence Davenport sitting in that chair at that camp. I'll tell Intel that I want blowups of this area and let you know if I think you ought to see them when I get them. Good job, Molly. We're planning a possible action at that location and I'd sure like to get Davenport, and hopefully alive."

•

CHAPTER 30

▼

Senator Davies was sitting on the verandah of his riverfront mansion drinking tea. He had shot eleven squirrels, eight crows and someone's apparently lost cat. Shooting had not improved his mood, and his staff, including his assistant, Beau Lawrence was staying out of his way until sent for. He had sent for Beau and he approached Davies hesitantly. "Where the hell is Winters?"

Beau glanced at his wristwatch. "It's only two-fifteen. Winters said he'd be here at two-thirty."

"Call him and tell him to hurry up. God damn it. Doesn't anybody care that Silver is killing me? That bitch, Morton's wife should have called me. I'd have given her more money than she can get out of Bill's estate. God damn it. We had it done. The votes were there." Davies picked up his rifle that had been leaning against the porch railing, sighted down the barrel and snapped off a shot at a passing Yorkshire terrier. The dog yelped as the dirt in front of its face kicked up and it then ran off back down the road.

"Jesus, Senator, that's Paul Mahoney's dog. It's a good thing you missed it."

"I didn't miss it. If I wanted to kill the damn dog I would have. Did you call P.J. yet?" Beau shook his head. "Well what the hell are you standing there for. Do it." P. J. fired his rifle again and a squirrel fell out of a pine tree.

Fifteen minutes later P. J. Winters drove up in his Lincoln limousine. He waved at Davies as he approached and said as he looked at the pile of dead squirrels, "Been big game hunting, I see."

"I'm in no mood for any bad jokes. You know I had the Senate votes for impeachment until that bitch consented to the use of the tapes."

Winters nodded that he did.

"I got this big staff of lawyers and advisers, nobody ever says why don't you have Badderley issue a gag order. It would have been the easiest thing in the world. Nobody tells me that as Morton's Administratrix she has the legal right to consent when he's dead. Nobody tells me that Silver sent that bitch that used to work for you to put pressure on her. If I don't think of it nobody does. They're worthless. They're nothing but a bunch of useless, shiftless bloodsucking niggers."

"I'm sure you didn't ask me down here just to listen to you complain. What do you want to talk about?"

"You remember our talking about killing Silver?"

"Of course."

"I'm ready to reconsider. I got to get rid of that son of a bitch."

"Sorry, Jeb. The man we were thinking about using isn't available. His condition deteriorated and he gave up his press credentials."

"Get someone else."

"What do you think, I got people like that in inventory?"

"I don't need your sarcasm. I need to figure out a way to get rid of that bastard and I need to do it now."

"I'll look around for another assassin, but it'll take a little time."

"I just said I don't have time. So far, only five or six Senators have heard that tape. If it gets released to the public, I won't be able to push Silver's impeachment."

"I said I'd try and find someone, but assassins like that can't be manufactured."

"If I knew Kendall was going to play the tape for a group of Senators, I could have pushed for a quick vote in the Senate. We had it made. I guess your staff is as bad as mine."

Winters scratched his head. "I'm not following you, Jeb. I have a very good staff."

"I assume no one told you they wanted access to the tape because you would have told me if they did, right?"

"Of course I would, and no one can get access to that tape without my knowing it. Fact is that tape is exactly where it's always been. No one came in for it. They must have listened to a copy."

"You have the original?"

"No, but I know where it is."

"Where?"

"The evidence room at the Department of Justice."

"You sure it's there?"

Winters picked up his cell phone and punched in a number. "Walter, check to see if the Morton tapes are in the evidence room. I'll hold on." Three minutes later, Winters pressed the phone to his ear. He listened a moment, grunted, ended the call and said, "It's right where it's always been. No one signed in to listen to it or even look at it"

"Then this should be easy for you. Bring it here and I'll personally destroy the damn things."

Winters shook his head. "I told you I wouldn't fall on my sword for you. There are systems in place that make that impossible." Winters could see a scowl beginning on Davies' face and said, "Forget it, Jeb. It can't be done." Winters put his hand up. "Don't say another word about it. I don't want to discuss it."

"Okay, okay. Could you at least say it's not genuine? I'm sure you can find some expert to back you up. Most of those guys will say anything for a price."

"I don't have the expertise to make that statement. I could recommend someone to you, but they won't have any credibility, and frankly, I don't think that's a good idea because if you rely on a crackpot you won't be taken seriously. That's why I won't do it."

"So, what are you telling me? Are you saying that there's nothing I can do? I can't accept that." Davies adjusted his cufflinks and then sat back on the wicker sofa. "Why couldn't we have a fire? The tape could be destroyed in a fire. Burn down the damn building if you have to."

"It's sprinklered."

"There has to be something."

Winters rocked back and forth in his chair a moment, nodding to himself.

"What is it? You think of something?"

"Yes, but it can't be politically suicidal for either of us. I've got a possibility in mind, but I'll have to check some building plans and there might be a little delay in getting it done."

"What is it?"

"I think there's a building maintenance inspection scheduled to take place some time next month."

Davies shook his head. "I may not be able to keep the impeachment simmering that long."

"Okay, then I'll forget about it."

"No, no. What is it?"

"I'll have to check out the building plans, but maybe, during the inspection, when we test the sprinkler system, the pressure can cause a little water leak right where that tape is kept. I might have to relocate some of the evidence storage facilities after I look at the building plans, but I think it can be done."

"Would that destroy the tape?"

"Probably not, but it might damage the quality enough to interfere with the voice identification testing."

"They have copies."

"I'm talking about damaging the original."

Davies adjusted the crease in his trousers with a puzzled look on his face and then fidgeted with his cufflinks. He turned to Winters and smiled. "You are a fox. You're thinking about disqualifying the tape under the Best Evidence Rule."

"Exactly. Put the case in front of the right judge and you're right where you were before Mrs. Morton authorized the use of the tape, and from what you said before, that ought to put you in a position to reclaim whatever votes you need."

Davies sat nodding for a moment, and then smiled. "This calls for a little cele-bration." Davies bellowed, "Beau, get someone to bring out a magnum of Piper and champagne glasses and you can join us." He turned back to Winters. "You can even smoke one of those foul smelling cigars of yours. I've got to make a phone call."

"Moments later he said into his phone, "Senator Davies calling for Senator Smithers…I don't care what he's doing. I want him now…I said now…Good." He tapped his fingers on the arm of the sofa while waiting and when Smithers got on the line he said, "I won't take much of your time. Just hold the fort in the Senate because we aren't dead yet…No, I can't tell you what and how. It's better that you maintain deniability on this…Winters?…Yes, he came up to see me," Davies could see Winters frantically waiving no at him, "but he has nothing to do with anything. We just talked but it went nowhere…Honest to God, I wouldn't lie to you. Someday when this is long since passed I may tell you about it, but for now, it's better for you that you don't know."

Winters said, "I was worried for a minute."

"I'm insulted. You got to know that everything we talk about is just between you and me. What do you think I am, stupid?"

"No, but we hadn't talked about that."

"No need to. Enough shop talk. Here comes Beau and the champagne. He and others like Smithers may guess, but they'll never know for sure."

It didn't take long, and by the next day, Smithers had started working on the Senators, and his and Davies upswing mood had been noticed and commented upon on the hill, by the media and at the White House. Spenser Cameron, Ben's Press Secretary brought it to Ben's attention. "I don't know why, but Davies and his impeachment supporters seem to have taken a new lease on life and nobody, not even his supporters know why."

"That can't be good news for us," Tom said.

Cam continued, "It doesn't seem like anything is going to happen this minute because there's no full court press on, but there's definitely something brewing."

CHAPTER 31

▼

It was after midnight at New Salman Pak, a time when Clarence knew he would not be disturbed. He went on-line and checked to see if Molly Pemberton had replied to his e-mail warning. She had.

Clarence opened the letter, read it, reread it four times, and then printed it and read it again. The more he thought about it, the more puzzled he became about what he should do.

He studied it some more. As he did, he thought, she says she knows I'm still alive, even though everyone else believes I'm dead and that, he looked at the letter, "it's better that way". That must mean she really cares about me. Then she tells me she takes the warning seriously but will have to go into the Rose Garden if the president wants her to. She explains how she had a fight with her boss when she worked at the FBI and that Director P.J. Winters fired her and wanted to put her in jail. I didn't know that. I thought she was rewarded for finding me. Then she says that the President protected her against Winters and that now she needs the job with the President. Why is she telling me all this? It's like I was an old friend. He thought a moment, maybe I am an old friend or maybe she wants my approval. She has to explain why she can't stay out of the Rose Garden like I told her to. "Shit," he whispered to himself, "I really don't want anything to happen to her, but what can I do?" He thought some more and looked at the letter again. Here she tells me President Silver and I think alike about the reforms I wanted to see. It's obvious that she admires him. He reflected. Does that mean she admires me? Yes, it has to mean that. It felt good when I sent Molly the warning, and now I feel good and bad.

What the hell can I do now? Clarence put the letter away and sat back in his flowered armchair. He thought and decided he felt good because she obviously cares about him and bad because he was going to be responsible for killing her. How could he let that happen? He couldn't, but what could he do about it. He looked at his wristwatch and did a fast mental calculation. It's late afternoon in Washington. I think I remembered reading a news report that President Silver had left Washington to testify at the murder trial of his chief of staff, Tom Andrews in Dedham, Massachusetts.

Clarence went back to his computer, tapped a few keys on his computer and then stared at the screen. Yes. He's in Boston. That means no Rose Garden tomorrow and that he had time to decide what he should do about Molly and the Rose Garden. Clarence returned to his armchair. He knew what he'd like to do. Could he find a way to have her sent to London? If he could, he'd get there and grab her and they'd live together someplace. He shook his head. A great dream, but impossible. Maybe he'd have some better idea tomorrow.

As Clarence prepared to go to sleep, Neil quietly slipped into the tent they shared. Clarence said, "She kick you out or was she a bad lay?"

Neil held his index finger over his lips and whispered, "It's nothing like that. Actually, I'm glad to see you're still alive."

Clarence felt the Colt 45 under his pillow, the knife strapped to his calf and then reached under his bed for an AK 47. "What's going on?" he whispered back.

"I've been hearing things. The religious fanatics are gaining control of the camp. They're planning to kill one of the more secular Iraqi leaders and when that happens they may expand the killing to include anyone they think is not a true believer."

"What set that off?"

"The daughter of one of the Wahhabi clerics committed adultery and they're talking about stoning her to death like they say the Koran requires, and they want to include the rest of the women who aren't fanatics like them with her. They'll soon be talking about how they have to rid themselves of all Western influences before they corrupt everyone. They always get into that every time they talk about replacing civil law with *sharia*."

"They're not there yet?"

"No, but I know they soon will."

"Are you the one she did it with?"

"No. That's not why I think it may get out of hand and they might come looking for us."

"Then why us?"

"You remember hearing Al Qaeda talk about the 'near enemy' and the 'far enemy'?" Clarence nodded that he did. Neil continued, "Well, we, me, Rabbani, you, all secular Muslims, we're the 'near enemy' and don't you ever forget it. In their eyes, we're no better than the Jews, Christians, Hindus and Buhhdists. It's just that they'll make temporary alliances with us, in fact with anyone, but they'll knife us in the back whenever it suits them."

"You think we ought to leave now?"

"We could but tomorrow night would be better. I have to make arrangements for the Lear to pick us up and they'll need a day to do that. I don't expect anything to happen tomorrow during the day, and we should leave here tomorrow before midnight. You'll have to leave everything because if they think we're leaving for good, they'll probably make their move right then and there. I'll stay here for the rest of tonight. One of us should stay awake. You want to take the first watch?"

"Okay." An hour and a half later, Clarence heard a sound outside the flap of his tent. He silently rose from his armchair that he had positioned to the right of the entrance. He had his knife in his left hand and a garrote in his right. He waited quietly.

A figure in a long robe and Arab headdress slipped through the flap. He was carrying a sword with a curved blade. The Arab began tiptoeing towards the cot where Neil was asleep. He whispered, "Khalil, Khalil."

Clarence sprung from behind the Arab, slashed the man's hand where he was holding the sword. It fell to the ground, and as the Arab started to turn, the garrote was whipped around his neck and tightened. He reached up for it to release the pressure and tried to struggle, but Clarence kicked his feet out from under him. The Arab fell to the ground with Clarence on top of him. Clarence finished him off with his knife, cutting the Arab's throat from ear to ear.

As Clarence wiped the blood off his knife on the dead Arab's robes, he whispered, "Neil," then a little louder, "Neil. For God's sake, Neil, wake up!"

"What? What? Good God, what happened?"

"What do you think happened?"

Neil, now fully awake, got out of his bed. "Those dirty bastards. They told me nothing would happen until tomorrow night, if at all." Neil rolled the dead Arab over on to his back and looked at his face. "Son of a worthless dog. He was supposed to be my friend. This is the bastard that told me that nothing would happen at all, and that if it did, the earliest it could be was tomorrow night after midnight."

"Looks like he lied to you. But maybe he is your friend. He thought it was me asleep in that bed. Killing you would have been a mistake."

"Perhaps, but they wouldn't kill only one of us."

"I guess we'll never know, but what now? We can't stay here with his dead body in my tent."

"You're right, but the jet won't be available until tomorrow. Let's move him into a cave I found. There's a big drop inside it and he'll disappear."

Clarence and Neil picked up the Arab's body and carried it outside and then in back of the tent. Neil said, "He's a heavy son of a bitch. The girl I was with earlier tonight, knows a short cut to the cave. She'll help us." They picked up the dead Arab, and each supporting one arm, walked the body towards the neighboring tent of the woman with whom Neil was supposed to have spent the night.

At the entrance to her tent, Clarence stopped Neil from entering and said, "You trust her?"

"Totally. She's sick of being treated like a third class person. I promised I'd take her to London when we left."

"Do you really intend to?"

Neil shrugged. "I don't know. Maybe I'll send for her when we get back." Neil drew back the flap of the tent and almost immediately exited. "Come in here. Take a look," he whispered.

Clarence removed his knife from its sheath and then ducked into the tent. He looked where Neil was pointing. The woman was spread-eagled on the bed. Her throat had been cut and her body mutilated.

Neil whispered, "They must have sent someone in here to kill me the same time they sent that other bastard to kill you."

"What now?"

"I don't know. You got any bright ideas?"

"Whoever tried to kill you here knows you're still alive somewhere. He probably intends to meet the one that tried to kill me and when he doesn't return, he'll probably go looking for him in my tent. Let's get back there and take him out when he shows up and then leave both bodies here. We can make it look like they got into a fight over the girl and ended up killing her and each other. What do you think?

Neil nodded his head as he considered Clarence's suggestion. "Yes, some will believe it and others will not. It should keep them busy arguing for most of the day and night and give us long enough to get out of here tomorrow night."

"You don't think we should leave tonight?"

"No, if we do, they'll decide that we killed those two and that could hurt our plan. We'll have risk it and wait until tomorrow."

Clarence and Neil brought the dead Arab into the girl's tent. They removed his headdress and robes, rearranged the girl's body and then returned to Clarence's tent. They didn't have long to wait. They quickly killed the Arab with a knife thrust to his heart and brought the body to the girl's tent. They arranged the scene and prepared to leave. Neil paused at the tent flap and said, "What do you think? It looks like the one we just killed came in, found them screwing, killed her and him, but not before the other one got lucky and managed to stab him right in the heart."

"The cut on his hand looks like it could be a defensive knife wound and there's the mark from the garrote on his neck. It wouldn't fool a good forensics team," Clarence smiled, "but they don't have one. Let's go, and stay alert. It's still two hours before sun up."

The camp was a beehive of activity in the morning. The bodies were discovered and while many suspected Neil and Clarence, when they went to see them, they were working as usual and both seemed surprised by the news. The other plotters involved in the attempt to kill Neil and Clarence couldn't talk without revealing that they were involved in an attempt to kill two important guests at the terrorist camp.

Clarence spent the morning downloading all the information on his computer onto a CD and several floppy discs. There was nothing else that he needed. He made a small bonfire and destroyed all paper copies of everything including the pictures of Molly that he had downloaded and printed. As he watched the pictures of her curl up and then burn, he decided that he couldn't allow these fanatical vermin to destroy her. Akmed and Yusif were nothing, but would he be betraying Rabbani and Neil? They were his real future. He could daydream about Molly, but that's a fantasy. Besides, they were blood relatives and they had been honest with him so far, and he couldn't do that either. He would have to decide before he left New Salman Pak tonight. He looked around. Maybe not, he'll take his cell phone and that small palm held computer. It'll be good enough to send a small message if that's what he decides to do.

CHAPTER 32

▼

Fire Protection Services Agency performed their semi-annual inspection of the building that housed the Department of Justice's evidence room without discernible incident. The pressure caused leak in the sprinkler system passed unnoticed until the tape of the Davies Morton conversation was retrieved following Senator Smithers demand for its examination to assure the Senate of its authenticity and that it had not been tampered with. When the D.O.J. clerk opened the drawer containing the tape, she found it sitting in a pool of water. She dried it off as best she could and then turned it over to the forensics experts for examination. Unfortunately, some of the tape was ruined beyond repair, and the bulk of it was sufficiently damaged in the opinion of experts to make it unreliable. At that point, Davies called Speaker Thurston, "Did you hear? We had a bit of good luck. The tape of me talking with Morton got damaged."

"I heard." Thurston said. "I don't know for sure, but I'd bet you made your good luck happen."

Davies laughed. "No comment. With that having happened, I think it's time to crank things up again. You ready to present the case against President Silver to the Senate?"

"I've been ready for weeks, but what does Senator Smithers say? You got the votes locked up? No sense to move until you do."

"I agree, but I think we ought to get the House and the Senate to hold a quick hearing and rule the tape inadmissible in the Impeachment proceedings because of its being water damaged and that copies of it are not acceptable."

"Good idea. I'll get the hearing done in the House tomorrow and coordinate the language of the ruling with Smithers so the language is the same in both Houses."

"Right, and once that's done, I'll have Smithers tally up the votes. Without that tape screwing me up, I can put the pressure on and get the sixty-seven votes we need."

"You should have them. They were there before Mrs. Morton consented, so you ought to have it now unless someone changes their vote."

"Don't worry about it. If I have to I can strong arm a few more of my associates."

After the resolutions discrediting the Davies-Morton tape were passed, Senator Smithers took his informal count in the Senate. As soon as it was completed, he went to Davies' office in the Senate Office Building. "We're stuck at sixty-five, Jeb."

Davies frowned and then sat back in his chair adjusting his cufflinks. "Who'd we lose?"

"They're not exactly lost."

"Who are the sons of bitches that reneged?"

"It was Sal Grilli. He wants to wait until the verdict comes down in the Lindsay Cabot murder case and Dan Borden agreed that waiting was a good idea."

"That's ridiculous." Davies picked up his intercom. "Beau, reach out for Sal Grilli. I want him in my office and I want him here now."

An hour later, Senator Salvatore Grilli was seated opposite Senator Davies. "What kind of a game are you playing with me, Sal? I know Kendall grabbed you, but you better remember. I told you I'd see to it that your kids are convicted of insider trading and that you're ruined politically, and I'm one phone call away from doing it."

"Calm down, Jeb. I can explain. The kids aren't the issue. The worst that can happen to them is a suspended sentence, but for me, it's my Senate seat. If you saw my mail, you'd understand why I have to wait for the Cabot trial. My constituent mail and local media is overwhelmingly opposed to any Impeachment based on the President's relationship with Mrs. Cabot unless the President was involved in the murder. They want me to wait for the trial. Dan Borden has a similar problem."

"And what if Andrews is found not guilty?"

"Then we got to bite the bullet."

"You speaking for Borden too?"

"Yes."

"I don't like it, Sal."

"Jeb, go with me on this. You can destroy my political career if you want to, but that won't give you the vote you want, and if I do what you want I'll be destroyed anyway. If Borden and I hold off until after the trial, we got a good chance of preserving our seats in the Senate and you get what you want. The trial starts next Monday, and from what I hear, they got a good case against Andrews and trial won't go more than three days."

"I still don't like it, but I'll hold off on doing anything until the trial is over."

Tom Andrews' trial for the murder of Lindsay Cabot started at the Norfolk County Superior Court in Dedham, Massachusetts at nine A.M. The prosecution's case went in fast. Kelly's confession and testimony was entered in evidence and corroborated by the physical evidence of the matchbook and shell casing with Kelly's fingerprints that placed him at the scene of the crime. That was followed with airline ticket evidence indicating when Tom Andrews arrived at and left from Boston's Logan Airport and his statements placing him in Worcester at the time of the meeting that Kelly described. The District Attorney next introduced the ballpoint pen with the White House logo on it that was found in Kelly's apartment. Defense counsel's objections to its presentation were overruled by the trial judge who ruled that it was up to the jury to determine how much weight should be afforded to that evidence. The presentation of evidence of Andrews' motive, terminating media criticism of the President's relationship with Jane Cabot and making it possible for the President and Jane to marry, was quickly concluded. That was followed by testimony by Senator Davies who said that Ben's relationship with Jane formed a basis in the mind of some Senators for Ben's impeachment. Over the objections of Defense counsel, he went on to suggest that Ben was having improper sexual relations with Jane and, possibly because Jane and the President were rarely together anymore, with others like his assistant Molly Pemberton, and that these things were occurring in the White House. The final prosecution witness was Lindsay Cabot's Attorney. He testified about the meetings he had with Tom Andrews and of his refusal to prejudice his client's rights by agreeing to the divorce desired by Jane and the President. At the conclusion of the attorney's testimony, the prosecution rested and the court recessed for lunch.

Ben and Tom were seated in a court house conference room having lunch and waiting for Ben to be called as a character witness. Ben was to testify that Tom had not been instructed to murder Lindsay Cabot and had never been told that it was urgent that Jane be free of her marriage. Tom said, "Mr. President, that judge allowed Davies to talk about your relationship with Mrs. Cabot, so I don't think you should testify. They'll ask you questions like they did in the House, and there's no need to put you or Mrs. Cabot through that."

"Tom, your attorney says I should testify, and after what Kelly said this morning it's even more important."

"Kelly didn't say anything we didn't expect."

"Yes he did. He described the man he met as having a big shock of white hair under his hat. That's new. That's something he never said before, and that describes you."

"And a lot of other people."

"Tom, face it, it was a bad idea to require this speedy trial."

"I know neither you nor Peter wanted me to do this, but it was my decision and you'll see it was the right one."

"I certainly hope so, but we keep hoping that the Worcester police might find some one besides your family who saw you with them when Kelly claims he was meeting with you."

"They aren't going to. I didn't see anyone I recognized, and since no one has come forward by now, I don't expect they'll find anyone. Besides, whose more believable, my family or a convicted murderer?"

"I hope your right, Tom."

After the noon recess, Ben and then Jane testified. On cross examination, they each testified, as they did before the House, that they maintained an adult relationship with all that was entailed in that kind of relationship, and refused to describe it further. The judge was asked to hold them in contempt, but refused, thereby avoiding a Constitutional crisis. Since Senator Davies had suggested that Molly Pemberton might have had an improper relationship with the President, she was allowed to testify and deny any impropriety. The balance of the afternoon session was taken up with testimony by Tom Andrews and his family. Tom denied any knowledge of the Lindsay Cabot murder and his mother, father, sister and brother-in-law testified that one or the other of them were with him from the time he stepped off the plane from Washington until he got back on it. By the end of the day, all that was left for the second day were closing arguments and jury deliberation.

Senator Davies left the Dedham courthouse right after he completed his testimony and returned to Washington. That evening, Davies watched a tape of the trial with P.J. Winters. Davies said, "What do you think?"

"Hard to say. You never know what a jury will do. Andrews' family were very believable, but they're family. I got to hand it to you about getting Kelly to testify about the white hair. I sent Walter to the trial to observe and remind Kelly about the deal. He called and said that some of the jurors seemed to be impressed with that evidence. That little detail may be just what's necessary to get the conviction."

"What did you think of the job Andrews' lawyer did on Kelly during cross?"

"He did as good a job as can be done, but people don't confess to being a killer for hire and Kelly was well prepared. The prosecutor will argue that the deal Kelly got was because the FBI determined that it was in the national interest to get the case resolved as quickly as possible. We've tested that out on a number of demographics and practically every one buys that argument and I think this jury will. We'll know soon enough. The case goes to the jury tomorrow."

The jury deliberated for two days. When court re-convened, the courtroom was packed with media from every TV network and major newspaper in the nation. The judge looked at the slip of paper and then handed it to the clerk. The clerk read the verdict. It was, "Guilty."

CHAPTER 33

▼

John Wallace and Rahsheed Evans had puzzled over the assignment Ben and Tom gave them. They had examined every inch of the Rose Garden and every entrance. They had found nothing even remotely suspicious. They had spent the last hour reviewing the White House site plan, a landscaping plan of the garden area, utility installation drawings and architectural plans of the façade of the building. If they were terrorists, they would have abandoned the idea of mounting a terrorist attack in the Rose Garden. The only other possibility was an attack by an employee who worked in the White House or on the grounds or a visitor and they had already checked all employees and there were no suspects among them either. They couldn't discount the warning since it came from the President, but they also knew that Ben, Molly and Tom didn't know where the warning came from. They said it might be from Clarence Davenport, but why would he suddenly warn Ben of a possible terrorist attack when he had tried so hard to kill him so many times in the very recent past?

As the day wore on, John looked up and said, "I've re-examined the FBI file on every member of the domestic staff, the groundskeepers, the White House staff, everyone that has access to the grounds. I haven't found anyone to even suspect. I suppose we could ask for permission to interview them, but the President doesn't want anyone to know what we're doing. You see anything on your last tour of the grounds?"

"No, and people are beginning to ask me what I'm doing."

"What do you think of the President's idea that the warning is genuine and came from Clarence Davenport?"

"If the President thinks it's possible, that has to be good enough for me." Rahsheed looked at his wristwatch. "It's time for another patrol of the White House grounds. I'm going to borrow Ace and Deuce so if anyone asks I can say I decided to give the dogs some exercise."

"You do that. I'll check the vendors and delivery people again, but this is getting very boring."

Minutes later, Rahsheed was patrolling the perimeter of the garden again. Ace the English bulldog was on one leash and Deuce, the black pug was trotting along beside him. As they made their turn, Deuce's ears perked up, and she looked up into the sky and started barking. Almost as if on cue, the bulldog also looked up and started growling. Rahsheed looked up in the same direction as the dogs. He saw a distant speck in the sky coming towards them and wasn't sure what it was. He looked through the binoculars that had been hanging around his neck and continued staring at the little speck, watching it grow larger as it slowly flew towards the White House. Now he could make out what it was. It was a model airplane. It looked like a model of a World War II style fighter plane, maybe a P-51. He watched it turn from its approach towards the Rose garden, and continued watching as the little plane flew lazy circles, coming no closer to the White House. After a few minutes, Rahsheed let the binoculars drop back onto his chest and said to the dogs, "Okay you two. Nothing much to look at, just someone flying a model plane. Let's head back." He started to move, but Ace sat down and refused to budge. Deuce looked at him. Rahsheed gave Ace's leash a harder tug and the bulldog got to his feet and started to accompany him. Deuce remained rooted to the spot, looking up into the sky. Rahsheed said, "Come on, Deuce. Time to go." She refused to budge. "Come on, Deuce. Be a good girl now and come." She continued staring into the sky and refused to move. Rahsheed reached down, fastened a lead on her collar and she then started walking back to the White House with him.

When Rahsheed returned to the White House, he gave the dogs back to Secret Service Agent Marino. "Thanks for letting me borrow them."

"They behave all right?"

"Sure, why do you ask?"

"I see that Deuce is wearing her leash. She hardly ever does."

"Yes, that was kind of a funny thing. She's usually so obedient. I started back and told her to come, but she refused, so I put it on her."

"What was she doing?"

"Nothing. Looking up into the sky and barking."

"It must have been that model airplane. Neither of them like that model plane."

"You've seen it before?"

"Yes, starting a few months ago. Sometimes I see it flying around four or five times a day."

"I wonder who it belongs to."

"Beats me, probably some kid whose father works around here."

Rahsheed nodded. "Probably."

Later that afternoon, Rahsheed and John got together to discuss their lack of progress at discovering anything. Rahsheed told John about the model plane and the reaction of the dogs to it. "Rahsheed said, "What do you make of that model plane? Marino told me he's seen it flying around any number of times."

"How close was it?"

"Not close at all and it was just flying around in circles."

"No stunts? I used to fly model planes when I was a kid. My favorite was a P-47 and we all liked to do fancy dives and turns."

"Nothing like that, and it was a model of a fighter plane."

John Wallace shrugged. "I can't see how it can be a problem if it just flies around and doesn't come near the Rose Garden." He looked at Rahsheed. "I know that face, Ray. What's bothering you?"

"I don't know. I'm going to talk to Molly. I wonder if she and the President have ever seen something flying around."

"She's in Boston with Tom and the President. Tom's trial is going on over there."

"Let's call her. I want to ask her if she saw the plane, whether it ever came at all close to where they were in the Rose Garden." Rahsheed dialed Molly's cell phone.

"Hello," Molly said.

"Molly, this is Rahsheed and John. I want to talk to you about the Rose Garden thing."

"I can't talk to you now. Tom was just convicted." She started to cry. Rahsheed could hear her say, "It's Rahsheed, Mr. President."

Ben took the phone. "Rahsheed. We're all in a state of shock. Tom was found guilty not five minutes ago. The bailiff has taken him away and Molly is a wreck. Let me talk to you later."

"Yes, sir." Rahsheed hung up the phone. He turned to John Wallace. "Shit, Tom Andrews was convicted. Can you believe it! They took the word of a life-long criminal over that of a career guy who never did one thing wrong in his whole life."

"Andrews in prison. They must be going to file an appeal. Maybe he can win his appeal."

"Maybe, but I doubt it. You followed the trial. I didn't see any grounds for reversal. Did you?"

Wallace shook his head. "No."

"Jesus, I wonder where he'll be sent. Guys like him and us have a lot of enemies in the prison population. I hope to hell he can survive it."

"Molly got to be a mess."

"She is. The President didn't sound so good either. Did you think what this might do to the Impeachment case in the Senate?"

"Oh, God. That's right." Wallace said, "Thurston becomes President. When that happens I quit."

"We won't have to quit. We'll be fired.

"Let's see if Martha knows anything. Maybe she's heard from the President."

Rahsheed and John walked over to the anteroom in front of the Oval Office where Ben's assistant Martha worked. Rahsheed said, "You hear about Tom." Martha turned her tear stained face towards Rahsheed. Rahsheed said, "I see that you have."

"I just can't believe it. Is it on the news already?"

"No, we called Molly to ask her a question about something and she told us."

"Poor darling. It's so unfair." Martha dried her eyes, blew her nose and squared her shoulders. "What did you want to ask her? Anything I could help you with?"

"I don't think so. Just about whether she ever noticed a model airplane flying around near the Rose Garden."

"She must have. I've seen it and so has Mrs. Cabot. She mentioned it to me a while ago."

"What did she say about it?"

"Only that it seemed to be flying straight towards them."

"How close?"

"Pretty close."

"And then what?"

"And then nothing. They went in and it must have gone away."

"Was it flying towards them when they went in?"

"I don't know. I suppose it was. Is this something important?"

"I wish I knew."

After they finished talking with Martha, Rahsheed and John Wallace continued talking about the model plane. Rahsheed said, "Tomorrow, if that plane is back, let's find out what we can?"

"Okay, but remember, The President told us we can't say who the source is or do something that would tell anyone that we have a source if this is some kind of a plot."

"I know. Everyone except Molly and maybe the President and Tom think Davenport was killed in that boating accident in Ireland. I kind of thought that maybe the President and Tom were humoring her about Davenport. You think Davenport could be the source? They haven't told us how they received that warning, and that has to be because they're trying to protect their source."

Rahsheed shrugged. "I don't know. Like the President said, maybe it is and maybe it isn't, but they think it's a good source."

"If it's Davenport, what the hell are we protecting him for? He needs killing. I never believed and still don't that the President was involved in the assassination, but if he's protecting Davenport, admit it, Ray, it makes you wonder."

"Not me. He got to have a good reason for what he's doing."

"Like what?"

"I don't know. Say it's Davenport. Maybe the guy's feeling remorse and giving us some counter-terrorism information."

"You never met with him. He's a cold fish. He doesn't know what remorse is."

"All I can say, John, is if the President wanted us to know who the source was and why he doesn't want to give him away, he would have told us, and that applies even if Davenport is the source."

"I guess you're right. What do you want to do tomorrow? Could be the person flying the plane is the son of some diplomat or maybe even some Congressman or Senator."

"We'll find where it's coming from and see if it's a kid or an adult. If it's at all suspicious, I got some friends on the D.C. Police. I'll have one of them stop them and find out what he can."

"Stop them on what grounds?"

"I don't know, maybe a traffic violation or maybe a broken tail light."

"You can't tell him anything."

"I know, don't worry."

The next morning, Rahsheed and John Wallace were in a small single engine Piper. They had received all necessary clearances to fly around the District on a surveillance mission. At ten A.M. they watched as a small model plane flew towards the White House, flew circles near an approach to the Rose Garden and then flew back towards a Ford Expedition. John and Rahsheed peered through their binoculars as two men retrieved the small plane, and an hour later launched it again.

Rahsheed said, "That begins to look suspicious to me John, two Middle-Eastern looking men."

"Just because they're Middle-Eastern looking."

"Don't give me that politically correct crap, John. In case you haven't noticed, I'm black and a Muslim."

John Wallace smiled. "I hadn't noticed, but now that you mention it."

Rahsheed smiled back. "You got me. Let's fuel up and watch them for the rest of today."

"The President should be back from Boston this afternoon and maybe he'll be in the Garden."

"I don't want him out there."

"We're Secret Service, we ought to be able to arrange that. Let's check the license plate. I'll read the numbers, and you mark them down."

Rahsheed phoned the numbers in to Agent Marino who called them back ten minutes late. Marino reported, "It's a Ford Expedition, rented from Avis over two months ago by a man named Yusif Ahmed. He's a student at American University and has a Lebanese passport. What's he done?"

"Maybe nothing. Thanks for your help." Rahsheed ended the call and after he told John Wallace what Marino had reported, he said, "You watch him for the next few hours. Let me know when they start to leave. I'm going to make arrangements with a police officer I know to stop those guys and I want to be there.

John continued watching the two men fly the little plane for the rest of the day. At six fifteen, the men started up the Ford SUV and pulled out onto the road. Three minutes after that, a police car pulled up behind them with its siren blaring and then pulled along side and motioned for Yusif to pull over. He did so.

Rahsheed in a car behind the police cruiser watched.

Akmed, sitting in the rear seat of the Expedition, hugged the plane to his chest and said, "How can they know anything?"

"Don't panic! Let me handle it. It's probably nothing."

The police officer walked over to the Expedition. "Out of the car, please. You too, in the back."

"What for? What do you want?" Akmed said.

Yusif said, "I'll handle this. You be quiet." He smiled at the Police Officer. "What seems to be the trouble, officer?"

The policeman took a step back and removed his gun from its holster. "I don't want to have to say it again. Out of the car. Now."

Akmed shouted, "We die as martyrs." He pressed the transmit button. The plane he was hugging against his chest exploded.

Rahsheed watched with horror as the Expedition exploded and burned and exploded again when its gas tank went. He ran over to the police officer and extinguished the flames on the policeman's body. Rahsheed wanted to report what had happened to the President, but first he had to call John Wallace.

When Wallace answered, Rahsheed said, "They had explosives in their car. They're both dead. Get a team over to their apartment in Baltimore and clean it out before the local police can get there. If we're lucky, maybe there's something we can learn about who sent them and if there's anything else planned." The next thing Rahsheed wanted to do was to make a condolence call. Officer Miswali whose charred body was lying at his feet was his wife's sister's husband. He wanted to explain what had happened and how he happened to be there, but he couldn't. He had been sworn to secrecy. That would have to wait. He had burns on his arms and a cut on his face from flying glass fragments that needed medical care. Rahsheed took off his jacket, walked over to the still smoldering body of officer Miswali, closed, his staring eyes and covered the body with his bloody jacket. Rahsheed then wearily sat on the side of the side of the road listening to the wail of an approaching police car and an ambulance.

The Washington Times reported

> *Yusif Ahmed, a Lebanese student attending American University, an unidentified man said to be his friend and D.C. police officer Kareem Miswali were killed in a freak accident and explosion earlier this evening. A passing motorist reported that Officer Miswali had apparently stopped the rented Ford Expedition driven by Yusif Ahmed for a minor traffic infraction. As the police officer approached the car, it suddenly exploded, killing both occupants of the car and the police officer. The cause of the explosion is being investigated.*

A similar story appeared in The Washington Post and was picked up by the wire services and on their web sites.

On the day Akmed and Yusif died, Clarence arrived in the UK. As he looked at the nameplate of Charles Rabbani in the entry foyer of his newly rented London flat, he wondered how long it would take him to get used to his new identity. Uncle Rabbani had arranged for the death of someone in a plane accident in Switzerland who would be identified as Khalil Yomani. He wondered if it would be someone who died from natural causes or a willing martyr whose family would now be taken care of. It really didn't matter and Clarence decided not to waste any brain cells thinking about it. He had never felt comfortable in that role and hoped that this one would fit better.

The first thing Clarence did in his new apartment was rearrange some of the furniture by placing an overstuffed armchair covered in a flowery damask print in front of his computer workstation. Fatima had made a great selection. Next, he went on line to check the news. He wanted to see where President Silver was going to be. If it were in Washington, he would have to decide whether to warn Molly or remain loyal to his uncle.

The front-page headline story was Tom Andrews' conviction for murder. A half-hour later, buried in the local news from the Capitol, he found the story about the death of Yusif and Akmed. Clarence breathed a sigh of relief. He wouldn't have to make a very hard choice after all.

Twenty minutes after that, he began reading the account of Tom Andrews' trial. When he read Senator Davies accusation linking Molly Pemberton and President Silver in an amorous relationship, he sat up straight. Could that possibly be true? He found and read the transcript of Molly's testimony. Did he believe her denials? And what difference did it make anyway? But somehow, he felt it did. Later that night he saw a TV news broadcast covering the trial and saw Ben with his arms around Mrs. Cabot and he knew Davies was lying about Molly.

CHAPTER 34

▼

Senator Davies' meeting with Senator Smithers took on a celebratory tone. Smithers reported that they had gone over the necessary two thirds in the Senate and now had sixty-nine votes. Ben Silver's short term as President was all but over. All that was left to be done was to present the evidence in the Senate and vote.

Smithers said, "Finally, Jeb, Andrews' conviction did it. It's over. We can present the case in an hour and call for a vote tomorrow."

"I know, but for the sake of history, we have to submit a thorough and compelling case to the Senate and then ask Silver to resign. By then, even Senator Kendall will have to fold. If Silver refuses, we throw the bastard out. We got seventy-five, maybe eighty percent of the public with us now. I want ninety percent."

"You're probably right. What's another week." Smithers rose and shook Davies' hand. "I'll get things started in the Senate and tell Thurston to get ready to move into the White House. It'll be a relief getting rid of Silver and putting one of our own kind in the White House for a change. I can see Thurston filling out this term and then two of his own. By then we ought to be able to reshape this country the way it ought to be."

P.J. Winters had been listening to the conversation on Davies' open intercom line in a small office in Davies' suite. When Smithers left Davies' office, P.J. entered. "Hard to believe that someone as stupid as him could be elected to the Senate of the United States."

"He's not the worst."

"If you need anything to keep him in line, I got a file on him."

"What you got?"

"On his personal life, he's a 'peeping tom'. No convictions, because they were settled out of court, but we got statements on a bunch of cases."

"How many?"

"At least six or seven, plus we have information that he has a secret camera installed in the guest bedroom at his house and in the bathroom."

Davies adjusted the crease in his pants. "I'm not surprised. He doesn't have enough courage to really do anything more than just look. I have information like that myself."

"You got anything else?"

P.J. nodded. "He's taken a lot of illegal campaign contributions, some from people directly concerned with legislation he was pushing."

"So have many others."

"True, but he wasn't smart about it. He had one group run an investment account for him. All he had were winners and the reports came in annually. He made three million dollars on a ten thousand-dollar original investment. We got a clerk at the investment house on an embezzlement charge and went easy on him for statements explaining the real deal on Smithers' account."

"It's nice to know, but I don't think I'll need it."

"You got it if you do. What do you think the time table is on your becoming President and me becoming Vice President?"

Davies fixed his cufflinks and sat back in his chair, "I see Silver gone in a week, ten days at the most. Thurston becomes President the next day and within thirty days, I become Vice President." Davies turned and looked at Winters. "During that thirty days, I'm going to need you to get all the copies of the Morton tapes, do something to them and then announce that they're all phonies. Can you do that for me?"

Winters frowned. "I can never be sure that I've found all of them. What I can do is say they were maintained in an insecure environment and could have been tampered with, and then mess with the ones we find. That's more believable and should be good enough to satisfy the media."

"I know better than to argue with you on things like that and agree the media will buy what you tell them."

"Okay, so you're Vice President. What happens after that?"

"We wait, maybe six or seven months, no more. Then Thurston will resign."

"Why?"

"He will. I got something on him so he'll do whatever I tell him."

Winters sat looking at Davies a moment. "I got a file on Thurston. There is evidence that he's probably gay. If that's the kind of thing you have on him, I'm a little nervous about your being able to keep him in line. There are openly gay members of Congress now and he seems to keep it under wraps."

Davies fidgeted with his cufflinks and then the crease of his trousers. "I may as well tell you. Beau is the only other person that knows about this, except of course for Thurston." Davies then told Winters of the evidence he had of Thurston murdering a young man in a San Francisco bathhouse. When he finished, he said, "I could show you the photographs of Thurston strangling the guy and the tape I made of Thurston admitting it."

"Not necessary. If it's what you say, that ought to do it. But you could get in trouble for being an accessory after the event by not turning him in."

"I was acting as his attorney."

"Then how do you threaten him now?"

Davies laughed. "So have me disbarred."

Winters nodded. "He gets life for murder and you might, at worst, get your license to practice law which is something you don't do anyway, suspended for maybe six months. I like it."

"There's no statute of limitations on murder."

"I know." P.J. continued. "When do I become your Veep?"

"I and a lot of other Senators were critical of Silver for failing to promptly get a Vice President chosen, so I'll do it pretty quickly. I don't see any problem in getting you approved in the Senate, do you?"

Winters smiled. "With what I have on so many of them? Don't be silly."

"How long do you think you'll need to get everything cleaned up in your office so you can accept."

"I promised Walter Wagner he could have my job. If he gets it, I could take it immediately, because I'll still be running it."

"Consider it done."

"When you're finished, you back me for the Presidency."

"That's the deal."

"How many terms you want?"

"I'll finish this one, then one more. After that, I'll decide whether I want to do another four years, but whenever I'm out, I'll do my best to make sure that you're next."

CHAPTER 35

▼

Ben was behind his desk in the Oval Office and Molly Pemberton was sitting in front of him, her eyes still red from crying. They had just returned from Boston. Ben's first visitor, waiting in the anteroom for their return, was Senator Kendall. He had told Ben and Molly the not unexpected news that, as a result of Tom's conviction, Davies now had enough votes to force Ben's removal from office. Kendall said, "I understand that they'll present their case to the Senate and then give you a chance to resign before they take a vote. Do you want me to try and negotiate a graceful exit for you as best I can before they start the presentation?"

Ben sat quietly for a long minute. "What do you think is in the best interests of the country?"

"I honest to God don't know. It could be best for you to resign and not have to go down in history as the first President to be removed from office."

"Like Nixon did?"

"I suppose so. What do you think?"

"I don't think so. Resigning is tantamount to my admitting that Impeachment was a Constitutional remedy being used properly. I'd rather historians look back at this and perhaps some day see it for what it is, a wrongly conceived remedy for unproven allegations."

At this point Molly broke down again and wept. Ben rose to console her and she waived him away. Moments later she said, "Excuse me Mr. President. I'm so sorry."

"Take some time, Molly. Come back when you feel a little better."

"No. No." She wiped her eyes. "I'm all right. I'll manage. Go on."

Senator Kendall said, "Why don't I leave you for a few minutes. I can be back in fifteen minutes."

Molly turned to Kendall. "No. It's okay. I didn't mean to do that. I hate to act that way."

Ben said, "It's okay to be human Molly."

"Please continue on. This is a personal sorrow. You're talking about more important things."

"Molly, I insist," Ben said, "go lie down in you office That's a Presidential order. When John Wallace and Rahsheed get here, I'll call you. I'll need you for that."

Molly smiled. "Okay, it's probably for the best."

After Molly left, Kendall said, "How the hell did Tom get convicted? I don't understand it. Was the jury rigged?"

"I don't think so. All I can say is that juries are unpredictable."

"Are there grounds for appeal?"

"It was filed, but counsel isn't optimistic unless they can come up with some new evidence."

"Like what?"

"I don't know. We couldn't manage to get him released pending appeal, but we pulled some strings to have him placed in a secure lockup for the present. I'm worried that when he has to join some general prison population he won't last very long."

"You're probably right."

"That's why I'm going to try and get the Governor of Massachusetts to grant him a full pardon."

"He can do that?"

Ben nodded. "He can. I already spoke to him. The problem is he needs the consent of the governor's Council. They're a difficult and very political group. The governor will see what it would take to get them to go along, but I'm prepared to play ball with them."

Kendall shook his head. "Don't do that. You'd be violating every principle that you've stood for all your life and disappoint everyone that has looked at you as an example of honesty and morality in government. Please, I understand how you feel, but we were just talking about what's best for the country. If you can arrange the pardon, it may make you feel better, but as you've said, it's not the job of people in government to make their own lives better by using the prerogatives of their office. I feel bad about Tom. I believe he was unjustly convicted, but using the Presidency to get him a pardon is wrong and you know it."

"I know your right, Bob. But I'm at a point where maybe I no longer care. The worst of it is, the governor isn't that optimistic he can get it done."

"Consider this too. Giving Tom a pardon will be taken as confirmation that he was acting for you when he killed Lindsay Cabot. I can just see Davies and Winters leaking to the media that they were working on turning Tom to implicate you in the Cabot murder, and that you misused the Presidency to keep him from doing that."

Ben said wearily, "I suppose that's a story the public would buy, but Tom never killed Cabot and, he'll probably be killed for something he didn't do while in jail. I don't see how I can just sit here and not try to prevent that from happening."

"Tom's a pretty tough guy, and maybe we can arrange for him to go to Eglin or some other minimum security prison. You can't play politics to try and get him a pardon. Everyone that supported you, me included, will feel betrayed. You got a week. Maybe the appeal will come through. Maybe someone else will confess to the Cabot murder. I don't know. Promise you won't do anything until we talk again."

"Okay." Ben looked at his wristwatch. I think I'll have Jane call Molly and have Martha look in on her. I wish I knew how to make her feel a little better. I feel responsible for Tom's conviction and her unhappiness."

"You can't fix everything and you're not responsible for everything."

Ben smiled, "Easy for you to say. In this job it seems like you are."

"You advised Molly to take a break. You ought to do the same."

"I'd like to, but there's a national security thing Molly and I are working on that needs some attention. We have to meet with a couple of our agents and after that, I'll have to fill you in on it. It's important that someone I trust in government know about this before they boot me out of here."

As soon as Senator Kendall left, Ben instructed his secretary that as soon as Rahsheed Evans and John Wallace arrived at the White House, Molly was to be sent for and they were to be expeditiously sent through to the Oval Office. Molly was the first to arrive. When she came in, Ben said, "You know how awful and guilty I feel about Tom, Molly. I feel like it's all my fault."

"But it's not. I just know that P.J. Winters and Davies are behind this somehow. They framed Tom."

"I don't know, but if they did it was because of me. I got him into this and I'd like to get him out of it."

"It's not your fault."

"I don't want to get your hopes up, but there's a possibility of a pardon. I've talked to the Governor of Massachusetts about it."

"What did he say?"

"He said if it were up to him, he'd do it, but he needs the consent of the governor's Council and he doesn't know if he'll be able to persuade them to go along."

"A pardon. That means that even though he's guilty, he's excused." Molly shook her head. "You know the way Tom is. I don't know if he'd want you to do that. He still wants to prove he's innocent."

"I understand, but I don't want him to stay in prison."

"Neither do I." Martha buzzed Ben at that point to ask if John Wallace and Rahsheed Evans should be sent in. As Ben responded, telling Martha to have them come in, Molly said, "Good luck. I hope you can get it done and if you can, that you can persuade Tom to accept it."

Rahsheed and John came in and sat down. Rahsheed had a large white bandage across his forehead and another under his right eye.

Ben said, "I heard you were injured in that explosion. Are you all right?"

Rahsheed smiled wryly. "This is the least of my problems. The police officer that was killed was my wife's sister's husband. I feel terrible about enlisting him in this and getting him killed."

"That's the way I feel about getting Tom in trouble."

John Wallace said, "Maybe it's easy for me to say this, but I've known Tom Andrews for most of my working life. He knew the score and that certain risks went with the territory in government. When he was in the Secret Service and took the job of protecting the President, he knew he could be called upon to give his life to save the President. Tom was always willing to do that. That's the kind of guy he is. You never know exactly the kind of risk, but you know they're there, and the same goes for your wife's brother-in-law, Rahsheed. He knew the risks when he became a cop."

"Sure, but you feel terrible anyway," Rahsheed said, "but let's move on."

John continued. "We have some important things to tell you. The tip you gave us was first rate. The guys that blew up the Ford Expedition and killed themselves and Rahsheed's relative had been flying a model plane over to the White House. It was loaded with explosives. They were two Middle-Eastern guys living in Baltimore. We picked up a bunch of documents and a computer at their apartment that we're still going over. What we know so far is that they were trained at a base called, New Salman Pak by some guy with a bandaged face named Khalil Yomani. This Khalil Yomani is a key Al Qaeda operative and came up with the plan of loading a model plane with explosives, and installing a GPS system and a miniature video camera in it. They were to fly the plane around the White House, and when they saw you in the Rose Garden, they were to fly the plane towards you. When it was within a certain range, they would make the plane explode and kill you and whoever was out there with you."

"That would work?"

"Yes, sir. Our experts think so. I hate to bring it up right now, with Tom in jail and the Impeachment on the way, but can we get any more information from your source. One of the instructions they received asked them to delay implementation of their attack on you, sir to coordinate it with other planned attacks. They were later told to proceed independently, but something big is in the works." John hesitated a moment and then continued, "Is your source Clarence Davenport?"

Ben looked at John Wallace. "Honest to God, John, I don't know. Molly and I think it might be, but if we said so, who'd believe us? The FBI, the CIA, all the intelligence services, everyone says that Davenport is dead, and the world believes it. None of them will ever admit they were wrong, and what difference does it make any way. It doesn't change anything."

"You're right."

"Molly and I have a way of communicating with our source by e-mail. We'll try and see if we can get anything out of him about whatever else is being planned. I'll promise you and Rahsheed this, John. Before I'm kicked out of office, I'll fill in you and Rahsheed and a group from the Congress that Bob Kendall puts together so that you'll know everything that Molly and I know. This is too important to be left to a Thurston administration that'll be run by Davies and Winters."

"Thank you, sir. Is there anything Rahsheed and I can do for you now?"

Ben shook his head. "No. Molly and I have to compose a message to our informant and hope that we persuade him to give us some more information."

After John and Rahsheed left, Molly and Ben sat across from each other not saying anything for a few minutes. Ben broke the silence. "I know your heart's not in it at this moment, and neither is mine, but we have got to craft a response to the letter we got from Davenport."

"You said you're not sure it's him. I thought you were."

"Ninety-nine percent, but that's not something I wanted to discuss at that point. Let's consider what Clarence knows. He follows the news and knows Tom was convicted. As far as I know, the media has not picked up your relationship with Tom. Davenport probably knows that Davies claimed you and I are having a relationship."

"I wondered about that. Davies knows that's not true."

"He's been spending a lot of time with Winters, and Winters doesn't like you from when you worked at the FBI and refused to withhold information from the Secret Service that they were supposed to deliver to them, and he hates Tom. He probably wanted to embarrass you and Tom and make me look like a lecherous old man. I don't think they needed it for the impeachment, but we don't have time to speculate about that. As hard as it is, we have to think about what we say to him now, because I think Davenport knows a lot more than he's given us. We've got to try and stop whatever the attack might be that the Al Qaeda are planning."

Molly sighed. "I'll do my best, sir."

"Let's remember that he admires you, not only for your looks but for your intelligence, and that he hates Davies because Davies was involved in the cover-up of what happened at Kamisiyah."

"Right, he tried to kill Davies with a car bomb and killed his secretary instead."

Molly and Ben spent the next two hours drafting and re-drafting an e-mail letter to Davenport. They printed and read the final draft. It said,

> *Dear Friend,*
>
> *Thank you so much for your warning. I managed to figure out where the attack would be coming from.*
>
> *The assassins managed to destroy themselves and the evidence of what they were doing and I managed to persuade the President not to allow the news of how we discovered the plot to be released to the media. He agreed it was the least we could do to protect my "friend".*
>
> *Receiving your warning and preventing the attack on the President and me was the only good thing that has happened.*
>
> *You probably saw that the President's chief of staff, Tom Andrews was convicted of the crime of murdering Mrs. Jane Cabot's husband. Just as I know you're still alive, I know he never committed that crime. He had to have been framed by Senator Davies and FBI Director Winters. They've been trying to destroy the President and Mr. Andrews ever since the President took office. The President and Mr. Andrews are two of the finest men I've ever known.*
>
> *Davies even tried to discredit me personally by saying that the President*

and I had a sexual relationship. How disgusting. You know I admire the President. He truly is a brilliant man, but he's old enough to be my father. He treats me like one of his daughters and his daughters treat me like a sister. I've gotten to know Mrs. Cabot and she also treats me like a daughter. No one could have a better family than I have with the President and Mrs. Cabot and their children.

But the worst thing is that most of the country thinks the President was involved in the Lindsay Cabot murder and it now looks like he will be removed from office by the Senate. That means all the reforms planned by the President, most of which were described in your Manifesto, don't have a chance at being adopted. I could e-mail you copies of the bills the President's legal staff was working on and you would have approved.

It now looks like Elliott Thurston will become the new President. We think that means Davies will be running the country.

Your friend,
Molly

After Molly left, Ben sat at his desk, too tired to walk over to the residential quarters. He had never felt so helpless. Ben rarely drank, and when he did, it would generally be a glass of red wine or a vodka and tonic at a festive occasion to be sociable. He felt like having more than his quota right now. He finally got up, walked to the residence and straight through to his bedroom. The phone rang. No, he didn't want any dinner, thank you very much. No he didn't want anyone from the wait staff to remain in case he changed his mind, and yes he knew he could call the kitchen if he got hungry.

Ben had been sitting quietly, staring at the fireplace when the phone rang again. He felt a moment of irritation, but then recognized that they were calling because they were worried about him. He took a deep breath and answered the phone. This time it was the Governor of Massachusetts. "Sorry to call so late, Mr. President, but you said to call, whenever I had an answer."

Ben brightened with hope. "I didn't expect to hear from you this soon. I hope you have good news."

"They said okay, but with strings attached. Some want Federal and some state judicial appointments that frankly they're not qualified to hold, and they know it. What's more, I doubt you could get the Senate to approve them."

"They're just playing games?"

"That's how I read it. They want the offer in writing, signed by you. I think it's to set you up for a corruption charge and prosecution."

"Thanks for trying, you can tell them to…"

The Governor interrupted. "I know what to tell them, but what's the sense. They were trying a sting operation and it didn't work. Leave it at that."

"You're right," Ben said.

As Ben finally went to bed he said, I'm so damn tired my hair hurts. I didn't want this job, when I took it, I only took it because I had to, and I wanted to quit a dozen times. For that very brief time when we exposed Davies and thought Davenport killed himself I thought maybe I could actually do something positive and useful in this position. What a perfect fool I am.

CHAPTER 36

▼

Margaret Kelly normally dressed very carefully for church and took great pains to fix her once auburn and now white hair into as attractive an arrangement as possible. Father Jim was not surprised that today she came to church in an old housedress, without lipstick and with her hair barely combed.

The priest said, "I can see that you are troubled, Margaret."

"Yes, Father, I am. I never thought that nice Mr. Andrews would be convicted. How can something like that happen?"

"You know the answer to that, Margaret. It was your son that betrayed the man that tried to help him."

"Like Judas, Father."

"Do you think the analogy fits?"

"I don't know."

"I think you do."

"What am I to do?"

"You know the answer to that question."

"How can I betray my son? He's been trouble all his life, but he's my son."

"How can you betray the principles you've lived by all your life. How can you see an innocent man spend the rest of his life in prison when you have the power to prevent that injustice?"

Margaret sat quietly in front of Father Jim not saying a word. Finally she said, "What can I do. Is it too late?"

"It's not too late to do the right thing. Call the lawyer representing Tom Andrews. His name is Peter McGlynn. You should speak to him."

"Would you go with me, Father?"

"Of course."

"You're telling me to do this?"

"I'm telling you that it's the right thing for you to do. You are the one who must decide to do it."

"What will happen to Red?"

"I don't know."

"Surely, you know more about these things than I do, Father. What do you think might happen?"

After a contemplative pause, Father Jim said, "I suppose the conviction for murdering Lindsay Cabot would have to be set aside. I don't know what other charges for other things may surface. At the very least, he could be prosecuted for perjury for saying he did the murder when he was sleeping it off in your house."

"Can I get in trouble for not telling the authorities before?"

"I don't know, but I suppose you might."

She shrugged. "That's of little importance. They can do with me what they will. I think I'll be in trouble with God if I don't."

"You know what's right and what's wrong."

"I'll have to tell Red."

"Would you like me to go with you to see him?"

Margaret Kelly dabbed at her eyes with a wadded up Kleenex. "I don't want to see him until after I see that lawyer. Red will talk me out of it."

"Are you ready to call attorney McGlynn now?"

Mrs. Kelly took a deep breath and said, "Yes, Father. I am," and accompanied Father Jim to his office.

Once there the Priest looked up McGlynn's phone number, dialed it on the old rotary phone in his office and said to McGlynn's secretary, "This is Father Jim Voss. I have a parishioner with me that needs to speak with Attorney McG-lynn on a matter of extreme urgency."

When McGlynn got on the phone, Father Jim confirmed who he was and said, "I am with one of my parishioners, Mrs. Margaret Kelly, the mother of Red Kelly. She has something she wants to tell you."

Father Jim passed the phone to Mrs. Kelly. She told her story as McGlynn lis-tened quietly. When she finished, McGlynn started to tell her what he wanted her to do. She interrupted saying, "I'm really unable to get anything straight right now. Tell Father Jim what I'm to do and then I'm sure he'll explain it to me," and then passed the phone back to Father Jim.

Father Jim listened for a few minutes, then hung up the phone and turned to Mrs. Kelly. "He wants us to come to his office in Boston so you can sign a document stating what you told him. He said he would come out to Worcester if you want."

"I want to get it over and done with."

"It'll be quicker if we go in to Boston. I'll drive you in. He can prepare the affidavit while we're on our way."

"Thank you, Father. That would be best. But can I change my clothes? I can't go into Boston looking like this. It'll only take five minutes."

Almost true to her word, she emerged from her house ten minutes later wearing a tailored navy blue suit, with her hair combed and fresh lipstick painted on. Five minutes later, they were sitting in Father Jim's late model Chevrolet travelling east on the Massachusetts Turnpike. For most of the fifty-five minute drive, Mrs. Kelly sat quietly in the front passenger seat, occasionally dabbing at the corner of her eyes with her ever present wadded up Kleenex. Father Jim twice attempted to start a conversation with her only to be rebuffed by her shaking her head. She finally said, "I appreciate all that you're doing for me father. It was wrong of me to not come forward when this first happened, but I never knew what the right thing to do was when Red was growing up, and this was the same. Maybe if I hadn't made excuses for Red and covered-up the bad things he did as a boy, he would have turned out better. I don't know, but I couldn't let it go on."

"You shouldn't blame yourself, Margaret. He went to Catholic schools, he went to church, and he had plenty of lessons in morality. The justice system had plenty of chances to rehabilitate him. Perhaps many failed, but the biggest failure was Red's. He chose to do the things he did and no one knows why. He came from a good home, your husband made a good living, your other son and your daughter all lead good and productive lives."

"You're right, Father. I've got to stop blaming myself. I'm only glad that his father, God rest his soul, isn't here to see this day. The man tried everything to get Red to mend his ways and nothing worked. Red broke the dear man's heart."

At last they arrived at McGlynn's law firm. His secretary ushered them into a nicely furnished corner office and offered coffee or tea. McGlynn was a slightly balding man who seemed to exude energy and competence. He greeted Father Jim and Mrs. Kelly warmly. "Thank you both for coming into Boston. I would have been happy to come to Worcester."

"You must be angry with me for not coming forward before," Mrs. Kelly said.

McGlynn smiled. "I would have liked it better if you had come forward before the trial, but you're doing the right thing now and that's what's important." He slid a two-page document across his desk to Mrs. Kelly and a copy of it towards Father Jim. "I want you to take your time and read this very carefully. I hope it says exactly what you told me. If there's anything, anything at all that isn't exactly what you said, let me know and we'll change it."

Mrs. Kelly picked up the affidavit and then put it down. As she fumbled in her purse, she said, "My arms aren't long enough to read this without my reading glasses."

McGlynn laughed politely and said, "If you can't find yours, you can borrow mine."

She found her glasses, perched them on her nose and then started reading. Her lips formed the words as she went along. A few minutes later, she took off her glasses and let them hang on her chest. "You've got it exactly right. Do you want me to sign it?"

"Yes, but wait until my secretary comes in. She's a notary public."

After Mrs. Kelly signed three copies of her affidavit, McGlynn nodded to his Secretary. She picked up the documents and said, "Do you want me to make that call now, Mr. McGlynn?"

"Yes." He turned towards Mrs. Kelly, "There's someone that wants to speak to you. I hope my secretary can get through to him because he's usually very busy."

A minute later the phone in McGlynn's office rang. Peter picked it up, listened a moment and then said, "She's sitting in front of me. I'll put you on speaker."

A moment later, the voice of Ben Silver came through the phone. "This is Ben Silver, Mrs. Kelly. I want to thank you for what you did. I can understand how difficult it must have been for you."

Margaret Kelly sat transfixed staring at the telephone. She made the sign of the cross on her chest and then whispered to Father Jim, "Is that himself? Is it really the President of the United States?" Father Jim nodded that it was. Mrs. Kelly resumed staring at the phone.

Ben continued, "You've made a lot of people very happy. By tomorrow at this time, Mr. McGlynn will have filed a motion for a new trial. We're hoping that the motion will be allowed and that Mr. Andrews will be released on bail pending the new trial. Peter, you'll keep me advised?"

"Yes, sir, Mr. President."

"Very good. Thanks again, Mrs. Kelly. I've got to go now. I want to call Mr. Andrews' mother, and there's a young lady that works for me here in the White House who will want to know about this."

Ben's final call was to Senator Bob Kendall. Kendall couldn't wait to get off the phone and start calling members of the Senate. Late that night, he called Ben, weary but happy to report that it looked like Davies no longer has the sixty-seven votes he needed. Kendall said, "I don't like to count him out, because Davies is a resilient bastard. He seems to have more lives than a cat, but for the moment, the impeachment won't make it. He's been meeting with his staff ever since the news broke about Tom and even ran over to the Hoover building for a meeting with P.J. Winters. I'd love to know what that was about."

"That makes two of us, but let's just enjoy the good news about Tom for now."

CHAPTER 37

▼

Not everyone considered Mrs. Kelly revelation good news. When attorney Peter McGlynn filed a motion for a new trial with Mrs. Kelly's affidavit attached, a clerk in the Superior Court immediately leaked the news to a reporter from the Boston Herald. The news rocketed across the country. Senatorial aide, Beau Lawrence saw the news while munching a Crispy Crème lemon-filled doughnut. He didn't finish it, and immediately informed his employer. Senator Davies' face turned red with rage. When he recovered enough to speak, he called FBI Director P.J. Winters and broke the news to him and then made a rare trip to the Hoover Building to talk with him.

They met in P.J.'s office. When Davies entered, Winters was smoking a Cuban cigar. Winters exhaled a cloud of smoke and tamped out his cigar as Davies sat down. "Sorry about the cigar, Senator, but I just lit up when you called and didn't expect you to get here so fast."

"Light up another one for all I care. It stinks of those damn cigars whether you're smoking one or not. It's against the law to smoke them inside of federal buildings, you know."

"You come to lecture me on smoking?"

"Sorry, P.J. I'm pissed. Son of a bitch, can you believe it? We had it made. Silver was dead meat. Now, I can just see votes for impeachment disappearing."

Winters scowled, "That's the least of our problems. If Kelly figures out how this happened and they turn him, we'll have a really big problem."

"I thought you said Kelly didn't know we arranged the whole thing?"

"He doesn't, but I never said he was stupid. There'll be a lot of smart people trying to figure this out. Mrs. Kelly's affidavit says that she told that priest in the confessional that Red couldn't have committed the murder long before the Andrews trial, and the priest just confirmed that. They'll wonder why Kelly didn't use the alibi and why he'd confess to something he didn't do? Initially, Kelly probably figured that we just wanted to claim credit for solving a high profile murder case. Fingering Andrews didn't mean that much to him. He'd think we just took advantage of the situation, or that maybe we knew the President had it done and that we just couldn't prove it. But if they start probing, Kelly may begin to figure that maybe Walter Wagner wanted to get Andrews and the President so bad, that he created the whole situation and caused the murder. From there they could connect me and then you."

"You trust Wagner, don't you?"

"Sure. But he's human."

"You'd never let him turn on me, would you?"

"If he turns on you he turns on me. If I thought that was possible, I'd have him killed right now, but forget about Wagner. The pressure will build and Silver, Andrews and the rest of them aren't stupid. They could put it together."

"What are we going to do?"

"I'm not sure, and whatever it is, it's probably best you don't know. You do what you can to stop the bleeding and I'll see to it that Kelly isn't a problem."

After Davies left, Walter Wagner came into P.J.'s office. P.J. said, "You heard him on the intercom. What do you think?"

Wagner shrugged. "He's pretty nervous. You think he's a stand up guy?"

P.J. shook his head. "He'd give us up in a heart beat to save his scrawny ass."

"You think he ought to be terminated?"

"Not right now. Nobody would deal with him to get you or me, and besides, maybe all we got to do is cut the link to you."

"Kelly."

"Yeah. We were going to close that door pretty soon anyway."

"How do you want it to be? Same way as we planned, the unknown prisoner in a prison fight or you got something else in mind?"

P.J. frowned. "I'd like an accident, but we don't have time to work that out. It's got to happen almost immediately."

"I think that's doable. The guy I made the arrangement with doesn't come up for parole for two months and he was going to do it a week before, but if I up the price a little, I think he'll cooperate. Kelly is always getting into fights so I think the plan will work just fine. I can reach him by e-mail and I'm sure he'll be able to do it tomorrow or the next day."

Winters nodded. "I assume the e-mail is untraceable."

Wagner smiled, "Give me a little credit, P.J. and even if they traced it, they wouldn't be able to understand it."

"You have a code with him?"

"Of course. I'll up the price for immediate delivery. Like I said, I'm not stupid and this isn't the first time."

P. J. nodded and blew out a cloud of smoke. "Just being careful, we can all get a little careless sometime."

"You're right."

"And I assume you'll close the door on the guy that does it pretty damn quick?"

Wagner nodded. "The guy's a total loser and a heroin addict. When he gets out, he'll have plenty of cash, so you got to know that getting high is the first thing he'll do. I bet he kills himself with an over dose inside of two weeks."

"And if he doesn't?"

"I can always help him along. Give him some stuff that's too pure, too strong. Trust me. He's not going to be a problem. I worry about Davies. There's nothing he can do for us anymore, and he could be a danger."

"I don't think so, Walter, and besides, don't write him off. Even if this impeachment falls through, he'll keep trying to find a way to get rid of Silver and put himself in the White House. Some day, even if he can't get rid of Silver right now, he could be the President, and if that ever happens, I'll hold him to the deal we made, and that's good for both of us. You go take care of business, and keep me advised."

Walter did take care of business. The next day and then two days after that, the Washington Standard carried two related stories, but not many realized the second was a result of the first. The first story was:

> ***Presidential Chief of Staff, Tom Andrews, convicted in the murder-for-hire killing of Lindsay Cabot, the husband of Presidential girl friend, Jane Cabot, by confessed shooter Francis "Red" Kelly, was granted a new trial today in a hearing at the Norfolk Superior Court in Dedham, Massachusetts. The court's action resulted from the startling revelation by Kelly's mother that Kelly could not possibly have been the shooter because he was asleep at her home when the alleged meeting with Andrews was supposed to have taken place and when the actual shooting took place. In another surprise move at that same hearing, convicted murderer, Tom Andrews was released on bail pending his new trial. The District Attorney's office has discounted Mrs. Kelly's affidavit. Assistant District Attorney Simpkins issued a statement saying they would launch***

an investigation with the FBI into the reasons alleged by Kelly's mother for Kelly's confession which was witnessed by officers of the Quincy, Massachusetts police force following an investigation of the Cabot murder by local police and the FBI.

The second story, carried in the same location in the same newspaper two days later read:

Francis "Red" Kelly the confessed shooter in the murder-for-hire killing of the husband of Presidential girl friend, Jane Cabot, was killed today by an unknown assailant in a prison house fight. Kelly had a history of involvement in jailhouse altercations. Kelly's mother had recently claimed that Kelly was asleep in her house when the murder took place. A spokesman from the District Attorney's office has stated that at no time during the course of their investigation had Kelly ever claimed that he was asleep at his mother's home at stated by her. Prison authorities will conduct an investigation into Kelly's murder.

Very few people other than Margaret Kelly mourned the death of Francis "Red" Kelly. President Silver called and sent flowers, and Father Jim visited to offer condolences. Red Kelly's siblings arrived to be with their mother, but they really didn't mourn his passing. For them, their brother had died long ago. For Margaret Kelly it was different. She couldn't help it. She blamed herself for her son's death, even though she knew she had done the right thing. Father Jim's visit helped, but he couldn't destroy the gnawing guilt feelings and overwhelming sorrow that threatened to destroy her.

CHAPTER 38

▼

Clarence Davenport was puzzled. The letter he received from Molly Pemberton had a lot in it that he had to think about. He sat in his flowered armchair with a printed copy of her e-mail note in his lap to think it over. Every letter from her left him more confused than the last.

She thanked him for his warning and said it enabled them to prevent Akmed and Yusif from carrying out the attack he had planned. He felt good about that, but bad that his plan had been foiled. He felt good that she thanked him, but he didn't tell her very much, only to stay out of the Rose Garden. She figured out the rest from that. He knew she was very smart and he liked that, and he liked that she didn't want to tell anyone about him, but what did she have to tell anyone? She thinks he's alive, but no one would believe her.

Then there's the story in the news that Akmed and Yusif were killed. Is that really true? Perhaps the authorities told the media they were dead to preserve the story that was now being told that Akmed and Yusif had no known connection to other terrorist organizations. Maybe they were captured and told the authorities about New Salman Pak and enough to make them wonder about who planned their attack. If they did, it's a good thing that he and Neil aren't there anymore. He checked the news on his computer. No attacks reported. Does that mean the story in the news was correct? Maybe, and maybe not.

If they are dead, was it an accident, like the news story intimated, or were they killed? How could he ever know? Perhaps she's telling him the truth. Nothing in the news suggests they were there to kill the President.

Clarence stared at his computer wishing it held the answers to the questions he had. He read the news of the trial and knew that Andrews was convicted, but

Molly says he was framed by Davies. Why'd she tell him that? Maybe she thinks he cares. Well, he doesn't and she's wrong about that. But he decided that he does care that Davies treated her badly by claiming that she was having an affair with the President and that he believes her denials. As he thought about it he shook his head and decided that he had never believed the statement Davies made about her and the President. He knew she would never do that. And he was glad that she felt that the President and Mrs. Cabot and the President's children were like family to her. Family is important.

Then she talks about the impeachment destroying the chance for the reforms in government he wanted and that Davies is behind that and that he'll be the power behind Thurston when he becomes President. That may have changed with today's news about Margaret Kelly's affidavit. But what's inescapable is the fact that Davies still wields a lot of power. He had participated in the cover-up of the Gulf War Syndrome claims of his men in the Senate following the 1991 Gulf War. As Clarence sat and thought about all he had done, he decided that he did not regret killing President Butler and all the others. The only regret he had now was the one he told Molly about when she came to his house to arrest him, and that was his killing Senator Davies' secretary instead of Davies, not that he minded killing her, but Davies was the real target. He thought some more. Did he regret his failure to kill Ben Silver? Yes, he did. Does he regret it enough to regard it as unfinished business? Perhaps not, but he did regard Senator Jeb Davies as unfinished business. Clarence glanced at his wristwatch. It would have to stay unfinished and he didn't have time to think about Molly anymore right now. Rabbani had called and they were to meet at the Dorchester for lunch. They hadn't seen much of each other since he went to New Salman Pak and this would be their first meeting since he arrived in London two days ago.

Clarence stretched his legs and looked through the windows of the old fashioned looking, tall, black taxi as they rode through the busy streets. God, but it felt good to be back in civilization. The thought of how nice it would be to see London with Molly Pemberton jumped uninvited into his head. He wondered if she liked theatre. They have great theatre here in London. He had to stop thinking of her. He would try to concentrate on other things. He'd see Fatima in a day or two, or maybe he wouldn't. He was going to the Dorchester. He tried to remember. Was the Dorchester targeted for destruction this fall? He was primarily concerned with targets in the United States, but there were several attacks planned on London facilities. Was one the Dorchester? He didn't think so. There was the Albert Hall and what else. He couldn't remember, but he had downloaded all that information onto the disc he took with him when he left New Salman Pak.

The cab turned into the little alley leading to the hotel and minutes later he was ushered into a very private dining room. Neil Rabbani and uncle Rabbani were seated at the dining table. His uncle greeted him warmly, "I apologize for being unable to see you until today."

Clarence smiled. "I needed some time to get the stench of New Salman Pak out of my system."

Rabbani nodded. "I understand. And how is my other favorite nephew? Have you had time to enjoy the comforts of London I hope?"

Clarence smiled. "Missing something makes you appreciate it even more."

"Speaking of missing something, Fatima wonders why you haven't called her yet. She worries that some desert flower may have captured your heart."

Clarence frowned. "No, no desert flower. I've had enough of the desert, enough to last two lifetimes. I'll call her tomorrow, maybe."

"Good. We must keep our women happy." Uncle Rabbani pointed at the bar set up in the corner. "Help yourself. There's wine, some Scotch gin, vodka and Irish whiskey." As Clarence poured himself a gin and bitters, Rabbani said, "What do you want for lunch? Neil and I have already ordered"

"Would you be offended if I ordered pork chops?"

Neil said, "That's what I ordered. Funny but whenever I return from spending time with those religious fanatics, I have to eat a lot of ham, bacon and other pork dishes. You must be feeling the same thing, and I drink more for a few days."

During and after lunch, Uncle Rabbani discussed his plans for his and their future. Eventually, there would be a secular Middle Eastern empire stretching from Istanbul to Cairo with outposts as far away as Siberia, Indonesia and Morocco, but for now, the problem was still the takeover of Saudi Arabia and its petroleum wealth. Its economic strength would make the rest of it happen.

Rabbani said to Clarence, "Perhaps it can't all happen during my lifetime, but if not, it will be up to you to carry it out after I'm gone and after you, it will be Neil's job or you will have children to take over. It is my job to begin. The plan to carry out a series of major attacks on the United States, the United Kingdom and other western targets around the September 11th anniversary date has been completed. It will happen and will be a major disaster for them." Rabbani raised his glass. "You did a magnificent job and helped make this happen. I salute you, Clarence. Oh, excuse me. I shall not make that mistake again. From now on you are Charles Rabbani."

"It suits me, uncle."

Uncle Rabbani continued, "After we will stage a supposed assassination attempt against me. After it fails, our expatriate group will then find a traitor among the assassins and seize a computer containing the plan for the attacks and the people responsible for carrying them out, delineating the chain of command and implicating the Saudi Royal Family. You, as my nephew, Charles Rabbani, will go to the United States and present that information to Mustafa Al Sabin. He will be suspicious because he is a supporter of the Royal Family, but he will be convinced by it, and he will present that information to the President and to the British Prime Minister. It will convince them that they must rid the world of the Saudi Royal family and see to it that a new regime is installed. Any questions?"

Clarence said, "You know that according to the Washington papers, Yusif and Akmed were killed in an explosion."

Rabbani nodded that he did. "Unfortunate, but true."

"So the plan to kill the President in the Rose Garden must be dead." A concern for Molly flashed into Clarence's head. "Do they plan to send someone else?"

"No. They think that plan could have been compromised. Someone searched their apartment and their computer was missing."

"Wasn't that a part of the plan."

"Yes, but not vital."

"The impeachment proceedings may not succeed now. Does it matter who the President is?"

Rabbani nodded. "The impeachment has probably run out of petrol. You may not know this, but a neighbor of Mrs. Kelly has corroborated her statement that her son was in her house at the time of the Cabot murder."

"The neighbor didn't want to say anything because Mrs. Kelly didn't. That's a strange situation."

"Agreed. Why Kelly confessed and how the shell casing and pen got to be found and why Cabot was killed is being investigated, but no one seems to have any answers. The smart money is betting that no one ever solves those mysteries. The story being floated in Washington is that an anti-Semitic, right wing Militia group in the United States tried to pin it on Andrews to get rid of President Silver. What do you think?"

Clarence shook his head. "I don't buy it. Someone had to have access to a cartridge shell with Kelly's fingerprints and a White House logo pen. It's very unlikely that any of those Militia group crazies could put that evidence together."

"Who do you think was behind it?" Rabbani asked.

Clarence thought about what Molly had said. "I think it's more likely that Senator Davies and FBI Director P.J. Winters were behind it."

Rabbani frowned. "Davies hates Silver enough to do it, but he doesn't have the ability to do it." Rabbani scratched his head a moment. "Now, Winters could have access to that kind of evidence, but why would he do it? No, I don't see it. Any other questions?"

"You think I can go back to the United States and no one will recognize me?"

Neil said, "Look at yourself in the mirror. You wouldn't recognize yourself. Uncle looks like he was our father and you look like my older brother. You look more like an Arab than most Arabs."

Rabbani added, "The only danger is that you give yourself away. Don't embellish your background with things that can be checked out. Stick to the history we gave you and you'll be fine."

Clarence nodded. "About that disc with all the information about the attacks," he was just about to tell them he had a disc with some of that information when he decided to keep that information to himself. Instead, he said, "Where and when and by whom the attacks will be done, how do I get that?"

"I'll get it to you when the time comes. It's on two discs. Our group has one that we deposited it in a time vault that can't be opened until a week after the attack."

Clarence frowned. "Why did you do that?"

"It was witnessed by an Al Qaeda representative who deposited the second disc in the vault at the same time. We all fear that there could be a traitor in our group. This way we make sure that no one has access to all the information. You may remember a little bit of some of the U.S. plans, Neil knows something about the UK and Europe. Nobody outside of New Salman Pak knows the whole plan. If any part of our plan is betrayed, we'll have a good idea who the traitor is. Anything else?"

Clarence and Neil remained silent.

Rabbani said, "Good, let's enjoy our desert. I'll send for the waiter." After they ordered desert, Rabbani said, "Soon, you'll be back in Washington. Speaking of Washington, I have some sad news for you. I know you liked your grandfather on your birth mother's side."

Clarence smiled, "Grandfather Hammonds, yes, he's the only one I missed. I didn't know any of the others."

"And they didn't want to know you."

That's also true. Did something happen to one of them?"

"I didn't have a chance to tell you before, but Mr. Hammonds died two days ago while you were returning from New Salman Pak."

"No! What happened?"

"He was old. I understand it was a sudden heart attack. He never knew what hit him."

Clarence said nothing. He only nodded with the realization that Rabbani and Neil were the only two relatives of his that he liked and that liked him, except for Fatima, and she was his uncle's niece, but not really related to him. He felt saddened, and wondered if that was what loneliness felt like. Could he create a family with Fatima? Did he want to create a family with Fatima? He knew the answer to that question, but didn't want to admit it. "Have they had the funeral?"

Rabbani shook his head. "No, I understand it will take place the day after tomorrow. Why?"

"I must go."

"Are you crazy? That's insane."

"Why, you both agreed that no one would recognize me and I need to pay my respects to the old man. I'll be very careful."

Rabbani frowned. "All right, but Neil will go with you. You have an apartment we rented for you at the Watergate. We'll tell our associates you went to see the apartment and set it up with the computer system you want so you can obtain secure instructions from us during the critical period following the attack. But I'm telling you both. Be very careful, and remember, there may be FBI or Secret Service Agents that attend the funeral."

Two days later, Neil and Clarence were outside the funeral home where Walter Hammonds funeral was taking place. Neil had gone inside, looked around and was reporting to Clarence. "I think it's too dangerous for you to go in there. I recognized that woman who helped find you, Molly Pemberton and she's with that Secret Service Agent that she used to work with."

"John Wallace."

"Yes. We have no cover story. Sorry, but we agreed with uncle before we left that if I thought it was too dangerous, we wouldn't go in."

As Neil talked, Clarence felt the need to at least see Molly. He sighed and said, "Yes, yes, I know."

Clarence looked like the world had come to an end. Neil stared at him a moment and said, "We can go to the cemetery and pretend to be visiting a nearby grave when the funeral party arrives. That's the best we can do."

"Okay, but how about this. We watch them leave the funeral home, and while they're all gathering to proceed to the cemetery, we get ourselves there and do what you suggest."

"All right. I don't know why you want to stay here across the street and half-way down the block instead of going now, but if that'll make you happy."

"I'll feel like I kind of attended the funeral service if we do that." Clarence thought there was no need to tell Neil that he was afraid that Molly might not make the trip to the cemetery. If she does go, he'll get to see her twice. Once coming down the stairs and then again at the cemetery.

Thirty-five minutes later, he saw her walk down the steps of the funeral home. John Wallace was with her. She stopped momentarily in front of a black limousine parked at the bottom of the stairs. When they rolled the window down, Clarence could see two men inside holding a camera and filming the people as they left. After that she walked over to her car and affixed a funeral sticker to the windshield.

Good, she's going to the cemetery. As Molly got into her car, he turned away from her and said, "You were right, Neil. It would have been too dangerous. They're filming from that limo in back of the hearse. Even if nobody recognized me, that'll will give them time to check out everyone that was there and they'll be suspicious of anyone they can't identify. Okay, let's go to the cemetery."

Twenty minutes later, after stopping to buy some flowers, they arrived at the cemetery. They quickly picked a spot and a grave that gave them a good view of the grave selected for Clarence's grandfather. They didn't have long to wait. Ten minutes later, the funeral procession arrived. Clarence watched Molly walk to the gravesite. Clarence was fortunate. Walter Hammonds had outlived most of his friends. Only his children and grandchildren were at the cemetery and Molly was in the front row, on the end closest to him. Clarence stared at her. She was magnificent. Shiny blonde hair, fair complexion, a wonderful athletic body. It was a warm, early September day with a little breeze that blew her hair back and made her clothes cling to her body. He snapped a quick picture of her and continued watching her until the burial was completed and she left the cemetery.

Immediately after the funeral, Clarence and Neil boarded a British Airways flight for their return to London. As their plane took off, Molly began a meeting with Ben. "Sorry sir, but no one attended the funeral service or the burial that could be Clarence Davenport. We have photographs of everyone there we can study, but no plastic surgeon could have made him look like anyone that was there."

Ben shrugged. "It was a long-shot at best. Nothing unusual at all?"

"Not at the funeral service, but I felt like someone was staring at me at the cemetery."

"Was there?"

Molly frowned. "I don't know. There were two men who were at the cemetery when we arrived visiting a nearby grave. They looked like they could be brothers. I left to keep this appointment with you, but I asked John to take a look at the grave they were visiting. He called me while he was riding back in the limo with the film crew. There were fresh flowers on the grave they must have left and the grave was that of a woman that died about a year ago. They could have been her sons. Want us to check it out?

"What did they look like? Could you get any pictures?"

"I couldn't tell and they didn't get any pictures. The sun was in my eyes and they were wearing broad-brimmed hats. They were looking down most of the time."

"You can check it out, but there's no rush.

CHAPTER 39

▼

Fawzi Almihidi, the Saudi Arabian, Al Qaeda co-leader of the New Salman Pak terrorist training camp was seated in the upholstered armchair he took from Clarence's tent. Clarence was right. He felt wiser and more powerful than the Sunni and Shiite co-leaders of the camp who were squatting on rugs in front of him. He said, "We must discuss the problem we found in the tent of the Syrian woman. Her death is of no consequence, but two of our comrades were found dead in her tent. That is a great loss, and if there's anything suspicious about it we must look into it and dispose of it before the meeting of the full camp council. You both agree?"

While the Sunni and the Shiite leaders were both from Iraq, they seldom agreed about anything. This time, they looked at each other and then both nodded in agreement.

Fawzi said, "We originally concluded that the men got into a fight about the woman, that one of them killed her and then they killed each other, but yesterday I heard that some of our people think that was not the case. What have you heard?"

The Sunni said, "I have heard the same. Neither of them was of us, but they were soldiers in our cause. If they were killed by our people, we must find out why, and if not justly done, they must be punished."

Fawzi said, "It happened when we were discussing ridding ourselves of the non-true believers in our midst after the glorious attack. Perhaps someone acted early. Were they too secular, maybe not faithful to the teachings of the Koran and killed by some of the more fanatical members of our society?"

The Shiite leader said, "They were most devoted to the Koran and faithful to all Shiite teachings." Turning towards Fawzi, he said, "They differ with your Wahhabi teachings and the Sunni only in the way all Shiites do. It could not be for religious reasons that they were killed unless someone broke their oath to suspend all such arguments until the infidel have been driven from all sacred Muslim lands."

Fawzi said, "We remain agreed that anyone of our people who violated that oath will be executed?" The Sunni and the Shiite solemnly nodded in agreement.

Fawzi turned to the Shiite. "What do you hear from your people that makes you believe your men did not kill each other as it appears?"

"They are saying that it was he, with the bandaged face, and his friend, Neil Rabbani that killed them and that is why they left without a word, like thieves in the middle of the night."

Fawzi shook his head. "I don't think so. I received a message from Neil's uncle that Khalil Yomani of the bandaged face and Neil Rabbani were urgently required in London. That is why they left. There was a similar message found in their tent. Why do they say it was Neil and Khalil that killed your people?"

The Shiite shrugged. "Let's bring some of those chattering old women before us and we will ask them."

Minutes later, two wiry Shiite men with scraggly, black beards and wearing foul-smelling robes appeared before the three camp leaders. The Shiite leader said, "You have been saying that Abdul and Mahi were killed by he of the bandaged face and his friend. Why do you say this and don't lie or I'll cut your tongues out." The two Shiites looked at each other. Neither spoke. The Shiite leader drew a knife from his robes and said, pointing to the elder of the two men before him, speak now or I'll cut your tongue out right now."

The man said, "It is because of the woman. She was a mattress for Neil Rabbani."

The Shiite leader scowled in disbelief. "You think he would kill two of our comrades in our *jihad* because of a woman?"

"I don't know. He was very Western. They think of women differently in the West."

"You agree with that?" the Shiite leader said to the other nervous Iraqi foot soldier.

"I only know that Neil Rabbani often slept in the woman's tent."

Fawzi asked, "Which of the two dead men was interested in the woman?"

Neither man spoke. The Shiite leader thundered, "Answer him you spawn of a dead camel."

"I don't know," the younger Iraqi said.

"I don't know either," the other one said.

The two very nervous Iraqis were ordered to withdraw temporarily while Fawzi and the other two camp leaders conferred. After they left, the Sunni said, "I agree with my Shiite colleague. I also find it hard to believe that Neil and Khalil would kill two men for a worthless woman. We really don't know very much about Khalil, and if he was the one with the woman, maybe I could believe Khalil might do something like this, but not Neil. I've known him a long time. He's a Saudi. He would never kill those men because of some whore. He thinks like we do when it comes to women."

The Shiite said, "There are many who say that Abdul and Mahi did not kill each other. Let us question some more of our people."

Minutes later the two men they had interrogated appeared before their leaders once more. As they knelt in front of the camp leaders the Shiite said, "We wish to question all those who believe that Abdul and Mahi did not kill each other. You will send them to us and say nothing of why you were here or why we want to speak with them."

One by one they came. A few thought that Abdul and Mahi may have killed each other because of the Syrian woman, but most would not believe that the two men would ever fight about a worthless woman. One close friend said, "They were like brothers. If both wanted that kind of a woman, they would gladly share her, but I don't believe either of them wanted her. She was a disgrace, acting like a Western harlot, freely admitting Neil Rabbani into her bed while her husband is languishing in an Israeli prison. If she had been stoned to death as proscribed by the Koran, I could believe that Abdul and Mahi would do that. I do not believe they would kill her and mutilate her body the way it was."

Another Iraqi they questioned was dressed notably better than the others. His beard was neatly trimmed and his robes were spotlessly clean. When asked if he believed that Abdul and Mahdi killed each other over the Syrian woman, he almost snickered. Fawzi noticed the unusual reaction and said, "You find the question silly?"

The man shrugged. Instead of the shrug producing a tirade as the other leaders expected, Fawzi gently asked. "There is something you are reluctant to say." He gestured inclusively to his colleagues, "We all insist that you be frank and complete in your answer."

The man looked towards the Shiite camp leader who then said, said, "Speak you son of a camel. Now."

The man nodded. "I can not believe that they would fight about a woman, any woman. Now, if it were a young boy they both wanted, I could believe they'd fight about that."

Fawzi said, "You know they take little boys?"

"Yes,"

"And how do you know this?"

"I have seen each of them with young boys."

"And do you do that too?" The Shiite leader said

"No. I do not."

Fawzi then asked, "You have said they are very devout. If that is true, they must know the Koran disapproves."

"They say that the Koran says many things. They are scholars of the Koran, and they and many others like them say the Koran allows it."

"And what do you say?" the Shiite camp leader said.

"I am not a scholar. I do not approve of what they do, but my cleric said I should do and say nothing."

"Why is that?"

"It is not my place to question him."

The three camp leaders nodded in agreement and then dismissed him.

The Sunni leader said to his Shiite colleague, "Do you believe the cleric told him to say nothing?"

"Yes. Let's be honest with each other. Despite anything we can say, there will be those among us who like young boys, some who like young girls and Sodomites who like only other men."

Fawzi and the Sunni agreed. Fawzi said, "It is said by many that the Prophet took Aisha as his wife when she was six years old and consummated the marriage at age nine. We do not allow our women to have sex with anyone who is not their husband. They are stoned to death under the *sharia* laws, so most obey. When they can't have women, there are many of our young men that look for substitutes. I saw when I was in Afghanistan, that the Taliban tried to stop it. They failed. It continues in Pakistan and throughout the Muslim world, as it does in the West."

The Shiite said, "If it happens in the West where all the women are harlots, then it can't be because of the *sharia* rules."

"It's not the only reason, but it's a major cause of the problem."

"What should we do about it?"

Fawzi smiled. "Nothing. We should adopt the policy of the West. Don't ask—don't tell. But, enough of that. After listening to that man, I believe him and I no longer believe that Abdul and Mahdi killed each other."

"Then who killed them?" the Iraqi Shiite asked.

"I don't know for sure, but it could have been Neil Rabbani and Khalil Yomani."

The Sunni said, "I thought you didn't believe they would do that over a woman."

"Neil Rabbani wouldn't, Khalil had nothing to do with the woman, and from what we heard, Abdul and Mahdi didn't know Neil or Khalil very well. In other words, Khalil and Neil had no reason to kill Abdul or Mahdi, and they both need a reason to kill someone."

"Yet you say you think they may have done it," the Shiite leader said. "Why?"

"Think back. Several days before this happened, a dispute started in the camp. There were many that felt the camp should be purged of those who were very secular in the practice of their religion and who believed civil law should replace *sharia*. The secular Muslims maintained that the strict religionists are fanatics and that we are held back by the refusal of many of our people to modernize their thinking." The Shiite and Sunni started to say something, but Fawzi held his hand up for silence. "I agree with you, but I have no desire to go back over this argument again. We resolved it by agreeing not to raise those issues until the war is over, and we all agree that is best. I recall that Abdul and Mahdi were among the main spokesmen for the views of the strict religionists. While neither Neil Rabbani nor Khalil Yomani participated in that argument, they were looked at as the prime examples of how much more effective we could be if we were to modernize."

The Shiite leader said, "What you say about Abdul and Mahdi is true. I will tell you, that if we didn't have our agreement in place and we didn't need them, I would have taken great pleasure in killing Neil Rabbani and Khalil Yomani even though Khalil worked very hard for our success."

"Perhaps Abdul and Mahdi felt the same way, and perhaps they didn't like the agreement. After all, we don't need Neil or Khalil any more. Maybe they decided they would try to kill Neil and Khalil and they failed and Neil and Khalil killed them. What tends to convince me that it was them that killed Abdul and Mahdi is the way they disguised it. I can't think of anyone else in this camp that would be that clever."

The Sunni and Shiite camp leaders sat quietly for a moment. The Shiite said, "I think I agree with you."

"I do also," the Sunni said. "What do you think we should do about it?"

Fawzi sat back in his armchair and smiled. "He of the bandaged face was right. I think better sitting in this chair." He sat up straight and said, "I think we should do nothing. Most of the men in the camp except those that knew them best, are willing to accept the conclusion that Abdul and Mahdi killed each other for whatever reason they had or that the Syrian woman somehow managed to inflict a fatal wound in each of them."

"Why? Neither had anything to do with her."

"Perhaps we can say Mahdi and Abdul decided to punish the Syrian harlot and have her stoned to death as required by the law. She resisted and maybe some other harlots in the camp aided her. They managed to kill Abdul and Mahdi after they killed the Syrian slut, but the other harlots killed them."

The Sunni said, "I like it. If I didn't know otherwise, I would accept that story completely."

The Shiite said, "I too like it, but let's gather together all the harlots in the camp and stone them to death."

"Good," Fawzi said. "It adds authenticity to our explanation. Tomorrow morning, we will start the meeting of the full council with the explanation we have agreed upon about the death of Abdul and Mahdi. We will suspend the meeting to stone the harlots and then review the status of the attack plans on the United States, the United Kingdom and the rest of the Crusaders in Europe."

The meeting of the full council began early the next morning. Fawzi presented the conclusion they had reached and the Shiite and Sunni both demanded that all the harlots in the camp be stoned to death. The full council agreed and immediately sent men out to collect the women and dig pits in the earth. Eleven women were then buried chest high in the sand as required by **sharia** law. The Shiite threw the first stone and the Sunni the second. After Fawzi threw the third stone, the remaining members of the council threw theirs, and then the entire camp joined in, hurling stones until the eleven women were dead.

The council watched the women bleed to death and listened to their screams as they talked and pointed to the bloodiest women and the ones that screamed for mercy the loudest. When all the women were dead, the council reconvened. They applauded as they heard that the foot soldiers and martyrs of the planned attacks on the West were gathering at the designated places, and that soon, the council could give the command to attack. Nothing could stop them now.

However, their thirst for blood had been whetted and the delay grated on them. The most devout among them wanted to do something now to sate their blood lust, but there were no more harlots to kill. Instead, they argued that since they no longer needed the technicians and planners, they could safely purge from their midst all those supposed Muslims who were no better than infidels and claimed that man made civil law should govern them instead of the laws of *sharia*. No one said no.

News of the massacre at New Salman Pak quickly spread throughout the mosques of Islamic communities everywhere and was greeted with pride by strict religionists everywhere. Wahhabi clerics sponsored by Saudi funding were among those who were most in favor of what had occurred, and none were more pleased than the strict religionist clerics of the Muslim community at Brixton in the United Kingdom. They lectured that their community must resist all the Sodom and Gomorrah temptations of New York and London and rid their community of those influences. If the time was right for that to be done at New Salman Pak, then this was the time to cleanse their own communities.

CHAPTER 40

▼

Clarence had become comfortable with his new face and his new identity as Charles Rabbani. He looked at the picture on his new Swiss passport and saw no resemblance to the remembered face of Clarence Davenport. He was Charles Rabbani, he liked who he was and he was ready to do his part in seeing to it that his uncle's plan to cause the downfall of the Saudi Royal Family and its replacement by a secular government headed by his uncle was accomplished. Returning to the United States to represent the interests of his uncle and his group of Saudi expatriates was an important step in accomplishing that goal. His uncle expected Al Qaeda to overthrow the House of Saud following the attacks on the West, and without intervention by the United States, Al Qaeda would remain in power. Clarence was a little nervous about his role in bringing about United States intervention, but if his uncle thought he could do it, he wouldn't fail.

Clarence thought he might even see Molly while he was there. Would that be good or would it be painful? Could he possibly win her affections? Would she recognize him and if she didn't, could he ever tell her who he really was? He would want to, but no, he couldn't tell her. She might not give him away, but it would create a difficult, if not impossible situation for her. He would make it his business to see her and he would either get over his infatuation with her, or he would try to win her over as Charles Rabbani. If he tried to win her over and failed, he would accept that and get on with his life. Either way, he would have a good rest of his life.

Clarence whistled happily to himself as he called a taxi to take him to uncle Rabbani's house. He would get his final instructions, and his first class plane ticket, direct to Washington.

As the cab approached the square where Uncle Rabbani lived, traffic, always a problem in London, was hopelessly snarled. Clarence paid the cabby, hefted his suitcase and began walking down the street to his uncle's. As he rounded the corner, he saw multiple police cars and ambulances in front of his uncle's house. He broke into a sprint. Moment later as he approached the house, he was restrained by an uniformed bobby. "Sorry, sir, but there's been an accident."

"I'm Charles Rabbani. This is my uncle's house. What happened?"

The policeman said, "Can't say, sir. I'll get a detective."

Moments later, Clarence again identified himself to a Scotland Yard detective as Charles Rabbani using his passport. The detective said, "Sorry, Mr. Rabbani, but there's been an explosion inside the house."

Clarence looked up and saw the window frame in his Uncle's home-office jaggedly pointing out towards the street and shards of glass scattered everywhere. "Was anyone hurt?"

"Sorry, but I'm afraid there were."

"Who?"

"An elderly gent and two younger men."

"They'll be all right, won't they?"

"Sorry, but two are dead and the other might as well be."

Clarence was stunned. Could it be his uncle and Neil? He turned to the detective. "What happened." The detective said nothing. Clarence said, "Was it a gas leak?"

"Come see for yourself," the detective said. "Perhaps you can confirm the identity of the victims." Clarence accompanied the detective into the house. The office was a wreck, debris everywhere. His uncle's torso was on the floor near his desk. Separated from his body, uncle Rabbani's legs were lying across the legs of another man. The other man's head was near the fireplace, and part of one arm was across the other side of the room.

The detective pointed to the body of Uncle Rabbani. "Is that your uncle?" Clarence nodded. Pointing to the head near the fireplace, the detective said, "That head belongs with what's left of that torso. Do you know who that is?"

Clarence looked at what was left of the face of the third man. He shook his head. "No. I don't know who he is. I never saw him before."

"Can you identify this person?" The detective pointed to where a group of medical technicians were working feverishly. "He's still barely alive, but they don't think he'll survive."

"Yes. That's my half-brother, Neil. What happened?"

"We can't be sure, but it looks to us like the one you can't identify was a messenger, there's a bike with a messenger service sign on it chained to the wrought iron fence outside. We think he was admitted into the office by the younger man, your half-brother. He knifed him and then approached your uncle. We think he was wearing a belt of explosives. He put his arms around your uncle and then blew himself up, like those Palestinian homicide bombers."

Clarence looked around the room dumbly. The explanation given by the detective was consistent with the appearance of the room.

The detective said, "Sorry sir, do you know whether your uncle was involved in anything?"

Clarence looked at him and said nothing.

"I mean was he Jewish or something like that? This is the kind of thing some of the Palestinians do against the Israelis."

"He was a citizen of the United Kingdom. He came here from Saudi Arabia."

"Was he political?"

Clarence nodded. "He was a leader of the C.D.A."

"And that is?"

"The Community of Democratic Arabians. It's an organization like a club for expatriate Saudis who oppose the Saudi Royal Family."

The detective shook his head. "Can't see the Royal family doing this sort of thing."

Clarence shrugged. "I wouldn't think so either."

"It definitely looks like one of those Palestinian bombings. Perhaps your uncle was mistaken for a wealthy Jewish gentleman."

Clarence shrugged. "I suppose that's possible."

"What bring you here today, Mr. Rabbani?" The detective asked.

"I came to say goodbye to my uncle and my half brother."

"May I inquire as to where you were going?"

"To Washington."

"May I see your ticket?"

"I was picking it up here."

The detective said in a loud voice to the assembly of forensic technicians in the room, "Anyone find an airline ticket?"

A technician wearing white, latex gloves came forward holding a glassine envelope inside of which was a bloodied paper envelope. Gesturing towards Uncle Rabbani's body, he said, "He had this in the breast pocket of his jacket. It's a first class ticket to Washington, D.C. in the name of Charles Rabbani."

"Can you tell us the purpose of your trip to the United States?" The detective asked.

"I was to meet with other Saudi expatriates in the United States to discuss matters of common interest."

"I see. When were you to leave?"

Clarence looked at his wristwatch. "In three hours."

"Can you postpone your trip for a few days?"

"Yes."

"Good, it shouldn't be long."

That should be all right, Clarence thought. I'll still have enough time to do what I have to do before the attacks on the West begin.

The detective asked, "Do your uncle or your half-brother have a wife or other family we should notify?"

"No. There was a niece and me. I'll notify her."

The detective looked at his notebook. "Would her name be Fatima..." He paused trying to pronounce the strange assortment of vowels and consonants that comprised Fatima's last name.

"Yes, yes, Fatima. I'll tell her. She lives not too far from here."

"I'm afraid that won't be possible sir. Sorry, but it seems she was here when the messenger arrived. We believe she opened the front door, and that he killed her and put her body in the library off the foyer before he went upstairs and did that suicide bombing."

Clarence stared at the detective. "My God, her too? I can't believe it."

"You have any idea who could have done this?"

"It has to be political enemies, but I have no idea as to who they might be."

"You don't think it would be supporters of the Saudi Royal Family?"

"I don't know. My uncle has been in exile a long time and that had never been a concern of his."

"Perhaps a rival in that," the detective looked at his little black notebook, "Community of Democratic Arabians?"

"I'm reluctant to rule it out, but I wouldn't think so. It's more likely to be some other dissident group like Al Qaeda that want to replace the Royal Family."

"Excuse me, sir, but didn't I understand you to say that your uncle opposed the Royal Family. Does that mean your uncle was in Al Qaeda?"

"No. My uncle and all of his associates oppose Al Qaeda."

"I see."

"It's complicated, but you can look into my uncle's activities and his associates. I'm, sure you'll see that they had nothing to do with this murder and that they are opposed to Al Qaeda."

"Rest assured we will. We should finish up in here by this evening. We will probably want to talk with you again tomorrow, and most likely, after that, you will be free to go to the United States if you wish. We will have to retain that ticket so let us know when you want to leave and we'll call British Airways and arrange for them to issue a replacement. One more thing, when we leave, you may want to call someone in to repair the window and examine the wall for a structural fault. There seems to be no one else to take care of that, and you ought not to let a nice place like this get ruined."

Clarence nodded mechanically. "I suppose that's so." After sitting a moment, he walked over to where the technicians were still working on Neil. "How's he doing?"

One of the technicians looked up. "Not very well. It'll be a miracle if he makes it to the hospital. We've done all we can here and will be leaving in a few minutes."

Clarence sat down again, watching the forensic and other police technicians work. He accompanied the medical attendant as they brought Neil out and placed him in an ambulance. He went back in the apartment and tried to make sense of his uncle's murder. He told the detective that it could have been Al Qaeda, but Al Qaeda leadership wouldn't do anything right now that might impede the attacks on the United States and the West and ruin their chance to take over in Saudi Arabia. They were crazy, but they weren't that crazy. Perhaps it was some rival in the C.D.A. or a case of mistaken identity as the policeman had suggested. Uncle had been sympathetic to the cause of the Palestinians, and it was unlikely that they would want to kill him.

It was late evening before the police and their experts left the house. Clarence left for a little while and got something to eat and then returned to await a carpenter he had called. He sat in an armchair in his uncle's office watching as a carpenter boarded up the window. The wall had been examined and was sound. Some new plaster, paint, a new bow window and it would be just as good as it ever was. As soon as the carpenter left, Clarence went to his Uncle's steel filing cabinet. It had survived the explosion remarkably well. The false bottom in the bottom draw of the first cabinet contained an envelope containing the numbers and all information necessary to gain access to his uncle's numbered accounts in Switzerland and the combination to the wall safe in his uncle's bedroom. He pocketed them. The police had removed his uncle's desktop computer and all the documents in the filing cabinets, but Clarence knew they wouldn't contain any information concerning the planned attacks on the West. All that they would find would be information about Rabbani's law practice. He knew Uncle Rabbani kept all sensitive information in the bedroom safe and in the laptop he kept stored in the safe.

When Clarence went up to the bedroom he found the mother lode of information. A floppy disc with his name on it contained the detailed instructions Rabbani had intended to give him to coordinate the attacks in the United States. The laptop hard drive contained files with all of the locations to be attacked, the identity of the attackers, where they were to gather before the attack and the time of the attacks. Rabbani must have somehow made a copy of the information before he ceremoniously locked it away in the time vault. It was all there. Clarence saved all the information onto a disc that he placed in his computer case, and then deleted all information dealing with the attacks from his uncle's computer.

Next, Clarence went through the other documents in the safe. He read his uncle's will and learned that all of his uncle's accumulated wealth was to be divided equally among Fatima, Neil and him. The next folder contained a copy of a document sent to all the leaders of the Community of Democratic Arabians. It decreed that in the event of his death, Charles Rabbani was to assume all of the positions of authority and leadership that Uncle Rabbani had at that time in that organization. Attached to it were pledges by all of the leaders to accept that direction by Rabbani. Clarence was stunned. He looked at it almost with disbelief and read it again. Uncle Rabbani had told him those were his intentions, but he never quite believed him. He would have a lot of money, more than he needed or ever wanted, and possibly have his chance to be the head of sovereign nation and make it the type of government he had wanted the United States to be.

Clarence worked furiously. Uncle Rabbani had lived almost all of his life as a loyal citizen of the United Kingdom. Clarence decided he would see to it that his memory would remain unsullied and that everyone would believe that he died as a loyal subject of the Crown.

Before leaving, Clarence decided he would open his uncle's e-mail account. He didn't know the password, but fortunately it was stored in the laptop. He found one unopened message. It was from someone named Farook Tiksit. Clarence didn't know who he was. He opened it and read a long letter describing the stoning deaths and subsequent slaughter at New Salman Pak. Clarence wondered if his and Neil's killing of Abdul and Mahdi had resulted in what occurred at New Salman Pak. He shrugged. Those Islamist radicals were a strange group, but he couldn't think about that right now. He had to study the detailed instructions from his uncle that he had downloaded, and as a tribute to him, he would carry them out to the letter. Neil was to have gone with him, but he can do what has to be done alone. He picked up the phone and called the hospital to inquire about Neil. He was on the phone with the hospital less than ten seconds. At least Neil was still alive.

Tonight, Clarence would sleep in his old flat. He'd try to summon the energy to read the instructions from his uncle. He looked at his wristwatch. It was after midnight, and tomorrow he was expected to be at New Scotland Yard at nine. After that he would have to make funeral arrangements for his uncle and Fatima. Poor Fatima. Should he cancel the trip to the United States? He sat down and forced himself to read his uncle's instructions. He stopped half way through. If he were to honor his uncle's life's work, he had to go to the United States for a very important meeting that could not be delayed. As he was about to leave, Clarence decided not to risk anyone learning anything from the files in his uncle's laptop. He slipped it into his suitcase, hurried down the stairs and left.

CHAPTER 41

▼

Senator Davies' office was not a happy place. The meeting with Senator Smithers and House Speaker Elliott Thurston had just begun. Smithers said, "You know I'd do anything for you, Jeb, but we got a problem. It looks like the impeachment is in trouble."

Davies glared across his desk at them. "I can bring Senator Grilli back. That Dago wop owes me big time. He'll vote the way I tell him."

"Sal isn't the only one. A couple of the guys have caught a lot of flack from constituents about the Morton tapes."

"They were damaged."

"I know, but a copy of it made the rounds and a lot of people accept them as genuine."

"Silver must have leaked it. We ought to launch an investigation and have him held in contempt of Congress."

Smithers shook his head. "A leadership group in the Congress demanded a copy from Silver and he gave it to them. They're the ones who leaked it and the media knows it. Go after them and you'll make a lot of enemies in both Houses."

Davies frowned, "The tape of Morton talking with Washburn is hearsay and the one of me and Morton is worthless. We ruled it inadmissible."

"Come on, Jeb. It's just the same as the parts of the original that are still audible. We pushed it as far as we could. There's a substantial number of the people willing to accept it as accurate, and a few Senators who are up for reelection had to jump ship or probably not get re-elected. When you add a few more who are beginning to think that Tom Andrews was framed and that Silver had nothing to do with the murder of Lindsay Cabot, the problem gets worse. Even if we were willing to push it all the way and burn our bridges behind us on this vote, we'd end up a few votes short."

"God damn it. That's just unacceptable. There's has got to be something we can do."

Smithers turned to Thurston. "Help me out here, Elliott."

"Jeb, we go back a long time. You know that I'd do anything for you even if it were to cost me my seat in Congress. You know what I'm saying, and that there's no limit on what I'd do for you. I've been talking to people in the Senate and pledging House support for their favorite constituent projects to keep them in line. I agree with Senator Smithers. Call for a vote and we'll be short."

Davies scowled. "By how many?"

Smithers said, "A few."

"I said how many?"

"Eight."

Davies turned to Thurston. "How many do you say?"

"By my count, nine, and that's after pulling out all stops. I'm sorry, Jeb, but we're going to have to accept reality. There's no way Senator Smithers and I or anyone can get two thirds of the Senate to vote our way. The Impeachment is dead for now. Maybe if he screws up something we can try again, but this isn't going to fly."

Davies adjusted his cufflinks, fixed the crease in his pants and said, "Okay, you're both telling me that we're beating a dead horse. I'll have to accept that. Maybe Silver will screw up. Maybe someone will do us all a favor and kill the son of a bitch, or maybe we have to wait until the next election. I want us to keep discrediting him every chance we get. I may still be under too much of a cloud to run for President, but starting now we'll see to it that Elliott is our party's candidate and I'm Elliott's choice for Vice-President no matter what else happens." Davies turned towards Thurston. "You agree, Elliott?"

Thurston nodded. "Of course."

"We'll build you up so much that you'll get what ever you want, and you want me. We understand each other?" Thurston nodded in agreement. Davies turned to Smithers. "You got a problem with anything I said?"

"No. If the leadership thinks you're a problem, it'll be your decision to go along with them or tell them to go to hell. I got no problem with that."

"The way I see it, we'll be the people that oppose Silver, and we'll designate the other party as the party that's soft on Silver. If we do this right, then no matter who else is running, we win."

"Now that's something we can do," Smithers said, "and I want to assure you that you will have my full and total support in that campaign. I congratulate you for the brilliance of that plan and for the restraint and statesmanship you're exhibiting. In all my years of political campaigning, I've never seen a more gracious acceptance of an unfortunate but inevitable catastrophic event with an intelligent master plan for the reversal of cruel fortune."

Davies held his hand up to still Smithers. "Thanks but there's no need to say any more."

After talking a few more minutes, Smithers and Thurston shook hands with Senator Davies and left his office. As soon as he left, he picked up his phone and pushed the intercom button. "You hear everything all right, P.J.?"

"Perfect."

"We're just going to have to accept the fact that a political solution is not feasible at this time."

"I agree. That Smithers is something. I don't know how you can stand that old gas bag."

"Sometimes I think people do what he wants just to get him to stop talking." Davies laughed. "But he's useful. He's got a lot of seniority and I can control him. What about the other solution to my problem with Silver? You said you might have some good news for me about that this week."

"I will, but I'll know more tomorrow."

"Oh, what kind of good news?"

"You know we started looking for someone new right after the man with the press credentials died."

"You found someone?"

"Sort of, but all I can tell you right now is that I'll know more about it very soon. We have information that something is being planned, and the best part of it is that we have nothing to do with it. The whole deal will go down with no real involvement by anyone associated with any of us."

"How does it get done?"

"I don't have all the particulars yet. We infiltrated a terrorist cell and from what I've heard from them and another source we have under surveillance, I think they must have an excellent possibility of succeeding. I don't know how they do it or when, but I expect to have those particulars by Tuesday night."

"You're sure about this?"

"I'm quite confident. We could get together Wednesday morning. I ought to know a lot more by then. I can be at your office at nine-thirty."

Davies had more questions he wanted to ask, but knew better than to press Winters further. He said, "That'll be fine P. J. See you on Wednesday morning."

The next two days passed slowly for Davies. When Winters arrived at his office, Davies was anxious to hear what he had to say and hopeful that Winters had found someone to kill Ben Silver. Since there was still no Vice-President, that would put House Speaker Elliott Thurston in the White House and after a few months, he would become Vice-President and then President. Davies smiled as he thought he might yet snatch victory from the jaws of defeat.

Winters arrived a few minutes after nine-thirty, and Davies could tell by the smile on his face that he had good news. As Winters lit up a Cuban cigar, he said, "With what I got to tell you, you won't mind my blowing smoke in your face."

Davies smiled. "I'll be the judge of that."

"Fine. I'll tell you the whole deal. You know it's the job of the FBI to do background checks on everyone that gets hired to work in the White House?"

Davies nodded that he did.

"An opening came up for a gardener and a Filipino immigrant named Jose Matera applied for the job. We checked him out like we check out everyone. Walter Wagner saw the file and a picture of the applicant and thought the man didn't look like a Filipino and that he looked sort of Middle-Eastern. He brought it in to me and I agreed with him. I saw that the man was from Cebu City and remembered that we had another source telling us that Middle-Eastern terrorists were trying to infiltrate someone with the code name of 'Okie Farmer Friend' into the White House. We decided to check it out ourselves."

Davies, listening intently said, "You think this guy from Cebu City is 'Okie Farmer Friend'?"

"Yes."

Davies looked puzzled. "Can I ask why?"

Winters smiled. "You remember McVeigh and Nicholls?"

"The guys who did the Oklahoma City bombing."

"Right. Nicholls made repeated trips to the Philippines and when he did, he went to Cebu City and stayed in a boarding house. This guy stayed in that boarding house when he was a student there. I don't know whether they knew each other, but it's very possible. Cebu City and that boarding house are known strongholds of Islamic radicals. It was in Cebu City where we think Nicholls learned how to make the bomb they used in Oklahoma City out of fertilizer and diesel oil."

"I didn't know that."

"Not many people do and it's not for publication so keep it to yourself."

Davies nodded that he would. "You approved the guy."

"Of course. He's working as a gardener at the White House right now."

"Fantastic, but the Secret Service is all over the place. How the hell is he going to do it, and when?"

Our source that told us about the plan to infiltrate Okie Farmer Friend into the White House also told us that the plan is to kill the President in the Rose Garden with a fertilizer bomb. Nobody notices those guys walking around with wheelbarrows and gardening equipment and he wears a cross around his neck. At this point, he's been there long enough so that everyone knows him."

Davies nodded. "That's true. Those people walk around and no one pays attention. But when is it supposed to happen?"

"Sometime shortly before 'glory day' in September."

"What and when is 'glory day'?"

"I don't know for sure, but it's probably the anniversary of September, 11. In any event, it can't be far off because this is the end of August after all."

"You really think this is going to happen?"

"I figure 'Glory Day' must be the day they try to kill Silver. If they succeed, super."

"So you think it can happen?"

"Yes, Lots of fertilizer has been ordered and already been delivered to the White House. The best thing about it is that no one can trace anything back to us. Jose Matera, alias Okie Farmer Friend, was approved in the normal course and the fertilizer purchase was approved and paid for through normal channels. There's nothing to interest anyone about anything, and we are totally in the clear. If anyone gets blamed, it'll probably be the Secret Service."

Davies frowned. "Not so fast. What about your other source, the one that told you the Okie Farmer Friend code name. He reports to you. Could he implicate you and Wagner?"

"I don't think he could have made the connection, but we don't have to worry about it. He was killed last night by some Islamic fanatic who thought our man wasn't religious enough."

Davies sat back on the sofa. "It's a little early in the day for me, but this calls for a drink and I think I'd like one of your cigars."

Winters grinned as he handed over one of his Cubans. "I agree. This is better than women."

CHAPTER 42

▼

As soon as Clarence arrived in Washington, he went to the apartment in the Watergate that his uncle had rented for him and set up his laptop. He had read the first part of the instructions Uncle Rabbani had provided back in Rabbani's apartment, but had been too tired and then too busy to finish them. The day after the suicide bombing, he was busy at New Scotland Yard and then with Neil at the hospital and with funeral arrangements for his uncle and Fatima. Neil's condition was still unchanged and the doctors said every day he survives is another miracle.

Clarence barely had time to make his flight. He had been tempted to open his laptop and read them on the plane, but even in first class, there were too many prying eyes to chance it. He opened the file and read the instructions for tomorrow's meeting with Mustafa Al Sabin.

Dear Charles,

Your meeting with Mustafa Al Sabin is very important and it is critical that it takes place as scheduled. Al Sabin is an old acquaintance that believes as I do that the Saudi Royal Family is a disgrace and that fundamentalist Islamic rule would be a disaster. He has continued to support the House of Saud as the lesser of two evils and because he believes our organization would fall before the militant fundamentalists. He knows nothing of our temporary alliance with Al Qaeda and the other fundamentalists and is never, I repeat never, to be told about it or our participation in the planning of any of the scheduled September events.

Your initial meeting with him is to be purely social. I have told him that you are coming to the United States to represent my interests there and that I would appreciate any help or advice he could furnish. He will be most gracious and will be happy to meet with you.

Al Sabin can be most useful to our cause. He has a long-standing good relationship with the United States government and was a confidant of former President Parsons as well as a friend of current President Silver.

As you know, following the September attacks, we expect the Wahhabi to seize power in Arabia and kill as many members of the Royal Family as they can find. When that happens, you are to see Al Sabin again and work on him to persuade President Silver or whoever is in the White House to send the military into Arabia to destroy Al Qaeda and install our organization as the new temporary rulers. This is vital and everything depends on your success, but we think they have no real other choice. Al Sabin knows that if Al Qaeda rules Arabia, it will have the financial ability to destroy Western Civilization. If we have to and as a last resort, we can make available the secret Al Qaeda documents planning the attack. I wish you good luck. After your meeting with Al Sabin, call me on a secure phone so we can discuss everything.

Your loving uncle,

Rabbani

PS Destroy this message after reading it.

Clarence destroyed the message as requested and then glanced at his wristwatch. Time for a quick lunch and then a cab to Al Sabin's office. At precisely two o'clock, Clarence walked into Al Sabin's office. Al Sabin stood to greet him. "You must be Charles Rabbani."

Clarence extended his hand. "Yes, I am."

Al Sabin shook Clarence's hand. "I was so sorry to hear of the death of your uncle."

"Thank you. He was a wonderful man."

"Actually, I'm surprised that you came."

"I debated myself about it, and I'm returning to London for his funeral the day after tomorrow, but there were rather urgent matters for my uncle's business that couldn't be put off."

"It was a shock. His murder and some others like it were a warning to all of us."

"Oh, I'm not sure I understand. What others?"

"Secular Muslims everywhere have been attacked by Islamic fundamentalists."

"I didn't know that."

"Isn't that who killed your uncle?"

"When I left London the police didn't really have a theory. They said they thought it might be the work of some Palestinian suicide bomber who thought my uncle was too friendly with the Israelis."

Al Sabin shook his head. "Perhaps, but since your uncle was killed, there have been twenty-three attacks on secular Muslims by those Islamic fundamentalists who want the world governed by the laws of *sharia*. That's the same kind of insanity that caused the assassination of Anwar Sadat in Egypt. Your uncle and I and all those Muslims that were attacked oppose that and want a democratic and representative system of civil laws."

"You're sure that's who's doing it?"

"Yes. They caught some of those assassins and made them talk. In some places they do not mind using torture and drugs. Believe me, there can be no question about it, and I assumed your uncle was part of that attack."

Clarence sat back. He had to think about this. If Al Sabin was right, the militants who were going to carry out the attacks on the United States that he had planned were the people who had killed his uncle, most likely Neil and Fatima. He said to Al Sabin, "Excuse me. I didn't realize what was behind my uncle's murder. Perhaps you didn't know it, but when they killed my uncle they also probably killed my half-brother and best friend, Neil Rabbani, and a woman I had dated who was my uncle's niece. Perhaps the attack was directed against Neil for something he had done."

Al Sabin said, "Yes, I heard they were there. I'm so sorry. I knew Neil slightly, but not the young woman. He was a nice young man, a bit of a womanizer by reputation, but I don't believe he was the intended victim."

Clarence didn't believe it either. He nodded, "And he enjoyed life. Damn, but those people are crazy. I'm so damn mad and confused right now, I don't know what to do. You're sure about all this?"

"Absolutely. Your uncle and I always agreed that the Wahhabi strict religionist point of view was the biggest problem that kept any real reform from happening in Arabia. I think that they and Al Qaeda have teamed up and they'd like to kill all us moderates."

Clarence nodded. "Yes, my uncle thought so as well."

"If you want to take my advice, you'll be extra careful yourself. I understand your uncle made you his heir and political successor. It wouldn't surprise me if some assassin decided to make you another victim of the current purge."

"You may be right. Thanks for the warning. I wonder, do you think the attacks against secular Muslims could be a precursor of an attack by Al Qaeda and the other extremists against the Royal Family?"

Al Sabin thought for a moment. "I suppose that's possible. Fourteen of the twenty three Muslims recently killed by Muslim extremists were Saudi Arabian exiles living here, in London like your uncle and many others places around the world. Six more that were killed were more moderate members of the Royal Family who were killed in Saudi Arabia, so twenty of the twenty-three that were killed were from Saudi Arabia."

"I'm curious. My uncle told me you're an expert on U.S. and Saudi relations. What do you think the reaction of the United States would be to an Al Qaeda take over?"

Al Sabin frowned. "It all depends on when it happens and on what's going on here. I don't think President Silver could do anything. Congress wouldn't allow it."

"And if he were impeached?"

Al Sabin mopped his brow with an immaculate white handkerchief. "That would probably even be worse, but that looks dead, at least for now."

"You say that is worse. Why?"

"Because House Speaker Elliott Thurston would become President and Jeb Davies would be the power behind the throne, so to speak. I know them both fairly well. They would most likely make a deal with Al Qaeda that would leave them in power and promise cheap oil to the United States. Once Al Qaeda solidified their position, they would acquire nuclear capacity and renege on their deal and the United States would be unable to do anything without precipitating a nuclear holocaust. I think that would be the end of Western Civilization as we know it."

"What would President Silver want to do if he stays in office?"

Al Sabin sat back in his chair and steepled his fingers a moment. "He would not allow Al Qaeda to remain in control. He would move militarily and look to someone like your uncle to become the temporary ruler until they had an election."

"If they asked you, is that what you would have advised them?"

"Yes, but with everyone that's been killed, that is no longer available." Al Sabin looked at Clarence. "I know your uncle designated you as his successor, and the United States might even have accepted that if you were accepted by the leaders in exile and those moderates who were in the country. Together, you could have formed an administrative capacity to govern the country, backed up by the United States. But I don't know if that's possible now. It's going to take some time for a moderate leadership to replace all those that were killed, so I don't know what they might do. It seems to me that the only choice the Americans would have would be to find a member of the Royal Family somewhere and reinstall the old, corrupt bureaucracy that worked hand in glove with the Wahhabi clerics, and that would end any move towards greater democratization." Al Sabin shook his head, "There's no sense in thinking about it, Charles, because even if the impeachment dies, and it looks like it will, with Thurston running the House and Davies and Smithers in the Senate, it's doubtful Silver could reinstall the Monarchy even if he wanted to."

"What about the U.K. and the rest of Europe?"

"The Brits would probably want to move, but Parliament wouldn't allow it without the United States, and you can forget about the rest of Europe. They'll all accept whatever temporary bone Al Qaeda wants to throw them."

Clarence felt discouraged and decided that there was nothing more he wanted to say to Al Sabin at this time. He needed to sit by himself in that nice flowered armchair in his apartment at the Watergate and think about what he should do. He said his good-byes and left.

Once back in his apartment, he sat and thought. He wanted to carry out his uncle's wishes, but it seemed that Al Qaeda was always one step in front of him. They must have anticipated the possibility that the United States would move against them when they deposed the Saudi Royal Family, with or without the help of the rest of the world, and decided to get rid of the moderate Arabian leaders. They might have understood the situation with the U.S. Presidency and be counting on that as well. The timing for them is near perfect.

Clarence wished there were someone to talk with. He had been a loner almost all his life and it had never bothered him, but now he needed to talk with someone. He decided to take a look at his uncle's laptop and check his e-mail. Perhaps there was some old letter from one of his uncle's inner circle that he might find and he could contact that person. He had purchased a newspaper and had the names of all the exiles that were killed.

Clarence retrieved his uncle's laptop and opened his e-mail account. There was one new letter that had been sent on the day Uncle Rabbani was killed by someone he didn't know. Clarence read it.

My dear Rabbani,

I learned today that Al Qaeda have managed to place one of their people in the White House. He is a Wahhabi convert who lived for some time in

the Phillipines, speaks Spanish fluently, and has a Filipino passport.
He is employed in the White House and his assignment is to kill the Pres-
ident in the Rose Garden with a fertilizer bomb. It will be similar to the
one used in Oklahoma City.
The attack on the American President is to precede the main attack
against the United States and should take place very soon.
Is this consistent with our plan, or is Al Qaeda doing this on its own? I
thought you should know.
Your faithful colleague,
Farook Tiksit

Clarence read the letter a second time. There can be no doubt about it. Al
Qaeda was one step ahead of them. All his uncle's work was wasted and his mur-
derers would be in charge of Arabia instead of him. Were there clues that he
missed? He remembered they wanted to delay his plan to kill Silver until they
were ready to launch their main attack. He thought it was just because they
wanted to add to the chaos created by the attacks and that they agreed to go forward, because it was too good a plan to pass up. But maybe it was also because
they feared President Silver might send the military into Arabia even if Congress
opposed him. The military has always strongly supported him. When Akmed and
Yusif were killed, they came up with a new plan to kill Silver and that plan would
probably succeed in killing the President and Molly along with him. Clarence
pounded his fist on the arm of his chair. No! No! They succeeded in killing his
uncle and Fatima and probably Neil, but they will not kill Molly.

Clarence walked over to his desk and sat at his computer. He began to compose an e-mail letter.

Dear Molly,

There is a new plan to kill the President with a fertilizer bomb in the
Rose Garden. The assassin is a newly hired Filipino gardener.
A Friend.

Clarence paused before clicking the send icon. That would save Molly, but
what does he do about his uncle, Neil and Fatima. Failing to kill the President
would not prevent the attacks on the United States and would not prevent Al
Qaeda from seizing power in Saudi Arabia. He could not allow them to win this
battle. He can not allow them to kill his entire family and remain unpunished.
He must avenge Uncle Rabbani, Neil and Fatima.

Clarence returned to his e-mail letter to Molly. He added a paragraph.

There is another plan to attack the United States and the West. I am attaching a detailed description of what is planned and by whom. It is part of a plan for fundamentalist Islamic rule of Arabia and the rest of the Muslim world. This threat to world peace must not be allowed to occur.

He attached the files he had downloaded from his uncle's computer and deleted all mention of Charles Rabbani. Clarence then sat back a minute. He took a deep breath. Should he send it?

He clicked the send icon.

CHAPTER 43

▼

Molly was in her office when her computer signaled that she had mail at the address that was used only for messages from Clarence. She opened it immediately and read the warning about the Rose Garden.

Molly turned to her phone and called Ben Silver's office. Ben's aide, Martha, answered the phone. Molly blurted, "Where's the President?"

Martha recognized Molly's voice. "Mrs. Cabot just arrived and she and the President are having tea in the Rose Garden."

"Get them the hell out of there this minute."

"I thought that threat was over."

"It's not. Get them."

Martha ran out to get the President.

Molly then read the second paragraph of Clarence's note. She said out loud, "Holy Shit!" as she slipped a disc into her computer, down loaded the message and then down loaded the attached files. Even with her high-speed connection it took over five minutes to complete the download of all the attached files. Molly then grabbed the disc out of the computer and ran to the Oval Office past startled clerks and interns who tried to ask what was going on. Molly ignored them all. When she arrived at the anteroom, she sat at Martha's desk and slipped the disc into Martha's computer and printed the warning letter from Clarence. Next she started printing the down loaded files he had sent her. As they came off the printer, she placed the pages in Martha's Xerox copier and started running off copies. She was hard at work when Ben, Martha and Jane entered the anteroom at the Oval Office. Without saying a word, Molly handed Ben a copy of Clarence's warning. Ben sat on the corner of Martha's desk and read it.

Ben said to Molly, "You printing the attachment?"

"Yes. I've printed about a dozen pages." She handed Ben a sheaf of papers. He scanned a few pages and then said to Molly, "My God, it's the mother lode." He turned to Martha, "Get Tom Andrews, Rahsheed Evans, John Wallace, the Attorney General and Tony Julian from Homeland Security. I want them in my office as quickly as they can get here, and I don't care what they're doing. I want them now. Oh, and call Senator Kendall. I'd like him here too. After you do that, take over for Molly and get the rest of the documents printed. I want one complete copy in my office as fast as you can do it and enough additional copies for everyone I've sent for." Ben then turned to Jane who had been standing and watching Ben act like the President. Ben said to her, "I'm so sorry, Jane, but this takes precedence over everything. I'll explain what's happening as soon as I can."

Jane smiled, "Don't worry about me, You go and do what you have to."

As Jane left the Oval Office for the residential quarters, Ben said, "I want Secret Service Agent Marino to send an agent to stay in the residence with Jane until I say otherwise."

"You worried about the Filipino gardener?" Molly asked.

"Yes. He's apparently on the grounds. Then have Marino arrest the gardener." Ben took a sheaf of papers containing everything that had so far been printed and copied, and walked into his office. He paused at the threshold and said, "I pray to God we can get this creaky damn bureaucracy organized with enough efficiency to intercept these attacks and that it doesn't get leaked to the press before we can round them up."

As Ben read the materials he had brought with him, his phone rang, It was Martha saying she had Agent Marino on the line. Ben picked up the phone. Marino said, "Agent Walton is with Mrs. Cabot in the residence, sir and I saw the Filipino gardener. I looked him up. His name is Jose Matera and he appears to be a legal immigrant. Don't I need a warrant to arrest him?"

"Have a couple of Marines detain him on my authority. He could be an enemy combatant. While they're doing that, go to his house and search it. Take someone from ATF because there could be explosives there. Let me know what you find immediately."

Moments later, Martha called Ben again. "Sorry, Mr. President, I've got Mrs. Kendall on the phone. Senator Kendall is at the golf course and must have turned his phone off. Do you want me to try and reach him there."

"Let me speak to her." After Martha transferred the call, Ben said, "This is President Silver, Mrs. Kendall. I need Bob at the White House as fast as he can get here. Get the head pro or the starter. Tell them to tell Bob it's a family emergency and he has to call you immediately. I hate to do that, but I don't want rumors to start flying all over the Beltway. When he calls, tell him I need him immediately. Thanks." Ben hung up the phone and returned to the documents. The pile of unread papers kept growing faster than the ones he had read. After reading a page, Ben picked up his phone, "Martha, tell Admiral Williamson I need to see him immediately."

Before Ben could resume reading, Ben heard an explosion from the direction of the Rose Garden. He ran out of his office and started through the anteroom when he was stopped by Secret Service Agents. One of them said, "Sorry Mr. President, but we need you to stay right where you are until we find out what happened." The agent pressed the receiver in his ear and listened intently. He reported to the President, "There was an explosion in the Rose Garden. When they went to detain Mr. Matera, he set off a bomb in his wheelbarrow. One of our agents and two Marines were killed. So was Matera."

"Damn," Ben turned to Martha. "Find out who they were. I'll want to speak to the families. Have Spenser Cameron tell the press that a suspicious acting gardener employed at the White House killed himself, the two Marines and the Secret Service Agent with a homemade bomb when the Secret Service went to question him. Make it clear that I was nowhere near the Rose Garden at the time of the explosion. I don't want to say too much and alert anyone about what we may know."

As Ben started to return to his office, he said, "Molly, let Martha finish that. I want to talk to you." She and Ben entered the Oval Office. Ben said, "There can't be any question about it. The first part of Clarence's warning was accurate. If he's right about the rest of what I read so far, we have an enormous problem. Al Qaeda and a lot of other terrorist organizations have joined forces to attack various targets in the United States." Ben paced around his desk and then stared out the window a moment. "Everyone will want to know how we know what we say we know, they'll demand a copy of what we received, it'll get leaked to the press and we'll lose the chance to break up that organization." Ben stood up and said, "No. We have to break this up and get all those people so they can't be reorganized again. Everyone will want to know who your letter writing 'Friend' is and I'm not sure anyone would even believe us if we said it was Clarence Davenport. The FBI and the CIA and Interpol all decided that he died in the Aran Islands. And what sense does it make to say it's him. We don't know where he is and can't apprehend him, and maybe he will continue to provide us with information. We can't forget that." Ben stood up and walked over to the sofa against the far wall near the entry. "Sorry, but I'm just kind of thinking out loud. Damn, but I hate the idea that I can't tell everyone the whole story."

"For what it's worth, I think your right, and I know how to keep a secret."

"Keep the notes from 'A Friend' separate from the attachment. When we have to give out copies we'll separate out the part that they're concerned with and not reveal our source. That way, no one will know it comes to you and they may not ask you if you know who the source is. If they do ask us, we have to say it's top secret and can't be disclosed. If we say we don't know, they won't believe us and insist on a congressional investigation."

Five minutes later, Tom Andrews arrived. He was followed by Rahsheed Evans, John Wallace, Homeland Security head, Tony Julian and the Attorney General. Admiral Williamson and Senator Bob Kendall were the last to arrive and they came together, explaining that they were playing golf together when summoned to the Oval Office.

Ben waited until they had all arrived before starting to explain why they were called. "On a routine review of the recent hire of a Filipino gardener we noticed a discrepancy in his papers. We went to check the information and the man detonated a fertilizer bomb killing himself and unfortunately killing two Marines and a Secret Service Agent."

Senator Kendall said, "I'm certainly pleased that the plot was discovered, but telling me about that can't be the reason you wanted me to be here right now."

"Your right, Senator. What I told you is the public message we will issue. Actually we were tipped off by a source I cannot reveal. I've told you about the source because it demonstrates the accuracy of the information we received from that source."

"There's more?" Kendall said.

"Lots more. I received the Al Qaeda plan of attack. One part of it calls for them to launch 'drone' aircraft carrying chemical weapons from tankers out at sea. That's the easy part and that's why I asked Admiral Williamson to be here. We have the locations from where the attack will be initiated and I'm sure the navy can avoid that attack."

"Where did Al Qaeda get 'drone' aircraft?" Tony Julian asked.

"Probably from Iraq. They never found all the 'drone' aircraft the Iraqis had during the 2003 Iraqi War. Williamson turned towards the President. "Do we know when the attack is supposed to happen?"

"Our information is that it's to take place 'On the anniversary of that most glorious day in September', so I assume it's scheduled for September 11."

"Then we have a week."

"On the outside, but there are many more attacks on the United States, that are supposed to take place on the same date."

Admiral Williamson said, "Do you want me to alert Generals Crandall and Lee?"

"I will for the attacks on our foreign Air and Army bases, when we finish up, but most of the attacks are planned against civilian targets in maybe a dozen states. That's where I have a decision to make." Ben turned to Senator Kendall, "What I'd like to do is send a task force of Secret Service, ATF, military and selected FBI Agents to roll up all these terrorist cells that are poised to carry out the planned attacks."

The Attorney General said, "You know you can't do that within the United States. Maybe you could if you declared Martial Law, but that would expose the situation. Give me the names of the terrorists and where they are, and the basis for your conclusion that those individuals are planning to commit acts of terrorism and I'll send as many Assistants from my Department as are needed to get arrest warrants and search warrants. I'm sure the judges will cooperate."

"That's the problem. I can't tell you who the source of the information is. I can only tell you that it's the same source that warned me of the Rose Garden attack."

"That's not much to go on, but it may be enough."

"That's encouraging, but what worries me is that the judges' clerks and other court personnel may leak this information and then Al Qaeda pushes up the date or scatters their people and they try again later. Do you think you can keep a tight lid on what we have to tell the judges?"

The AG furrowed his forehead in thought and shook his head. "Candidly, no I don't."

"I didn't think you could. That's why I said selected FBI. You know this town leaks worse than a sieve." Ben sat back and addressed the assembled group. "The problem is the courts, the Attorney General's office, and the FBI. They're all dedicated to investigating crimes and punishing the perpetrators, not to crime prevention. I've got to prevent this from happening." Ben turned back to the Attorney General, "Since we agree that going to court and trying to get warrants presents a risk that what we're doing would be leaked, I can't do that. There may be hell to pay, but it's my job to protect the people of this country and that's what I'm going to do, even if I get impeached for exceeding my powers." Ben grimaced, "I don't like it much, but so far as I'm concerned, the planned acts are acts of war and the people named to carry them out are enemy combatants."

The AG said, "There's lots of judges who won't see it that way."

"I know, but I have to do it. I want you to research the law, and be prepared to defend what I'm going to do, as best you can. No one other than you is to know that this is anything more than a hypothetical issue. If we mess this up, it could result in hundreds of thousands of civilian deaths, maybe millions, and the ruination of our economy, so I've got to do it this way."

"Yes, sir," the AG said. "I'll do the best I can, but you'll have the A.C.L.U. and other civil liberty groups screaming about your violating the Constitution, not to mention the media."

Ben smiled grimly. "That's what makes this a great country. Most of the people we'll take into custody will be illegal immigrants. See if you can draw some distinctions between citizens, legal immigrants and illegals. Perhaps the founders intended that the rights be different than the courts have said. Do the best you can, and I think you had better get started now. I don't think you have any need to know any more about this at the present time. Do you disagree?"

"No, sir. I'll get started now." The AG rose and walked towards the door.

Ben said, "Thank you, and let me know how you're getting along and if I can help in any way."

After the Attorney General left, Senator Kendall said, "I wish him good luck, but the information you're proceeding under better be right. I assume you considered it could be some hoax or plan by Davies to get you to make some blunder that ramps up the impeachment again?"

"I don't think it is, Senator. The Rose Garden tip was one hundred percent right, and we've had others from the same source that were just as good and none that were bad."

"Could be a ploy, a sting. Hate to say it, but I wouldn't put it past Davies to have set it up. Between him and Winters, I wouldn't put it past them to find some suicidal bastard to try and pull this off."

"You think they're that tight?"

"Yes, a Senate colleague confided in me that Winters used information against him to pressure his impeachment vote that could only have come from Winters."

Ben shook his head. "I appreciate your concern, Bob, but even if it is a scheme of theirs, I can't risk the deaths and destruction that I think results from inaction. They're planning to blow up over twenty bridges and tunnels connecting Manhattan to the rest of the country and destroy the electric power grid, and while the city its isolated and in the dark, they plan to fly drone aircraft carrying chemical weapons to spray the city." Ben turned towards Admiral Williamson. "It's going to be your job, Ted, to intercept the tankers carrying the planes and if they manage to launch any, to knock them down." Ben turned back to his audience.

"They got plans for similar attacks in Seattle, Los Angeles, Miami and Chicago. They plan to isolate Detroit from Canada, and attack Texas cities with drones launched from Mexico. They've targeted the multi billion dollar "Big Dig" project in Boston, an oil refinery in St. Croix in the U.S. Virgin Islands and lots more. There are targets in London, Paris, Berlin and Moscow, and strategic targets like the harbor tunnels in Hong Kong and the Hein Tunnel in Holland. All that takes place before they overthrow the Saudi Royal Family."

Kendall asked, "You planning to contact the Europeans, the Saudis and the folks in Hong Kong?"

Ben thought a moment. "I'll contact the Brits. I trust them to keep it to themselves. But I'll wait on the Europeans and the Saudis until after we roll up the operation here."

Tom Andrews said, "That'll piss them off, especially if it doesn't give them enough time to protect themselves."

"I'm not happy doing it that way, Tom, but I don't trust the leaders of those countries enough to tell them. Any one of them might sell us out to Al Qaeda. My primary obligation is to the people of this country, and I'm not going to risk their lives by trusting people that are not trustworthy." Ben addressed the group he had assembled, looking first at Tom Andrews, next at Secret Service Agents Rahsheed Evans and John Wallace, then at Homeland Security head, Tony Julian and finally at Admiral Wilson. "I'm going to want you to separate the planned attacks into tactical operations and plan how we approach each of them. Admiral, you get help from Generals Lee and Crandall as required and designate some military planners to work with us on the planning. Select some military bases where we can hold the people we round up and interrogate them. Tom, you know the agencies. Select any help we need from ATF and the FBI that you know we can rely on. Even though this is a war and I regard the people we move against as enemy combatants, we'll be moving in civilian areas and I want to alarm the general population as little as possible. There's a copy of the information we have for each of you. Study it and then get together. We don't have a lot of time. The faster we can do this and complete the United States operation, the longer lead-time we can give the Europeans and the Chinese. Molly and I are going to work on an Executive Order designed to protect you and the people working with you from criticism."

"You mean so it all lands on you," Senator Kendall said.

"Yes, as Harry Truman is supposed to have said, 'if you can't stand the heat, get out of the kitchen.' Well, I'm in the oven, but no one else has to be. Okay, let's get started, but I'd like Molly and Senator Kendall to stay."

When Ben, Molly and Kendall were alone, Ben said, "Bob, Molly and I think our information comes from Clarence Davenport."

Kendall stared at Ben. His mouth hung open. For a minute he couldn't say anything. "I don't believe it. You can't be serious."

"But I am."

"Jesus, they'll be asking if you communicate with a ***Ouija Board.***"

Ben smiled. "You see why we can't tell anyone who our source is. Molly and I never bought that story about his drowning in the Aran Islands." Kendall continued staring at Ben and shaking his head as Ben continued. "I figure he's a little nuts and seems to have become infatuated with Molly."

Molly smiled, and punctured the tension as she said, "Thanks a lot, Mr. President."

Ben blushed, "Not that you have to be crazy to fall for Molly, but I really think that's what happened. You remember that story about the two middle-eastern men who blew themselves up in their SUV not too far from here?"

Kendall nodded that he did. Ben continued, "That came out of a similar tip from the same source. They were supposed to kill me in the Rose Garden and our source was worried that Molly would be near me and be killed."

Kendall said, "I suppose men have done unexpected things because of women before. It sounds odd, but I know you too well to think you're nuts."

"I want you to know the whole story. I suppose there'll be a lot of rhetoric from Congress, because as I see it, we'll do what we have to do here and hopefully prevent anything terrible from succeeding. I won't be able to break the news immediately as to what we discovered because the Europeans will want some time to do what they have to do. I'll trust your discretion on this. I'd like Congress with me, but I want you to only talk with people you know will be quiet until we finish what we have to do."

Kendall frowned. "There'll be a few, but I agree that we can't risk premature disclosure." Kendall shook his head. "Are there targets in Washington?"

"Yes."

"What?"

"The White House, The Capitol, the Supreme Court."

CHAPTER 44

▼

Four days later, at four-thirty A.M., Eastern Daylight Savings Time, President Ben Silver was in the situation room in the basement of the White House with a full staff from the military and from civil law enforcement. He took a deep breath, and said, "Now." On his word, task forces coordinated by Admiral Donald "Ted" Williamson, moved against Al Qaeda terrorists being readied to attack Army, Air Force and Naval bases in Europe, the middle-east and the United States. At the same time, FBI, ATF, Secret Service and military forces coordinated by Tony Julian, head of Homeland Security, raided terrorist cells in twelve cities in eleven states.

In the United States, eleven terrorists were killed and thirty-two were wounded resisting arrest, and another two hundred and twelve were taken into custody. Two U.S. Army corporals were wounded. Eleven thousand tons of fertilizer and other materials for making explosives that were to be used to attack tunnels and bridges in Manhattan were seized in Elizabeth, New Jersey, and another eight hundred tons were seized in Hudson, New York. Lesser amount of explosives were seized in Brooklyn, Everett, Massachusetts, Miami Springs, Florida, Detroit, Dallas, San Antonio, Oklahoma City, Chicago, Seattle, Washington, Los Angeles and San Francisco. Additional raids were conducted by U.S. forces in two Mexican and two Canadian border towns after ten minute notice to local law enforcement authorities in those communities. While the raids were successful, and Ben called the Canadian Prime Minister and Mexico's President as they commenced, the incursion across national borders by U.S. police and military gave rise to official protests from both governments.

Ben knew that the operations were too massive to pass unnoticed and he scheduled a press conference for ten o'clock in the morning. The scheduled press report could not head off the early news telecasts and radio broadcasts, and they reported that United States military and civil law enforcement agencies arrested hundreds of people across the nation. As it soon became established that law enforcement officials armed with warrants did not conduct the actions, Ben was attacked for employing fascist methods and violating the Constitutional right of all those detained.

When Senator Davies called P.J. Winters, he found Winters so angry at not knowing what had happened and learning that FBI agents had participated in the action without telling him, that he could hardly speak coherently. Winters said, "Heads will roll. That son of a bitch in the White House assigned some of my people, my people, to Homeland Security with instructions that they not tell me anything about it. He went too far this time. I say impeach the bastard. The people he picked up have rights and they're being kept incommunicado at military bases. I ought to send some of my people to the White House and arrest the son of a bitch Jew."

"He says they're terrorists."

"Where are the warrants, where's the probable cause? How did he know who to pick up and where to find them? He says they're terrorists, but we have zero information about that. He's just trying to make me look bad with this. I'm the God damn FBI and any information about terrorists in the United States has to come to me."

Davies adjusted his cuff links. "Look on the bright side. Maybe he screwed up royally this time. If he did, we can get the impeachment going again. Let's hear what he has to say at ten. We'll talk after that and maybe get together and discuss the situation." Winters agreed.

At ten o'clock in the morning, looking haggard from lack of sleep over the last four days, and exhausted from a series of phone calls to Paris, Berlin, Moscow, Beijing and other capitols, Ben walked into the pressroom in the West Wing. The tension was so heavy, Ben almost seemed to be swimming upstream as he walked towards the dais emblazoned with the Presidential seal, and then gripped its sides for support. The room quickly stilled.

"Ladies and Gentlemen of the media and in the television audience, at my direction, this morning, naval forces of the United States intercepted an oil tanker flying a Panamanian flag. It was carrying drone aircraft and chemical weapons, and was tasked, we believe, to attack targets in the United States. At the same time, forces assigned to the Department of Homeland Security captured a large number of enemy combatants at various locations in this country and seized a large quantity of materials from which explosives can be manufactured. We believe that many of the people being detained are here illegally and that they were planning to carry out terrorist activities in our country. We picked up a number of people who were infected with small pox in varying stages who were prepared to infect a large number of other terrorists who were to then invade our churches and synagogues, our symphony halls, sporting venues and other locations. The largest operation we interrupted was aimed at the City of New York and its inhabitants." Ben seemed to gather strength as he went along. "A similar raid was conducted in the United Kingdom. As soon as we can analyze the results of these operations, we will inform you further. I can't say that we have destroyed the threat of terrorism in our nation, I wish I could, but I can say that the United States is a safer place today than it was yesterday. Thank you very much."

As Ben prepared to leave, the press corps erupted. "No, Mr. President. Mr. President, you can't leave. We have questions."

Scott Jackson shouted louder than the rest, "Why was the FBI left out? You can't do this without arrest warrants and search warrants. Did you get them?"

Another reporter shouted. "The people you arrested have rights. Were they advised of their rights? Do they have lawyers? Are any legal immigrants or citizens?"

As the questions rocketed across the room, Ben returned to the dais, held his hands up for silence and looked out at the audience of newsmen and women and television cameras. After the noise level subsided, Ben said, "I believe most of the people captured are illegal aliens although some may be here legally and a few may be citizens. I don't know. However, we believe they are all enemy combatants. We believe they are all here to kill as many of the innocent citizens of this country as they can." As a buzz of protest began to rise, Ben said over the noise, "I'll make it clear. They have not and will not be offered the protections of the Constitution available to citizens and residents of this country. Their status is a legal question and the Attorney General is prepared to defend what was done in court if necessary."

"That's a violation of their civil rights. It's indefensible." Scott Jackson shouted.

Ben said, "There is precedent for their detention."

Shouts of, "That's unconstitutional! It violates the Bill of Rights!" and "What kind of precedent!" were heard.

Ben held his hands up for silence. He wondered if he would have agreed with the irate members of the media before he became President that what he did was terrible and violated the Constitution. Maybe not. Ben took a deep breath and then said, "For example, Nazi spies and saboteurs who landed here from submarines during World War II, they were treated in that manner." Ben could have referenced the detention of Japanese Americans after the attack on Pearl Harbor, but chose not to. Instead he said, "This is not the place to debate law cases."

Jackson shouted, "Couldn't you get the FBI to go along with that. Is that why P.J. Winters wasn't involved?"

"It was my decision as President in view of the threat I saw, to take the steps we took to protect us all. No single Agency or Department was able to handle the entire threat, and so I established special joint task forces to blend the talents of what everyone does best. So far as the FBI is concerned, they're primary function is the investigation of crimes and the apprehension of criminals. We have a military whose function is primarily to protect us from foreign attack from abroad and a Department of Homeland Security whose function is in large measure to protect the nation from attacks from within by terrorists. Everyone we used did what they do best."

Gavin Hunter, a well-respected member of the White House permanent press corps waved at Ben for attention and said, "Excuse me Mr. President. Is it true that you authorized raids in Mexico and Canada without receiving permission from those countries?"

"Yes, it is." A gasp went up from the assembled media. Ben held his hands up for silence. "Since the completion of those operations, I have spoken with the Mexican President and Canadian Prime Minister. Understandably, they are not pleased, but I felt it necessary and I believe our relationships with those countries will remain satisfactory."

"Why in the name of heaven did you do that?" Hunter asked.

"I'm glad you asked," Ben said. "I did it to protect the people of this nation. That's my job. I certainly don't want to offend anyone, least of all two neighbors with whom we enjoy cordial relations, but when attacks on American citizens are about to be launched from a foreign location, it is my job to prevent it from happening. I considered our intelligence too sensitive to share." Although he wanted to Ben didn't add the phrase, "...with political leaders who haven't demonstrated their full support for our war against terrorism and our efforts to protect ourselves."

"Just one more question, if I may, Mr. President." Ben nodded for Hunter to continue. Apparently, the information you acted upon didn't come from the FBI, so where did it come from?"

"Sorry, Mr. Hunter, like you gentlemen of the press, I have to protect my sources. It would prejudice its effectiveness if I were to disclose that information." Ben looked out at his hostile audience. "That's all the time I have right now. Thank you for coming and for your attention."

As Ben began to walk off the dais, Polly Shore of CNS News Service said, "Just one more question, please, Mr. President." She had always been fair with Ben, and he stopped and looked in her direction. "Okay, and this really has to be the last one."

"Thank you, Mr. President. You had just managed to avert trial of the Impeachment charges by the Senate and your possible removal from office. Don't you think your proceeding the way you did without warrants and the rest will give ammunition to those that want to see you removed from office?"

"Even if it does and it results in my removal from office by the Senate, I couldn't have acted otherwise. It's my job to protect the people of this country. The threat I saw to the people of this country was so terrible, so severe, and so catastrophic, that there was no choice. Even if what I did is prohibited by the Constitution in the opinion of the Supreme Court, what I did had to be done to avoid hundreds of thousands of deaths in this country. I would do it again, exactly the same way."

"That's not good enough," Scott Jackson shouted. "The people have a right to know what's going on and why these police state tactics are being employed."

Ben shrugged and continued walking towards the exit.

As Ben entered his West Wing office, Peter Clemmons, his Acting Secretary of State met him. He said, "After you spoke with the heads of state in France, Germany, Russia and China, their foreign ministers started calling me. Their intelligence services may have contacted Al Qaeda because they all want to know how you learned what you say you know and who the source of your information might be. If I won't tell them, they say they'll conclude it's unreliable."

"If they had acted six hours ago when I first called them, they probably could have apprehended most of the terrorists that were planning to attack targets in their countries. By now, the information could be unreliable. If I were Al Qaeda and I heard that the planned U.S. operations were discovered and the operatives captured, I'd probably tell the people planning the other operations to scatter." Ben frowned. "Tell them I will not give them that information."

Clemmons smiled. "I thought you might say that and I told them I doubted you'd agree. They told me if they are attacked by anyone, it will be on your head because you refused to tell them what they wanted to know."

"You know what to tell them, Peter."

"Yes, to perform a physically impossible act."

"Exactly. They probably have talked with Al Qaeda and Al Qaeda may well back off, after what we did, but Al Qaeda can't control all the loose cannons that are out there."

Ben was right, and during the rush hour in Paris, four Peugeot vans carrying fertilizer based bombs exploded near the Arc de Triomphe, killing forty-seven French citizens and wounding one hundred and sixteen more. The President of France attributed the failure of the French police to prevent the attack to the United States' refusal to share intelligence with them.

During the afternoon and evening following Ben's press conference, Senator Davies and P.J. Winters assessed the mood of the nation. While the press was incensed at Ben's actions and his refusal to tell them how he knew what he said he knew, the general public seemed confused by all the sound and fury coming out of Washington. The first reaction in Congress was to start up the impeachment again, but by evening, they began hearing from constituents. As it became more and more apparent that a substantial threat to the nation had been averted, outside the Beltway the feeling grew that maybe the President had done the right thing. Impeachment was out. Winters and Davies were incensed. Davies called Winters. "We got to talk some more. We can forget about impeachment, and the plan to kill Silver that you told me about didn't work. We got to do something about him, and we got to do it damn soon. I'm thinking we get somebody to do a hit, like the Lindsay Cabot deal. We frame Al Qaeda. We use a rocket or something. I'll be at my cottage tomorrow. Come over around eleven. I'm sure we'll come up with something."

Winters agreed. "I'm going to look around. I may have some materials around we can use to pin it on Al Qaeda, and we picked up a hit man with a bad habit. He's an expert with all kinds of weapons. He's a possibility. We'll talk tomorrow morning and I'm sure we'll find a way."

CHAPTER 45

▼

Ben Silver sat on the living-room sofa in the residence. His laptop was in his lap. He had wanted to draft another note from Molly to Clarence. He wasn't sure what he should say and was having trouble focusing on it. He didn't want to admit that he was too tired to think about it. After four days of around the clock planning, they had successfully prevented the terrorists from launching the attacks against New York City and the other terrorist targets across the country. The destruction of the New York tunnels and bridges combined with the chemical weapons from the drones and missiles on the oil tanker they stopped would have killed millions of people trapped in Manhattan. The best guess estimate was three million dead. That crisis over, Ben had run out of gas and he fell asleep. His glasses were perched on his nose and his English bulldog, Ace was snoring at his feet. The black pug was asleep next to him. Jane had returned to Boston, but was scheduled to return tomorrow. Ben's final thought before falling asleep was how nice it would be to have nothing to do and wouldn't it be nice to go someplace nice with Jane. He was the President and should be able to do whatever he wanted, shouldn't he. As he drifted into sleep, he saw himself and Jane in St. Croix, enjoying the vacation they planned that was interrupted by Clarence Davenport's assassination of President Butler. They were dining and dancing at the Ha'Penny Bay Beach Club. It was a pleasant dream.

When Ben finally woke up, it was seven-thirty in the morning and Molly was expected at eight. They were supposed to compare ideas on what to write to Clarence, and Ben hadn't had one thought about it. Perhaps Molly would have some bright ideas. Ben hustled into the bathroom to get ready and reappeared in the living room as Molly was ushered in. Ben smiled at her. "I overslept and fell asleep without a single idea."

"I did too. I just couldn't stay awake. I was kind of nervous coming here and telling you that. I tried, but I passed out and didn't wake up until quarter of seven."

"You're entitled to a little vacation after what you did. This country owes you a big debt of gratitude and I'd love to tell the world about what you did."

"What we did."

Ben shook his head. "You're the one that caused Clarence to do what he did. He did it for you, not me."

Molly blushed. "Even so, we can never tell anyone. They'd never believe it."

"Unfortunately, you're probably right. When the bureaucracy comes to a particular conclusion and tells the world their version of something, it's almost impossible to ever change that. We'd have to produce Clarence Davenport and have fingerprints or DNA evidence to prove that he was who we said he was before anyone would believe us." Ben shook his head. "There's an interesting story about two women who did a tremendous job that I want to tell you. One looked into the 1993 World Trade Center bombing, and the other worked on the 1995 Oklahoma City bombing." Ben clicked a few keys on his computer. "I've kept this piece from the Wall Street Journal. It starts with a quote by Former CIA Director James Woolsey." Ben peered at the screen of his laptop and started reading,

"When the full stories of these two incidents (1993 WTC Center bombing and 1995 Oklahoma City Bombing) are finally told, those who permitted the investigations to stop short will owe big explanations to these two brave women (Middle East expert Laurie Mylroie and journalist Jayna Davis). And the nation will owe them a debt of gratitude."

"In my judgement, what Woolsey said about those two women can equally be said about you. Unfortunately, they still haven't gotten the credit they deserve and the bureaucracy continues to ignore the work they did. Unfortunately, you're not going to get the credit you deserve either. Much as I'd like to start a manhunt to capture Davenport and bring him to justice for the terrible things he did, we'd lose whatever credibility we have if we said we believe he's alive and had provided us with the information that enabled us to do what we did. The best we can do right now is to try and continue to use him as a resource. He has to be highly positioned in the terrorist hierarchy to have access to the information he provided."

"What do you think finally made him send us that master plan of their operations? Maybe his peculiar concern about my personal safety made him send the information about the Rose Garden bomb, but what about the rest of it?"

Ben thought a minute. "There was a story about his uncle being killed in London by a suicide bomber a few days ago. The report I saw said they thought it was a Palestinian terrorist that thought Rabbani was an Israeli. That never made any sense to me. So, maybe it was an Al Qaeda operation. Maybe Al Qaeda got rid of Rabbani. Davenport didn't like it and he decided to defect. Al Sabin told me that Rabbani was opposed to Al Qaeda so they had reasons to want to get rid of him." Ben paused as a waiter came in with a tray of coffee and Ben's breakfast. Ben said, "Help yourself if you want anything."

"I'll just have some coffee."

After the waiter left, Ben said, "I think we're going to have to forget about getting Davenport, at least for now. Let's just send him a brief thank you note. He'd probably appreciate that. Something like, 'Thanks so very much for what you did. You must have seen the results by now. You saved a lot of lives, and for that you will always have a warm place in my heart. The best thing I can do to show my appreciation is to keep our secret. Molly'. What do you think?"

"I think it's perfect. He's too smart to buy into an all is forgiven-come home kind of note."

"Do you want to add a line saying you hope you'll continue to hear from him?"

Molly wrinkled her forehead. "No, I don't think so. In a few weeks, maybe a short note saying I hope he's well and that I miss hearing from him."

"Good, do it, and you'll let me know if you hear from him." As Molly rose and started to leave, Ben said, "And Molly, thanks. You've done a terrific job."

"Thank you, sir. That means a lot to me."

"If there's anything I can do for you, just ask."

Molly paused a moment. "Well there is something. Tom and I plan to get married soon. Would you be willing to give the bride away?"

"I'd be more than proud."

While Ben and Molly were talking about him, Clarence Davenport watched Senator Jeb Davies climb into an armored limousine. Clarence discreetly followed the limousine, but before long, it was apparent that the limousine's destination was the Senator's country house. Clarence had been watching Davies for the last two days and this was the first time he had left to go anywhere other than to his office. Clarence turned off the road and drove to a self-storage warehouse. He went inside and shortly returned carrying three boxes. Two were quite small.

One was very large but appeared not to be very heavy. He stowed them in his SUV and then returned to the warehouse and soon re-appeared with two medium sized boxes that he carried very gingerly. He put both boxes on the rear floor of the SUV and then fastened one in place with Velcro. He then leisurely drove out towards Davies' country house, parked on the opposite side of the river and watched as another limousine approached Davies' cottage up a winding driveway. Clarence looked through his binoculars as someone got out of the limousine. It was P.J. Winters. It couldn't be better. He'd love to wind his garrote around their necks and squeeze till their eyes bulged, but each had a bodyguard and they were undoubtedly well armed.

Clarence withdrew to an unoccupied house one street back from the river, then got out of his SUV and assembled the model airplane in the large box, installed a small TV camera and the GPS system, and then added the battery and explosives. He was ready. He launched the Model P-51 fighter plane, maneuvered it with the console and watched its progress on the TV screen. He didn't really need the GPS system, but it was there. With the camera's eagle eye he could see Davies and Winters in deep conversation. He brought the plane in closer. Winters looked at the plane. Was he upset? Would he understand the danger that was approaching? Winters started to rise and say something to Davies. Was the model plane close enough? Clarence pushed the button and immediately heard an explosion. His picture vanished. Had he succeeded?" Should he chance driving back to where he could see Davies' house, and if he did, what would he see? He wouldn't know if he had succeeded even if he could see the porch where they had been sitting and he saw their bodies on the ground. No, he'd leave very quietly and find out later.

On his way back to his apartment, Clarence detoured into Virginia and disposed of the boxes that had contained the materials he had purchased for today's attempt to kill Senator Davies in a pond near where he had grown up in Alexandria. He had tried to kill Davies once before and only succeeded in killing Davies' receptionist and part time sex pal, Laverne Templeton. He hoped this time that he had taken care of that little piece of unfinished business.

All the way from Maryland to Virginia and then back to the Watergate, Clarence listened to the news, but he was not rewarded with the news of Davies' death. Finally, at ten thirty-seven, the network programming Clarence kept on but wasn't listening to or watching was interrupted for breaking news. A breathless reporter announced, "This is Andrea Black with breaking news. Presidential foes, Senator Jebediah Davies and FBI Director P.J. Winters were killed late this morning in an explosion of undetermined origin at the Senator's riverside mansion. The President could not be reached for comment. Press Secretary, Cameron Spenser said that he had informed the President of what had happened and that the President was shocked at the news.

The next night, Molly called Ben shortly after midnight. "Sorry to call so late, Mr. President."

Ben shook the sleep out of his eyes. "I know it's important or you wouldn't have called."

"Yes, sir. I just got a message from Clarence Davenport."

"Do you want to come over?"

"Up to you, sir. It's pretty short."

"Read it to me and then we can decide."

Molly read,

> *I had unfinished business with Davies. P.J. Winters was an unexpected bonus for you. I didn't like the way he treated you.*
> *A Friend*

"You're not blaming yourself for what that mad man did are you?

"No, sir. Frankly, I'll shed no tears at the death of either of them."

"Good." Ben smiled. "You know what that means, don't you?"

"No, what?"

"It means that Davenport was in the United States, in the D.C. area two days ago and that we missed our chance to get him."

"Would it be awful, Mr. President, if I said I was glad that he's gone again?"

"Not to me, but how do we know he's gone."

The End

Author's Postscript

Some readers of my previous novel, **After Kamisiyah**, and of the manuscript for **The Accidental President** have asked me where I got the idea for the novels and how much of them is fact and how much is fiction. If you are also interested, read on. Otherwise, your work is done and you have finished the book. Whether you read on or not, if you liked **The Accidental President**, loan it to a friend, or better still buy them a copy.

Both novels are, of course, a blend of fact and fiction. My goal as a novelist is to entertain the reader, and mixing fact and fiction has been a methodology to achieve that result used in varying degrees in novels like the **Da Vinci Code** and by writers like Ken Follett and Jack Higgins to name only two. You are the judge of whether and to what extent I succeeded.

My interest in writing **After Kamisiyah**, the prequel to the **Accidental President** arose out of a slow to develop news story about claims of returning veterans that they had contracted strange diseases in connection with their Gulf War service. The George H. W. Bush administration and then the Clinton administration insisted that the mysterious illnesses had no medically discernible foundation. Like many Americans, I first believed the complaints were not genuine. I thought it was most likely just another case of people looking for a free ride, this time American service people. As the complaints multiplied, I began to suspect there was more to it. What I learned was shocking.

We may wish it weren't so, but during the five-year period following the end of the 1991 Gulf War, the U.S. Government consistently denied that the illnesses of our service people, lumped together as "Gulf War Syndrome," could have resulted from exposure to chemical or biological weapons. It was not until February 1997 that the Pentagon finally acknowledged that it had been previously warned that chemical weapons were stored at Kamisiyah, and not until July 24,

1997, that it admitted that almost 100,000 American troops had been exposed to Sarin gas and other contaminants. Congressional investigations to determine what happened at Kamisiyah remain to this day frustrated by bad memories and "lost" government records. That is fact.

As the story of the cover-up developed, I began to think about writing *After Kamisiyah*. Before I finished the novel, more of the truth became known, although the whole story has still not been discovered. For those interested, more of the facts concerning the cover-up at Kamisiyah are compiled in the Foreword of *After Kamisiyah* and for those who want more information about Gulf War Syndrome, I recommend they visit www.gulfweb.org., an excellent non-profit web site for Gulf War veterans and their families.

While the Government's failure to heed the warnings it had received that chemical and biological weapons were stored at Kamisiyah could have been excused as a tragic blunder, treating the many and varied illnesses of our returning servicemen and women with denials of responsibility and deception was a national disgrace. Those events helped create the fictional antagonist of the prior novel who continued to play a major role in this one.

This novel borrows from another series of likely mistakes by the U.S. Government, which may have had and may continue to have serious consequences. Many believe that the lack of cooperation between the CIA and the FBI and other agencies may have contributed to the disaster of September 11. That failure to cooperate is undeniably true. But there are other errors that also have played a part and bureaucrats within the Federal government have again met those errors with denials of responsibility and deception.

Could avoidance of criticism and career advancement considerations have led to those bad memories and "lost" records that resulted in depriving our Gulf War returning servicemen and women of the support they had earned? I can find no other explanation. Are those forces again at work in the aftermath of September 11 as they were in the aftermath of Kamisiyah?

It should be no surprise that the twin evils of careerism and of the denial of responsibility that affect business corporations may reach into government agencies as it did with the Kamisiyah cover-up, but, where the security of the citizenry is involved, the stakes are too high for it to be tolerated.

I believe that those evils and the long-standing denial of state sponsorship of terrorism caused the continuing mishandling of investigations into prior attacks against the people of the United States and that those errors contributed to the Sept. 11 disaster. Perhaps September 11 could not have been avoided. Congressional investigations have been frustrated and we may never know all of the truth, but the failure to seek the truth and remedy the failures may result in more disasters like 9/11.

The U.S. Government, primarily through the CIA and FBI, has denied that the September 11 attack and those that preceded it were state sponsored despite the growing wealth of materials from reputable sources casting doubt on that conclusion. Could the critics of the CIA and the FBI be correct? We would hope not. But whether the critics are right or wrong, there are lessons to be learned from their criticism.

New York Times journalist William Safire, writing about a warning pertaining to the activities of Mohamed Atta received from Czech intelligence sources about four months prior to September 11, said on May 9, 2002,

> *A misdirection play is under way in the C.I.A.'s all-out attempt to discredit an account of a suspicious meeting in Prague a year ago. Mohamed Atta, destined to be the leading Sept. 11 suicide hijacker, was reported...to have met...with Saddam Hussein's espionage chief...If the report proves accurate, a connection would exist between Al Qaeda's murder of 3,000 Americans and Iraq's Saddam...Accordingly, high C.I.A. and Justice officials—worried about exposure of the agency's inability to conduct covert operations—desperately want Atta's Saddam connection to be disbelieved...They are telling favored journalists: Shoot this troublesome story down...Everybody jumped aboard the C.I.A bandwagon.*

The Washington Post, Newsweek, Time Magazine and several others attacked the credibility of the Czech intelligence services. Safire writes in his May 9 article that the New York Times discredited the Czechs report of the Atta meeting by reporting,

> *a senior Bush administration official appeared to close the matter, saying F.B.I. and C.I.A. analysts had firmly concluded that no meeting had occurred.*

Generally unreported, except by Mr. Safire in a May 29 column and a few others was the response to those efforts to discredit the Czech intelligence information. He reported that the Czechs continue to stand by their report that Atta met with the Iraqi espionage officer in Prague prior to the Sept. 11 attack. Safire asks,

> *Whom do you believe—a responsible official on the scene speaking on the record, with no ax to grind, or U.S. spooks who may be covering up a missed signal from Prague about Sept. 11...?*

Is it possible that the CIA could miss important warnings like that sent by Czech intelligence? One would hope not, but consider this December 11, 2002 MacNeil/Lehrer Productions copyrighted Online NewsHour report. In it Democrat Senator Carl Levin of Michigan asked the CIA,

> *My question is do you know why the FBI was not notified of the fact that an Al Qaeda operative...was known in March...2000 to have entered the United States? Why did the CIA not specifically notify the FBI?*

An unnamed spokesman for the CIA responded,

> *Sir, if we weren't aware of it when it came into headquarters, we couldn't have notified them. Nobody read that cable in the March time-frame. It was an information-only cable from the field and nobody read that information-only cable.*

Rather surprisingly, it seems that some of the intelligence materials coming into the CIA is simply filed and not looked at.

In that same report, PBS' Gwen Ifill questioned Florida's Democrat Senator Bob Graham the chairman of the Senate Select Committee on Intelligence about the report of the committee's investigation into September 11.

> *GWEN IFILL: Senator Graham, are there elements in this report, which are classified that Americans should know about but can't?*
>
> *SEN. BOB GRAHAM: Yes,...I was surprised at the evidence that there were foreign governments involved in facilitating the activities of at least some of the terrorists in the United States. I am stunned that we have not done a better job of pursuing that to determine if other terrorists received similar support and, even more important, if the infrastructure of a foreign government assisting terrorists still exists for the current generation of terrorists who are here planning the next plots.*
>
> *GWEN IFILL: Are you suggesting that you are convinced that there was a state sponsor behind 9/11?*

> *SEN. BOB GRAHAM: I think there is very compelling evidence that at least some of the terrorists were assisted not just in financing—although that was part of it—by a sovereign government…*
>
> *GWEN IFILL: Do you think that will ever become public, which countries you're talking about?*
>
> *SEN. BOB GRAHAM: It will become public at some point…but that's 20 or 30 years from now…*

While the official position adopted by the Clinton administration and followed by the subsequent Bush administration is that there was no state sponsorship of 9/11 or any prior attack on the United States, not everyone is willing to accept that pronouncement.

Micah Morrison, a senior editorial page writer at the Wall Street Journal wrote a September 5, 2002 article about two women who refused to accept that government conclusion. One is former Clinton White House advisor Laurie Mylroie who asserted that Iraq was probably involved in the 1993 World Trade Center bombing. The other is former Oklahoma City TV journalist Jayna Davis who believes that Iraq was most likely involved in the 1995 bombing of the Oklahoma City Murrah Building. In his article, Morrison quotes former CIA Director James Woolsey saying about the two women,

> *…when the full stories of these two incidents are finally told, those who permitted the investigations to stop short will owe big explanations to these two brave women. And the nation will owe them a debt of gratitude.*

The Justice Department prosecuted and convicted four Muslim individuals it apprehended who moved in extremist circles in the New York area for their participation in the 1993 World Trade Center bombing. Ms. Mylroie claims, and is probably right, that others were involved. According to Mylroie, one other was an Iraqi named Abdul Yasin. He was picked up after the bombing, but managed to talk his way out of a FBI interrogation and then immediately left for Baghdad. Mylroie claims that another conspirator in the bombing, Ramzi Yousef, entered the United States with an Iraqi passport and left with a Pakistani one in the name of Abdul Basit. She claims that Ramzi Yousef is an Iraqi agent and that the bombing was probably "an Iraqi intelligence operation with the Moslem extremists as dupes." A growing number of people agree with her. Morrison also writes in his Wall Street Journal article,

> *She [Ms. Mylroie] says that the original lead FBI official on the case, Jim Fox, concluded that "Iraq was behind the World Trade Center bombing." In late 1993, shortly before his retirement, Mr. Fox was suspended by FBI Director Louis Freeh for speaking to the media about the case…Ms. Mylroie says that Mr. Fox indicated to her that he did not continue to pursue the Iraq connection because Justice Department officials "did not want state sponsorship addressed."*

In a May 29, 2002 article in National Review on Line, Ms. Mylroie wrote,

> *A decade ago major terrorist strikes on US targets were considered to be state sponsored. For all practical purposes, that meant Iran, Iraq, Libya, and Syria. Yet that is supposed to have changed with the first attack on the World Trade Center, in February 1993, one month into Bill Clinton's first term…The Clinton administration claimed that the bombing represented a new kind of terrorism that did not involve states…And thus was born the notion that major terrorist strikes were carried out by individuals, or "networks," without the support of states. The predictable happened. Terrorism continued. In fact, it grew far worse because the state sponsor…was never identified…Like the FBI, the CIA accommodated Clinton's aversion to hearing that Iraq was attacking the US and is now committed to its past…Senior officials are now involved in what William Safire politely terms, "covering their posteriors." That exercise is so irresponsible as to defy belief.*

It is beyond the scope of this Postscript to fully present all the evidence Mylroie has compiled of Iraq's complicity in terrorist activities. To those of you interested in learning more of Ms. Mylroie's views concerning the Iraq connection to the 1993 attack on the World Trade Center, I recommend her book, *Study of Revenge: The First World Trade Center Attack & Saddam Hussein's War against America*.

The materials compiled by Oklahoma City journalist, Jayna Davis indicating state sponsorship of the Oklahoma City bombing are equally if not more compelling than the arguments of Ms. Mylroie about the 1993 World Trade Center. Assigned to cover the Oklahoma City bombing by the TV station that employed her as an investigative reporter, Ms. Davis had no agenda other than to discover what she could about the Murrah Building bombing and then report it. It was soon apparent to Ms. Davis and the rest of the world that the perpetrators of the Oklahoma City bombing were former army buddies, Tim McVeigh and Terry Nichols. Official assurances soon followed that the guilty parties had been apprehended and we were told that the perpetrators were angry white men, upset by the US handling of the Waco and Ruby Ridge cases. We were assured they acted alone and that no foreign terrorists or governments were involved. Those assurances did not fit with the earliest announcements by the FBI and were contrary to what Ms. Davis discovered in her investigation of the tragedy.

Ms. Davis had utilized a FBI bulletin, arrest warrant and sketches of two men seen together as leads. One of the sketches was of Tim McVeigh. The other sketch and description was of a middle-east man with a tattoo on his left arm. Ms. Davis found a man matching the description with the tattoo and she obtained affidavits from many witnesses who placed him near the Murrah Building shortly before the explosion and with Tim McVeigh. The Wall Street Journal reported that when the person Ms. Davis identified sued her for libel,

> *the judge ruled that Ms. Davis had proved that [the man she identified] "bears a strong resemblance to the sketch"...including tattoo on his left arm, that he was born and raised in Iraq, that he had served in the Iraqi army, and that his Oklahoma City employer had once been suspected by the federal government of having "connections with the Palestine Liberation Organization."*

The Journal article continues and states,

> *Evidence supporting Ms. Davis' suspicions surfaced during...the McVeigh trial. A FBI report...records a call...from Vincent Cannistraro, a retired CIA official...He told Kevin Foust, a FBI counter-terror investigator that...there was a "squad" of people currently in the United States, very possibly Iraqis, who have been tasked with carrying out terrorist attacks against the United States...[Cannistraro's Saudi source] claimed...that the first on the list [of targets] was the federal building in Oklahoma City, Oklahoma.*

> *In dismissing the...libel suit [against Davis]...Judge Leonard pointedly noted the indictment of McVeigh and Nichols included a charge of conspiracy" with others unknown." In sentencing Nichols, U.S. District Judge Richard Matsch remarked, "It would be disappointing to me if the*

law enforcement agencies of the United States government have quit looking for answers."

That is of course precisely what they did, only worse. They refused to accept the "gift wrapped" package of evidence meticulously put together by Ms. Davis. As in the 1993 World Trade Center attack, official Washington didn't want to hear about a state sponsor for the Oklahoma City attack. Could it be that the strategy Mylroie suggests Iraq employed of blaming the 1993 World trade Center bombing on a group of extremists was followed by them again in 1995 when McVeigh and Nichols were blamed as the sole perpetrators? Intelligence sources indicated that blaming terrorism on non-Muslim, American born natives, "lily-whites," was a terrorist strategy.

None of us want to believe that U.S. government officials who are supposed to protect our interests would so badly fail in the performance of their duties, but yet, even some of those very officials tasked with that obligation support the charge of failure by their agency.

Consider briefly the revelations by Coleen Rowley, Time Magazine's 2002 co-person of the year, and an employee of the FBI's Minneapolis office. Time reported,

> *When Rowley walked into her office on the morning of Sept. 11 and saw the Twin Towers burning on TV, she immediately thought of Moussaoui. For three weeks her office had been trying—and failing—to get FBI headquarters to allow a request for a search warrant of his computer...Minneapolis agents pushed headquarters for approval to dig deeper, fearing—before Sept. 11—that he might be part of a larger scheme to hijack commercial jetliners.*

According to Time, Rowley who went public with her complaints about the FBI's handling of the Moussaoui case was treated as a pariah by the higher ups in the FBI for her disloyalty to the Bureau. Perhaps Rowley's loyalty to the people of the United States exceeds her loyalty to the Bureau. It's reported that Rowley said,

> *The bureau could be great,...if only it put the goal of protecting Americans above the goal of protecting itself...*

It seems that Moussaoui may not have been the only September 11 terrorist the FBI refused to permit its agents to act against and that MS Rowley was not alone in feeling frustrated by FBI procedures. From a Dec. 13, 2003 Washington Post story by Dan Eggen, we learn,

> **FBI lawyers refused to allow criminal agents to join an August 2001 search for Khalid Almidhar, who had entered the United States and would later help commandeer the airliner that crashed into the Pentagon...information about Almidhar's ties to al Qaeda obtained through intelligence channels could not be used to launch a criminal investigation. An angry New York FBI agent warned in an internal e-mail that was later revealed during congressional hearings that "someday someone will die" because of that decision.**

A December 19, 2002 ABC NEWS.com story by Brian Ross and Vic Walter states, that two veteran FBI investigators claimed they were ordered to stop investigations into a suspected terror cell linked to Osama bin Laden's al Qaeda network. It was reported that in their interview they said,

> **"September the 11 [th] is a direct result of the incompetence of the FBI's International Terrorism Unit...You can't know the things I know and not go public. "...Wright says that when he pressed for authorization to open a criminal investigation...his supervisor stopped him. "Do you know what his response was? 'I think it's just better to let sleeping dogs lie,...' Those dogs weren't sleeping. They were training. They were getting ready."**
>
> **The move [refusing to prosecute anyone] outraged federal prosecutor Mark Flessner...Flessner said, 'There were powers bigger than I was in the Justice Department and within the FBI that simply were not going to let it [a criminal case] happen. And it didn't'.**

According to the referenced Washington Post article, under previous FBI protocols, intelligence gathering and criminal case development were to be kept separate and sharing of information was limited and "overseen by legal mediators from the FBI and Justice Department..." Will this change improve their performance. Perhaps, but the Washington Post reports,

> **"To civil liberterians and many defense lawyers, the changes pose a threat to the privacy and due-process rights of civilians because they essentially eliminate, rather than blur, the traditional boundaries separating criminal and intelligence investigations.**

In a precursor to the disclosure that Muslim interpreters and clerics may be acting as spies in their dealings with the detainees at Guantanomo Bay, Cuba, ABC NEWS stated that according to Flessner and Wright, an FBI agent named Gamal Abdel-Hafiz seriously damaged the investigation.

> *...Hafiz, who is a Muslim, refused to secretly record one of [the] suspected associates, who was also a Muslim. Wright says Abdel-Hafiz told him, Vincent and other agents that a 'Muslim doesn't record another Muslim.'...Far from being reprimanded, Abdel-Hafiz was promoted to one of the FBI's most important anti-terrorism posts...*

Do the reported statements of Abdel-Hafiz reflect the view of mainstream Muslims or are they the opinions of a fundamentalist minority? We hope and believe that the vast majority of American Muslims are like *The Reluctant President's* Rahsheed Evans, Americans first and Muslims second.

In a manner consistent with William Safire's claim that the bureaucracy is engaged in a disgraceful "cover your posterior" mode of operation, ABC NEWS reported that

> *the FBI...defended the agent saying he had a right to refuse because the undercover recording was supposed to take place in a mosque. But former prosecutor Flessner said that was a lie and the mosque was never part of the plan. 'What he [Abdel-Hafiz] said was, it was against his religion to record against another Muslim. I was dumbfounded by that response...and I had perfectly appropriate conversations with the supervisors of his home office and nothing came of it.'*

The statements reported by ABC NEWS describing the way the FBI dealt with two veteran agents from the Chicago office are consistent with the way the FBI dealt with Ms. Davis when she attempted to deliver evidence of criminal activity to the FBI, even to their attempting to misrepresent what she did. And what about that evidence?

Responding to criticism of her work by federal appointee, Cate McCauley who termed it a "very small package of information", Ms. Davis wrote the following:

> *Twenty-two witness affidavits supported by 25-hundred pages of corroborative evidence is hardly a 'very small package of information,'...McCauley is wholly unqualified to criticize the complexities of the investigative dossier because she has never reviewed it.*

I interviewed nearly 80 potential witnesses, but I deemed only two-dozen to be credible because the veracity of their testimonies could be independently corroborated and their stories did not conflict with the government's timeline of the movements of the Oklahoma City bombers. All confidently identified eight specific Middle Eastern men, the majority of whom are former Iraqi soldiers, collaborating with McVeigh and Nichols during various stages of the bombing plot. They have signed sworn affidavits confirming their testimonies.

After a thorough vetting process, this investigation has earned the ringing endorsement of...former Deputy Director of the State Department's Office of Counter Terrorism Larry Johnson, former Director of the CIA James Woolsey, former Chief of Human Intelligence for the Defense Intelligence Agency Colonel Patrick Lang, the Director of Congressional Task Force on Terrorism and Unconventional Warfare Yossef Bodansky, and the editorial board of the Wall Street Journal, including senior editorial writer Micah Morrison.

Former CIA analyst and Deputy Director of Counter Terrorism for the Department of State, Larry Johnson, has determined that 'without a doubt, there is a definite Middle Eastern tie to the Oklahoma City bombing. As a Fox News consultant, he has expressed publicly his concern that the Islamic terrorist network, which assisted McVeigh and Nichols, is still operational and poses a threat to national security.

In addition to comprehensive coverage published by the Indianapolis Star and the LA Weekly, I have been invited as a guest to discuss this investigation with Lou Dobbs of CNN, Fox News (Bill O'Reilly, John Gibson, Greta Van Susteren, and John Scott). The credibility of my work has also been recognized by nationally syndicated radio show host Glenn Beck as well as numerous talk radio programs. in several major markets (New York, San Fransico, Minneapolis, Philadelphia, Pittsburgh, Tampa, Miami, Nashville, and Richmond.)...

Jayna Davis
Yukon, OK

Philadelphia talk show host, Michael Smerconish is another seasoned media person impressed with the materials compiled by Ms. Davis. He did yeoman work to have those materials seriously looked at by Congress, but unfortunately, without satisfactory results. He wrote of Ms Davis,

> *Davis identified a group of Iraqis living in Oklahoma City, one of whom...sported a tattoo on his left arm that Davis said indicated he likely served in Sadam Hussein's Republican Guard (this was before the rest of us ever heard of the Republican Guard)...Davis has not gotten the credit she deserves.*

Frank J. Gaffney, Jr. writing in townhall.com on November 19, 2002 said of the materials compiled by Ms. Davis,

> *Unfortunately, it appears that at least some of the agencies charged with addressing the threat posed by Saddam's operatives and their sympathizers fail utterly to comprehend the challenge the targeted groups and individuals constitute. For example, the Times reports that "according to the CIA," there is no evidence that Iraq has engaged in terrorist activity against the United States" since 1993, when Iraqi agents tried to assassinate former President George H.W. Bush in Kuwait. This statement is deeply disturbing...It...evinces an obliviousness to the historical record that raises a question as to whether the existing intelligence and law enforcement agencies are up to the task at hand. That record includes the impressive investigative research conducted by Jayna Davis, a former reporter with Oklahoma City's KFOR television station. Since the Murrah Building was destroyed in April 1995, Ms. Davis has been tirelessly collecting, sifting and analyzing evidence (including some 80 pages of affidavits from more than twenty eyewitnesses and 2000 supporting documents) of precisely the sort that the CIA says does not exist.*

Another Journalist, Jim Crogan writing in the Indianapolis Star on February 17, 2002 reviewed evidence that the Oklahoma City bombing had Middle Eastern connections compiled by Davis and described it as "compelling." Any reader of his column would have to agree. He went on to say:

> *Over the past seven months, I reviewed all of Davis' documents,...I also conducted my own follow-up interviews and found no holes in her investigation...According to her attorney...Department of Justice attorneys prosecuting Nichols rejected Davis' documents in 1997 because they didn't want more material to turn over to the defense...Is this a case of FBI incompetence, political interference or the Justice Department's*

desire not to complicate a seemingly open-and-shut case...I don't know. I do know that too many questions remain unanswered. And I wonder if the FBI had followed through on these leads, might agents have turned up links to sleeper cells or networks that planned the Sept.11 massacre?

I urge anyone interested in learning more about the Oklahoma City bombing visit Ms. Davis' web site at ***www.JaynaDavis.com*** and purchase her book on the subject scheduled to be published in the spring or summer of 2004.

In doing research for this novel, I learned of a terrorist training camp that had been situated at Salman Pak, Iraq. Some of the action in the novel occurs at a fictitious terrorist training camp I've called New Salman Pak. In doing so, I drew heavily from a PBS Frontline interview of an Iraqi defector named Sabah Khodada who had worked at Salman Pak, Iraq that was about 30 miles from Baghdad. In the interview, Khodada said that the camp trained Iraqis and non-Iraqis, mostly from the Gulf. While the Iraqis were kept segregated from the foreigners, they were trained by the same Iraqi intelligence service trainers. The training included what Khodada called,

...hijacking and kidnapping of airplanes. And...how to belt themselves...with explosives...

After stating that the training of Arabs was much harsher than the training of Iraqis, he was asked why and responded:

Arabs...who come to train...are going to be sent to very dangerous and important operations...Those Arabs are real volunteers. They come in small numbers, and they come with the intention to do some real suicidal operations.

When asked if he thought some of the people trained at Salman Pak participated in the Sept. 11 attack on the United States, Khodada replied,

I assure you, this operation was conducted by people who were trained by Saddam...this kind of attacks...has to be organized by a capable state...there's a real whole 707 plane...standing in the middle of the training area in this camp.

According to the UK's Guardian Unlimited, another defector, a former Iraqi intelligence service colonel code-named Abu Zeinab claimed he had worked at Salman Pak. The Guardian reported that he said,

> *...separated from the rest of the facilities...was a barracks used to house Islamic radicals, many of them Saudis from bin Laden's Wahhabi sect, but also Egyptians, Yemenis...Zeinab said the foreigners' camp was controlled directly by Saddam...The method used on 11 September perfectly coincides with the training I saw at the camp. Yesterday their [Zeinab's and Khodada's] story received important corroboration from Charles Duelfer, former vice-chairman of UNSCOM, the UN weapons inspection team. Duelfer said he visited Salman Pak...He saw the 707 in exactly the place described by the defectors.*

Does the Salman Pak training base explain how the nineteen hijackers of four airliners managed to break into the cockpits of those airplanes and subdue the crew of each plane without one crew member on any flight being able to manage to say one word to the control towers monitoring the flights? It will for me until I hear a better one.

If you think so too, we are not alone. On May 7, 2003, a U.S. District Court judge ruled that Salman Pak, played a material role in the Sept. 11 attacks on America. NewsMax.com in reporting the ruling two days later said,

> *In a bombshell finding virtually ignored by the American media, a U.S. district court judge in Manhattan ruled Wednesday that Salman Pak, Saddam Hussein's airplane hijacking school located on the outskirts of Baghdad, played a material role in the devastating Sept. 11 attacks on America...only the Philadelphia Inquirer and the Chinese news service Xinhua mentioned Salman Pak by name...Meanwhile, the New York Times and the Washington Post, which opposed the war in Iraq, have so far declined to report the first official ruling linking Saddam to 9/11...*

Among the obstacles that had to be overcome in the case, according to the story, was the CIA's public denial that Iraq played any role in the Sept.11 attack and CIA Director George Tenet's failure to include Salman Pak in his presentation of evidence tying Iraq to Al Qaeda. The article continues:

> *Tenet's decision to ignore the critical role played by the camp is said to be based in part on friction between the CIA and the Iraqi National Congress, which helped several Salman Pak veterans defect to the U.S. and*

made them available to the media.
Tenet's opposition is believed to have been key in the decision by the Bush administration not to spotlight Iraq's 9/11 role, leaving White House officials with the sole argument that Saddam Hussein threatened the U.S. with weapons of mass destruction.

Ms. Mylroie wrote with an impressive degree of prescience concerning the debate on weapons of mass destruction,

George Bush...seeks to finesse the problem of the bureaucracies commitment to their Clinton-era positions by ousting Saddam on the basis of Iraq's flagrant and undeniable breach of the UN sponsored cease fire: Its retention of proscribed weapons of mass destruction. That may work, if we're lucky.

Unfortunately, that hasn't worked well. Self-styled liberal columnist Tom Friedman, writing in the Nov. 30, 2003 New York Times, decried the antiwar fervor he witnessed while in London. He explains it by saying,

It [the liberal left] can't see anything else...other than...the...original sin of launching the Iraq war, without U.N. approval or proof of Iraqi weapons of mass destruction...

In considering whether Ms. Mylroie is correct in suggesting that the denial of state sponsorship for the attacks of the 1990's is a continuation of the fiction invented by the Clinton administration, natural cynicism demands that we ask: why would President Clinton invent that theory? For me, that question is preceded by another puzzling question. Why did the Clinton administration continue to deny for so long that our troops were exposed to chemical weapons contamination at Kamisiyah? We know that denial continued throughout the Clinton first term, and there was certainly no desire to protect the first President Bush. There may be a single answer to both questions.

We know that President Clinton wanted to make his mark in history by bringing peace to the Middle East. That laudable goal would be defeated by a Middle East war. State sponsorship by Iraq of acts of terrorism like those that occurred at the World Trade Center in 1993 and at the Murrah Building in 1995 would be acts of war against the United States. Their commission would require that the United States go to war against Iraq, even if the flagrant Iraqi violations of the 1991 cease-fire for failing to account for the chemical weapons such as were destroyed at Kamisiyah were disregarded. It would seem then, that to pursue the Clinton goal, it would be necessary to avoid the necessity for armed conflict and therefore deny state sponsorship of acts of terrorism and of the cease fire violations. The federal bureaucracy obliged. In retrospect, it was a bad gamble.

We can understand why CIA and FBI personnel may feel trapped by their prior denials that terrorism had a state sponsor, but why did the Bush administration go along?

Initially, the Bush team was opposed to adopting a policy of regime change and nation building, but after Sept. 11, the new Bush administration had a problem. It had to recognize that the Clinton era policy of denial of state sponsorship wasn't working and that its announced policy spurning nation building was destroyed in the ruins of the twin World Trade Center towers. The Bush administration and an almost unanimous Congress agreed that war was the only alternative. Al Qaeda and its home base in Afghanistan was the first target. Once the armed forces had achieved what they could there, the Bush administration looked at Iraq, probably as the major state sponsor of terrorist attacks against the United States. The problem was that the CIA and FBI were not going to admit they had been wrong in the past about state sponsorship and risk being held responsible for the Sept. 11 disaster. Perhaps it seemed to the Bush administration that insistence that Saddam Hussein account for his stockpile of chemical weapons (WMD) like those found at Kamisiyah would be a good compromise. It would be acceptable to the federal bureaucracy; and it would seem that the U.S. State Department agreed, believing that WMD would be seen as a unifying problem to most of the members of the UN in seeking international support. While there was a general feeling of sympathy towards the United States after Sept 11, it was primarily regarded as a U.S. problem. In any event, as is now abundantly clear, assigning concerns about weapons of mass destruction as the major reason for war against Iraq to obtain UN support was also a bad decision.

Perhaps the failure to obtain UN support should have been anticipated since the UN and several key nation members of the UN were earning substantial sums running the oil for food program that followed in the wake of the 1991 Gulf War. Those nations then lead UN opposition to the United States plan to enforce its own resolutions. We can never know, but did European opposition to the US persuade Saddam to refuse offers of asylum and lead him to believe the US would only wage a bombing campaign that would leave him in power? Has their opposition aided those forces that still oppose Saddam's removal from power?

In any event, the Bush administration continued the Clinton era denial of state sponsorship of acts of terrorism. Was it solely the reluctance of the CIA, FBI and other federal bureaucrats to admit their mistakes that led to that result? Perhaps, and again, we cannot know for certain, but there may be additional reasons. Perhaps it's because there was more than just Iraq involved in those acts of terrorism. Many believe there was also state sponsorship by elements within the government of Saudi Arabia. If so, could that explain the refusal to release portions of the Senate's investigation of the Sept. 11 disaster? Why would that information not be revealed? Could it be because of some personal relationship with members of the Royal Family or because of our dependence on Middle East oil? Perhaps those are factors, but I think it is much more likely that, as is suggested in the novel, what would replace the royal family in Saudi Arabia would be a Wahhabi sect regime that supports Al Qaeda in its avowed *jihad* against the United States and western culture.

In the news and in the novel, we find the word *jihad.* What exactly is meant by that term? It sometimes refers to an individual Muslim's internal struggle to lead a good and moral life, but there is a second meaning that, according to the World Book,

> *developed in part from the example of Muhammad and his early followers. They launched a number of military campaigns to spread their faith. It also developed based on certain passages in the Qur'an—the holy book of Islam. The doctrine is based on three related ideas. First, Islam is a universal community. Second, God and Muhammad have commanded all free and physically able male Muslims to spread their faith, even by waging war against non-Muslims when necessary. Finally, Muslims must spread their religion until all people have converted to Islam or agreed to live under an Islamic government.*

We should also recall that Osama Bin Laden is waging a *jihad* against the West, principally the United States and that he issued a *fatwah* or order to all his followers. He said in that order,

> *we issue the following fatwa to all Muslims. The ruling to kill the Americans and their allies—civilians and military—is an individual duty for every Muslim who can do it in any country in which it is possible to do it,...*

Many refused to believe the avowed purpose of Nazism was expressed in Hitler's *Mein Kampf.* To our sorrow, we know that was a terrible mistake. Let us not make the same mistake with the Muslim terrorist declaration of *jihad*. The novel assumes a well-organized and well-trained cadre of terrorists dedicated to the destruction of the United States. Is that fact or fiction? Will the now captured Saddam Hussein furnish any proof of Iraqi complicity in prior attacks against the United States and whether he does or not, can you believe anything he says? What kind of proof is required to make the case? You are a member of that jury.

Is there state sponsorship of terrorism that must be dealt with in Syria, Saudi Arabia and elsewhere? Will we have to resort to military regime change? Let us hope there are other alternatives. Perhaps the apparent move towards a more open society by some of the youth and women's groups in Iran is a hopeful sign. Perhaps success can be achieved in Iraq and a democratic society can be built which will inspire a similar yearning for freedom in the Middle East. We should work towards that result, because it may be that producing regime change to our liking by the military in Saudi Arabia where the prevailing power structure is composed principally of Wahhabi fanatics might make the difficulties in Iraq look like a walk in the park. Those things, if they happen at all, will be very costly and they will not happen overnight, but is there an alternative. Writing in the Boston Globe on October 2, 2003, op-ed columnist Jeff Jacoby opined,

> *...if the war in Iraq were a single, discrete moment in US foreign policy, unconnected to the larger war against international terrorism or to the prevention of another Sept. 11......it might indeed seem crazy to go on pouring tens of billions of dollars into Iraq. But the reality is very different...Iraq is only one battle, in what will be a grueling campaign...World War IV, some have called it...The Cold War was World War III, and the United States had no choice but to fight and win it. There is likewise no alternative to fighting and winning the war we are in now...We cannot ignore the region's virulent anti-Americanism and the militant Islamist radicalism that feeds it...For a long time we did all those things. We played see-no-evil, subsidized corrupt governments, turned the other cheek to terrorism. And Sept. 11 was the result.*

New York Times columnist Friedman seems to agree with Jacoby's assessment of the danger and the Mylroie and Davis assertions that the terrorist offensive preceded September 11, if not in the United States, at least in other places, saying,

> *...we are seeing—from Bali to Istanbul—the birth of a virulent, nihilistic form of terrorism that seeks to kill any advocates of modernism and pluralism, be they Muslims, Christians or Jews. This terrorism started*

even before 9/11, and is growing in the darkest corners of the Muslim world.

Are generally regarded conservative columnists like Jeff Jacoby alone in recognizing the dangers presented by the militant anti-Western Muslim declaration of *jihad* and that W.M.D. is not the real issue? Liberal columnist Tom Friedman wrote in his December 7, 2003 column,

> *Where did Mr. Bush's passion for making the Arab world safe for democracy come from?...A cynic might say that...with no W.M.D. having been unearthed...the President felt he needed a new rationale. And so he focused on the democratization argument.*

In that column, while admitting to that possibility, Friedman states that the, *"Freedom and democracy argument was [for him] the only compelling rationale for the Iraq war."* He then went on to favorably compare President George W. Bush's abandonment of the W.M.D. rationale and emphasis on the democracy goal with similar actions by other presidents. He first cites Abraham Lincoln's replacing his initial reliance on the twin goals of opposition to secession and preservation of the union with the "larger purpose of the Civil War—namely freedom and the elimination of slavery." A second Friedman example is Woodrow Wilson's turn around from campaigning on a platform of keeping the nation out of the European War in 1916 to asking for a declaration of war against Germany in 1917 to make the world "safe for democracy."

Cynic or not, W.M.D. or not, would failure in Iraq mean the re-establishment of training bases and state sponsorship and assistance to future generations of terrorists? Is it possible that having committed to a decision made during the Clinton years that there was no state sponsorship of the prior attacks on the United States that the FBI and CIA are still unwilling to admit they made a mistake? Is it possible that a desire for advancement has so corrupted the performance of those agencies that even now they refuse to deal with reality? If W.M.D are never found and if the FBI and CIA continue to deny state sponsorship, will that lead to a possibly regrettable and premature exit from Iraq and the war against terrorism and another September 11? In the novel, one was tried and it failed.

Will they fail in real life? We hope so, but only time will tell.

0-595-30688-8